THE TRANQUIL ARK

THE
TRANQUIL
ARK

Stewart Vassie

The Book Guild Ltd
Sussex, England

First published in Great Britain in 2001 by
The Book Guild Ltd
25 High Street
Lewes, East Sussex
BN7 2LU

Typesetting in Baskerville by
Acorn Bookwork, Salisbury, Wiltshire

Printed in Great Britain by
Antony Rowe Ltd, Chippenham, Wiltshire

A catalogue record for this book is available from
The British Library.

ISBN 1 85776 620 2

The Tranquil Ark is dedicated to *Laura Jones* and *Joseph Vassie*, and my other grand children who have taught me so much about the joys of childhood.

CONTENTS

1

The Reverend Hartwell Leaves

There are no beginnings without ends, and so the end of Reverend Lionel Hartwell's tenancy as Administrator of St Margaret's Comity represents the beginning of our story.

There was little or no rancour in his decision to leave the post, and it may justly be said, if his tenure as Administrator had been marked by a rambling liberality in all things concerning the running of the Comity, the cause of his leaving had undoubtedly not been this liberal approach but rather his ingrained untidiness in the administration and it has to be said that, as a consequence of his vacating his position, he was to bequeath an untidy situation to the trustees who had control of the imprecise, yet charitable foundation under his charge.

The last days of the Reverend Hartwell's residency at St Margaret's Comity were largely unremarkable if a shade sad, for he was well regarded and was comfortable with his own tenancy.

The Comity, as it is known locally, has had a chequered history. The land upon which the Comity had been built was owned by St Margaret's Church, which was one of two fine churches in the village of Newell under Lea. It was, for sadly it is no more, the furthest church from the centre of Newell under Lea and was built late in the Victorian era by a wealthy industrialist, Joshua Stanwich, who had purchased a great tract of land in the area, and had erected upon this land a splendid country house, Stanwich Manor. Having few bad habits and a large consciousness of his own ability as a dilettante architect, Stanwich had decided that he should build a church on his own land, to complement both the manor and the vista from his drawing room. The dedication stated that St Margaret's had been built for the good people of the village and as a living proof that great architecture was only fit for God.

Sadly, both the elegant house and the church, whilst well designed, lacked constructional soundness. As a result of the poor materials used and the poor skills of the builders employed, Stanwich Manor only just managed to survive its builder's death before the roof collapsed, causing a great fire which gutted the home of the Stanwich family, they had then sold up and left the area. The land which Joshua had given to St Margaret's included an area for a sizeable churchyard. Nobody had been buried on this land, as it had not been consecrated, and so the parish council decided to offer it for building, to a charity. The only charity interested was an obscure clerical foundation dedicated to helping distressed clergy widows, it was given the land, but failed to raise enough money to build.

During the Second World War a Spitfire clipped the spire of St Margaret's and the church had simply collapsed, much as Stanwich Manor had, and was demolished to make it safe. The other church in the village, St John's, had been renamed, St Margaret's and St John's. At about this time, the charity that owned the churchyard site had leased the land to the Radio Retailers Association's Welfare Fund – RRAWF. In 1950 this welfare fund commissioned the building of the Comity, as a group of small dwellings with an extensive community building at the centre. The plans of the layout of the Comity resembled a letter 'U', with six small single-storey terraced homes in each arm of the 'U' and the community building at the base joining the two terraces. This community building was designed to have two storeys, with the second storey containing an office and a flat, which under the terms of the lease should be let to a retired or destitute clergyman who would act as administrator and carer.

The cottages were to be let, at peppercorn rents, to retired members of the radio retail trade who, for one reason or another, had fallen upon hard times.

The Reverend Hartwell had, or so the advisers to his Bishop asserted, suffered a nervous breakdown following the death of his wife, and whilst he avowed that he still felt his calling, it was considered that he was unable to run a parish. The post of Administrator of the St Margaret's Comity became vacant some two months before the 'Hartwell crisis' and in this fashion, the Reverend Lionel Hartwell had been suggested and accepted, mainly on the grounds that his only daughter lived in Salisbury and was married.

Thus in 1978 the Reverend Hartwell had taken up the post of Administrator of St Margaret's Comity and, if I were to be totally honest, had allowed the affairs of that place to slide and to slip. That being said, the residents of the Comity had no complaint whatsoever, nor did they find the Reverend Hartwell in any way unharmonious. As a group, the residents were content with their untidy, kindly Administrator. The widows mothered him, the widowers found him a good friend and the married couples enjoyed his company, and he merged and melted into the daily life of the residents of the Comity.

Of the man himself, he was nothing very special or striking, round, bald, clean-shaven with glasses and more than a little deaf. One thing, however, about Lionel Hartwell was noteworthy and that was his smile, when the Reverend Hartwell smiled it was as if angels flew around his head. His smile could, I believe, have melted snowcaps on mountains and certainly the hearts of his sternest critics.

His smile, however, had not been sufficient to prevent his forced resignation. As so often with untidy people, the Reverend Hartwell had encountered that which a more ordered man might have met and easily resolved.

The matter that had proved the straw on the camel's back was the matter of a fire exit in the very office in which, had he been a more ordered man, he would have spent more time and thus moved the desk that had been pushed in front of that all-important door. The fire officer had, I believe, been sympathetic on his first visit, and indeed on his second and third, but the insurance company finally threatened to refuse to renew cover for the Comity unless and until the fire officer's recommendations had been implemented.

All this might have crossed the mind of Lionel Hartwell as he climbed the steps of his pulpit for the last time, but his mind was on his sermon. The text he had taken from Proverbs chapter 12, verse 3: 'A man shall not be established by wickedness: but the root of the righteous shall not be moved'. And the congregation of St Margaret's and St John's were once more moved by the warmth of his smile and the powerful insight of such an unprepossessing-looking man.

Few from the Comity were in the congregation, for although they respected the Reverend Hartwell, they were not much taken with religion or moral thoughts.

Concerning St Margaret's Comity, it is not, I think, a charming structure and cannot be said to be of the highest architectural standard. It was designed in 1948 by Simon Taklock Associates of Gray's Inn Road, London, and finally built in 1952. Simon Taklock had wanted the plan of the Comity site to resemble a medieval illuminated manuscript letter 'U' full of serifs and curlicues. His first drafts were formed thus with the illumination made up of lawns and flower beds, while the buildings would wear fine woodwork and fanciful brick courses. In reality, the budget, combined with the architectural climate, corrupted the idea and produced a utility capital letter 'U', sans serif and sans elegance, or indeed any ornamentation apart from a rather sad string course of yellow brick at the height of the gable ends. The only aspect of the whole edifice that warrants a second look is the actual Comity building at the base of the 'U' shape.

The cottages that form the two arms of the 'U' resemble, as far as the internal layout of each dwelling is concerned, a postwar 'prefab', although the terraces are built with red brick and have pitched roofs and stable doors.

The Comity building is of a more ambitious design, having two storeys with, at its centre, an elegant clocktower rising from its roof. Under the clocktower there is a single storey high arch that allows access to the two terraces, this arch being wide enough for just one vehicle, which can park on the gravel at the back of the Comity building.

In the centre of the 'U' which each terrace faces, there is the Comity Garden, this takes the form of a lawn with several large forest trees and some round beds. At each end of the lawn, four flowering cherry trees stand. On the sides facing the cottages, wisteria grows along iron frameworks. The cottages have no front or back gardens, neither have they any backdoors.

The single-storey arch that leads into the Comity is closed at night by two large white wooden gates that fit the arch completely at the end facing the road. At the other end of the arch, supported by two removable metal poles, a chain is looped, effectively stopping any vehicle driving beyond the confines of the arch when the main gates are open during the day.

The Comity building is more opulent. A suite of rooms on the ground floor on the left side of the arch was intended for the boardroom and offices of the RRAWF. It had never been used for this purpose and is now hired out for functions. On the right-hand side of the arch on the ground floor another suite of rooms is used for residents' communal activities, there is also an extensive kitchen.

On the second floor of the building, which is reached by a staircase located in the arch, there is a suite of three rooms, which is the Comity's administrative offices, with interconnecting doors, the rest of the second floor is the Administrator's flat.

This then is how the Comity looks today and indeed how it has looked for the whole of its 39-year history.

One thing more the you should know about this unremarkable set of buildings. St Margaret's Comity faces onto the A354 and is about one mile from the centre of Newell under Lea. The Comity sits neatly sandwiched between two large rolling hill fields owned by different farmers who covet the land it inhabits and dislike it mightily as it impedes their ease of access.

Following his sermon Lionel Hartwell returned to the Comity and spent his last night in the flat. He did not eat an evening meal but had a sandwich that had been prepared earlier for him. He read for a little while and then watched television. At ten thirty, he went downstairs to check that the gates were closed and turned the lights in the arch out. The gates were locked with a simple Yale lock to which all the residents had a key. Having satisfied himself that the gates were locked, he walked around the garden, noticing that spring was starting to show itself on the trees, dusting them with a green mist of buds.

Most of the cottages' lights were still on. As he walked back he passed the Halls' cottage and saw that John Hall was standing by his front door smoking his pipe and seemingly just looking up at the sky. He slowed down and acknowledged the oldest resident.

'Evening, John. Fine night.'

'It is that, Reverend Hartwell. I can never look at the stars without thinking about the way we've landed on the moon and even walked on the place. It seems so far away, so other worldly, if you know what I mean. It's hard to believe man's been there, somebody just like you or me, actually walked on it and looked down at us – this world. When I was a kid, nobody would have ever believed we'd have been to the moon. It's wonderful to just think about it, makes me regret I'm as old as I am.'

'Oh you've had a good innings, John, seen a lot, done a lot, you've fought the battle and come back safe to Doris and your children. You wouldn't want to start all over again, would you?'

'No, as you say, I've seen my share of fights and stupidity and I reckon I'm better off here than out there flying to the moon or fighting off the competition. Shopkeeping's changed, like everything else, you don't sell televisions now, you sell the maker's name. You're off tomorrow then?'

'Yes, I'm off tomorrow. I'm going to be looked after instead of looking after you lot and it's just down the road from my daughter Jane. I'm looking forward to seeing her and the grandchildren more. I'll be more like you, John, peacefully watching the world go by.'

'Who's taking your place? We haven't been told.'

'It's not been settled yet. The trustees are meeting tomorrow afternoon.'

'You'd have thought that they would have settled your successor weeks ago. I can't think what's holding them up, Reverend. After all, they knew you were leaving, didn't they?'

'Oh yes, they knew all right. Well, I'm off to bed. Goodnight John.'

'Looking at that sky makes me think that regardless of what we look like from up there, down here in Newell under Lea we

6

carry on without much change, things stay more or less the same, or have done since we've been here. You know that my daughter called my granddaughter Fidelity because when my daughter was a little girl and used come to my shop Fidelity radios were the most beautiful things she saw – because they had them on big display boards in elegant room settings. She said to me, 'I couldn't call her John but I could call her Fidelity to remind us of you, Dad, and how beautiful your shop was.'

Lionel Hartwell started walking back to his flat and John called after him.

'Goodnight, Reverend and good luck with tomorrow.'

'Goodnight, John. Sleep well and my regards to Doris.'

Back in the flat, Hartwell lay in bed thinking about how change is only ever noticed when it comes in big dramatic lumps, we don't notice that every day change streams in upon us all and nothing stays the same from day to day. Change, he thought, is the witness of time, and with that thought giving him some comfort, he slept as soundly as all the other residents in St Margaret's Comity.

In the morning, Lionel Hartwell rose early, went downstairs and opened the gates. As was his habit, he walked round the garden checking the front of each cottage. Mrs Patel was already up and sweeping the front doorstep.

Mrs Patel was a recent arrival at the Comity, her husband had died a year ago, and in a strange way he felt an affinity with her which was not reciprocated. He knew that her husband had been one of the Asians who had been thrown out of Uganda and had lost a considerable fortune in the process. They were both Christians, although Sangita Patel had told him that she had not been brought up in the faith but had been born into a Jain family and converted when she married. She had confided to him that because of her very pale skin she had often fantasised as a child that she was in fact the daughter of a white father, a sort of female Kim. However as she grew up and got to know her mother better, she realised that this was totally impossible. Her husband had married her because, she sometimes felt, she was to all intents and purpose white, especially when dressed in European clothes. They had arrived in Britain penniless and had established a small radio and TV rental business. Success had followed and they had ended up with five shops, all located in Asian areas. She had adopted the habit of dressing in a sari to help the business. Her husband had died of a massive heart attack and she'd given the shops to her son, who had sold them and left her more or less destitute. She turned to the RRAWF to try to get help to sort out her affairs and they had found her a place in the Comity. After about three months she had fallen into the rhythm of the place and had made friends, although she still dressed in a sari and seemed content not to revert to the more European mode of life she had lived in Uganda.

At nine o'clock Jane arrived with the removal van to move his things and finish the packing. By eleven o'clock every trace of the Reverend Lionel Hartwell had been packed or swept out of the flat, and after saying his goodbyes he left with Jane, sitting beside her in her car.

A breeze blew round the Comity as Hartwell left for the last time, but apart from the soft spring wind, there was no other sign that for the Comity the world had tilted on its axis and speeding down the A354 was what remained of the settled life that the residents had come to know.

2

A Matter of Selection

In the afternoon, at two o'clock, five people met at the Comity ostensibly to select a successor to the Reverend Hartwell. The panel comprised representatives from the RRAWF, the Diocese, two people from the local Social Services and the vicar of St Margaret's and St John's, the Reverend Palmer.

Mr Eric Fribble and Ms Rosemary Kickshaw were old hands at committees. Eric Fribble, as the Secretary of the RRAWF, chaired or attended committee meetings almost every day of his working life. He was on the staff of the Radio Retailers Association Welfare Fund, and handled all matters concerning its interests.

Ms Rosemary Kickshaw was the Diocesan representative for clergy welfare and charities. Her presence at the selection of a new Administrator of St Margaret's Comity was a formality rather than anything else, although it was accepted that she represented one vote should the selection require it.

The local Social Services department fielded two representatives, a Ms Felicity Eristic and Mr Simon Tottery. Ms Eristic was the junior member of the pair, having only lately qualified as a social worker, Mr Tottery was the notional head of department.

It would be fitting to explain why I say that Simon Tottery was the 'notional' head of the department of social welfare for the Council. Mr Tottery had worked for the Council almost the whole of his working life. Apart from his two years' National Service, Simon Tottery had been in the employ of the Council. He had worked his way painfully slowly up the ladder of a council career, serving in his 37 years under Conservative,

Liberal, Labour, Residents and hung councils. He was appointed head of Social Services under the last Conservative Council and had been head of department when the new Labour Council had been elected. His new 'Chair' had, however, seen in Mr Tottery a man wedded to the past and, moreover, a man out of touch with the latest thinking in social welfare administration and had therefore split up the social welfare department into several independent sub-departments dealing with specific areas of welfare resource, and these she had awarded various priorities according to the fashion prevailing in welfare thinking amongst the political left of the Council. The exact role that Simon Tottery now filled was unclear, and a stronger and younger man might have resigned rather than put up with the odium that was now the lot of the head of department. Mr Tottery was neither strong nor a young man and, with his pension in sight, he coasted along, trying, wherever possible, to be invisible by going out of his way to hold no opinions whatsoever on any matter of importance. His presence at the Comity selection meeting had occurred because another more difficult meeting was taking place at the Town Hall and Simon Tottery felt in his bones that it was better not to be available for that other meeting.

It might perhaps seem strange that there was only one candidate to be interviewed. The suspicious reader might smell a rat or see evidence of skulduggery, but in reality the reason was not the result of any kind of overt fix, but rather a common-sense arrangement between all the members of the selection panel.

It is well known that selecting the best candidate for a post is about the most thankless of all committee work. The committee knows full well that any selection it makes will be faulty because each separate member knows that he or she has no way of knowing which is the best candidate. Further, they are also aware that the other committee members will all be seeking some attributes in the candidates that they find totally irrelevant, while the qualities they consider important will be an anathema to the rest. Add to this the fact that they will all reject any candidate who exhibits the slightest degree of questioning the status quo, truthfulness or radical attitudes toward the establishment, and the die is cast for mediocrity and mendacity.

On the part of the candidates, they understand that their particular qualities and talents will not be discovered, rather they will be questioned on the current and mindless fashions of the particular disciplines of the job they are seeking; on these they will be expected to lie convincingly. It is also vital that they exaggerate their experience, because selection panels only ever select people who have been doing the same job somewhere else. Candidates therefore expect the selection procedure to be a game unrelated to the job they will have to perform should they be selected; a game that has to be played with great skill and cunning but that has no bearing whatsoever on the role that they will, if successful, eventually fill in the real world of employment.

For these reasons the suggestion that the short list should be reduced to one candidate had come about by skilful manipulation through Ms Felicity Eristic, who understood these matters and was able to use the compliance of the members of the selection panel to further her ambition to obtain for Mr Puritan the post of Administrator of St Margaret's Comity.

We will hear more of Ms Eristic later and therefore it might be as well to consider this formidable lady. Felicity Eristic is by any measure a powerful woman. Tall and thin, she dresses in the uniform of most social workers, that is to say in jeans and sweatshirt with trainers and sometimes a knitted waistcoat. Her hair is short and cut to be managed easily by simply brushing it into place. As to her face, it is strong, with a strong chin and small dark eyes. The eyes of Ms Eristic are the dominant feature of her strong face, they burn with the zeal of a fanatic, they dart, they spy, they glare and they hunt for weakness. Ms Eristic's eyes give her away and once the thoughtful observer notices them they know all there is to know about Ms Eristic and her social welfare philosophy.

Ms Eristic's looks out upon the world and sees its terrible weakness, its terrible liberality and lack of conviction, its foolish loves and petty habits, its imperfections and hopeless disorder; and she sees that her secret knowledge of what is best for the world is possible to obtain, providing she is strong and doesn't falter. What Ms Eristic does not see through those censorious eyes is that the world sometimes looks at her and does not like what it sees.

Felicity Eristic, at 39 has only recently obtained her degree in sociology. This is her first salaried job, but not her first 'community' involvement. On leaving school she went to university and read politics and economics, gaining a poor third. While at college she fell under the influence of a radical set bent upon bringing revolution to the country. Totally convinced of the imminent collapse of the capitalist system, she moved into a squat in a fashionably poor North London suburb and started to work for immigrant and homeless causes, setting up cells of activists to demonstrate against whatever government legislation happened to be fashionably targeted. After several brushes with the law and many affairs with other activists, she had fallen in love with Richard Puritan, one of her more capable activists, and had only fallen out of love with him when she discovered that she might be a lesbian, which was then an important issue amongst her peer group. Richard Puritan had then left the group and gone to university to study sociology.

Five years later she too had searched her heart and found that she was really heterosexual and getting nowhere fast, and so, remembering Richard Puritan, had followed his example and returned to university to take a degree in sociology. On gaining her degree she had called upon all her political acquaintances who were in a position to help her, and by this route she had landed her present job.

On seeing Richard Puritan's application for the advertised post of Administrator of St Margaret's Comity, she had contacted him and decided to do all she could to secure the post for him. Thus it was that there was only one candidate to be considered by the panel that afternoon.

It is entirely possible that the reader might see in all this the seeds of a conspiracy, especially on the part of the awful Ms Eristic, and I have to confess that this ignoble thought was much later actively entertained by the residents of the Comity. However, to be fair to Ms Eristic and Mr Puritan, there were other considerations that weighed heavily upon the circum-stances of the selection.

There was, for example, the little matter of the insurance company's demands for a fully worked out and implemented fire safety policy, a subject about which the Reverend Palmer, Rosemary Kickshaw and even the committee expert Eric Fribble had not the slightest working knowledge. There was also the matter of the medical provisions of the county, which were in a continual state of reorganisation with the closure of the local friendly hospitals in favour of large town-based hospitals that provided a fat living for the consultants and administrative staff, but a meagre resource for the largely rural population. Added to this there was the reorganisation of the local doctors' practices into primary care groups. Newell under Lea now shared one such group practice with the next village about ten miles away.

The police had also been reorganised to satisfy the Chief Constable's desire for better equipment with which to fight a hardly noticeable rise in crime. The local police station had been closed and the area was now covered by fast police cars that were, however, unable to respond to rural crime because of the traffic congestion. The fire service had likewise reduced its local cover for a centralised fire station in the town, and had also equipped itself with fire-fighting appliances that could not easily negotiate the narrow, twisting roads and thus its service had, in effect, been hugely reduced.

The ambulance service had followed the other services and relocated its resources to the major town and assured the rural population that with its new helicopter it could meet any emergency call faster than ever before. It could not, however, supply a service to take patients on routine visits to hospital.

These and other factors Ms Eristic had explained with delib-erate slowness to the other members of the panel. She had, however, omitted to include in her explanation the fact that the local Council Welfare Department had diverted a sizeable sum from its budget for the 'provision for the elderly and infirm' to a budget for the construction of lesbian and gay flats, and thus welfare cover for the Comity could no longer include home helps or some other mobility services previously provided.

Naturally the smooth-talking Ms Eristic blamed all the woes upon the Government, whose lot in life was to suffer never-ending calls for more money.

It was therefore against this background that the selection panel had decided that the appointment of a candidate who enjoyed the confidence and support of the Council was the ideal answer to the challenges that the Comity faced in the light of the various changes that the new climate demanded.

For Mr Puritan, matters could not have been better suited to his need to obtain both housing and paid employment, albeit on a nugatory salary. The reassurance Ms Eristic had given him that the job was his had helped him to face the selection panel with a high degree of equanimity.

As to Mr Richard Puritan, it would be best to leave his character to be explored by the events following his appointment. I should, perhaps, explain a little of his background and describe his appearance at this important juncture.

Trousers do not much figure in the great architecture of history, indeed, any close and detailed analysis of history will reveal very little in terms of trousers, either for or against. The Scots, it has to be admitted, have been largely famed for the kilt, and the Amazons are usually depicted in skirts, as are the Romans and the Greeks. Trousers have not, however, been noted as playing any crucial part in the development of mankind's heedless drive towards perfection.

This is certainly unfortunate, because the first thing anybody notices about Mr Puritan is his trousers. Exactly where he purchases these garments is unclear, nor can I tell readers where, should they be so ill-advised as to want to wear such weird-looking trousers, they should shop. Mr Puritan's trousers are unique to him. Sometimes they seem to be the regulation social worker jeans, but at other times such as the Selection Panel interview, they are corduroy. The jeans are always blue but the corduroys come in several colours, the most popular being crimson, but bottle green, brown and blue have also been seen gracing the bottom of the worthy Mr Puritan.

Exactly why Mr Puritan's trousers are such an important part of the man is not difficult to explain, for Mr Puritan has a very

14

large rear end. Were it some other part of his anatomy, he might be said to be deformed, but because it is his bottom that is out of proportion with the rest of his body, common decency prevents people commenting and thus they notice rather his trousers and wonder at the tailor's art in being able to hang so much cloth round such a uniquely difficult shape. For the rest of his appearance, his hair stands out because it grows in all directions and seems unwilling to come to terms with the shape of his head. His eyes are the eyes of a zealot, staring and with a tendency to water. Apart from his base, he is thin and not given to any pretensions about dressing to inspire or impress. He usually wears the social worker's obligatory T or sweatshirt and trainers.

It is not Mr Puritan's dress that is noteworthy, because he wears the uniform standard to all other community politicians and activists. The thing that is important about Mr Puritan is his mind, or rather intellectual mindset, for he is the product of his education and training, laced throughout with a burning zealotry and, strangely, an ordered administrator's ability. Had he been born in another age he would have become a bank clerk or a clerk in an office, where he would have risen to be in charge of administration and been an essential nuisance to the more creative people around him.

His adult education had been firstly in the politics of Marxism and then in community action. Later he had been active with Ms Eristic on her various 'community fronts' and then he had taken advantage of more formal education and had selected a university that was known for its political correctness and left-wing tutors in social studies. It is a fact in his favour that throughout all this great lump of learning he had consistently been very critical at the lack of administrative tidiness on the part of all those who had instructed and guided him. 'Life,' he was fond of observing, 'should be run like clockwork, with every cog meshing with every other cog to drive society towards ordered and civilised goals.' By this he meant the goals he set for society rather than the goals society might like to set for itself.

This ability to be an administrator as well as an inclination towards revolution and political correctness had been the thing that had first attracted Ms Eristic to his application for the St Margaret's post, and then the realisation that this Mr Puritan was the very Mr Puritan who had once been the intimate of her earlier days had effectively assured him of success.

The interview was formal because Mr Fribble could not image any other kind of interview. A table was set in the middle of the interview room; behind this the members of the selection panel sat. In front of the table a chair had been placed facing the panel; all the other furniture in the room was pushed against the wall, thus giving the impression that all matters of importance that were taking place within the room happened in the centre at the table.

Ms Eristic sat appropriately on the extreme left of the table and acted as secretary to the panel. She was therefore the person who ushered Mr Puritan to the seat in front of the table and then returned to her seat behind it. Mr Fribble acted as panel chairman, and opened the interview.

'Good afternoon, Mr Puritan. As you probably already know from the advertisement, this is a charitable foundation, by that I mean that St Margaret's Comity is owned by the Radio Retailers Association Welfare Fund. This is a charitable fund, however the head lease of the property is owned by a Diocesan charity, and as a consequence, it has been a condition of the lease that the post of Administrator is awarded to a clergyman. You, I see from your application form, are not a member of the cloth. However, we are prepared in this instance to consider a candidate who has not been ordained. Should we make such an appointment, it would not be a permanent position, although it is very unlikely that we would search for a new candidate should the appointment prove satisfactory. However, if a suitably qualified clergyman were to become available we would naturally have to seriously consider dispensing with any non-ordained Administrator in favour of an ordained person. I trust that is understood?'

Mr Puritan understood and indicated this fact. Ms Kickshaw then asked her prepared question:

'Mr Puritan, I represent the Diocese's interest in this matter. Are you a Christian?'

Mr Puritan squirmed, Mr Puritan shifted uneasily in his chair, Mr Puritan stroked his chin and then his nose, Mr Puritan looked at Ms Eristic and found no assistance or seeming support. Mr Puritan understood then the meaning of being flummoxed.

'Well,' he began, 'I certainly believe in many Christian ideas, I believe in many things that are or could be said to be Christian, like Christian ideas and things.'

'Yes, but *are* you a Christian, Mr Puritan?' repeated Ms Kickshaw.

The Reverend Palmer attempted a rescue: 'Do you attend a church, Mr Puritan?'

A light dawned in the candidate's brain, a route to safety flashed in his memory. 'I was baptised at St Saviour's, Gravesend.'

'Mr Puritan, are you familiar with the sheltered housing legislation passed in the last five years?' Ms Eristic had come to his aid, had moved off the question of faith, of belief, of Christianity, of loving and caring, of human concern and support, and on to the real business of laws and regulations, of making things ordered and orderly. By this question the whole matter of humanity had been side-tracked and the untidy, unpredictable, uncertain and unhelpful topic of people had been conveniently swept out of sight. Now, thought Mr Puritan, we can get down to the real business of my suitability to bring the affairs of this organisation within the rules and laws set down in buff booklets and advice pamphlets sent out by councils and authorities.

'Yes, I am very familiar with this legislation and indeed with the regulations governing such designated properties and structures.' His voice was confident, his demeanour was confident, his ample bottom firm upon the chair and his head erect. Mr Puritan was certain of his ground and sure now that the interview was turning in his favour.

'I am familiar with the Health and Safety legislation and the amendments under the European Union's regulations covering fire safety, VDU screen usage, dangerous chemicals commonly known as VOCs, of the disposal of mercury vapour lamps and of chemical waste.'

'Yes, yes,' interrupted Mr Fribble, 'but how do you stand with the frail and the vulnerable?'

'I think the question is about the provision for the elderly,' paraphrased Ms Eristic.

There is no need to continue the record of the interview. Ms Eristic steered the question always towards Mr Puritan's subject of regulations and rules and Mr Puritan answered with a string of mnemonics and initials that would have blinded even the keenest brains.

After 45 minutes the panel was exhausted and retired to another room to confer, leaving Mr Puritan to cool his heels, which, as he wore sandals, did not take too long.

In the committee room the panel supposed it had the job of giving its collective opinion upon the candidate. Ms Eristic, however, felt that the matter was settled, and so it was.

3

Mr Izzat

John Izzat studied the papers that Eric Fribble had given him earlier in the afternoon. Mr Fribble always wrote his minutes up directly after a meeting and therefore it was usual for him to deliver a copy to the President of the Welfare Fund by the next afternoon.

Sitting in his conservatory in his house in Wimbledon High Grove, Izzat concentrated fiercely on the minutes, as was his habit. He had long ago found out that it was only by reading and re-reading the details of the things that crossed his desk that he was able to obtain his legendary advantage over his competitors and rivals. Now, although there was not the urgent need to soak up so much of the detail as previously, he could not break the habit that had served him so well in the past.

The post of President of the RRAWF was honorary and had fitted in well with his plans for a gentle run-up to retirement in two years' time. The presidency of the RRAWF went with the chairmanship of the trade association, and he had consented to taking the chair of the Association when he had finalised his plans for retirement. It meant that he spent roughly one or two days a week on the Association's or the RRAWF's business, which fitted in well with his plans to allow his heir apparent in the company to field the company's affairs while he was still in the picture and active with the board.

The fact that he was working on RRAWF affairs at the weekend was normal for him, another habit that he found convenient to continue as long as it amused or engaged his attention. With his daughter Laura now down from university, he felt that he more or less had to stay in the house at weekends to keep her company and act as a buffer for the memories that she probably had of better times in the house that his wife Elizabeth had named Ideality, a made-up word to express all their love of the place.

The Izzat house in Wimbledon is by almost universal agreement an elegant and a highly desirable property. To some, it is a house where some stinking rich nob lives, whilst for others it is a tangible sign of the kind of rewards that hard work and a prudent lifestyle can produce.

For Izzat, it is simply his home which he now shares with his beloved daughter Laura. Indeed, he is probably right in this idea as it is the work of his late wife Elizabeth, who chose the furniture, fittings and decorations, whilst her husband spent long hours building up his chain of radio and television retail shops, and then managing a national chain of such shops following the acquisition of his business by National TV Retailers, or NTR, as it is known in the high streets of Britain.

When his chain of shops was acquired, Izzat was sold along with the business, for it was recognised by the board of NTR Group that Izzat was both an exceptional businessman and a very talented manager of retail operations. Thus the outrageous figure which they offered him for his company had included in it a sizeable sweetener to ensure that he took over as managing director of the whole of NTR's retail operation. Later Izzat had been promoted to the group board and still later he had won the Chief Executive post, and in this position had powered the group into the position of one of the top five UK companies, and then into a top slot in the list of top companies in the world. Izzat knew that he was by any measure a major asset, but he still intended to retire in two years' time.

His rise and success had mostly happened while Elizabeth had been alive and thus the money had allowed her to indulge her slightest whim. In the ten years between Izzat's appointment as MD of NTR Retail and Elizabeth's death, the house had undergone a further series of transformations, and what had been of passable quality prior to his appointment had been replaced with the very top of the range.

Seven years ago Elizabeth had learnt that she had cancer and that it was inoperable. Within two years she had died and the house that had once been in a constant process of renewal and change had, ceased to change in any way. Neither John Izzat nor Laura could contemplate changing any detail as it was to them a monument to Elizabeth and to the loving past when Elizabeth shone from the corners of every room and beamed down a history of delight and improvement both to their lives and to Ideality.

Izzat reached the report on the Comity appointment meeting, and scowled. He appreciated the reason for the single candidate and understood why the Reverend Hartwell had been forced to resign, but he found that there was something about the whole matter that disturbed him and generated unease in what should have been a trivial matter.

He had been used to talking over such concerns with Elizabeth, and now he called Laura and she came to his side. 'This doesn't ring true, girl, doesn't seem right.' He handed her the minutes of the selection meeting. She read them while he sat and stared into the garden.

'It certainly is strange to only have one applicant for an interview,' she conceded. Her training as a lawyer, although only partially completed, had already taught her to be cautious with opinions and weigh matters much as her father did, without taking sides immediately.

'Hartwell was right for the place although he was no administrator,' he observed, 'and now there is a suggestion that the Council will have more of a hand in the running of the Comity. I'm not sure how well that will fit into the Association's interests, and I am not impressed with that Mr Puritan; he seems all rules and regulations. That place is not about regulations, for God's sake, it's sheltered housing, a place to ease away problems not generate them.'

Laura regarded her father with a mixture of care and admiration. He seemed to her to be able to see depths and complexities where she only saw facts or situations. If only he had been able to prevent her mother's death ... The thought flitted across her mind, but she dismissed it immediately, as she always did.

To look at Laura through her father's eyes might be considered

21

to produce a partial image of the young lady. However, in truth, the girl that her father's eyes saw was almost exactly the same as most other people's view of her. This does not mean to say that her father did not see his daughter through a mixture of rose-tinted lenses, happy memories and indulgent love, these were always the filters on his eyes.

Interestingly, even those who viewed Laura without these filters generally agreed with her father's estimation of her, namely she was very near to being a paragon.

Moderately tall, well covered but neither too fat nor too thin, with a mane of beautiful dark brown hair, Laura could drive even misogynists wild with passion and love. Her face radiated health, her eyes were light blue and set wide apart, her nose was just about as perfect as it is possible to get and her mouth, generous without being wide, was framed by soft red lips. Her complexion might, on others, have seemed a little swarthy, but on Laura it was like the colour of a summer rose – just wonderful.

To some it might seem unnecessary to comment upon Laura's figure, but her shape and the disposition of the various parts of her – so often the object of other people's envy and admiration, deserves comment. Like her personality and her face, Laura's figure was delightfully in proportion. Her bust was large enough to generate sighs from men and small enough not to be the object of sympathy or comment from women. Her waist was also small enough to make dressmakers envious, whilst her legs were long enough to elicit vast admiration from all and sundry. Laura was desirable in every aspect and yet was modest enough not to flaunt her beauty or to tease her many admirers.

That every man who met her fell in love with her and every women admired and envied the good fortune she obviously had received from an indulgent God did not cause Laura to wonder or question. She had been the object of great love from the very moment of her birth. The remarkable thing about her was her modesty and the fact that she was, whilst not surprised that men threw themselves at her feet, always sensible of the kindness that such devotion produced and grateful for the welfare and generosity that came her way.

I have described Laura as a paragon, and have not exaggerated, she is not pompous or prudish, she is not rash or opinionated. Thoughtful, educated, modest and beautiful, is it possible for any girl to be so perfect, seemingly without fault or flaw? This question most men asked their friends and themselves and were seldom able to reach any other answer than yes!

However, Laura, perfect in every other way, was flawed, for she had a temper that when roused, which seldom happened, would distort her otherwise perfect exterior and turn her into the nearest thing to a demon with a pretty face, full of spite and retribution. Should you ever get on the wrong side of Laura, then you would never return to the right side.

Her choice of the law was a career that suited such a stunning person, for all who knew about the profession reckoned that she would be able to twist almost everybody, in wig or gown or in the jury box, round her little finger.

I know of very few people who were on the wrong side of Laura, which is to the good because the experience is less than happy and the prospects dismal for anybody who crosses that Rubicon, that boundary between the acceptable and unacceptable to Laura Izzat.

Her course at university was just the start for her; she fully intended to gain her LLB and then eat the required number of dinners at one of the better Inns of Court. Her father John had already secured the promise of a place in chambers for her, and so to all intents and purposes her progress from university to paid employment was mapped out and foretold.

Laura's view of her father was one of great warmth. Throughout her childhood, he had been, as is so often the case with daughters, a figure who was powerful and yet blurred. He had not been at home a great deal of the time, but when he was, he had been an immense presence that affected the whole house and family. Whilst never in awe of him, she had grown up with a highly developed sense of his importance to the family and her existence. On the death of her mother, she had felt that she was given a role that she hardly knew how to fill. She could never be a replacement for Elizabeth in her father's life and yet she had a duty to him that was never explained – even to herself, in her own mind. A consequence of this feeling of inadequacy haunted her relationship with her father, for she always felt that she had not done something that she should have done for him, to make his life better, or a least more tolerable and less stressful, less lonely, less isolated.

When he had asked her to look at the minutes and give him her opinion, she had done so happily and had exhibited the same fierce concentration that he always gave to any matter. It was, she sometimes felt, a quality of being an Izzat, a person with a funny name but a lot of clout.

'I think the members of the selection committee were being manipulated by the Council appointee Eristic,' she said after some more thought and having handed the minutes back to him. 'Is it legal to have just one candidate in this instance?'

John Izzat lit a cigar. 'That must be a very fine point indeed, I should imagine. The committee agreed before the meeting to allow Ms Felicity Eristic to weed out the applicants and draw up a short list. They also agreed that the requirements of the job demanded a person who could work closely with the Council's Welfare Department. Given those two factors, Ms Eristic seems to have chosen just one candidate who fitted the bill. As so often, Laura, the die is cast before the meeting ever takes place and the lines of action are constrained by the objectives agreed prior to selection. What happens is that they make the door so damn small that only those they want can squeeze through. It seems that this is a prime example of fixing the results before you've done the research.'

'But is it important, father? After all, it's only the appointment of basically a warden for a sheltered housing complex, hardly something that will shake the world.'

'It is the hardly important things that often turn out to be events that shake organisations to their very foundations, my love, and I am very uneasy about this one, although for the life of me I can't work out why. What have you got on in the next few weeks?'

'Nothing that matters. Why?'

'I wondered if you could drive down there and just look around, speak to some of the residents, see what they feel about things generally, get the feel of the place.'

'What possible reason could I have for being there, father?'

'I'll ring Fribble and tell him that I'm sending you down there as part of your university vacation project, just to see the place and talk to the residents. I'll tell him that I wanted you to get a little country air and increase your interviewing skills. That will satisfy him and the new management of the Comity and not arouse any suspicion.'

'What should I look for specifically?' she asked.

'I can't tell you, little one. What I would like you to do is to produce a kind of snapshot of the way the place is, how it feels and the attitudes of the residents and anybody else involved.'

'Oh, I can do that. I'll drive down there and see for myself.'

Izzat continued reading the minutes and Laura went to prepare dinner for them both. She still felt that her father was more concerned than he needed to be, but she also knew that he was seldom wrong when he felt this kind of unease, and she looked forward to being able to do something tangible for him.

John Izzat finished reading the minutes and tried to order his thoughts and feelings about the wretched Comity developments. He had no reason to think that the appointment of Mr Puritan would be a bad thing, nor that the selection by Felicity Eristic of a Council-sponsored candidate would prove anything other than good. But he had to admit to himself that he was disturbed by the appointment. Perhaps, he thought, he was getting old and conservative in his attitudes, but he would have been so much happier if a cleric had been selected. It seemed to him that the Comity needed a cleric rather than a hot-shot regulations man. It was after all, a sheltered housing complex, set in the heart of England and a place where residents had a right to expect little change in their lives as they saw out the years that remained to them.

At dinner that evening both Laura and John Izzat were more or less preoccupied with their own thoughts. The fact that both their thoughts revolved round the Comity was not a reason for them to discuss it further. Both father and daughter respected each other's privacy and talked only on a social level.

John Izzat would have spoken to Elizabeth, but daughters

were different and where a wife could be expected to put up with her husband endlessly worrying at something and going over the same ground time after time until he had sorted it out in his own mind, he felt that this was too much to expect of a daughter, and so he steered the conversation on to things that he thought would be of interest to her.

Laura, for her part, also believed that for her to raise the subject would be to almost question her father's opinion on the matter. It was not her place to quiz her father on his business, and so she picked up his signals and chatted about social things that she felt would interest him.

Now you might deduce from this behaviour that both father and daughter were not close, were separated by the generation gap or some other fashionable psychobabble analytical explanation, but you would be wrong, they respected each other to the point that the other's privacy was paramount to them. Their love, each for the other, caused them not to invade the boundaries of individual privacy until and unless invited.

After dinner, John Iazzt telephoned Eric Fribble. The Secretary was happy to arrange Laura's visit and expressed no reservation or indeed surprise at his Chairman and the President of the Welfare Fund's wish to send his daughter down to the Comity to improve her interviewing skills. He asked if the Chairman would like him to be there to greet Laura and show her round. Izzat declined his kind offer, having noticed that Mr Fribble, like most of the other men he had introduced to his daughter, became all moony-eyed and silly about her.

He called to Laura to tell her that the visit had been arranged and that Mr Fribble would have notified the Comity people of her intended visit so that she would be expected.

She came into the lounge and they worked out a route for Laura from Wimbledon to Newell under Lea. She asked about the history of the place and he told her what he knew of how it had been built.

They then watched some television and at eleven o'clock went to bed.

John Izzat hadn't been sleeping well since Elizabeth's death and so he had taken up reading, something that he had abandoned many years before. Now he found great pleasure in reading in bed with the radio playing softly and the light over his bed just bright enough to light the pages of his book. With Laura in the house he found that he felt more peaceful and was able to sleep more easily than when he was in the house by himself.

Earlier in the evening at the Wilton Arms at Newell under Lea, the subject of the appointment of a Mr Puritan was on the bar's agenda, especially amongst the residents of the Comity who had decided that the Wilton Arms was the ideal place to discuss the latest ripple in what had been a fairly rippleless life. John Hall normally went to the Arms, as it was known locally – the only pub in the village. Also in attendance were Phil Dabster, Des and Sheila Truckle, Arni Pule, Rachel Malapert and Ray Paladin.

'I don't think he will be very good for us.' said Arni Pule.

'We'll just have to try to work with him,' said Sheila Truckle, and her husband Desmond nodded his head in agreement. These two were known firstly for the almost gestalt agreement between them on every subject known to man and secondly for the way they would buckle under any seemingly unreasonable demand by anyone, to, as they were fond of saying, 'rub along, which means give and take, doesn't it?

Rachel Malapert snorted with impatience. 'You two can try to work with the fool if you will; for my part, the idiot can do what he likes, it won't make the slightest bit of difference to me. Did you see the fool's wine corduroy trousers? Did you see his bum? My God, it was like the side of a brick how's-your-father. My Philip would have called him rabble food, and that's just about what he is.'

Doris Hall clucked at the topic of Mr Puritan's bum. 'What a person looks like doesn't mean much, does it? The Reverend Hartwell never looked very, er, er, imposing, did he? But a sweeter, more gentle man you couldn't meet, and clever too. A clergyman and a real gentleman, that's what he is, and I wish he hadn't resigned.'

'He didn't resign, he was sacked,' observed Arni Pule,

27

'because he didn't take enough notice of all the new laws and regulations. They sacked the poor sod because he didn't fit into this new political correctness nonsense, and I expect they will get rid of us too.'

'You shouldn't call the Reverend Hartwell a poor sod, Arni,' interjected Desmond Truckle. 'He's an ordained person, a member of the cloth. Show some respect, do.'

'Respect! He's not here, is he? I don't know what you're going on about respect for, I was not being disrespectful only accurate. He was sacked because of the regulations.' Arni Pule glared at the Truckles.

'Oh, I didn't mean to say you were disrespectful, Arni, did I, dear? No, I simply meant ...' But neither Desmond Truckle nor yet Sheila Truckle could not think of what they wished they had said instead of what they in fact had meant and said. 'We have to rub along together, that's all I meant, old son, we have to rub along.'

Roy Paladin finished his drink and placed it on the table. 'He was sacked, was Hartwell, because of the fire regulations. Mrs True told me. He kept saying he'd do something but didn't and the trustees couldn't get insurance on the place. That's the way of it and that's why he had to go.'

'So how come we haven't got another vicar? Why have we got this guy with his vast corduroy trousers and his sandals?' John Hall asked the question with possibly more anger than he felt, but the Truckles always brought out the worst in him.

'Search me, John, I always thought it was a condition of the appointment of Carer to the Comity, but it would seem that it is not,' replied Ray Paladin. 'So it seems that we are stuck with Mr Puritan, love him or hate him.'

'Oh we'll rub along with him, I'm sure. After all, you don't have to be a clergyman to be a nice person, do you? No you don't, and I'm sure that we'll find that Mr Puritan is a thoroughly nice person, you'll see if I'm not right. We'll rub along with him, won't we, Desmond?'

Desmond Truckle agreed with his wife as he always did and nodded his head. 'Yes, I'm sure we'll be able to rub along with Mr Puritan just fine, just fine.'

28

As with so many things about the Truckles' life, this optimism would turn out to stretch the meaning of the words 'just fine' to the very far edge of contradiction.

The Truckles had reached the Comity by way of the most dire of dire circumstances. They had demonstrated time and again that their business acumen and their life skills were so poor that no matter who tried to help them, they always managed to create failure, no matter how hard they were pushed into the jaws of success. The only abiding constancy in their joint lives had been the Church, which had been responsible for their being given a cottage at the Comity on the flimsiest of reasons – Sheila Truckle had once worked in the Birmingham Co-op's radio and TV department for a three-week period. It was upon this pretext that the vicar of their local church had applied and shepherded their application to the RRAWF, and with some pull from the Bishop, whose son was in the TV retail business, they had been awarded a cottage.

Ray Paladin smiled, and seeing that all the residents had finished their drinks suggested that they should all walk back together.

Landlord Roger Blithe was preparing to close the bar as they left and wished each and every Comity resident a good night's sleep.

Still discussing the appointment of Richard Puritan, the residents made their way along the Newell under Lea high street and down the road past the point where the street lighting stops and the pavement gives out.

They walked along the A354, on the grass verge, in single file because the road, even at that time of night, was busy and cars and lorries drove by at speed, without slowing in Newell under Lea. On reaching the Comity they wished each other good night.

4

Mr Puritan Starts with a Bang

I would not be unkind if I say that Mr Puritan had never enjoyed the benefits of a proper home since his rather unfortunate childhood ended with his latest 'uncle' explaining to him, at the age of 14, that his mother, and indeed the 'uncle', preferred his room to his company. It was, explained the 'uncle' to the lad, not so much a matter of his not being loved or wanted, but rather that the first wonderful flush of love between his mother and the 'uncle' was sorely strained by the presence, in the one-bedroom family flat, of a 14-year-old boy. Young Puritan, it has to be said, was tempted to say that he had lived there first and had accommodated the new 'uncle' without fuss. But weighing up the size of the new 'uncle', he had decided to say nothing, after asking his mother if this was what she wanted, and hearing her say, with a giggle and a smile, that it was.

From that moment, Richard Puritan had lived in shared rooms and in squats until he got his place at university, and then he again shared with a rather lordly student who had the happy knack of claiming the best bed, desk and anything else that required a division.

Mr Puritan thus had very little in the way of possessions beyond several pairs of corduroy trousers and some sweaters, jeans, trainers, sandals and books. These he had been in the habit of keeping in a rather large wooden box that he had made himself at school. The box was stout and well made, with strengthening members which had been added at various times when Mr Puritan had thought his compatriots had been attempting to break into it. The box was very heavy, large and without handles, but with a very strong padlock. Normally the

30

box was not moved, but if and when it was, it needed two people to move it, and then only by dint of great expenditure of effort, wind and stamina could a pair of able men negotiate the box into the desired position.

Having brought his personal effects, namely his sleeping bag and his cooking pots and food on his bike to the Comity, Mr Puritan had paid a taxi driver to bring the box and had helped him load it on to the taxi's roofrack. The taxi had then driven off, leaving Mr Puritan to cycle to Newell under Lea with the rest of his belongings, which didn't amount to much.

The taxi driver, having insisted on payment ahead of time, had arrived at the Comity and pulled the box off the roofrack in the arch by the stairs. He had then driven off, leaving the box neatly blocking the entrance to any emergency vehicle.

This had been noticed by Philip Dubster, who had thought it unwise to leave it blocking the drive to the Comity, but had rightly felt that he was neither strong nor officious enough to interfere with somebody else's box. What is more, and this was odd considering it was Phil Dubster, he had forgotten that Mrs Reck, the community nurse, was scheduled to visit Mrs Truckle to dress the burn she had on her arm. Mrs Reck was a cheerful, middle-aged stout lady who had a caseload a great deal bigger than it was her capacity to handle adequately. A consequence of her cheerfulness and excessive workload was that she drove her Rover Metro at a speed and with a lack of road sense that only the forgiveness of quiet country lanes and a lifetime of familiarity can allow.

Mr Puritan arrived to find his box in the middle of the archway a few minutes before Mrs Reck turned into the Comity at high speed, crushing Mr Puritan's bike and ploughing powerfully into Mr Puritan's box.

The battle between Mr Puritan's carpentry skills and the Rover designers and engineers who had constructed Mrs Reck's Metro proved an uneven contest; metal and modern aerodynamic styling won the day and Mr Puritan's treasures were rapidly distributed over the gravel drive. Mrs Reck's car, however, did not escape unscathed from the carnage, and what had once been a very serviceable front aspect of the Metro

31

took on the appearance of what she stated was 'a heap of old junk'.

Confrontation ensued, and I have to admit that in verbal terms alone Mrs Reck proved her point more adequately and sharply than Mr Puritan, who was unable to give a worthwhile or even intelligent argument to rebut Mrs Reck's assertion that neither the box nor the bicycle should have been in the path of oncoming vehicles.

Whilst Puritan and Reck went at it hammer and tongs, as is the way with traffic accidents, the residents who were within earshot of the event quickly assembled to witness the battle. Thus Mr Puritan's arrival to take up residence at the Comity was both marked and noted as a matter of some moment.

It was, I have to admit, not a propitious ingress. Nor, had I been asked, would I have advised Mr Puritan to use such low, immoderate language to Mrs Reck when he found that he could not win the argument with rational logic because, largely, there was no single logical argument he could muster in his own, his box or his bicycle's defence. It was assuredly not a good idea to liken Mrs Reck to the copulation procedures of Nazi extermination camp guards, nor yet was it clever to liken these same guards and Mrs Reck to the first lady Prime Minister of Britain. This intemperate, no, *coarse* language was noted by the assembled residents of the Comity, and I have to say they were both sickened and repulsed to hear such words, and Mr Puritan's stock plummeted amongst even those that had been prepared to give him the benefit of the doubt.

Mr Dubster, who had been there from the moment Mr Puritan arrived, had finally been able to prise Mrs Reck away from the car and the archway and had taken her to his cottage, where he had sat her down and made her a cup of tea. He had returned to the car and carried her nurse's box of drugs and dressings back to his cottage ready for her, when she had recovered her composure enough, to be able to dress Mrs Truckle's burn.

Mr Puritan had been left to collect his possessions and take them to his flat. He also was left to clear up the broken bike and bits of wood that had once been his treasured box.

The RAC were called by Mr Dabster to tow away Mrs Reck's car, and Mrs Patel was asked if she would taxi Mrs Reck back to her home when Mrs Reck had dressed Mrs Truckle's arm. Mrs Patel was the only resident to own a car, although Mr Paladin rode a very large and, most thought, dangerous Honda motorcycle. Mr Dabster had not thought it appropriate for Mrs Reck to ride on Mr Paladin's Honda, given the fact that she was probably already in shock enough from the accident.

Richard Puritan climbed the stairs to his new accommodation clutching his goods and the pieces of wood that had once been his beloved box, his last contact with his childhood.

He wandered about the rooms in his new domain feeling both angry and beaten, a not uncommon feeling and one that was always painful however many times he came face to face with it. Walking through the rooms of his new flat, he was appalled by the choice of wallpaper that Jane Hartwell had chosen for her father. It is, he thought, typical of middle-class people to choose flower patterns. His memory drifted back to his mother and how she had always like tricky, floral and cheap-looking things around her, ornaments covered in gold and with sentimental pictures on them. She had liked to have fluffy toy animals about her room and probably still did. Puritan hadn't seen his mother since he had been forced out.

Thinking about his mother drove his anger forward and he felt waves of despair tinge the anger. The 'uncle' had been too big and he had been too little, but the anger at his rejection still burnt like a red-hot knife in his chest, and he wished to be free of it, wished it would stop haunting him.

Oh how much better it would be, he thought, if we had a socialist society, an ordered society. A society where uncles weren't as big as walls and mothers wanted and cared for their children. Where large women in dreadful cars didn't destroy people's boxes and then accuse them of being thoughtless and careless. A socialist society where everything was the best possible and for the best possible good, where people cared about whales and factory farming and free access to common land and loved trees. Oh, he wished for a world where you knew what tomorrow would bring, where you knew somebody cared for you and watched over you, where somebody could see into your very heart and know that it was a good heart.

It would, I suppose, have been more comfortable for Puritan if he had enjoyed the faith of the former tenant of the rooms in which he stood. If he could have known the Collect for the fourth Sunday after Epiphany, he would have found a balm from the very first words: 'Oh God, who knows us to be set in the midst of so many and great dangers, that by reason of the frailty of our nature we cannot always stand upright'. Or he would surely have found comfort in the Collect for the eighth Sunday after Trinity: 'Oh God, whose never-failing providence ordereth all things both in heaven and earth. We humbly beseech thee to put away from us all hurtful things, and to give us those things which be profitable for us; through Jesus Christ our Lord'. But he knew nothing of such comfortable words, only the anger and pain and the oh so deep belief that a socialist society would rid him of the discomfort, wash away the hurt and provide for him an outward and tangible heaven right here amongst his and everybody else's frailty.

Indeed the simple restating of his dream of a perfect society, the lowly mental chanting of his own personal mantra-litany for a better world, calmed and comforted him, soothed and restored him to his more usual and sociable self. The contemplation of a better world worked to charge up the batteries of his optimism, and he gathered up his sleeping bag and determined to work in the office and find out more about his new position and duties.

He moved the desk from in front of the fire exist and sat at it and drew out of a drawer some poster paper and found some large felt-tip pens. On to this paper he wrote: THIS IS A NON-SMOKING OFFICE ... SMOKING KILLS THE YOUNG. On another sheet he wrote: WE DO NOT TOLERATE RACISM IN OUR COMMUNITY. On another he penned: WE BELIEVE IN EQUAL OPPORTUNITIES and on the last he wrote: THIS COMMUNITY IS GENDER EQUAL, ANY SEXUAL ORIENTATION IS O.K. HERE.

Having produced these large posters, he stuck them on the walls and experienced a feeling of extreme well-being. He stood looking at them and knew in his very heart that he would build

34

a new kind of society here at the Comity, a society that was as near as damn it, a socialist society. A place where his rule, his writ would run wide and deep; even, he thought, the whales and trees would be safe here under his protection, his rule. He would, he vowed there and then, stamp out the very last vestiges of racialism, sexism, smoking and even meat eating from the dark corners of the Comity. He would, he swore, search out and expel bigotry and prejudice. All wrong thinking would be expunged from the Comity under his rule, for he knew the path, he knew the way and he was now charged with the job of putting the Comity's collective feet upon that path, with taking each and every Comity resident along the road to a better and more beautiful world.

His eyes fixed upon the new posters, stuck upon the floral wallpaper that Jane Hartwell had chosen for her gentle and loving father. Puritan continued day-dreaming and then, dragging his eyes away, he once again sat down at the desk and started to plan how he would go about establishing his New Jerusalem. He worked rapidly and covered many sheets of paper, carefully placing them in a folder as he finished each sheet.

While he worked at the giant architecture of plans, the ever-present pain of his box, now in pieces, nagged at his conscious-ness. The box represented the man insofar as it had replaced his family, his mother and father – although who his father was he had never known. This man who had fathered him had long gone from the family by the time the young Richard could comprehend that other children had a father and he did not. It had been a subject that he had never been able to ask his mother about and he had had to make do with the succession of 'uncles' that came and went. Thus in many ways the box was his father, it was dependable, strong, contained his life history, was always there and was intensely practical; he could sit on it, even on occasions hide behind it and, come wind or rain, it was there for him and would never desert him. The box had often been stronger than he was, it had never let him down. If he had been a religious man he would have been able to pray to 'Our Father' and have found an echo in the psalms, praying, 'Hide not your face from me in the time of my trouble'. But he was not religious and his box served in its place and was now in pieces on the floor of the flat.

He got up from the desk and went into the flat and assembled the pieces. He had no tools and no nails or screws, but he did have some Sellotape and he bound up the box's wounds as best he could. Tomorrow he would see if he could get a handyman or a carpenter to mend his box and he murmured to it that he would make it as good as new.

It was now late in the afternoon and he had not eaten since his breakfast. Being a vegetarian, and an awful cook, he tended to eat either out of packets or cold salads. The only dish he could manage with any skill was boiled rice and vegetable stew. He had brought some with him, together with a saucepan, and so he searched out the bag of food and prepared his normal evening meal of boiled rice with boiled vegetable stew and Marmite.

His day had been lonely, troubled and obviously dreadful. It is true that he had written the posters and stuck them up, he had drawn up some plans and he had started to heal the box with Sellotape, but all in all his day had been awful and he was cast down. This was not the feeling he had expected on his first full day as Administrator of the Comity.

The arrival of Felicity Eristic in her Renault was marked by much throwing up of gravel as she attempted to sweep round the parking space in a wide arc, although there was not enough space to allow this, and so she had to brake and then reverse and complete the turn in three goes, leaving her just facing the arch.

Ms Eristic got out of the car and strode to the stairway in the archway. She had slammed the door of her car and set off the car alarm with so much noise that almost all 12 sets of curtains moved as the residents, unused to visitors in the early evening, peered out to see what was going on. Ms Eristic noted the twitching curtains.

Mr Puritan, however, not used to silence or peace in his environment, was unaware of the arrival of Ms Eristic until she banged on the door of the office. He opened the door and she barged in expecting to be welcomed and invited.

Eristic swept the office with an expert eye and took in the new posters.

'Richard, we should be more powerful on sexism. I've been re-reading Justin Covinous, the chapter on sexual inequality and the establishment strategies to keep women as second-class citizens. I think it applies here particularly, because women live longer and so are shunted off into places like this where they can't challenge the system. Do you see that?'

Puritan felt he had been found wanting – yet again. He had been satisfied with his posters but now felt that he had not done enough.

'Well, I thought I'd settle in a bit first before I tried any real action, Felicity.'

'But can we wait? You know as well as I do that Justin Covinous reckons that all systems take the players over and that they become part of the process rather than in charge of it. He has stated that it is the first 100 days that are crucial in any change of powerbase. We have to establish the tone of our leadership – you here, me with the Council. We know how things should be organised to empower the participants, not the holders of office or positions. You do agree don't you?'

Puritan agreed, Puritan believed in the words of Justin Covinous and his ideas, but he also believed in the power of regulations and order. 'First I will have to work to get this place in line with the regulations and then will be the time for a more powerful socio-political push. You know I agree with your and Covinous's ideas, but I have a responsibility to make sure that this place is safe and fully up to speed with the legislation and social policies of the Council, the Ministry and the EU. We'll have to do something about the archway. It's too narrow for emergency vehicles, and then there is the question of smoke alarms in every cottage, and I want a nurse-call system installed, and the gates will have to go, we can't have gates shut at night, just when the emergencies happen. And there's the parking. One of the residents has a motorbike and another has a car – they mustn't be allowed to park on the standing, that should be reserved for emergency vehicles and deliveries. I've also had a look at the kitchens; they would be ideal for the Council to use and so we would need more lavatories and staff. I rather thought we might take over one of the cottages for a council catering office and storerooms. What do you think?

Felicity thought nothing about Puritan's plans, for her mind was fixed upon a more pressing need. She recalled her nights with Puritan and the powerful urgency of his wanting her when they had first met. She remembered their love and the wonderful moments afterwards when she had his body, soul and mind in the palm of her hands as he lay beside her exhausted but receptive to her every suggestion. She pulled from her memory the gasping protestations that he had made, the vows he had sworn and the wonderful regeneration of their lust and the way they had watched the night's blackness ebb away and the dawn creep into the corners of the room before they had finally been sated with each other's passion. These were for Felicity Eristic sweet, fond memories, and the simple act of remembering them woke up feelings that she had not experienced for some long time.

'Have you got a bed yet Richard?'

'No, I thought I would use my sleeping bag on the floor here in the office for a bit. There's so much to do.'

Felicity decided that she was prepared to put up with the office floor just this once and started to undo the boilersuit type thing she was wearing.

'Do you remember that squat in Camden, Richard, that first night after we'd been to that ridiculous meeting about language and its power in revolutionary politics? Well, I now feel just like I did then – I want you.'

At ten thirty that evening John Hall closed the gates of the Comity, not knowing if the owner of the Renault had a key and not really caring very much. He was too cross and as he said to Doris, his wife: 'This never happened when the Reverend Hartwell was the Administrator.'

5

Covinous Leads from Behind

The comings and goings of what are known as the chattering classes are at best of very slight importance to the rest of England and of even less importance to the world. Silly academics closed in small worlds fulminate ineffectually, fashion leaders flap their hands, and the politically correct chatterers lay down absolute conditions to nobody in particular.

These people elevate themselves to a position of importance that has no foundation in fact or, indeed, reality. The chatter that they hiss in high-pitched tones or braying yelps to those who listen, either because they have nothing better to do or because their next meal turns upon their sycophancy, normally fades into the air already full of silliness.

Of even more pointlessness are the army of London-based champagne socialists, who, living a life of affluent and sybaritic indulgence, mouth off continually about the evils of the very life they enjoy to the full; yet never dream of changing themselves.

One such pair of chattering, champagne socialists is Justin and Tabby Covinous. Justin Covinous works for the Open University in the Sociology Department, where he helps to make educational programmes for mature students. His salary is such that he can live a great deal better on it than many people working in industry and generating wealth for the country. He also receives royalties from the sale of his books, which titles, by pure coincidence, find their way on to the reading lists that his Open University course issues to students each term. Notwithstanding this sizeable income, Justin Covinous maintains the fiction that he is simply a poorly paid teacher, living from hand to mouth.

To be fair, his hands and mouth do figure greatly in his life, as eating out in his locality – Hampstead – is a major hobby that both Justin and Tabby indulge almost every night, suffering as a consequence what their friends describe as a weight problem.

Tabby Covinous is wealthy in her own right, and her feminism is most notably demonstrated by the fact that she has all her own money in her maiden name in her own bank account, which is not the same bank as Justin's. The only child of a very wealthy Australian, Tabby is by any measure remarkably rich and owns the Hampstead house (again in her maiden name) which Justin calls 'my house' to his friends and 'my lodgings' in his published works. She also owns a large slice of a residential and retail estate in another fashionable part of London, as well as a farm in Surrey and a well-appointed house in Gloucestershire. Jointly they own a house in the South of France, a boat and a respectable portfolio of stocks, bonds and shares.

Tabby Covinous works tirelessly as a legal executive for Haringey Council, specialising in racial and adoption matters. She is a qualified solicitor but has always stated that she would never work in the non-state sector of the UK economy.

Justin has long held the same views on the private sector as Tabby, but working for the Open University has enabled him to write the books for which he is now famous, and the opinions expressed in those books have enabled him to appear on BBC TV.

It would be an injustice to Covinous for me to try to explain his incisive and clever philosophy. However, because the baleful influence of Mr Covinous's ideas were to act as a spur and yardstick for both Mr Puritan and Ms Eristic, I should perhaps provide readers with a tour of the more notable towers of Mr Covinous's philosophical architecture.

In his first book – *The Power of the Free Market to Inhibit Social Progress* – Covinous takes as his starting point that a demand market is driven simply by gross numbers. It is, he maintains, solely a matter of the greatest number of demands being met. Thus, he argues, as society works on the basis of 'now' rather than what is best, a market-driven society is always satisfyingly instant rather than deferred gratification. A market-driven economy has no mechanism for thinking about tomorrow's needs or even for a medium or long-term view.

In his second book – *The Establishment's Ability to Retain Power* – he postulates that the Establishment has a vested interest in letting the market economy hold sway, as it will, by so doing, be encouraging the 'now' factor and thus shifting the populace away from the idea that it is possible to change and to have a vision of a better world tomorrow.

The third book by Covinous carried the title *The Common Man's Inheritance*. In this mighty tome the writer explains that socialism lost its nerve under Stalin and others and allowed the cult of leadership to usurp its true power, which is democratically based. 'Leaders', he wrote, 'are seduced by power rather than facilitating in the growth of people power. Therefore the leadership must always be based upon small units that are led along the right road by communal discussion and continual debate. Leaders, he stated, 'must be replaced by Facilitators – people whose sole job it is to steer the group along the right path'.

The last book is titled *The Establishment* v *the System*. In this work Covinous examines the way his idealistic, socialist system would come about through winning key control over small independent units within society and replacing the market-driven impetus with what Covinous called 'longtermism'.

On the strength of this prodigious output, Covinous has gained a following amongst certain of the younger students of sociology and amongst BBC producers of the 'what a terrible country we live in' school of docu-drama.

Since the publication of his first book, Justin Covinous has become much more vocal in his left-of-centre views and has been heard on TV explaining how it is impossible to live on the level of income the miserable state pays teachers and others, how it is impossible for a person such as himself to enter the property market, and how his plight identifies the plight of thousands of ordinary people just like him.

Many of his readers, knowing nothing of his very comfortable circumstances and his and Tabby's very valuable and well-appointed Hampstead house, let alone the farm, bonds, stocks and shares, the boat and the French property, felt that he spoke directly for them in their poverty and misery. Justin encouraged such misconception by dressing deliberately like the squatters and the disaffected – but only for his television appearances; he also adopted a kind of cockney accent and sniffed a lot whenever the camera focused upon him. His catchphase, if a serious TV social commentator can have a catchphase, was ideally crafted to reinforce this 'man-of-the-people' image: 'I'm a beer man, not your wine and spirits Establishment leech.'

Tabby had also crafted a similar persona. Her wealth carefully hidden behind her husband's success on TV, Tabby fought for the disadvantaged and persecuted who came to Haringey Council, regardless of the merits of their case or the honesty of their statements. To Tabby, the very act of turning up was reason enough to believe in the injustice of the system and the rightness of the claimants' case. She too dressed down to her cases and also used a cockney type of accent in keeping with her peers in the council's employ.

When each came home to their Hampstead nest, all this pretence was sloughed off, and safely with their friends, they drank wines and spirits and ate out, happy in their anonymity. The only disappointment in their otherwise perfect existence came in the shape of Joe Staunch, Tabby's son by her first husband. Joe lived with Justin and Tabby. At 23 years of age, both mother and stepfather felt, Joe should have found his own flat. There was, though, no reason for the young man to live away because he occupied a separate, self-contained basement flat in the house and paid his mother a grossly subsidised rent for it.

The problem for both Tabby and Justin was that having educated Joe at the best private schools and then at Cambridge University, he was not the son they would have wished for. There was nothing of the man-in-the-street about Joe Staunch. He was already patrician in his manner and interested in every-thing that a classics education gives to a serious student. He was, in short, more than a little censorious of his stepfather and his mother. He lived on a generous legacy from his maternal grandfather and was a very talented painter and sculptor, although commercial success in these fields of activity was yet to find his address.

Joseph Staunch was unattached, and apart from a true affection for his cat Verity, love had not crossed his path, mind or even his dreams.

It was, therefore, something of a shock for Joe Staunch to find on his ansaphone a message from his mother to have dinner with them – actually in the house above. Normally, when the Covinouses invited people to dinner, they ate out at one of the more fashionable restaurants. This evening, however, Joe was intrigued to learn that he was invited to dinner, which would, he presumed, be manufactured by either Tabby or Justin. I use the term 'manufactured' because neither Tabby nor Justin could ever be described as cooks. Their lives and their causes were of much greater importance to them both than learning to boil an egg or roast a joint of meat.

In his childhood, Joe had discovered that if he wanted a cooked meal, when his nanny wasn't in residence, the only certain way of getting it was to cook it himself. As a result, he became a proficient cook and, having been forced to become a cook, he had grown to love the whole business of preparing and cooking a meal.

The receipt of his mother's invitation to a 'home cooked' dinner therefore was not calculated to set his mouth watering or his spirits climbing. He had not spoken to either Tabby or Justin for some days and thus felt it would be unreasonable to turn the invitation down. He determined, though, to make himself some edible snack which he could eat before he unlocked the internal door and paid his filial visit.

Joe Staunch did not like either his mother or stepfather. It would not be true to say that he disliked them, he just felt that they were not people he would ever seek out or choose to know. This distaste was really just that and was not an active dislike or indeed an active anything. Given the choice, he avoided them, and since taking up the tenancy to the basement flat, this choice had been exactly what he had exercised, for he had no wish to be part of Tabby and Justin Covinous's lives.

He probably had never really thought about this judgement, but were he to be asked, he would have probably stated that his parents' social life seemed thin and valueless, while their private life struck him as being indulgent and pointless. Regarding their political causes and stands, he remained aloof and disinterested for he was not a political animal, tending to lean more to religion.

In all this Joseph Staunch walked his own path and made up his own mind on all matters of moment. His education had equipped him to be discerning and, once programmed, he was unable to discard this mechanism for the sake of snap opinions or instant sound bites.

The problem of communication was not by any stretch of the imagination a difficulty between the son and his parents, as neither Tabby or Justin Covinous were ever able to comprehend or even hear any opinion that did not totally accord with their own personal view on life or society.

At 23 years of age, Joseph believed that he suffered from the generation gap. He also thought that sons always had little to say to parents and that was the way it had been since the dawn of time. The reality was that he saw through his parents' deceits and was not amused by the double standards that they both exhibited. He was, as most sons always are, critical of his parents because he had not seen too much of the world in just 23 years.

Tall and already graceful, with clear blue eyes and fair hair, Joe Staunch knew himself to be attractive, and having none of the weight problems of his mother and stepfather, he dressed out of fashion and, when not at home, wore a formal lightweight suit, coloured shirt and tie. Dressed like this, he unlocked the internal door and went upstairs to dinner.

In the long sitting room he found his mother, stepfather and two strangers who obviously were confidants of his parents. The first person to whom he was introduced was Norman Hircine, a lawyer who worked with his mother. He took an instant dislike to Mr Hircine, although the lawyer smiled broadly and shook the young man's hand affably.

The other man, Mr Palter, was a friend of Justin and was from the BBC. He asked Joseph to call him Eric.

'It's just pre-dinner drinks, sweetheart,' his mother told him. 'We are having dinner delivered from Wheelbites, that smashing new restaurant in the high street, and they promised to deliver it sharp at eight thirty, so you've plenty of time to get to know Mr Hircine and Mr Palter.'

Joseph smiled his most affable smile and accepted a glass of red wine which Justin assured him was so much better than anything you could get in England and was only sold in France to a very select group of customers.

'Ordinary people don't really understand wine, they have no nose for it and drink it like Coke. That's why this vineyard only sells to special customers. This is a 1986 Burgundy, Joe, and 1986 was a wonderful year for Burgundy, providing the grapes were not picked too early – as some unscrupulous producers did. Of course this is an *appellation Controlée*, it comes from a chateau just outside Dijon, but I refuse absolutely to say more.' He looked at Palter and said: 'Joe here's my stepson but I wouldn't even tell him the address, because he's a fabulous cook and a bon viveur, so mum's the word when I find a great, mind-blowing wine like this.'

'That's really exciting news from that council down in Wilts, Justin.'

Mr Palter was buzzing with his news and Joe realised that the impact of his arrival had quickly dissipated.

'The Council has set up its own development enterprise company to get round the legislation about tendering and going private, and they have appointed a young girl hot-shot called something like Esteric – in fact it is Eristic, I never thought I would remember the name, but I have. Anyway, this development enterprise company is owned and run by the Labour Party and the council has leased all its old people and sheltered housing properties to it, and the board of directors is the Labour Party big-wigs who are also on the council. There's pots of Government money for this sort of thing and they are awash with it, and any profits they make obviously go straight back to the party, or rather the big wigs. It's just brilliant, Justin, and this chief executive girl Eristic is an absolute fan of yours and they say she's planning to take over many of the charity homes as well.'

45

'Is that legal?' Joseph's question seemed naive as soon as he'd uttered it.

Tabby smiled at him. 'Well, not strictly legal, I suppose, but it's no more dishonest than the way justices' clerks run up over four hundred and thirty-two million pounds' worth of legal aid for solicitors or barristers. One hell of a lot of that is highly dubious, but it's Government money just like the sheltered and old people's homes funds are Government money. And to think of it, Norman, only some eleven point two million pounds of that goes on immigration legal aid; it's a pitiable percentage.'

Justin now took the opportunity presented to show himself off to his friends, not as a TV commentator but as a free-thinking spirit. 'Government money always goes either to the middle classes or to business, because they know how to handle it, to launder it so that it looks as if it's doing some good. They can talk it up, convert it to the language of "good" while living very comfortably on it. All the Labour council and local party are doing is using the system that the middle class has put in place for its own ends. That is justice, regardless of whether it is legal or not, Joe. The choice is between shovelling Government money into the middle class's pockets or the party's pockets, and I know which one I'd sooner see stuffed with Government money, eh, Eric?'

Eric agreed, as did Norman Hircine and Tabby.

'The beauty of the whole set-up is that this Eristic woman is an employee of the Council as well as Chief Executive of the Development Enterprise Company, so she just has to keep her mouth shut and be helpful. Mind you, she's getting a good salary from the council and a director's fee and performance bonus from the Development Enterprise Company. So she has everything to lose if she steps out of line. Apparently, I'm told, they are not totally sure of her on account of you, Justin, she keeps talking your stuff at them, and so you see your philosophy is sneaking into every corner of the land.'

'Well, if she succeeds or fails I'm into some TV appearances,' mused Justin.

There was a knock at the door and Tabby announced, after looking out of the window, that the dinner had arrived and left the room to arrange it.

Palter carried on talking about his news although Joe, Justin and Hircine grew ever more bored with the subject.

Hircine finally broke in and asked Justin about the house, was it really old and would he not like a more modern property?

'God no,' Justin replied, 'everything built after the First World War is rubbish. Builders have been busy reducing the heights of the ceilings and the sizes of the rooms, whilst at the same time filling the reduced space with built-in machines, and all this during an age when people have been getting bigger physically. Modern houses are simply little cells for the common herd to live in. I couldn't live in one, I need my personal space to match my imagination. The Victorians got it right, they built gentlemen's houses for gentlemen and workers' cottages for the rest. The only damn thing about it is that you have to be bloody rich now to live in this sort of house. Thank God, Tabby can keep it up. I couldn't on what the Government pays us chalk-face teachers. What's thirty-five thousand a year if you want to live in a place like this? It costs us nine hundred pounds just to have the hall painted, and the bloody man seems to be here for ever doing it.'

Justin Covinous would have carried on about how £35,000 a year was an impossibly low figure for a man of his worth to live on, had Tabby not announced that dinner was now ready and they should move into the dining room, where the white wine was nicely chilled and the red mercifully at room temperature. Wheelbites had produced a wonderful spread and Joe felt a slight pang of regret that he had snacked before he came.

The conversation over dinner was hardly interesting as Justin gave what had become his established dinner talk on the evils of the Establishment and Tabby talked totally about how the private sector of the legal trade enjoyed huge fees and milked the legal aid system dry.

For Joseph Staunch, the dinner proved to be as boring and uninteresting as he had imagined. At ten thirty he escaped to his basement flat and determined that he would not see either Justin or Tabby for another month or more. There must be something more to life that hearing those two bang on about the system and the legal aid bill, he told himself.

6

On Stony Ground

Eight weeks had passed since Mr Puritan took over as Administrator of the Comity. June was the second quarter-day when residents paid their rent in advance for the next quarter. The quarter-day was more a matter of the Administrator just chatting with each resident or pair of residents, as they handed over their cheque or rent money.

Rents were nugatory, indeed they were designed to be peppercorn rents. When the RRAWF had set up the Comity, it had been agreed by the trustees that all residents should pay a sum every quarter-day to establish the concept of their independence. The rent was, however, set according to means, with a ceiling being established of £5 per week for the richest resident. From that figure the Administrator was allowed to reduce the rent to 10s per week in pre-decimal coinage, 50p in 'new money' as it was called by the residents.

Amongst the residents at present in the Comity only the Truckles and Mrs Patel paid a reduced rent, all the others paid £60 per quarter. There had been talk of making the payment of the rent possible by standing order, but the Reverend Hartwell had opposed it on the grounds that it allowed him to discuss a degree of business with each resident in private. The trustees had seen the wisdom of this and so the ritual of the quarter-day rent collection had continued.

The Comity residents were therefore mightily surprised to find that their appointment slips on this first Puritan quarter-day showed the same time, rather than staggered times, and that instead of the Comity office, the location was the communal room on the ground floor.

They assembled punctually at 11 o'clock on the morning of the quarter-day in the Comity's communal lounge and were surprised to find 16 chairs set out in four rows of four chairs each row. In front of them was a table and two chairs were behind the table.

On all the walls of the lounge there were large wall posters printed with giant red letters. Each poster carried a different message, but all said more or less the same thing and that was that racialism, sexism, and smoking were wrong. Only one poster was not negative and that read that all sexual orientations were good.

The residents first read the posters with something very like amazement, and then a collective anger spread through them, although nobody said anything. Rachel Malapert stood up and walked towards the one that carried the slogan SEXISM FINDS NO PLACE IN OUR COMMUNITY and started to pull the corner off the bluetack. Just as she had got the corner free Mr Puritan came into the lounge, followed by Ms Eristic.

'Was it starting to peel off? That's right, press it back, Mrs eh, eh, that's right, press it, firmly dear.'

Had Mr Puritan known more about the residents, he would have known that nobody ever called Mrs Malapert 'dear' and would thus have saved himself first the withering look she gave him and then the scorn that filled her voice when she answered: 'I was taking the thing down. It's offensive, Mr Puritan, and should never have been put up.'

Mr Puritan and Ms Eristic had reached the table and turned to face the residents.

'Leave it alone and sit down please.' Ms Eristic spat the words out at Mrs Malapert. Mrs Malapert did so and looked hard at Ray Paladin.

'I've called this meeting to bring you all up to date with a number of changes and some great new ideas that I've been planning, and I've invited Ms Eristic from the Council, who, as you all probably know, is very involved in the provision of care for the elderly.'

Mr Puritan had dressed in his green trousers and a green denim shirt. To some of the more short-sighted residents he

49

looked more like a huge animated bottle of French table-water than the Administrator of the Comity.

'As you all probably know, there has been new legislation covering sheltered housing. This means that we have to make some changes to both your living units and to the way St Margaret's Comity is organised. Firstly there is a requirement that we should fit in every living unit a smoke detector, er alarm, together with a brand new nurse-call system.'

John Hall stood up and pointed the stem of his pipe at Mr Puritan. 'I don't want a smoke detector in my cottage and I won't have one, thank you, Mr Administrator. As for the nurse-call, I don't want one of them either.'

'It is not a matter of what you want,' replied Ms Eristic, 'it is a case of the legislation and our duty of care, and please don't smoke in here, we have all got to breathe the same air.'

Ray Paladin got up very slowly. 'Who, Mr Puritan, said this was a non-smoking room? Residents have always smoked in here. And also, while I'm at it, who asked you to put up those notices? Have you lost your reason? All of us are over sixty-five years of age, our sexual orientation has absolutely nothing whatever to do with anyone. I am embarrassed, Mr Puritan, to see such words plastered on the wall when there are ladies here. I am also embarrassed to see the notice about racism, that is irrelevant here as we believe in good manners not in crude slogans exhorting us not to do things that we would never entertain doing anyway. So, if you don't mind, I will remove them and then we can get on with anything else you wish to say.'

Ms Eristic became icy cold and spoke from her chair: 'Those posters will stay exactly where they are, Mr Paladin, isn't it?' 'Yes.' Those posters are not your property, nor are they a matter that is open for discussion, they are there to remind us all of what being part of a community means. We are not islands, Mr Paladin, we are all part of a great tide of humanity that has to share each with the other, the air we breathe, the ground we walk on, our common troubles and our genetic make-up. They are to remind us of those facts and also to remind us that we are not the be all and end all of our own lives. We have to depend upon each other, and the older we get

50

the more we depend upon the younger, stronger people around us. But there is a price we have to pay for this dependency, and those posters represent the price that is expected by the generation that will be providing you with the resources and strengths you will be needing if you don't need them already. Is that clear, Mr Paladin?'

Valerie Curst, one of the eldest residents and also one of the shortest tempered, rose from her chair under the poster calling for the eradication of sexism. 'I don't know who the hell you are, miss, or rather who the hell you think you are, but let me tell you straight, I certainly don't need any lessons from you about humanity, sharing or dependency. My husband lived for twenty years sitting in a chair unable to speak or even to pee without help, and I ran the shop and looked after him; but I never once allowed him to suspect that he was not the most important person in the place and that it wasn't a pleasure to be helping him. And, miss, let me tell you it was a pleasure for most of the time because I could do it for him and he couldn't do it for himself, and I knew which of those two alternatives I would sooner have. So if you want to lecture anybody, go and find some sexual cripples, they might be prepared to listen to you, but I'm not, I've better things to do.' Valerie Curst painfully made for the door. As she drew level with it she turned: 'Another thing, Mr Puritan, you can forget about the smoke alarms and the nurse-call. If there is a fire, John and Doris Hall, my neighbours, will wake me and call for help if I need it, so save your money to buy some proper clothes, like a jacket and some stout shoes.'

As she opened the door, most of the rest of residents also stood up and made for the door. Only the Truckles and Gerald Foozler remained seated, looking mightily confused and totally ill at ease.

Felicity Eristic watched 13 residents leave the room, with a mixture of rage and interest. The one thing Ms Eristic had learnt in life is that there is much to gain by keen observation of the situations associated with defeat. The fact that Desmond and Sheila Truckle and Gerald Foozler remained seated provided her with three potential allies, three potential weak links in the otherwise united front of the residents. She remained silently watching the residents leave; she looked only at the door as it opened and then shut.

Mr Puritan had stood up as Valerie Curst was speaking and he remained standing looking down at the table saying nothing, but feeling a sulleness creeping over him. A resentment grew in his heart that this should have happened in front of Felicity Eristic.

The silence in the room became oppressive and the Truckles got up, followed by Gerald Foozler. They were embarrassed and chose not to look at either Mr Puritan or Ms Eristic. They shuffled to the door and eased themselves out, seeking to leave unnoticed.

Outside they hesitated. 'Oh dear, oh dear, that wasn't very nice, was it, Desmond?'

'It certainly wasn't, Sheila love, it was very difficult indeed. What do you think, Mr Foozler? Nasty, wasn't it?'

Gerald Foozler looked desperately at the Truckles. Never a winner in life's lottery, Gerald Foozler had gone through life never understanding what was expected of him until it was too late. He had inherited his father's shop, had married and had watched the shop slowly fade. Too late he had realised that he should have been into marketing and hiring TVs and repairs and hire purchase. He should also have noticed that his wife spent more and more time out, and he should have noticed earlier that other married couples had children. All these things and many others he should have noticed but had not until forced to try to comprehend them as they fell apart about his ears. Always too late, always not understanding, always backing the wrong horse, these were the accusations his wife flung at him as she left him to live with the man who ran the shop next door.

'I think,' stammered Gerald Foozler, 'that it is a pity that the Reverend Hartwell left. I could always talk to him, he understood things, he understood.'

'But what about this meeting?' asked Desmond.

'Well, it was a shambles, wasn't it. The new Administrator doesn't seem to know much about us at all, does he, and that woman was so rude to Mrs Malapert and Mr Paladin, so rude, so rude.'

They walked slowly back to their cottages, each keenly aware that they had witnessed not the end of a tiff, but the start of a battle, the birth of umbrage, the ingress of hatred and anger into the normally calm waters of their Comity existence. There was fear and sadness in their hearts because they knew that they were probably unequal to the struggle which had started to pull apart the residents from their carer and administrator of the minutiae of their daily lives.

In the office in the Comity building Felicity Eristic strove to strengthen Mr Puritan's sinews ready for the battle which she knew would be both bloody and long. It was a battle she had to win because it was the first charity-based sheltered housing complex she had targeted for the Development Enterprise Company to acquire. Her reputation with the local Labour Party and the Council turned on her ability to resolve the problems and bring the ship of St Margaret's Comity safely home to the Development Enterprise Company's harbour.

'It's a blip, that's all', she told Puritan. 'They're old, set in their ways, they hate the new, they hate change. It doesn't change anything, though – what can they do? It will all happen regardless of them. They have no voice, no strength, no power. You have the power, your appointment gives you the power.'

'But they walked out, Felicity,' whined Puritan, 'before I could tell them about the anti-sexist festival and the fire pathways and the hot meals facilities.'

'Start a St Margaret's Comity newsletter, Richard, and then they will all know what's happening and won't be able to contest it. You need to pick each one off separately and a newsletter is the way to do it because they won't act in unison. Write and tell each one when it is their turn to have the smoke detectors and nurse-calls fitted – make it official. People always cave in if they think something is official. If you like, I'll give you some Council Welfare headed paper which can use. Remember, if you order people they do it, if you ask them they argue. That's Covinous's first law of social direction. And for God's sake be tougher, Richard. The law and the Council are on your side and you're in charge here, so *take* charge.'

Richard Puritan heard Felicity's words and they did stiffen his sinews. He was in charge, he did have right on his side, they were only powerless, crumbly old people and they had no power. The law, thought Richard Puritan, is above all and has to be obeyed, and it was the law that smoke alarms should be fitted and it was also the law that, there should be an anti-sexist festival at the Comity in September – his law and he was the bringer of law to the Comity. He determined to follow Felicity's advice and compose a newsletter and send out letters to the residents telling them that the contractors would be fitting alarms and nurse-calls.

That lunchtime at the Wilton Arms' saloon bar the 13 residents who had walked out of the meeting held what was a battle meeting.

Roger Blithe, the landlord of the Wilton Arms, had been pleasantly surprised to see his saloon bar suddenly fill up and had happily instructed Mrs Blithe to make the sandwiches that the Comity residents ordered.

Sharon Lubberly was the loudest voice in the mass of 'terribles', 'awfuls' and 'disgustings' that bubbled up from the group.

The Lubberlys had run a market stall in London's East End Chaple Market and had arrived at the Comity because they had not only sold radios and TVs but other more questionable goods. Because of their age, the judge had sequestrated all their considerable property and told them to get out of his sight. The property that was left and that which the courts and the Inland Revenue knew nothing about had been disposed of, and both Sharon and Sid had happily accepted the cottage at the Comity, with their now much reduced nestegg, safe in the knowledge that the Old Bill would remain on the outside of the Comity unless specifically invited in.

'It is,' said Sharon, 'nothing more or less than a diabolical liberty. Our cottages are private property and Puritan is no more allowed to come into them than any stranger. Isn't that right, Sid?'

'You're right, Shar, it's private property and not nobody can come in unless they have a warrant,' replied Sid. 'I don't know about the rest of you, but as far as Shar and me go, this Puritan man can stroll right on with his alarms and call systems.'

Sid Lubberly had caught the attention of the group, which had fallen silent.

'We didn't come here to be politically corrected, and there's no call for it neither. What we are has taken us years to reach and Shar and me don't intend to change into social workers, do we, Shar?'

Sharon indicated that she did not want to become a social worker or a politically correct person either. I have to note, however, that whilst the other residents had no desire for the Lubberlys to be politically correct, they did sometimes wish that both Sharon and Sid would indeed change, although the choice would have tended to be that they both entered a Trappist Order.

Valerie Curst was still steaming with indignation and although sorely incapacitated by arthritis, she had forced herself to keep up with the group as they had made their way to the Wilton Arms.

The conversation dwelt upon the events of the meeting they had just left, and the consensus was that Puritan had gone too far. The problem was that none of the group could come up with any one course of action that seemed to meet the problem, much less answer the pressing need for a response to the smoke alarms and nurse-calls. John Hall suggested that one of the group might call upon the Reverend Hartwell and ask his advice. He had his address and if Mrs Patel would give him a lift, he was prepared to act as spokesman. Mrs Patel, however, thought that to visit the Reverend Hartwell would be an imposition as he had officially retired. Her idea was that they would write to Mr Fribble or the RRAWF and put their case to him.

'But if it is the law,' ventured Arnold Pule, 'then it's the law and we can't do a thing about it.'

'Damn the law', chipped in Valerie Curst, 'we pay a rent and are entitled to privacy and a say in our affairs.'

Ray Paladin suggested that they should approach a solicitor for advice. 'If we all divvied in we could pay for a consultation and then we'd know exactly where we stand,' he suggested.

The cost, however, was not known, and the group felt that once you were in the hands of solicitors your money ran out of your pockets faster than ice melted on a griddle. Solutions were thin on the ground and they returned to the Comity without any idea of what to do.

7

An Old Problem

Old hearts and old attitudes harden. In the summer the sun
shines upon old heads and the very heat tells old bodies that
winter is most certainly around the corner.

Thus in the days following the quarter-day, the old minds of
the Comity residents tried desperately to cling onto the concept
that the world of the Comity hadn't changed and that, given
time, things would return to some kind of normality.

Such pious hopes were to be quickly dashed as Mr Puritan
rushed out his letters and, more importantly, his newsletters.
The letters were simply factual statements that told the residents
when the contractor would install the smoke alarm and nurse-
call system in their particular cottage.

The newsletter, entitled *St Margaret's Comity News*, was
altogether more vicious and damaging to the tranquillity desperately sought after by the residents. The first edition ran a
headline that screamed 'THE KILLERS AMONGST US'. It dealt with
the spurious dangers of passive smoking and was in reality a
single-issue tract on the dangers of smoking and how the elderly
were particularly at risk.

Puritan posted a copy through the door of every cottage in
the Comity, and in spite of the fact that it was badly written,
totally unresearched and full of the most dreadful and dire
warnings, the effect it had upon all the residents was totally
horrible. Ray Paladin, who smoked cigars and was the only one
who showed any fight, lit his cigar with it when he saw Mr
Puritan emerge from his office to instruct the builder to remove
the gates.

For John Hall it was a different matter. He had read it before breakfast and was consumed with guilt for Doris. Having smoked his pipe for something like 50 years, he now felt like a murderer – as indeed the newsletter told him he was. He forgot to make the normal pot of tea for Doris and just simply sat in his chair consumed by grief and guilt. Doris became alarmed and went to search for him and found him staring at the pipe he held in his hand. She asked him if everything was all right, but he couldn't speak to her, she put her arm around his back and he simply broke down and cried, great sobs of grief, great wails of pain and remorse. Doris became alarmed and ran next door to Valerie Curst. As they arrived back, they found John Hall slashing his wrists, and when he saw them he turned to Doris and with an anguished cry shouted: 'This is what should be done to killers.' He fell on the floor sobbing, blood gushing from his wrists.

Doris screamed and rushed to comfort him, Valerie Curst ran to the Comity office and, hearing the noise, Sid Lubberly pushed his way into the cottage, saw the blood and, gently lifting Doris off John, asked her to get some plasters. First, pressing hard on the cuts on one wrist, he was able to staunch the bleeding, while telling Doris to do the same on the other wrist. John was starting to lose consciousness, drifting in and out of a kind of dream state. He felt nothing, the pain of cutting his wrists had gone and only the terrible guilt remained. He was a killer, he had been killing Doris ever since their marriage, slowly killing her for 50 years, day by day, week by week. That was the pain that wouldn't go away and a fearful blackness came over him, a feeling of self-hatred, and if he had had the strength he would have snatched his arms away and pulled off the plasters that they were trying to stick onto his wrists.

He became calmer in his despair, he became cunning. He had been convicted, the newsletter told him so.

It is possible that readers will think that John Hall had acted too quickly, had believed the nonsense that Puritan had penned out of his shame at having been bested at the residents meeting on the quarter-day. Old men, however, are not always stable, nor always rational. They have lived long lives and have seen the most unlikely things happen, they have learnt that the world is a world of unpredictability. They have seen black proved white, they have seen the impossible made flesh and in their frailty they have recognised that man has a very slight grasp on what they assumed in their youth to be cast-iron certainties. Challenge such old men and they will back down, not from lack of courage, but from the certainty that there are no certainties. John Hall had read that he had been killing his beloved and much cherished wife by smoking his pipe and had believed it to be true, regardless of the fact that he himself was 78 and his wife two years older. He had believed the rash, stupid generalisations of Puritan, rather than the cold reality of proof that his and Doris's very age gave testimony to, and had judged himself as Puritan had wanted him to judge.

As he lay on the carpet in his cottage with Sid and Doris trying to stop the bleeding, John Hall felt he had to apologise to Doris, had to try in some way to tell her that whilst he admitted his guilt, he was sorry.

Doris kept asking him: 'Why, John love, Why?'

His voice seemed loud in his head, but it came out as a whisper. Doris and Sid had to bend their heads down to hear.

'It says I've been killing you all these years, my heart, my lover, I've been killing you, I'm a killer and I never meant to, you know, I never meant to.'

'Killing me? What does he mean? What do you mean, love? You've never tried to kill me, never.'

Sid could no longer hold on with the pressure needed to keep the wounds closed, his own strength was giving out. Doris, too, shocked at John's whispered confession, had released her grasp on John's wrist and the blood once more started to flow freely onto the carpet. Sid stood up and saw the newsletter with its headline.

'It's this rubbish, this sodding thing, Doris. It's this sodding newsletter – see.'

But Doris was too distraught, too bewildered, too frightened to see anything. All she could do was to cradle John's old head as he slipped out of consciousness.

Valerie Curst returned, followed by Mr Puritan. They came

59

into the room fearfully, uncertain what enormity they would find.

'An ambulance is on its way Doris love. How is he?'

'Stop the bleeding, you useless bugger, press on the wounds, stop the bleeding,' Sid Lubberly shouted at Puritan. But Mr Puritan was not good in emergencies, he was uncertain, hesitant and didn't like touching people, especially old people. Valerie Curst hated the sight of blood, it made her faint, so she was unable to do anything more than sit rather heavily down in John Hall's chair, breaking, as she did so, his pipe that he had dropped on the seat.

Doris could no longer remain in control of herself and she simply collapsed beside John, moaning softly, longing to do something to turn the clock back just 30 minutes, to have John upright, strong, in charge, with his pipe in his mouth and a smile on his face, bringing her the morning tea on the tray that he had brought her every morning as long as she could remember. Doris loved John with a fever of love that she had had ever since she first met him 54 years ago. It was his strength, his ability to withstand the tosses and turns of life, his even manner, his amused and thoughtful way. She lay down besides him now, looking into his face, hoping to see the familiar eyes, the half-smile, hoping to hear him call her name, but all she could hear was his gasping for breath.

Nobody in the room did anything now. Puritan, confounded by uncertainty, just stood and watched the man bleed. Sid was trying to regain enough strength in his hands to have another go at stopping the wounds gushing blood. Valerie Curst was unable to look and unable to move in case she saw. And Doris was broken and suffused in misery and pain.

How long it was before the ambulance arrived nobody could tell, and when the ambulance crew came into the room it struck them that they were in a waxworks, except for the lady on the floor calling and crying. Sid Lubberly explained what had happened and they started to attend to John, calling to him, asking him what his name was, but they received no reply. They bandaged his wrists tightly and set up a drip, they lifted Doris from the floor and sat her in a chair, they instructed Valerie

Curst to make Doris a cup of tea, and for once she did as she was asked without a tart rejoinder. They ushered Mr Puritan and Sid out of the cottage and explained to the policemen who had now turned up what seemed to have happened.

It being hot, one of the young constables took his helmet off and placed it, unknowingly, over the newsletter.

As they rolled John Hall onto the stretcher his heart arrested.

It was, I suppose, remarkably unlucky for John Hall that the ambulance that had been sent to the Comity that day was not the ambulance that was specifically equipped to deal with heart attacks. As the ambulance chief officer was to explain in a letter later: 'The cost restraints enforced by Government on the service only allowed three ambulances in the fleet to be fully equipped with this equipment.' The letter failed, however, to also mention that had the chief elected to equip the whole fleet with this equipment, rather than only three ambulances, and forgone the purchase of the helicopter, Mr Hall might have survived. The helicopter was the chief's pride and joy and could fly at night and indeed through thick fog, and it had also justified a large capital letter H to be painted on a specially strengthened roof of the main accident and emergency hospital in the area, which was more than the chief of the next area could claim. John might also have survived had the local hospital not been closed in order to finance the large central hospital with the strengthened roof for helicopter landings.

John Hall died on the journey from the Comity to the modern, gleaming hospital 30 miles away.

John Hall's death in the ambulance was shocking to Doris, but as she told Valerie Curst later, she was with John when he died, holding his hand, stroking his brow and telling him she loved him more than life itself.

John Hall's time had come, but had it been hastened by the newsletter that Mr Puritan had slipped under the door of each and every cottage?

Many residents of the Comity felt that it had. Certainly Sid Lubberly felt that the newsletter had been the cause and bearded Richard Puritan with the accusation in his office after the ambulance had left.

'You killed John Hall, you bastard,' he shouted at Puritan. 'You and that bloody newsletter, you killed him as surely as if you had taken a gun and shot him. He smoked a pipe which did no harm, but you with your witch-hunt killed him.'

'What about the rest of us? What about his poor wife having to breathe in his smoke? What was he doing to the rest of us'? countered Mr Puritan.

'Doris is eighty, you daft sod. At eighty you don't care about passive smoking or anything else except getting through each day together. That's what being human is all about, being together, getting through the days and being thankful for one more day together. We don't want causes, we want to see the world we know unchanging, safe.'

Sid hadn't waited for an answer but had left anxious to get back to Sharon. He might shout at her, for he felt so utterly desperate, upset, angry and above all frightened. He did not know if John Hall was dead, but he was afraid and he needed to see that his world was still there, to see that Sharon – probably with a fag in her mouth – was still his Sharon, in his cottage, with the breakfast things still on the table and the newspaper with tea stains where Sharon had spilt the tea, as she always did. He rushed back wanting to hear his front door bang behind him.

The death of John Hall and the manner of that death was not a matter that could easily be ignored. The police had been called and had seen that he had been cut and wounded; further, he had died in the ambulance, not at the hospital, and all this added up to the fact that an inquest would need to be held and witnesses heard.

Richard Puritan, when he heard the news later that day, understood these matters and knew exactly the regulations and procedures. He knew that there could be publicity and bad publicity over John Hall's death, and he knew that he had to alert Felicity Eristic and he also had to inform that dull and dried-up Mr Eric Fribble, the Secretary of the RRAWF.

In his own mind Richard Puritan couldn't make the connection between the newsletter and Hall's death or even Hall being upset. As to Sid Lubberly's accusations, these he found offensive and rude and he dismissed them from his mind. He had, however, to find a reason for this resident's bizarre behavour and this stumped him. Of all the residents John Hall was possibly the most stable, the most calm and measured, yes, even thoughtful. He was not a man given to strange behaviour, certainly he had walked out of the now famous meeting Puritan had called – but he had not led them out, had not said a great deal, although he had certainly rejected the smoke alarm, but that was all. Why, wondered the Administrator of the Comity, had the man slashed his wrists and before breakfast, which seemed almost a ritual to the residents of the Comity, why had he done this, what had caused him to be so upset?

Richard Puritan determined to ask the doctor, for there must be, he surmised, some medical reason for such action. Perhaps the clue lay in the fact that he had died of an heart attack.

The death of John Hall had caused Doris to be returned by ambulance as the shock had been very great, but she had insisted upon returning to the Comity and her daughter had been called. The hospital had informed Puritan that an autopsy would need to be performed and he had undertaken to tell Doris.

All this activity had exhausted Puritan and he felt that although the day was still young, he would need strengths that he did not possess to be able to see the remaining hours through. He needed to telephone Felicity, or better still see her, to be able to talk the events through and yet he could not contact her, could not reach her. He also needed to inform Eric Fribble but he felt that before he did this he should speak to Felicity. He now thought of the festival of anti-sexism and anti-racism that he had planned for the Comity. This was scheduled to take place in three weeks' time and the banners announcing it were due to be erected by the Council outside the Comity, facing the road, this very day. Should he stop this from happening, he wondered.

A car swept through the archway of the Comity and Puritan, hovering outside the Halls' cottage waiting for the Halls' daughter to arrive, assumed that it was the daughter and started walking towards the car. He was, however, astounded to see the stunning Laura Izzat emerge smiling.

Puritan's heart leapt, his jaw dropped, his mind spun. Never had he seen a woman so remarkably beautiful, so divinely put together, so utterly perfect.

'Hallo, I'm Laura Izzat. You must be Mr Puritan, the Administrator of the St Margaret's Comity.'

'Yes.' Puritan's grasp on conversation had left him.

'I think Mr Fribble told you that I would be visiting the Comity today?'

Puritan now remembered that he had indeed been told in a letter from Mr Fribble that Ms Izzat would be visiting the Comity.

'I'd like to speak to some of the residents, to improve my interviewing skills, if that isn't a dreadful imposition upon you and the residents, Mr Puritan. Do you think I could just chat to them?'

'I sorry but we have had a, a, an accident, em, em well, a death of one of the residents. Things are in a bit of turmoil, it would not be a good time at the moment, Miss Izzat.'

Felicity Eristic's battered Renault swept into the Comity, narrowly missing Laura's Rover 75. Felicity climbed out and walked over to Puritan. Ignoring Laura, she spoke directly to Puritan.

'I've just heard about that man Hall killing himself. What the hell happened? This will do us no bloody good if there is an inquest, you know that. Who are you?'

Richard Puritan introduced Felicity Eristic to Laura Izzat. 'Miss Izzat is the daughter of the President of the RRAWF, Felicity,' and turning to Laura, 'Ms Eristic is the Chair of the Elderly and Frail Committee on the Council, Miss Izzat.'

It is doubtful if two women have ever taken a more instant dislike to one another in the whole history of mankind. Laura Izzat was everything that Ms Eristic despised in rich women – she was beautiful, elegant, soft-spoken, exquisitely dressed, magnetic to men, and worst of all clever, educated, always at her ease and intelligent.

Felicity Eristic was for Laura the template woman she disliked, tactless, loud, ill mannered, poorly groomed, badly educated, self-opinionated and above all dowdy.

'How good to meet you, Ms Eristic.'

'Cut the crap, Ms Izzat. Richard and I have something important to discuss and we have no time to give you the Lady Bountiful treatment, I'm sorry.'

Laura Izzat looked first at Richard Puritan and then at Felicity Eristic. She offered her hand to Richard Puritan, who shook it and smiled weakly. She then turned to face Felicity Eristic.

'Miss Eristic, you say you're sorry, perhaps not as sorry as you will be. Good day.'

Like a flower closing when the sun has gone in, the beautiful face of Laura Izzat changed and a steel coldness shone from her eyes, and her smile, while still lovely, suddenly gave the impression of a snarl. Elegantly she walked to her car, stopping to look over Felicity Erisitc's battered Renault with an appraising glance and hint of a smile, eased the Rover round the Renault with consummate ease and power steering, and with the slightest increase in engine noise glided past the battered Renault and out of the Comity.

At that moment Richard Puritan knew that he was in love with Laura Izzat. He knew he was not in her class, knew that she was now the enemy, knew that she would never look twice at him and yet he also knew that he was hopelessly, utterly in love with her.

As Laura cleared the arch of the Comity, she saw the big, bold banner hanging over the entrance announcing that there was to be a 'Anti-Racist and Anti-Sexist Festival for the Third Age' at the Comity in three weeks' time, sponsored by the Council and something called the Covinous Society of Wiltshire.

8

A Gift for the Reverend Hartwell

At a meeting of the RRAWF trustees earlier in the year, it had been agreed that the Reverend Lionel Hartwell should be presented with a gift after he had retired.

The matter of the selection of the gift had been left to John Izzat, who had put it on his schedule. After some thought, he had determined to purchase on behalf of the RRAWF an original painting of St Margaret's and St John's in Newel under Lea. He had consulted various people in the art world and had been given the name of a painter, Lee Speer, who would produce a recognisable likeness at a reasonable price. Izzat had commissioned Speer and the painting was now finished, framed and ready for Izzat and Eric Fribble to view and agree the wording on a brass plate that would be fixed to the frame.

Lee Speer's studio was in London and Izzat decided to take Laura with him, as he felt she knew more about fashionable art. It was agreed that they would meet Fribble at the studio.

Speer's studio was in a run-down house at Archway, the only thing in its favour, thought Izzat, was the fact that it had a drive and so he could park safely.

When the Izzats arrived, Fribble was already waiting on the steps by the front door, and as he saw Izzat drive in he rang the bell. Mrs Speer opened the door and the party climbed the stairs to the studio. On entering, Laura noticed that Speer was talking to a tall young man with bright blue eyes and fair hair. Both men were perched on a builders' scaffolding board which fronted a massive picture of the face of a rather old, yet distinguished lady. The painting covered the total end wall of the studio.

Mrs Speer called to her husband as they entered and both men jumped down. Speer moved over to the window, where a gilt frame leaned.

'Here's the picture, Mr Fribble, finished and framed.' They crowded round it and the young man joined them.

'It really is very good, Lee,' said the tall fair-haired young man with the bright blue eyes. 'Where is the church?'

'Newel under Lea in Wiltshire, just outside Salisbury. I'm pleased with it, the sun was just right when I came to actually fill in the original sketch I made on the canvas, and so I could get the depth of colour of the stone which is a feature. Oh,' he looked at Laura and John Izzat, 'you don't know Joe Staunch, do you? Joe is a fellow painter, mostly portraits. I think he's very good, but the world sadly remains unconvinced. It's probably because he never paints famous people, just people that catch his eye. That's so, isn't it, Joe?'

Joe Staunch smiled and indicated his agreement.

'You should paint my father then, Mr Staunch. He's famous and I would have thought an ideal subject. Would you like your portrait painted, Daddy? He'll say no, but I would like a picture of him. Are you good at portraits, Mr Staunch?' Laura looked at Joe.

'Well, I think he is,' Lee Speer replied for Joe.

'This is excellent.' John Izzat had been studying the picture closely and was obviously deeply impressed. 'If you had painted two, Mr Speer, I would have bought the other one.'

'You can have the watercolour sketches that I made if you would like, I could get them framed.'

'Would that be a good idea, Laura?' Izzat turned to his daughter.

'I think it would be a wonderful idea, and we've got plenty of space for a watercolour or two.'

Eric Fribble and John Izzat then moved into another room with Lee Speer to arrange the final payment and the wording for the brass plate, leaving Joe Staunch and Laura alone to wait for them to complete the business side of the visit.

'Have you nothing to say, Mr Staunch, or am I so dull that your painter's eye causes you to be dumb?' Laura Izzat was not used to not being instantly courted.

'You know full well that you are intensely beautiful,' Joe replied. 'But beauty is not an end in itself, is it? You need more than beauty to live and succeed, you need intelligence, education, contacts, faith, talent, skills and ability.'

'You also need money, Mr Staunch, if you are to succeed royally, and power and iron determination. These are attributes that most painters, or so I read, dismiss, rejecting them for what they assert is the raw, red power of creativity.'

'That's so much feature-writer's nonsense as far as I'm concerned. Creativity seems to me to be little more than an eye that sees the total picture and a skill that can record that picture accurately, plus an opinion about the subject. It is this last thing that is most often called creativity, because it is the artist saying something about the subject that he is reproducing, be it a sculpture or a painting. When I paint a portrait I take sides. A portrait is a statement about the way, time and the sitter's lifestyle has changed the face they carry about with them. You can read the history of a person from their face. You can tell if they've been well fed, spent most of their days in comfortable buildings, been happy or sad, slept well, smoked too much, drunk too much, been clean or dirty. Once I've read that history, I then take the main points and display them in the portrait. But you've got me on to my favourite subject.'

'And what about love? Can you read love in somebody's face, and if so, what does it look like? Could you teach me to see love in a person's face?' Laura asked.

'Well, I can see goodness and evil, they are always very clear, I can see kindness and cruelty, I can certainly see pain and humour. So you mix and match those attributes and tell me what love is and I will show you how to read it on a person's face.'

'Well, that's a cop-out, Mr Staunch. Artists are meant to be passionate and hooked into the lifeforce, not cold and analytical.'

'Artists are also meant to starve happily in garrets and sing songs. My voice qualifies me as a non-artist, and as to starving, I simply refuse to eat less than three meals a day. Further, I would very much like to eat one of those three meals in your company? How about dinner?'

'That would be wonderful, but I'm a busy person and because my father and I live together, I would need to find a date when he is eating out.'

'When would that be then?'

'How can I tell you until you've given me at least three dates to choose from?'

Lee Speer, Eric Fribble and John Izzat returned to the room.

'Right, Laura, we've got the wording agreed and the picture will be delivered home by Speer towards the end of the week, so we can go to lunch now. Mr Fribble will provide you with the address, Mr Speer. Goodbye, Mr Staunch.'

John Izzat took his daughter's arm and left. At the door, Laura turned round.

'I expect to hear from you, Mr Staunch.' She waved and left.

'That is a pure dream, Lee, I've never seen anything so beautiful − Laura Izzat, what do you know about her?'

'It's the first time I've ever met her, but I agree she is a knockout. You spoke to her; what was she like? Dumb I suppose, beautiful people are normally dumb or plain stupid, it goes with the looks. If you're beautiful, you don't have to try at school, or at home, you're just beautiful and it gets you by, it's the way of the world.'

'Not at all, she seemed remarkably clever. But God, I haven't got her address or her phone number and I said I'd ring and invite her to dinner. What can I do? I have to see her again.'

Lee laughed. 'Are you in love, Mr Staunch? I've never known you to be the slightest bit interested in anybody like that before. I reckon it must be love.'

Mrs Speer came into the studio. 'Lee, it's Mr Fribble − he thinks he might have left his briefcase. Is it by the window?' The briefcase was by the window, and Mr Speer called down to Eric Fribble, who came up the stairs and into the studio.

Panting as he entered the room, he smiled when he saw Lee Speer with the case.

'Oh, thank heavens it's here, Mr Speer, I thought I may have left it in the taxi, not that there's anything vital in it except a copy of a notice for an autopsy, but that was faxed and so another could just as easily be faxed, couldn't it?'

Joe Staunch felt that luck, if not God, was on his side. Having failed to get Laura's address and telephone number earlier, he had now been given a second chance to obtain this vital information.

'Have you got Mr Izzat's address and telephone number, Mr Fribble?' he asked.

'Yes, he is the President of the Association's Welfare Fund.'

'Could you let me have it?'

'Why, I don't give that information out without Mr Izzat's permission, I'm sorry. You'll send the picture to Mr Izzat without fail by Thursday won't you, Mr Speer?'

'I will indeed, Mr Fribble, without fail.' Mr Fribble left, followed by Mrs Speer.

'Of course, you've got the address, Lee.'

Lee, adopting Mr Fribble's voice, said: 'I don't give that information out without prior permission, Mr Staunch. It's on the desk in the office, Joe, with the phone number.'

'Well, I don't feel like working on Flossy any more. Let's go to the pub and drink ourselves into a rather happy state of mind.'

'You mean rat-arsed, you daft bugger,' replied Lee Speer, dumping some brushes in a jar of white spirit as he followed Joe Staunch out of the studio.

Eric Fribble had given John Izzat a quick note about the death of John Hall. He stressed in the note that he hadn't heard the news from Mr Puritan, but from the vicar of St Margaret's and St John's, the Reverend Palmer. The vicar had made it clear that he had only heard one side of the story, namely Mrs Hall's and Mrs Curst's version.

Izzat passed the note over to Laura as they drove to lunch.

'This must have been what Puritan meant about death. It doesn't sound very nice, does it, Laura?'

'It is, as the vicar says, only the women's version, not the official account,' observed Laura. 'I think Fribble should ask for a copy of this notorious newsletter, father. It would certainly be strange for a man to cut his wrists simply because a newsletter attacks smoking; indeed, I would need a lot of convincing before I accepted it.'

'You become more timorous as you get older, Laura, less able to take new ideas as simple concepts; because you have seen a great deal and experienced a lot of things, what seems to young people just an idea, becomes reality for a lot of elderly people. They have seen an idea become a law in a matter of weeks, they have seen a rumour turn into a fact in front of their eyes on the television. Old people are aware of their frailty and are aware of the life that has flowed past them. We have all become much more science-based, we expect science to produce answers, and what if it produces answers we don't like and can't tolerate? The young still have time, although not as much as most of them think, to change, to adapt, the elderly do not have that luxury, time is the one thing they do not have in the bank.'

'Do you think it could have been the newsletter then, father?' Laura asked.

'I think it could have been the last straw, a bewildered and confused man does not need a powerful, well-argued justification to act irrationally – anything can be a trigger, even a rainy day. If what you saw, I mean the banner, is any indication, I would say that there has been, and is, a lot of pressure being put upon the residents of the Comity by the new Administrator.'

'Can you do anything, father?'

'No, not by my myself and not easily. You appoint an administrator to administer. It is not up to the President of the Welfare Fund to direct the Administrator's day-to-day activity. If he steals, or attacks a resident physically, he can be sacked, or if the police bring charges against him. We could sack him if he is criticised by the coroner at the inquest. But we can't sack him if his style is not to our liking, or if he is trying to change things for what he sees as improvements. He has all the rights of any other employee.'

'But what about the malign influence of that Eristic woman on the man? The Comity is an independent, charity establishment. she has no place there.'

'Even that is doubtful, she represents the Council, which has a duty of care over the people in its area of responsibility. The problem is that these things are all very complex when it comes to the exact legal definition of responsibility. To go head-to-head with any authority is always difficult: that is why, with something as sensitive as sheltered housing, where you are dealing with people, it is always better to compromise, you give a bit and expect them to give a little in return. When it comes to welfare, there are no hard-and-fast rules that should apply, therefore it is always best not to drive anyone beyond the line of legality; accommodate and compromise is the name of the game, but it all depends on both sides being of a like mind and equally anxious not to cause harm to the people involved. What worries me is that Mr Puritan and Ms Eristic may not care as much about the residents as they do about their pet causes.'

'The woman is a monster,' retorted Laura. 'She won't accommodate or compromise, it will be her way or no way, I know the type. We should try to get Puritan out of the Comity and get someone in who is more Hartwell than Puritan.'

'Did you really like Speer's painting, Laura, and more to the point, do you think Lionel Hartwell will like it?'

'I think it is a wonderful painting, and although I've never met the Reverend Hartwell, I am certain he will treasure it. Do you know anything about the other artist there, Mr Staunch, have you seen his work?'

Izzat shot a sideways glance at his daughter. She was not in the habit of asking about the various people they met unless they were main players.

'No,' he answered, 'I've never met him before nor ever seen his work, but if Lee Speer thinks highly of it, I suspect that it must be above average at least. Did you like him then?'

'What on earth does that mean, did I like him then?' said Laura. 'He was interesting, and I just thought that I would like to see what he was like as a portrait painter. Liking has absolutely nothing whatever to do with it. Why should I like or indeed hate him when I've only met the man once?'

They drove on in silence, with Laura feeling that once again her father had seen that she did indeed like Mr Staunch. John Izzat was amused to hear his daughter deny any interest beyond the man's ability as a portrait painter. Had he been a betting man, he would have put money on the fact that Laura was much more interested in Mr Staunch than she was prepared to admit to him.

As they drove, Laura could see that Mr Staunch could, or perhaps would be, the ideal person for her. Nothing as common as Mr Right, she told herself, but certainly the person with whom she could share her thoughts, concerns and even her ambitions. He was, she felt, a sympathetic man, a thoughtful man, although following the little lecture he had given her about beauty perhaps a shade didactic. He was also something else she thought, he was exciting, not run of the mill, not full of himself. Yes, she promised herself, she would go to dinner with him and see if this Mr Staunch could meet the expectations she had of him.

But what about meeting his parents, she thought. They could be dreadful, or they might take as instant a dislike to her as she had to that dreadful Ms Eristic. Her fear didn't last long, because they had arrived at the café and John parked his car and they had lunch.

Meanwhile, at the pub, Joe Staunch was talking about the wonderful Laura Izzat.

The fact that often such conversations are held in pubs is no coincidence, because the male human in love is not, whatever women might think, a sight to be seen or heard sober, except, that is, by the object of that love or by a friend so steeped in alcohol that the endless repetition of the wonders of Miss X or Ms Y blur into the drinks consumed.

Lee Speer has been in love and knew the symptoms, and understood that it is the friend's duty on such occasions to simply get quietly and totally drunk, while the great lover sketches the various parts of the campaign to woo and win with many timorous and ridiculous ideas.

'You know, Lee, she is of course much brighter than me. She's rich too, and just think of her father. He's important; why, they even write about him in the Sunday papers. She must meet thousands of really dynamic men and, looking as she does, an angel, well, I doubt very much indeed that she would want to know some poor, unsuccessful artist, would she, Lee?'

'Joe, you're not poor and you're only unrecognised, not unsuccessful, in fact.'

'It's true I'm not poor, I've plenty of money and I'm a good portrait painter, regardless of the fact that I've not painted the rich and famous. But why should a perfect angel like Laura be the slightest bit interested in me? She wouldn't, would she?'

Lee Speer took another drink and knew that he need not reply. There was never any need to reply to these rhetorical questions. No answer was possible, nor even was it a profitable line of thought to pursue, so he took another drink and ordered another one to follow.

Love, he thought gloomily, changed men from rational people into idiots, and only drinking provided the answer to the age-old question of why God had created love in the first place. Sex was no adequate answer, nor was bringing up children, all this could be done very well with just good humour and friendship. Why did God make love between men and women? It served only to change both people into selfish, silly, fixated creatures who rejected their friends while they went through all the stupidity of 'being in love'. And what good came of it? he wondered. None that he could see?

'I will ask her to dinner, even though, compared to her, I'm as ugly as sin. I will still ask her. After all, what can she say, except no?'

'But she's already said that she would say yes, you daft git.'

'I know, but I don't think she meant yes, she only said it so she wouldn't hurt my feelings.'

It would be foolish and unkind to record much more of the conversation. Most readers will have heard it a thousand times and many, if not most, will have even made the tortured speech themselves as they got drunker or watched their best mate slowly fall into a drunken stupor.

It is worth mentioning, however, that the day following Laura's and Joe's separate but long lunch, Joe did telephone Laura, and what is more found her in, and what was even more surprising to Joe, Laura graciously agreed to have dinner with him that same week.

9

Sangeta Patel is Offended

Martha Preen and Sangeta Patel had grown closer in their friendship following Mr Puritan's disastrous public meeting on the quarter-day.

Both Martha and Sangeta were widows, both had come to the Comity as widows and both were inclined to be – even in their old age – shy.

The difference between the two women was that whereas Sangeta had always taken an active role in her husband's shop, Martha had never taken any interest or role and had lived her married life as the wife of Norman Preen, rather than a partner.

Martha was always a very conceited person, concerned with her looks and little else. To Martha, turnout and dress were everything, and for all of her married life, Norman Preen had supplied the necessary money for her to indulge her taste in clothes. It was only after his death that she had been forced to face the fact that Norman had died massively in debt and that there was very little money available for her to live on. She had been offered a cottage at the Comity because of her circumstances whilst she was still comparatively young – 55 – and was both one of the longest-established tenants and also one of the youngest. The Preens had not had any children because of the likely effect it would have had upon Martha's figure. Both her parents had died and so she was, apart from a sister living in Australia, alone, and as she had no skills that could be used to gain employment, there had been little else that could be done for her except to take care of her housing and personal needs.

The friendship that developed between Sangeta and Martha came about because both women were basically hesitant about forming relationships with other members of the Comity, especially male residents. In all such situations, both women would avoid coming face-to-face or committing themselves to any project that might place them with any other member of the Comity family as it were. Thus it was almost by default that both women found themselves leaving gatherings early or turning down the offers of lifts in taxis or sharing bus seats.

By constantly bumping into each other they had struck up a relationship and over a very long period indeed this had flowered into almost a close friendship. On Sangeta's side, however, there were reservations about Martha's overwhelming vanity and obsession with dress, whilst on Martha's side there was a reservation about Sangeta's business knowledge, education and lack of dress sense.

These reservations were not, however, enough to prevent the gradual growth of the friendship and both Sangeta and Martha spent much more time together than either would have admitted. Recent events had served to cement the relationship and both seemed to draw power from it in order to avoid the unpleasantness that Mr Puritan generated by his every action.

The death of John Hall and the subsequent problems with the coroner cast a pall over the Comity. So much so, that residents had taken to meeting in their cottages rather than out in the Comity garden or in the community rooms. They all feared to meet Mr Puritan and so issued invitations to their neighbours or friends to visit them at home.

Martha, however, did not invite Sangeta into her cottage because she didn't 'have people in', and Sangeta did not invite Martha because she felt that as Martha was the longest-serving resident, it was obviously not the 'done' thing to have people in for visits. The two friends continued, therefore, to meet in the garden or to go to the shops together.

When they did meet they usually had much to talk about and would be seen standing together for long periods.

The habits of these two friends were known and understood by the other residents. Mr Puritan, however, was a man much concerned with his own single-issue causes and cannot be said to be observant unless and until his cause collides with a person.

Since Mr Puritan's appointment, both Sangeta and Martha, when they met and talked in the Comity garden, always kept a very wary eye out for his or Ms Eristic's approach, and should either of these two worthy people come into view they would immediately break off their conversation and fly off to their own cottages. They usually met at the end farthest away from the Comity building for such conversations. This allowed Martha to fly quickly to her cottage, which was the last one in the row. Sangeta's cottage was the second cottage in the row and therefore she had to fly up the path and hope to arrive at her front door before either Mr Puritan or Ms Eristic reached the end of the first cottage.

On the morning in question Ms Eristic and Mr Puritan had been meeting to discuss the forthcoming festival and the erection of a marquee on the Comity lawn. Just as Sangeta and Martha came out of their cottages to have their morning chat, Mr Puritan, Ms Eristic and the tent hirer emerged from the arch to survey the lawn. Martha, seeing the approach of the two worthies, didn't know what to do. Her instinct told her to run, however, she knew that Sangeta was already walking down the path towards her. In panic she ineffectually waved Sangeta back. Sangeta, in full sari and under full steam, didn't understand the wave and continued to advance.

Martha's waving became more frenzied, and as the two worthies started down the path to reach the lawn, Sangeta finally came within voice distance of Martha, who said: 'Puritan and that woman are coming, I'll ring you.' Martha then as near as it is possible ran from Sangeta to her own cottage. Sangeta, understanding the peril, turned abruptly on her heel and made off for her cottage as fast as her legs could carry her.

Both Mr Puritan and Ms Eristic witnessed this scene and, being single-issue fanatics, immediately interpreted it as overt racism on the part of Martha Preen, who had very clearly been waving Sangeta Patel away from her.

'There, Richard. Did you see that blatant racism against that Asian lady? It was disgusting.'

'Who would have thought we would have seen it – it was classic racism,' agreed Richard Puritan. 'I will have to do something. That is Mrs Patel, the poor woman.'

They both broke off their meeting with the tent man and went to console Sangeta, who had great hopes that she would reach her front door and avoid them both.

'Mrs Patel, please believe me,' said Richard Puritan, 'such racism is not tolerated here. I intend to take this shameful incident up with Mrs Preen directly. Believe me, I know how you must feel, how hurt you must be, how humiliated.'

Sangeta was taken aback. What, she thought, are they talking about? And why had they stopped her from reaching the comfort of her own front door?

'What racism, Mr Puritan?'

'There, that is a normal reaction to such racial rebuffs,' explained Felicity Eristic, 'it is denial. I understand, Mrs Patel, believe me I understand. But Mr Puritan will root it out, will make Mrs Preen see that it is wrong and cruel. We will not tolerate racism in this place or any other place under my control.'

'What are you talking about?' asked Sangeta Patel, now desperate to flee to the safety of her cottage.

'It is as Covinous says,' explained Felicity Eristic, 'the racism of superior whites against the imperial poor, and it is evil. Believe me, Mrs Patel, we have no sympathy with any kind of racism, just because of the colour of a person's skin, or their different accent, or different culture or religion. They must all be treated the same, as worthwhile people regardless.'

By this time, Sangeta Patel had heard the words that she didn't want to hear, had heard herself described as coloured skinned, as different in religion and different in culture, had heard the accusation that she spoke differently, and she did not like hearing these things. Firstly because they were not true, and secondly, because before these two fools had stopped her, she had experienced no such statements about her race, her colour or her culture. Sangeta became angry, Sangeta became very angry, Sangeta became incandescent with anger.

'How dare you say this to me?' she hissed at the two worthies. 'What have I done to you to cause you to be so rude, so offensive? First you insult us with your dreadful posters and then you pick on me, a widow, to insult and vilify. How dare you? It is intolerable. I am going to my home now, but I shall not forget this. You have neither manners nor grace.'

Sangeta walked slowly on to her cottage, pale with rage, boiling with anger. They had called her coloured, they had said she spoke in a funny way, they had said she was different. If her husband had been alive he would have fried them with his scorn, burnt them alive with his anger.

She entered her cottage and broke down in tears. She had been insulted in public by two people who should have known better. She had been disgraced, reviled and cheapened, and who could she turn to, who could help her regain her dignity? It is possible that Sangeta had never been so unhappy or so alone. Her phone rang. It was Martha, but she couldn't speak to her, she was too upset, too tearful. All she could say was – 'Oh Martha, oh Martha', and then she cried some more, holding the phone by her side and letting the pain find its own way into her sobs, into the tears that rolled down her cheeks. Great pain-filled sobs escaped her, as the shame of her situation, her weakness, her powerlessness, and above all, the fact that she was alone, far from the home of her childhood overwhelmed her.

On the other end of the phone, Martha was alarmed.

'What's happened, Sangeta? What's the matter?'

Martha heard only sobs and then heard Sangeta hang up. Never mind the fact that Mr Puritan and 'that woman' were still on the lawn, Martha resolved to go to Sangeta, to comfort her friend, to make her a nice cup of tea, and to help and console her, no matter what the problem was. Sangeta is my friend, she thought, my best friend, my only friend. I must go, regardless of the fact that Mr Puritan and 'that woman' are still there, still between me and Sangeta's cottage.

Martha opened her front door and started off down the path towards Sangeta's cottage. It took a lot of strength for her to go past the two worthies as she was a shy and certainly not a courageous person. She had never needed courage while Norman was alive, and after his death, the RRAWF had taken care of her. She had never needed courage at the Comity, and while the Reverend Hartwell was the Administrator she had felt that she would never need courage.

As she started to advance down the path Mr Puritan saw her and drew Felicity Eristic's attention to her.

'Here comes Mrs Preen, hell bent no doubt on more mischief. I shall head her off and also tell her about our anti-racism policy, although she should have known by now that we wouldn't put up with her kind of behaviour.'

'Is she healthy, Richard? We don't want any more heart attacks.'

'Strong as an ox, according to the doctor. No reason to worry, Felicity.'

It was fortunate for Martha Preen that Valerie Curst decided to go to the shops and left her cottage at the same moment that Martha started down the path. They met Mr Puritan together.

'A moment please, Mrs Preen,' said Mr Puritan, barring her path to Sangeta's door.

'What is it, Mr Puritan. I must see Mrs Patel,' explained Martha.

Valerie Curst had been forced to stop by the two, and waited, anxious not to miss something she could gossip about to the others.

'Ms Eristic and I saw your very unpleasant racial rejection of Mrs Patel when she was walking in the garden just now, Mrs Preen, and I am forced to say that there is no place for racialism here in the Comity, as our posters have made very clear.'

'My what?' asked Martha.

'Your racial rejection of Mrs Patel. We both saw it, waving her away and then turning away and hurrying into your cottage as soon as she got near to you. Ms Eristic and I saw it, Mrs Preen, and we won't have it. The Comity is against racialism, isn't it, Mrs Curst?'

If Valerie Curst had been given a birthday present on a plate, she couldn't have been more pleased than she was right then to be included in this ridiculous conversation. Already burning with a loathing of Mr Puritan and Ms Eristic, she had rehearsed a thousand times the things she would say to the pair of worthies, given half a chance – and here she was actually invited to give vent to all her views about Mr Puritan and 'that woman'.

'What in God's name are you blathering about, you clown?

Mrs Preen and Mrs Patel are friends, old friends, very old friends. The chance of Martha here doing anything at all to wound Sangeta is about as unlikely as the chance that you will do anything that is halfway intelligent or helpful. If Martha was waving at Sangeta it is probably because she wanted to remind her to get something or for some other reason. It would certainly not be anything to do with racialism, or as you put it, you ignorant fool, racism. You must be going off your head.'

Oh the joy that Valerie Curst felt at letting off the head of steam that had been building up in her irascible nature ever since she had first met Mr Puritan and Felicity Eristic.

'If you had more sense than you most obviously have, you would know that Martha and Sangeta are great friends and that friendship, you idiot, does not work on a racial basis. How dare you accuse Martha of being the same kind of snivelling half-wit as you, how dare you!'

During this tirade, Martha had made her escape, had slipped past Mr Puritan and reached Sangeta's front door and knocked gently on it and had been admitted by Sangeta.

Valerie Curst, however, had just started, had got up an head of steam to give vent to all the annoyance and anger that had been building up ever since Mr Puritan had arrived.

'Racialism,' exclaimed Valerie Curst. 'What do you mean by racialism, or sexism or gender orientation, come to that? Why, you've not lived long enough to understand what race you are, let alone anybody else's race. I even doubt if you have ever even won a race. How could you accuse poor Martha? You're off your head, you stupid man.'

Mr Puritan drew himself up to his full height and looked the irritable Mrs Curst straight in the eye. 'Mrs Curst, I happen to have attended ... gone on a two-week anti-racism course, so I think I can be said to know exactly what racism is and what it is not. I know the nature and structure of racism and I know full well what I saw.'

Valerie Curst snorted with exasperation. 'Mr Puritan, I have been to France for two weeks but that doesn't mean that I speak French, nor does it qualify me as an expert on France. I can tell you that what you saw could have been many things, but it was not what you call racism on the part of Mrs Preen, and if you can't get that into your thick head then you're a bigger fool than even I took you for, and that's the end of it.'

Valerie Curst's arthritis seemed to have flowed away from her as she had delivered her rebukes to Richard Puritan. She found that she did not need to lean upon her stick nor did she need to take little hobbling steps. She strode purposely out down the path and headed for the arch, leaving Mr Puritan standing well and truly told off.

Puritan was uncertain how to proceed with this grave matter of overt racism. Valerie Curst had been so definite, so certain, that he now felt doubts, perhaps there was another explanation for what had seemed such a gross act of out-and-out racism. Could he have been wrong? The question rose into his consciousness for fully one second, but then he remembered all the lessons he had learned, and he remembered that all white people were, according to the received wisdom of his lecturers, racists, no matter if they did or did not exhibit any such prejudice. Racism, recalled Mr Puritan, was a scientific fact, like gravity or the boiling point of water, and all white people were racists. If the Virgin Mary had been white she would have been a racist, he had been told this and knew it to be true. John Covinous had written about it and had explained that no matter what, the imperial past of the white English had infected every cell of their thinking with prejudice and racism, and it was only by recognising this fact that any way forward could be found. Every white English person had to admit to the sin and guilt of racism before there could be a wonderful and creative multicultural society where love prospered and wrong was outlawed.

Had Mr Puritan enjoyed the wisdom of his predecessor, he might have recalled the Collect for the fifteenth Sunday after Trinity, and acknowledged everybody's need for humility as embodied in the words ... 'and, because the frailty of man without thee cannot but fall, keep us ever by thy help from all things hurtful, and lead us to all things profitable to our salvation'. But he supped from the books of Covinous, not from the Book of Common Prayer, and knew nothing of the comfortable words that for centuries have held men back from rash and

82

hurried judgements, and so compounded his mistake with prejudice of his own making.

He walked back to Felicity Eristic, who was deep in conversation with the man who would erect the marquee for the festival of anti-sexism and anti-racism.

'Did she understand that racism will not be tolerated here, Richard?' asked Felicity.

'There's an awful lot still be done before this Comity is free of prejudice,' he replied, and Felicity Eristic nodded her head, knowing that they had embarked upon an uphill struggle but one that they would surely win for right was on their side. Felicity Eristic was confident that she knew the true path, probably better than Richard Puritan, for she had read John Covinous's latest book, which she knew Richard had not, because he had asked her to lend it to him.

In this way Richard Puritan and Felicity Eristic confirmed their beliefs and bolstered their determination to rid the Comity of all things bad, and, although they would have denied this, replace them with all things fashionable amongst their peers.

10

Preparations for the Festival

The day before the festival, had been planned by Richard Puritan to represent a dress rehearsal for all those taking part.

The first stage was the erection of the marquee and this had been scheduled for eight o'clock in the morning. Right on time the lorry with the marquee, poles, guys and flooring nosed its way into the arch.

It is with some sorrow that I have to say that there had been a major change in the shape of the arch between the time the marquee contractor had called to make the arrangements and the time when the lorry nosed its way towards the Comity garden. The change in shape had been brought about by Mr Puritan's wish to publicise the anti-racism and anti-sexist festival. To this end, Mr Puritan had caused to be erected, a large sign crowning the arch with the timeless words – 'Anti-Racist and Anti-Sexist Festival for the Third Age'. This remarkable prose was signwritten upon a very large wooden structure that cut off the top two feet of the arch. Suspended and attached to the framework of the sign was an additional board which stated that 'The Festival is sponsored by St Margaret's Comity and the Covinous Society of Wiltshire'. This secondary sign was only two foot deep but some six foot long and was screwed to the main sign along its bottom edge. In total, therefore, the archway height was reduced by roughly four feet.

The four-foot reduction of the archway would not normally have caused any problems, but the marquee lorry had a small crane for lifting the canvas off and on the lorry, mounted by its tailgate, and it was this crane which became entangled with the sign as it drove through the arch.

Richard Puritan had been up and waiting upon the arrival of the marquee for about 30 minutes, so when the lorry nosed its way through the arch, Richard leapt in front of it and waved it forward. By directing the driver in this way, the driver stopped being aware of the back of the lorry, concentrating on Mr Puritan's directions. In this fashion and by this means, the crane struck the sign and pulled it into the archway, effectively wedging the crane firmly into the arch and wrecking the sign.

As this happened, Arni Pule, Sid Lubberly and Ray Paladin were meeting to catch the bus to Salisbury to see a cricket match. The three men watched with amusement as Mr Puritan waved the lorry forward unaware that it was stuck fast behind. The lorry driver noticed that no matter how hard he accelerated he didn't move, and putting on the brake, opened the cab door to see what was holding his lorry fast. He was joined by Mr Puritan and for a few minutes both could not see what the cause of the trouble was, as they looked down the sides and under the lorry and saw nothing amiss.

It was at this point that Arni Pule reached the lorry and seeing Mr Puritan bending to look under the lorry said, in an over-loud voice, 'You won't find them there, Mr Puritan. You should have string round each leg so that they couldn't fall out of your trouser legs.'

For his part Mr Puritan did not have a great sense of humour and most certainly did not have Mr Pule's rather coarse, lavatory humour.

'Nothing has fallen off, Mr Pule. The lorry seems stuck and I'm looking to see what is holding it up.' Puritan commented.

Ray Paladin, having joined the party, pointed to the ceiling of the archway. 'I rather think the crane is holding up the arch rather than the arch holding up the lorry, Mr Puritan.'

At this point both the lorry driver and Richard Puritan looked up and saw the cause for the immobility of the lorry.

'Reverse, for God's sake, reverse. You've caught the sign in the crane,' screamed Mr Puritan.

'If he reverses, how do you know the arch won't fall in?' asked Sid Lubberly

'The whole building might fall down,' chipped in Arni Pule.

'Collapse onto the lorry and perhaps kill the driver,' mused Ray Paladin in a gloomy voice.

'Don't reverse,' shouted Puritan. 'We need to assess the situation before you move the lorry.'

'You know Nurse Reck is scheduled to see Mrs Curst this morning, Mr Puritan, and you know she never looks to see if the archway is clear before she hurtles through in that Metro of hers,' said Ray Paladin, enjoying the drama of the moment.

'Get out in front of the building and wave her down, Mr Paladin,' instructed Mr Puritan.

'How is he meant to get out front, through the arch? I wouldn't risk it, Ray. The thing might fall down and then you'd be crushed to death, or worse still injured for life,' warned Arni Pule.

Philip Dabster strolled up to the group and, sensing the joke, decided that he should join in.

'That lorry is blocking the entrance, Mr Puritan. You said you had to have the gates removed so that emergency vehicles could have free access twenty-four hours a day. How can an emergency vehicle have free access when a lorry is blocking the entrance?'

'The lorry is stuck, Mr Dabster. It can't be moved. It was an accident.'

'That's why we need access for the emergency vehicles, isn't it, Mr Puritan,' asked Arni Pule. 'In case there's an accident.'

'Yes', replied Richard Puritan, 'but the accident has occurred in the archway. Surely you can see that.'

'Oh, we can see that all right,' commented Sid Lubberly, 'but how can the emergency services get to us to free the lorry?'

'This endless talk isn't helping,' retorted Mr Puritan. 'Leave me alone to sort it out.'

'But what about our bus? We've probably missed it and that means we'll miss the start of the match. Shall we risk going through the arch, lads, even though it might fall on us and kill us?' Arni Pule enquired.

'Why not,' said Ray Paladin, 'It would save us from that bloody festival.'

'Nobody can go through until we've established that it's safe,' asserted Puritan.

'Well, that writes off the rest of the morning,' commented the driver.

Nurse Reck had now arrived at the Comity and, although not part of the festival, she had joined the others who were scheduled to set up their stalls and displays. Indeed there was by this time something of a traffic jam caused by those wishing to enter the Comity.

Nurse Reck, however, knew that she had a duty of healing, and whilst most of the others stranded outside waited with typically British patience, the nurse was anxious to see her patient and equally anxious to be about her other calls.

She peered round the lorry and called out: 'I have to see a patient. Would you move this damn lorry, please.'

Mr Puritan had, since his previous run-in with Nurse Reck, been inclined to avoid her and was, if I tell the truth, rather afraid of this formidable healer.

'Nurse Reck, I'm sorry but the lorry has got stuck on the archway roof and it can't be moved until we have made sure that the archway is safe. So I'm afraid you'll have to wait until a building surveyor has inspected the arch.'

'Oh it's you, Mr Puritan. I might have guessed that it would be you,' said the nurse, having squeezed passed the lorry and arrived in the Comity's grounds. 'I can't possibly afford to wait for any building surveyor, I've got patients to see. Illness doesn't wait for building surveyors, you know, nor does pain. Why did you jam the lorry in there in the first place?

'I didn't jam the lorry in the arch, Mrs Reck,' exclaimed Mr Puritan. 'It caught the sign.'

'Oh well, it's a damn stupid sign anyway, so it won't be missed will it,' Mrs Reck retorted.

'I happen to think it is, or rather was, a very good sign,' replied a now definitely dispirited Mr Puritan.

The men had taken the opportunity to squeeze themselves past the lorry and had left in the hope that the bus would be late. Those outside, seeing people squeezing in and out, now took it upon themselves to try the same passage through the arch.

'I should stop those other people coming through if I were

you, Mr Puritan. They could hurt themselves,' said Nurse Reck over her shoulder as she made her way to Valerie Curst's cottage.

Mr Puritan decided that he should try to send them back and rushed to block the one way past the lorry that they were trying to squeeze through. Sadly, a projecting bolt on the side of the lorry caught and snagged the back pocket of Mr Puritan's famous trousers. Unaware of being caught, Mr Puritan ploughed on and tore a great rip out of the seat of his pants. He spun round, hearing and feeling the tear, only to secure himself ever more tightly to the bolt. Desperately he tried to pull himself free and in doing so tore even more of the bottom out of his trousers.

He was now caught with his enormous bottom on display to any person coming from the Comity through the arch. In modern terms he was almost perfectly mooning, being unable to stand up straight without tearing even more out of the seat from his trousers. He therefore adopted a crouching pose and, displayed thus, presented to Sheila and Desmond Truckle a sight that they would rather not have seen so early in the morning.

'Good God, Mr Puritan,' exclaimed Desmond Truckle. 'Cover yourself up, man.'

Desmond Truckle could take most things, but things that drew attention to the fleshy humanity of each and every one of us filled him with horror and fear.

'We can't possibly squeeze by you like that, Mr Puritan,' explained Desmond. 'And if you would get them to move the lorry then we would not need to squeeze by you anyway.'

'The lorry is stuck in the arch, Mr Truckle, and I am stuck on a nail or something. Could you give me a hand to free myself? You stand close to me and hang on to the bit of my trouser that is caught on the nail, while I inch up and take the strain of the trousers.'

Desmond Truckle was not generally an unhelpful man. Although not a very far-sighted person, he would usually lend a hand if asked. However, the thought of standing very close to Mr Puritan with his arse hanging out was not a prospect that

Desmond Truckle could entertain, the more so when he recalled that this was the same Mr Puritan who was forever banging on about gender orientation, which Mr Truckle in his unsophisticated way thought meant homosexuals.

'I would help you, Mr Puritan, if I was on my own, but I've got Sheila here with me.'

'What's that got to do with anything, Mr Truckle? I'm not asking you to sleep with me, just to give me a hand to get my trousers off this nail.'

It would have been wiser of Mr Puritan if he had not mentioned sleeping with him, because this had the opposite effect on Desmond Truckle than he had intended and Desmond Truckle almost visibly jumped back a yard.

'No, no, I must take Sheila back to the cottage, Mr Puritan. I'm sorry, but I must go.'

Sheila during this conversation had been eyeing Mr Puritan with something very akin to disgust as well as interest. The needlewoman part of her was fascinated to see the actual anatomy over which Mr Puritan's trouser maker was able to drape so much corduroy. However, the sight of the actual anatomy was enough to generate in her sensitive spirit revulsion at such grossness.

Desmond took her arm and she was not totally sorry to be led away and back to the safety of her cottage.

'Thank you very much, Mr Truckle,' yelled Mr Puritan at the backs of the two residents as they walked away from a man caught in a web of circumstances beyond his control.

Happily the anger that Mr Truckle's rejection of his appeal for help caused in Richard Puritan was enough to make the already thin and stretched material at the seat of his trousers give up the unequal struggle, and with a satisfying ripping sound, the last threads that held Mr Puritan fast to the lorry broke and he was free and certainly bare arsed. With a cry he rushed round the lorry and squeezed past the driver's side of the cab and managed to wiggle his way to the stairs and up to his flat, where he pulled off the now useless trousers and pulled on his more usual jeans.

As he prepared to rejoin the lorry the phone rang in the office and he lifted the receiver. 'Richard, this is Felicity. What the hell has happened now? I'm outside with the other people and there's a bloody great lorry blocking the archway. Time's money, Richard, and I'm not prepared to hang about out here for ever.'

Richard Puritan rushed down the stairs and found that the Council's building surveyor had arrived and was standing on the lorry looking up at the roof. He pulled free a large bit of the sign which carried the legend 'SEXI' on it and threw it at Puritan's feet. He then called to the driver.

'Go on, inch it forward, go on,' and the lorry inched forward. He jumped down and walked round to the driver and told him that he was clear to carry on.

The archway was free and the driver immediately started unloading the marquee on to the Comity lawn. Men appeared and started putting the poles into the lawn.

Nurse Reck, having attended to Mrs Curst, walked past Mr Puritan on her way to her car. 'All this nonsense is upsetting the residents, you know, Mr Puritan. You shouldn't do it, people of their age don't want and don't need this kind of disturbance in their lives. Why can't you leave them alone and play at your festivals somewhere else?'

'I think I know my business best, Nurse Reck, but if I need any advice on dealing with corns, I'll be sure to call on you.' The smirk on Mr Puritan's face showed that this laboured irony was as near as he could get to humour.

'Well, at the rate you keep putting your foot in it, Mr Puritan I should think that you've already got corns,' snorted Nurse Reck, and that was the nearest she could get to humour. She walked off to where her car was parked and slammed its door with extra venom.

It was obvious to all the residents of the Comity that they would be deeply disturbed during the day of the festival. Not one of the residents intended to go to it, and even the Truckles, who had determined to 'rub along' with Mr Puritan no matter what, had been forced to draw the line at the Anti-Racist and Anti-Sexist Festival for the Third Age.

The local press had been alerted to the festival largely by the advertisements that had been placed in their papers announcing the event. On reflection, both Ms Eristic and Mr Puritan would regret this fact, but on the dress rehearsal day, optimism flowed like a great stream through the organisers and they rapidly became caught up in the hundred and one things that organisers have to deal with when a festival moves from the plans and into the marquee.

Many local single-interest groups said they would be attending, and at the setting-up stage lots of strange and downright weird people invaded the quiet solitude of the Comity garden carrying display boards, posters and various boxes of one kind or another.

It was therefore impossible for Mr Puritan to monitor everybody who passed through the arch and headed for the marquee. Even had he known the people, it is doubtful if he would have been able to keep an eagle eye on all the comings and goings that took place during the build-up period.

One group that almost certainly escaped Mr Puritan's watchful eye was three young teenagers who drove in on two mopeds, which they parked right at the end of the marquee, almost at the spot where Mrs Preen and Mrs Patel were in the habit of meeting for a gossip.

The marquee, once erected, shielded the last two cottages on either side of the garden from sight of the people entering or leaving the marquee. Thus safely obscured by the large canvas tent, the three youths were able to break into the cottages and, as the residents had been more or less driven out by all the noise and commotion, three of the cottages were empty and the youths ransacked and vandalised them.

The fourth cottage was, however, occupied. It was the Cenobites' cottage and this couple were never sociable people, keeping themselves very much to themselves. Mrs Cenobite had very poor eyesight and was nearly blind. Her husband David was a good bit older than his wife Grace, but apart from a slight deafness, David was hale and hearty and did most of the housework.

When the three boys broke into the Cenobites' cottage, both David and Grace were dozing in front of their television. Grace heard them force the door and woke up David, who immediately got up and found himself face to face with the three thieves each carrying a hold-all.

It is impossible to say who was more surprised, the thieves or David Cenobite. He asked them what they were doing, and the largest of the three pushed him back into his chair and threatened him and Grace with a knife. Transfixed with fear, the two old people just stayed where they were while the thieves went through the cottage taking what they wanted. As they left, the leader of the group, the largest lad, cut David's hand with the knife with which he had been threatening the couple.

'That's what you'll get if you tell the police, granddad, so remember.'

The thieves left on their mopeds and then David at last found a use for the nurse-call and pressed it.

Felicity Eristic noticed that the alarm was sounding as she sat in the Comity office talking to one of the groups who were exhibiting in the marquee. She shouted to Richard Puritan to turn that damn noise off, which he did, and then realised that it was an alarm call on his new system, so he set off to the Cenobites' cottage to investigate, preparing to tell them off for misuse of the system. On the way he was stopped by some of the people setting up their displays and asked questions about times and places. In short, he got side-tracked and regretfully forgot all about the alarm call and the Cenobites.

11

The Arrival of the Police Marks a New Low

The arrival of the police at the Comity on a criminal matter was an all-time first. Certainly the police had attended for such things as sudden death and to advise on crime prevention, but never in its history had the police been called because a crime had been committed within the confines of St Margaret's Comity.

Ray Paladin's cottage was one that had been broken into, as had Martha Preen's, Gerald Foozler's and the Cenobites'. But it was to Ray Paladin's cottage that the police had been called and to which two burly policemen reported.

Ray had not bothered to tell Mr Puritan, because relationships between Mr Puritan and the residents were at such an antagonistic level that neither side felt able to confide or even talk to the other unless forced by circumstances to do so. It had become an unspoken policy of the residents that wherever possible they would try to be independent of the Comity office and Mr Puritan. Thus, rather than calling on the office to ask Mr Puritan to call the police, Ray Paladin had called them himself.

As for the most part the police were unable to go anywhere without sirens sounding and blue lights flashing, Ray Paladin was not surprised to hear the siren sounding through the arch, nor was he surprised to see from his window the blue flash of the police car beacon reflected on the canvas of the marquee. Had Mr Paladin been living outside of the Comity community, he would have been very surprised indeed to find the police answering a break-in call on the same day, let alone within an hour. He had, however, lived in the Comity for some seven years and so remembered the police service as it was then, rather than how it has developed. He had therefore expected the police to come at once when he had made the 999 call to report that his cottage had been broken into and vandalised.

It is indeed so strange to write that the police responded within the hour to a call about a domestic burglary that I feel I have to give readers the reason for this altogether exceptional police response, or readers would accuse me of being wholly out of touch with the way things are in the land. The reason why the police arrived so quickly was simply because firstly, it was nearing the end of their shift, and secondly, the local force was mounting a surveillance on the A354 to specifically catch motorists who were exceeding the speed limit through Newel under Lea. A police car was therefore in the area, and the Comity was on their way back to their station.

If the siren and the blue flashing light was expected by Mr Paladin, it was a very great surprise for Mr Puritan, Ms Eristic and the stallholders still in the marquee setting up their stalls and displays.

The police, as is their way, drove at speed through the archway and executed a hand-brake turn on the gravel, thus blocking the entrance from the Comity to the road.

Faced with the fact that they didn't know how the numbers went, the two constables each took one side of the Comity 'U' and ran down it looking for Mr Paladin's cottage. Mr Puritan had gone to the entrance of the marquee, saw them arrive and saw them run down the two paths on either side of the marquee. He was bemused. What, he thought, can the police be doing at the Comity? He followed, and happily chose the right side of the tent so that he was able to see a policeman run up Mr Paladin's path and go into his cottage. He followed and entered the cottage just after the constable. It did not take him or the constable long to see what had happened. This did not stop him, however, from asking Ray Paladin: 'What has happened?'

Both Ray and the policeman turned to him and the constable replied: 'There seems to have been a burglary, sir.'

'Good heavens, who did it?' asked an amazed Mr Puritan.

'A burglar, I should think,' observed Ray.

The other policeman had by this time arrived, as had Mrs Preen, who burst through the door to tell the assembled group: 'My cottage has been broken into and everything is broken and all over the floor. Oh Mr Paladin, it's happened to you too.'

Before Ray could answer, Gerald Foozler appeared and stated that he, too, had been burgled and vandalised.

'What about the Cenobites?' asked Martha. 'If they have done mine and Mr Paladin's cottage and Mr Foozler's, they might have been to the Cenobites.'

'Oh my God,' gasped Mr Puritan, remembering the alarm call and making a dash for the door, 'the Cenobites set off the nurse-call alarm and I was on my way to answer it but...' and here Mr Puritan wisely didn't say, I forgot. 'Quick!' He ran out of the door but then realised that he would have to run right up the path and round the marquee in order to get to the other side of the Comity lawn and to the Cenobites' cottage.

'The Cenobites live in the cottage opposite and very seldom go out anywhere,' explained Martha Preen.

'So they might have witnessed the robberies?' said the policeman nearest to the door.

'Or been burgled themselves,' said Ray Paladin, making for the door.

The awfulness of the situation now dawned upon everybody in the room, and the two constables ran after Mr Puritan, followed by Ray Paladin and more slowly by Martha Preen.

Observing this police activity were the reporters of the *Wiltshire Times*, the local radio station and the local TV station, all of whom had been summoned by Ms Eristic for a press conference.

Mr Puritan arrived at the Cenobites' cottage first, followed by the reporters and then the police. Like all the other cottages that had been broken into, the door was open and so Mr Puritan was able to rush in, as did the reporters. The scene that faced them was Grace Cenobite and David Cenobite sitting rigidly in their chairs, obviously deep in shock. David Cenobite's hand was covered in dried blood and there was blood on his shirt and on Grace's face. Camera flashes went off and the picture was caught on video, as was Mr Puritan's exclamation: 'Oh God, what's happened to them?'

One constable, panting from the run, then ushered the reporters and Mr Puritan out, while the other radioed in to the station.

The policeman inside then very gently and calmly set about assuring David and Grace that all was well and that the police were there and there was nothing to fear. The second policeman, having made his report and called for an ambulance, then came back into the cottage with the first-aid kit from the police car. He cleaned the blood off David's hand and found that the cut was not serious. He then cleaned the blood off Grace's face and found that she had not been cut at all.

Both David and Grace were still rigid with shock, but otherwise were largely unharmed. A plaster on the cut was all that was needed, and slowly the Cenobites overcame their shock enough to be able to explain what had happened and give a description of the three young thieves. From this description the police were able to almost instantly put possible names to the thieves and radio the facts through to their station.

By this time the police back-up had arrived and a senior officer appeared with a crime team, who quickly established fingerprints and other evidence including a tyre print of one of the mopeds. The ambulance also arrived with full heart-attack equipment on board, but the Cenobites declined the offer of medical help and sent it away. Grace Cenobite did, however, ask Martha if she would ring St Margaret's and St John's and see if the Reverend Palmer would call. Martha called the church and was told that the Reverend Palmer was away but that a part-time curate, Mr Boon, would visit. The doctor was also called and prescribed a mild sedative for both the Cenobites, which they were given and then put to bed.

The police then set up an incident room in the Comity office so that statements could be taken from the residents and from anyone who had been in the Comity at the time of the break-in. The reporters had meanwhile filed their stories and interviewed the residents concerned.

The senior policeman in charge of the investigation was not

all sweetness and light. He was, to put no finer point on it, inclined to be censorious towards Mr Puritan. Why, he asked, had the gates been removed and why had the marquee been put up so that it obscured the last four cottages from the Comity office view? He also wondered aloud about the people who were in the marquee and asked what had Crystals for Psychic Health got to do with the Comity residents and why did Mr Puritan think that the residents were interested in the People Against Motorways or in Afro Beauty Products or even in Lesbian & Gay Counselling?

Felicity Eristic took grave exception to these questions, as did Mr Puritan. It was not a matter for the police to question how the Comity was run, nor was it any concern of the police who was invited to the Anti-Racist and Anti-Sexist Festival for the Third Age, she reminded the senior officer.

'It is a question of total policing,' he told them. 'We now look at all the constituents that contribute to crime, not simply at the crime itself. This total policing concept was extremely helpful in identifying factors that encouraged criminal activity in an area, and so the removal of the gates, for example, encouraged toe-rags and low-life to view the Comity garden as fair game.'

The mention of toe-rags and low-life enraged Ms Eristic.

'The problem with you fascist police,' she observed to the officer, 'is that you are in the pay of the landowners and moneyed classes. You are simply a tool to keep the vast majority of the population in its place, to let the rich sleep safe in their beds. I do not need a lecture from you about how a sheltered housing complex should be run.'

The officer took this onslaught without any sign of annoyance, probably because he had heard it all before from the Watch Committee, and commented, 'I seriously believe that the gates gave the residents both a feeling of security and a measure of it as well. Indeed, I would think very seriously about replacing them if you do not want a repetition of what has happened here today.'

Mr Puritan was not going to let Felicity Eristic be the only flail of the forces of law and order. He, too, had suffered at their hands at demonstrations and had been rudely treated when he had sat down in front of police cars.

'Happily, inspector, the welfare of the people in the Comity is not your responsibility, it is mine, and the regulations state very clearly that a complex such as this has to allow access for emergency vehicles twenty-four hours a day, hence the removal of the gates.'

'I think you will find that the regulation you quoted only applies to hospitals and medical centres not sheltered housing, Mr Puritan,' answered the inspector.

At this point in the argument a constable came into the room and told the inspector that two of the youths had been arrested with the stolen goods still in their hold-alls. The third youth would be arrested shortly.

'Well, it will be a matter for the courts then,' said the inspector. 'You will in all possibility be called to give evidence when the case comes to court, Mr Puritan. By the way, what was the result of the coroner's examination? I haven't heard from the court about that. Is there going to be an inquest?'

'No,' replied Ms Eristic, 'there is not going to be an inquest. The coroner was satisfied that death was by natural causes – a heart attack, in fact.'

'Well, that's lucky for you. Inquests can be very difficult and you can never be sure what will come out at them.' The inspector gave Mr Puritan a peculiar kind of look when he said this, and the look was not lost upon either Mr Puritan nor Felicity Eristic. They had disliked the inspector as soon as they saw him, and this distaste had grown during their conversation with him.

'There is nothing to "come out" as you call it, inspector,' Mr Puritan answered.

'No, sir, I'm sure there isn't, but it is good news that there will not be an inquest all the same, isn't it?'

'Inspector, we have nothing to hide or anything to reproach ourselves for, and so we feel completely neutral about the outcome of the coroner's examination.' Felicity said this through very tight lips.

'Indeed,' replied the inspector, and I am reminded that there are so very many ways to interpret the word 'indeed' when used in conversation that it is almost impossible to write the word down without implying something, which was, I suspect, the very reason why the inspector used the word.

Having arrested the thieves and having told the Administrator of the Comity exactly what he felt his duties were, both to his residents and to the community at large, the inspector had nothing more to do. Statements had been taken from those whose cottages had been broken into, the Cenobites had seen the doctor, the scene of crime officer had satisfied himself that all the evidence that could be gleaned had been gleaned, and a locksmith had been sent for to replace the locks and mend the doors. The inspector therefore closed down the investigation and vacated the office in the Comity, allowing Mr Puritan to regain possession and gaze again upon the posters that so eloquently explained how a new Jerusalem would dawn for the residents of the Comity.

I will not surprise anybody if I say that, as the lights went out in the Comity that night, peace and tranquillity did not attend the residents or Mr Puritan's sleep.

The breeze that blew through the marquee guy ropes and round the doors of the cottages and rustled the heads of the flowers reflected the troubled sleep of all the residents.

Mr Paladin did not sleep, for he turned over in his mind the way the quiet life of the Comity had suddenly become a never-ending round of fights and shocks, of misery and confrontations. There had been the matter of his parking his motorbike at the back of the Comity block, there had been the matter of the quarter-day meeting, the newsletters, the nurse-call system, the posters, the removal of the gates, the accusation against Mrs Preen of racism, the insulting of Mrs Patel and the laughable assumption that Arni Pule was a homosexual simply because he was a bachelor and had never married. At the centre of all this had been Mr Puritan constantly suggesting, changing and pushing the residents in directions that none of them wished to go.

Most important had been the death of John Hall. Everybody missed John, thought Ray Paladin. Not that others who had died at the Comity had not been missed, but they had died of a understandable illness or just of old age. John Hall had not died like that, he had died because the Comity had struck out at him, had turned on him, had tried to change him rather than accommodate him.

To some old people the will to live simply ebbs away and they just give up on living. Sangeta Patel, thought Ray, was in danger of doing this. Since her run-in with Puritan she had stayed more or less permanently in her cottage having other residents get her shopping and hardly ever going out. The Lubberlys had also almost given up living at the Comity and stayed with their children for weeks on end, only coming back for a day or two before they went somewhere else. Mrs Hall seldom went out and relied upon her daughter to bring her groceries. The Cenobites had never been sociable and always kept themselves to themselves, but since the arrival of Mr Puritan they had been even more solitary; now he would be surprised if they stayed on at the Comity at all.

Reviewing the events since the appointment of Mr Puritan, Ray Paladin decided that he would write to the President of the RRAWF and set it all out and ask him to do something urgently, for things could not possibly continue as they were.

He wrote his letter, often scratching out paragraphs and screwing up sheets of paper, but finally as the dawn started to light up the edges of his curtains, he had a version that seemed to him to say all there was to say about the affairs of the Comity.

He posted his letter that morning and it caught the first collection.

The dress rehearsal for The Anti-Racist and Anti-Sexist Festival for the Third Age, had been dramatic. Mr Puritan's trousers had been assaulted and had suffered greatly, Ms Eristic had met some important suppliers and had further cemented her position in terms of the Comity management and the residents had been ignored.

The actual event, the Festival in all its glory and high moral determination, demonstrated that the English have an in-built, possibly genetic, answer to those who aspire to shape and mould their thinking, it is called apathy. Visitors were very few indeed, the residents boycotted the festival and a trip to Salisbury was organised for lunch.

It was fortunate for Mr Puritan that Felicity Eristic's department had underwritten all the costs of the Festival, the loss was
therefore borne by the Council's Frail and Elderly Welfare
Department. Indeed so few visitors turned up that everybody
involved, with the exception of Ms Eristic and Mr Puritan,
decided at four o'clock in the afternoon, to go home and leave
the marquee empty and unattended.

Apathy was the major reaction to Mr Puritan's high minded
initiative. It would be rash to say that the people of Wiltshire
rejected the festival, the reality was that the people of Wiltshire
very sensibly ignored it and went about their business without a
second thought.

It was however a success, the minutes of the council meeting
reported it so, as did the report that Richard Puritan sent to Mr.
Fribble. The spin reported a success and so, as far as the world
outside of the Comity was concerned, it was a success.

12

Love and Laura

There is a common misconception that if you are rich, educated and intelligent then love is easy. In reality for somebody possessing these qualities, love is the very opposite of easy, it is fraught with too much introspection, too much thinking and too much imagining. Love is primarily about instinct and sexual drive, it is not about thinking, imagining or analysis. Money, again contrary to popular belief, does not help love, if anything it hinders it by taking away the magic of wanting and finding, replacing them with satiation and baubles. Money is no help to love, it provides at best a distraction that for a time obscures the point of love and at worst completely buries love in a fur-lined grave.

Perhaps that is why most people fall in love when they are very young, and out of love when sense and experience have taught them that friendship and loyalty, honesty and trust are altogether more valuable in man's travels through that brief history of existence that is called a lifetime. Love can bemuse, confuse and entertain but seldom, if ever, does it last long enough or go deep enough for there to be any remaining trace of it after it has passed on and left the lovers either married, wiser or embittered.

The slow dawning of love in Joe Staunch's and Laura Izzat's hearts was not without difficulty.

Joe was proud, inclined to be bookish, intellectual and scornful of emotions, whilst Laura was savagely independent, mannered, used to being adored, highly intelligent and well-read, confident and distrustful of sexual overtures. Combined, for both Laura and Joe, it was an uphill task for love to gain even a toehold, and it was only the raw emotion of youth and sexual attraction that kept the two lovers at the task that their hearts told them was right.

Added to their problems was the fact that neither of the two had been 'in love' before and so each new wave of confusion and demands broke upon two minds that were neither experienced nor prepared. If it had not been that love at its most basic requires little by way of sophistication and even less by way of intellectual effort, I am sure that Joe and Laura's love would have collapsed after the first dinner together.

Certainly they had felt that mutual attraction that lovers feel when they meet, certainly they had been hugely entertained by each other's witty and absorbing conversation, certainly Laura had not found Joe's tendency to give didactic lectures on every subject under the sun irksome, and Joe had not found Laura's ability to reach the point of the lecture before he had arrived at it wearisome. Nor, I have to admit, had Laura been altogether affronted by the fact that Joe's eyes were inclined to gaze at the top of the low cut dress she wore, whenever she leaned forward to make a point. For his part, Joe found it rather enjoyable to notice that Laura was inclined to touch his hand whenever there was the slightest excuse, such as when he poured the wine or offered her a dish.

When they were together the raw drive of sexuality, compatibility and amusement kept them in love, but when they were apart the interests of their lives and the events in their day-to-day business tended to sideline their attention.

On Laura's part she was more inclined to remember her undying love for Joe in those moments when she wasn't meeting friends, shopping, studying or running her father's house. Joe, however, was a person who did one thing at a time and did it very well by the simple expedient of devoting his whole being to it. Regardless if he was cooking, painting or sketching, Joe was always one hundred per cent engaged in the job on hand and this tended to crowd out any extraneous thoughts, even of the wonderful and beautiful Laura.

Because love always finds a way, the pattern that had emerged between Joe and Laura was that either Joe or Laura would turn up at the other's flat or house and wait until the object of their love appeared. In this way, as Joe tended to visit Laura rather more than Laura visited Joe, John Izzat often felt that he saw rather more of Joe Staunch than his daughter, but then fathers are inclined to resent their daughters being in love.

There was, though, a degree of truth in John Izzat's observation, and the two men had found that they had much in common when it came to intellectual matters and they also shared many tastes. The age difference didn't seem to matter either, which is often the fact with son-in-laws and father-in-laws.

The one thing neither the lovely Laura nor John Izzat knew was that Joe Staunch was the son of the Covinouses. Had they known, I am not sure it would have made much difference to John Izzat, but it would probably have made a great deal of difference to Laura, who enjoyed the youthful indulgence of holding very strong views on all things political.

The reason why the Izzats did not know this crucial bit of information was not because Joe Staunch did not want them to know, but rather because the subject had not arisen. Laura was not particularly interested in Joe's parents, until such times that she would need to met them, while John Izzat was not interested because he did not consider that his daughter was truly serious about Joe Staunch and, until she was, he would not want to waste his time.

Thus it was that the subject of Joe Staunch's relationship with the awful Covinouses did not raise its ugly head in the first heady weeks of Joe and Laura's love. They did, however, establish very clearly their views on the French nuclear policy of testing bombs in other people's backyards, of Spanish fishing ambitions and the European Union's monetary policies. They also worked out how world art was developing and came very near indeed to finding out the true meaning of life.

If readers think that I am making fun of Joe and Laura at this vital and wonderful moment in their lives, they are wrong. I am, perhaps, making fun of love or even casting a wry look at youth. Joe and Laura are altogether too decent a couple to warrant my poking fun at them, for they behave no worse and indeed a great deal better than most of the young lovers you see about you daily, behaving as if they had not only invented sex, but were hell-bent on demonstrating the finer points to the general public at large.

John Izzat liked Joe Staunch, as I have said, and he was prepared therefore to discuss with Laura certain of his business in front of him. This was particularly true of his RRAWF business, which was not, for the most part, commercially sensitive.

With affairs of the Comity becoming ever more tense, it was not surprising that John discussed the twists and turns of Comity events with Laura, particularly as she had been to the place and met some of the players. John Izzat was anxious to hear Laura's opinion on the letter he had received from one of the Comity residents, which had profoundly disturbed him. The problem was that Joe Staunch had been waiting for some time for Laura to return and when she had returned home, Joe and Laura had had a shouted conversation about which restaurant they would visit that evening, as Laura had rushed upstairs to shower and change.

In order to discuss the letter with Laura, John Izzat had suggested that they should have food brought in. Laura, sensing her father's wishes, had agreed to the three of them having dinner together at Ideality. They were sitting in the dining room when John had raised the matter of the letter.

'It is from Mr Paladin, and I have to say that the things he describes confirm my very worst fears about the appointment of Mr Puritan. It seems that the residents of the Comity are up in arms about almost everything Puritan has done since his appointment. There has been the death of Mr Hall, and some nonsense about racialism and Mrs Patel, Mr Pule has been told that he should come out of the closet and admit that he's homosexual, which Mr Paladin reports had so shocked the man that he now gets drunk once a week and screams abuse at Mr Puritan. The whole thing seems like a right mess and Mr Paladin asks me to do something about it. Here, read the letter and tell me what you think.'

He passed the letter over to Laura, who read it with Joe reading it over her shoulder. When they got to the part where

Ray Paladin mentioned the Anti-Racist and Anti-Sexist Festival for the Third Age, Joe saw the dread words 'The Wiltshire Covinous Society' and his heart sank there and then. He realised that he had not told either John Izzat or the lovely Laura about his relationship with the Covinouses. Indeed, it had never crossed his mind that he should mention them. He tended to think of them as irrelevant to his life, and while he had the basement flat, he saw enough of them to fulfil his duty as a son and no more. Now they had come to haunt him in the house of his love and he would surely have to mention that he was related to the object of the Wiltshire Society's admiration.

Laura read the letter carefully and then read it again. Her father was right: the folk at the Comity were being subjected to the most appalling propaganda and coercion. They were being used to further the political ambitions of that Eristic woman and Mr Puritan, they were being manipulated and dragooned into political correctness against their will.

'The influence of that Eristic woman is something that should be considered, father, along with the position of this "Wiltshire Covinous Society". There is no formal tie-up between the Council and the Comity, is there? It is an independent entity officially, although as you said the other day, there is the matter of the power of the Council over things like sheltered housing complexes. That is only a regulatory power, though, rather than a power of responsibility, isn't it?

John Izzat felt that Laura's analysis was probably correct, but was not sure that regulatory control and power of responsibility were vastly different things when it came to the facts of bullying old people for some politically correct ideal or ambition.

'If Puritan and Eristic agree on something, I would not like to arbitrate on the difference between regulatory power and power of responsibility, Laura. English law is, as you well know, based upon two parties contesting an issue rather than the French system of an investigation followed by defence. In these circumstances, the difference between regulation and responsibility would be splitting hairs, I fear.'

Joe meanwhile had grown anxious about the way the conversation might turn to the Wiltshire Covinous Society. Not that he had ever heard of the wretched group, but it was enough that his mother's name was the meat in the sandwich of the words that made up the society's name.

Love also flew about his head. He felt that this was 'precious time' when he could have been trading the sweet nothings of love with Laura, rather than considering the serious deficiencies of St Margaret's Comity. The urgency of love drove out, for Joe, the problems of the old in a distant sheltered housing complex.

If Joe's thought were turning towards love, Laura's were starting to burn with indignation. The injustice and the disturbance brought to the lives of the residents of the Comity became, for Laura, the seeds of a *cause célèbre*.

John Izzat had planned to work late in his study on some other matters of the RRAWF, and so made an excuse to leave Joe and Laura alone.

They cleared away the dinner things together and while this was being done, Joe was aware that Laura's mind was not on the prospects of love, she was preoccupied, and he dreaded the thought that he might have to admit his 'Covinous connection'. He also knew that if Laura had taken the plight of the Comity residents to her heart, he would have to take sides. He had a choice, he told himself. He could deceive Laura about the Covinous connection or he could confess it. He ruled out deceit; he had read enough novels to know that even white lies can lead to temporarily losing your lover, and as for great, monstrous, deceitful lies, well, they could end love for ever and a day. Further, knowing his mother and his stepfather, if it came to a fight and there was the merest chance of publicity, then his parents would jump into the ring with all guns blazing. Indeed, the only thing he admired about his stepfather was his public courage, even if it did mask a private cynicism and an intellectual arrogance.

Having cleared away and washed up, Laura and Joe sat on the terrace. In more normal circumstances, it would have been an ideal opportunity for love, but Laura's mood was far from such activity, although perhaps love is not just kissing and cuddling, but commitment and support as well, and if that is the case, then Joe was constrained by Laura's mood to indulge in the latter version of love rather than the former.

'We have to do something for those poor people at the Comity, Joe.' Laura was both determined and indignant. 'Those people running the Comity are ruining the last few years of the residents' lives. It's dreadful and something has to be done.'

Joe was sympathetic, he agreed, and what is more felt, if not as strongly as Laura, that such political correctness as that which Mr Puritan was forcing upon the Comity residents was silly and pointless. But he could not rid himself of the wish to hold the lovely Laura in his arms and breathe in the wonderful perfume of her, to touch her velvet skin, and feel her hair upon his face. If love in this was inconsiderate, then I can only plead that if it wasn't for such love, there wouldn't be lovely Lauras or the likes of Joe Staunch. Love is the engine that drives the human world, and even if it is sometimes little more than lust, then that must be the way it is, for it is the fuel of the engine, and if it makes us make love no matter whether the setting is right or the time appropriate, then that is the way it is.

Joe was sitting next to Laura, and a summer moon was shining and the night was still warm. He put his arm round her and gently pulled her towards him.

Now I cannot say if it was the wine, or the evening air or the closeness of Joe, but whatever it was, Laura's indignation and anger seemed very slowly to fade away, and it would not be right to pry upon them any longer as they sat on the terrace.

In the morning, however, Laura was just as determined and just as angry at the way the Comity was being run. Joe was also in the right frame of mind to bend his considerable intellect to the subject, and they attacked the problem together. Powerful as the combination of the two minds were, they both found themselves in more or less the same situation that John Izzat had found himself, namely, unable to think of any course of action that would resolve the problem or force Mr Puritan to leave the Comity.

'The key, of course,' observed Laura, 'is to find a cleric, because it was made clear to Puritan that if a suitable rector or vicar came along then he or she would be appointed and

Puritan would be out. But where do you find suitable clerics when you want one?'

'You could try the Bishop, I suppose. They have lists of vicars and such.'

'But I don't know any bishops and you just can't walk into a bishop's palace and say – "Here, Bishop, have you got any vicars in stock we want one for the Comity"!'

'Does your father know any bishops then? Perhaps he could ask?'

'I'll ask him,' said Laura. And she would have done so if John Izzat had not rushed into the kitchen where they were having breakfast carrying the morning paper in which there was the headline under a news-in-brief section: 'BURGLARS BEAT UP DARBY & JOAN AT ANTI-SEXISM FESTIVAL'.

'Look, Laura, the Comity has made the national newspapers.'

John Izzat was angry, and flung the paper down on the table. 'This is the last straw. I intend to call a meeting of the trustees and invite Mr Puritan to attend. I've had enough of all this social engineering and it is time Puritan faced the real world of his employer, rather than the loony world of local political correctness. It is time he understood that people at the Comity are not pawns in his ridiculous game. I'll phone Fribble and have him set up a meeting as soon as possible.'

He stormed out to make his phone call.

Laura had seldom seen her father so angry and she looked at Joe, who raised his eyebrows in sympathy.

'If it warrants a small mention in the nationals, just think what the story is getting in the regional paper, Laura.'

Laura could imagine, and she could also imagine what her father would say when the clipping service RRAWF employed sent the cuttings through and he saw the Comity spread across the front page, with quotes and pictures.

'There must be some way to find out if there is a suitable cleric available. Because if they force Puritan to resign, the problem will remain and that Eristic woman will simply find another puppet to replace him.'

'Why don't you go down to Salisbury and call on the Bishop, Laura? I'm sure that he wouldn't bite your head off and, knowing the Church, he will probably turn out to be an absolutely charming man, full of understanding and common-sense charity. Look, I can come with you, if you like.'

Laura was delighted at the thought of Joe coming with her and kissed him. Independent lady though she was, she welcomed a friend as she was still uncertain what she really wanted and what could be achieved. She told her father that they were off to Salisbury, but did not tell him the reason for the trip.

John Izzat was too busy and too angry to enquire and was pleased that Laura was going to be occupied while he attended to the matter of the Comity and Mr Puritan.

13

The Trustees Meeting

The RRA building is based in London in a large office block off Coventry Street. The outside of the building, which is a glass and steel structure and typical of modern architecture, consisting of nests of windows and an over-large lobby.

The RRA offices occupy the top two floors and are well appointed and elegantly functional. This was the citadel of Eric Fribble, who ruled over the place with considerable skill and not much humour. Eric Fribble was a man tied to structures, minutes, committees and procedures. Aged about 45, he fawned to the Association's Committee but to few others, and most of the RRA employees walked in almost total fear of the man. His strength, and indeed it was a strength, lay in his ability to rewrite the minutes to suit his strategies and tactics. Normally RRA affairs were run exactly as Eric Fribble wanted, regardless of what the Management Committee wanted or indeed requested. Fribble's other ability was to rig the elections to the various committees and ultimately the Management Committee so that 'his' men were elected and promoted.

The RRAWF was a sideline and served Fribble as a sink for those members who were elected against his wish, they served on the Welfare Fund Committee and usually faded away after one year.

This then is the world of Eric Fribble. How, you might wonder, did John Izzat slip through the Fribble net? Well, Izzat's company was a major, perhaps *the* major, contributor to the finances of the Association, and so regardless of Eric Fribble, the chief executive automatically sat on the Management Committee and in time became President. Added to this was the fact that John Izzat was a national business figure who was consulted by the DTI and was in line for an honour. Eric Fribble thus accommodated John Izzat with fawning attention to his every whim.

For his part, Izzat was well aware of how Fribble wielded power and how he changed the minutes to suit his own vision of the Association. Izzat corrected it where he wanted to and softened the effect of Fribble on the staff.

However, in his own offices, Fribble was a powerful man and more than a match for Mr Puritan, who had been summoned to the RRAWF meeting by a very angry Eric Fribble. Seldom in Mr Fribble's memory had a president ever told him to hold a meeting, and never dealing with matters of the RRAWF.

Steaming with anger in his office, Eric had confided to his secretary: 'This man Puritan has tarnished, Muriel, tarnished the whole image of the RRA and, worse still, has brought rotten publicity on us and, even worse, caused the President to call a meeting. Where will it end? It will be brought up at Management Committee and the President will take more than a passing interest in the minutes and why? Because this man Puritan has let me down!'

Little needs to be said about the other members of the Welfare Fund Committee. There are five members, including John Izzat, the Chairman; Eric Fribble is not a committee member but is the secretary to the committee without a vote. Normally the committee sits twice a year, once to agree the accounts and consider financial matters for the following year, and once to consider fund raising and any housekeeping matters. The day-to-day matters are handled by Eric Fribble in consultation with the President and the Chairman. It was therefore right that Fribble was angry at there having to be an extraordinary meeting of the Welfare Fund Committee, such an extraordinary event indicated that things had gone badly wrong.

Izzat had arrived early and had already spoken with Eric, at length, about the problems of the Comity and had indicated that he was far from happy and expected Eric Fribble to do something about it, indeed his very words were: 'Look, Eric, use your devious mind to shift this Mr Puritan. He has dirtied the image of the RRAWF and presented us with a problem that we don't need and certainly don't want, so I expect you to resolve the issue and with all speed. I hope you understand very clearly what I'm saying, Eric, because I would hate to have to face the prospect of finding a new Secretary of the Association.'

Eric Fribble understood clearly what the President was saying and deeply resented this threat to his job security, but was enough of a realist to know that in the real world, if the President wanted him sacked he would be forced to resign.

'Mr President, I totally agree with you about Mr Puritan. The man has indeed blotted his copybook and the Association is smeared with his failure and I shall remove him, but, with respect, sir, you know as well as I do, the legislation does not make it easy for him to be removed quickly, er, er, by – as it were by force. I will have to engineer his departure and it won't be easy. I need, sir, time to get Mr Puritan out. It cannot be done in a moment.'

'Eric, I know all about the employment laws – better, I hazard, than you – but that is not the issue. We can't sack the man, he's done nothing particularly wrong, but that is where your devious nature must come into play. We must, how shall I put it, engineer him into resigning. Use your bloody skill with minutes and memos, with procedure and the like, push him into breaking the rules and then bring the knife down with speed and skill. I don't want blood on the carpet or screams of pain, I want him out, broken and bowed down so low that he won't even look up to see the road ahead. I want him disgraced and ashamed, so ashamed that he will never want to remember the Comity ever again, and I want you to do it quickly.'

'Mr President do you want me to minute those instructions?'

'They'll be the very last minutes you write here if you do, Eric.'

'Of course I wouldn't dream of minuting this conversation, Mr President. Have you heard any more about this year's honours list?'

'Mind your own business, Mr Fribble, or I won't invite you to the celebration party. Let's get on with the meeting shall we?'

'Can I assume that you will support my minutes on this meeting, Mr President?'

113

'Yes, Mr Fribble, you can safely bet on it.'

They walked to the committee meeting room, with Eric Fribble thinking that if he managed this tricky assignment John Izzat would owe him a considerable debt, and with John Izzat contemplating how he would have to get rid of Eric Fribble if he succeeded in booting out Mr Puritan. John Izzat never left hostages to fortune if he could help it, and he could help it in this instance.

Richard Puritan was not invited into the meeting straight away, but was invited to sit in the outer office until the meeting had reached the matter of the Comity on its agenda. He sat on the edge of his chair, ill at ease and wishing with all his will that the meeting was over. Mr Fribble had simply told him that the RRAWF Committee was meeting and would welcome his attending. There had been no reply to the question what's the meeting about, Eric? Nor had there been any warmth in Mr Fribble's voice, when he had said that he was shockingly busy and would see him when he arrived at the RRAWF offices. He had indeed greeted Richard Puritan with the briefest of brief handshakes and the minimal 'hallo, Richard'. Now Puritan sat on the edge of his chair and worried.

In the meeting room John Izzat took the chair at the top of the table and Eric Fribble sat at a table behind and to the side of Izzat. The other members of the committee had arrived on time and had in front of them a paper, prepared by John Izzat, setting out his case against Puritan.

After opening the meeting, Izzat reviewed the events set out in his paper and then got to his point: 'The Comity is now in a state where not one of us here would be proud to have our name connected with it. It is no longer a peaceful and restful place, no longer a series of cottages where elderly members of our industry can pass their days without fear or problems, it is a battlefield where political correctness fights daily with old, inoffensive habits, where old ways of doing things are challenged and residents' thoughts are policed and their actions scrutinised for deviation from a political norm to which not one of us would subscribe. It is a place where the garden that should be a timeless place of ease is used for a festival of political correctness,

114

and the local louts terrorise and steal from the residents. The Comity is no longer a bright star on the Association's shield but a evil mark on its activities. We are here to ask the Administrator to explain why this is so and how this has happened, and if you question my description, then simply read the copy of the letter from Mr Paladin addressed to me and attached to your papers.' The members of the committee turned to the letter and registered their disapproval. 'Mr Fribble, perhaps you would invite Mr Puritan into this meeting?'

This was the first time John Izzat had seen Mr Puritan. I cannot say what he had expected, but Richard Puritan's entrance was not, contrary to Ms Eristic's coaching, powerful. This was in part due to the fact that Eric Fribble had given him a tray of coffee and tea cups to carry that were piled dangerously high, and further that the same Mr Fribble had preceded him into the room and not held the door for him, thus Richard Puritan's entrance was more that of clown at a circus than a powerful administrator. He backed into the room, pushing the door with his large bottom, and tried to turn faster than the door closed, and then rushed with the tray towards the table. As he got near the table Mr Fribble motioned him to a side table and then when he was halfway to it announced: 'Ladies and gentlemen, this is Mr Puritan, the Administrator of St Margaret's Comity.'

Was it by this stratagem that Mr Fribble devalued Mr Puritan's entrance and the first impression he made upon the committee? Only Mr Fribble, who introduced him before he could set down the tray, could know. What I know is that Mr Puritan was wounded by his entrance and the first impression he made upon the members of the committee. Having set down the tray, he turned and found all faces looking at him.

'I brought in the tea cups,' he offered, instead of the more usual 'good morning'.

'Good morning, Mr Puritan.' John Izzat's voice was as cold as ice and there was no welcome to the wretched Administrator from any of the faces that gazed at him.

'Please sit down.' Izzat indicated the only free seat at the other end of the table. Richard Puritan sat down and tried a smile on his neighbours, they did not return it.

'I'm John Izzat, the Chairman of the Welfare Fund Committee.' Izzat did not introduce the other members, but instead looked at Richard Puritan, allowing the silence to chill Puritan's mind. The silence seemed to stretch for several minutes, although Izzat's gaze bore powerfully into Puritan's face until the Administrator had to look away and then stroke his nose.

'Mr Puritan,' John Izzat's voice had a steel-like quality to it, 'I have received a letter from one of the residents of the Comity which has disturbed this committee very greatly. In this letter we are told of events and happenings that are profoundly worrying, of a resident's death, of a resident being insulted and of thieves being allowed access to the premises, of gates being removed and of posters being displayed that harangue the residents. These are elderly people, Mr Puritan, not some street rabble to be set against some imagined social ill, elderly people who want very little beyond peace and an unchanging life until they have to meet their maker. Why has this been happening, Mr Puritan?'

'Can I see a copy of the letter please?' Mr Puritan now saw what the meeting was about and his worst fears were realised. He needed time and he needed to hear a debate before he entered his defence.

Mr Fribble came from behind his table with a sheet of paper and gave it to Mr Puritan. 'This is a copy of the substance of the letter, Mr Puritan, I have been instructed to delete the name of the sender so you cannot identify the writer, and to have the letter typed.'

Mr Fribble did not even whisper this statement but said it out loud, implying Mr Puritan's guilt. This was not lost on Mr Puritan or on the committee. Mr Puritan read the letter and the committee waited for him.

'The old and frail often feel themselves to be targeted when in reality what is being done is for the best for them.' Mr Puritan spoke these words softly, seeking to regain the disadvantage of his entrance and to appear a sweetly reasonable person.

'Are the facts given by the writer wrong then, Mr Puritan?' John Izzat let a degree of puzzlement creep into his voice.

116

'The facts are not wrong but they are only half the facts,' replied Puritan. 'I think the writer misjudges the point about the gates being removed; this is required by the Health and Safety regulations, and the point about the death, the unfortunate death of Mr Hall, there was no inquest nor any suggestion from the police that there was anything wrong. As to the thieves, again the police found nothing wrong with the organisation of the Comity. Regarding the insult that Mrs Patel felt she had suffered, it was a misunderstanding, nothing more, and as for the posters, well, there are all kinds of posters on the notice-board, posters about dangerous plants from the Ministry, posters about the time of surgery at the doctor's and about pension entitlement.'

'It seems to me, Mr Puritan,' asserted John Izzat, 'that you are seeking to meddle, to change the lives of the residents of St Margaret's Comity, to force them into your view of society rather than theirs. Would I be right in this assumption?'

'I seek to show them that in certain ways we have all changed. We no longer allow certain race words to be used, nor do we like to see women treated as second-class people, nor yet again do we hound people who have different gender orientation than our own. They may be elderly, as you say John, but they have to live in today's world, they have not got permission to ignore the rules the rest of us live by.'

Richard Puritan should not have called Izzat by his Christian name; it was a mistake, although Puritan felt – as he had been taught – that it was a way of bringing the other person to see that you are his equal. John Izzat, however, saw it as an impertinence.

'Mr Puritan.' Izzat spoke slowly and stressed the 'Mr'. 'The Association finances the St Margaret's Comity. We have the lease, the residents' tenancies are contracts between the Association and each tenant. You, *Mr* Puritan, are an employee of the Association. We pay your salary, your rent, we even buy your damn toilet paper. The Association, *Mr* Puritan, makes the **rules**.' Izzat stood up and raised his fist level with his shoulder and then smashed it down upon the table. 'Not, *Mr* Puritan, the world, or society, or the Covinous Society of Wiltshire, or Ms

117

Eristic, or the Health and Safety authority, and not our employees, especially not our employees, but the *Association*, we make the rules. The Association sets the tone, determines the way St Margaret's Comity is run, because it is private property and a private charity and a discrete act of benevolence, paid for, Mr Puritan, by the Association's members and efforts. If you cannot find it within your make-up to work within those confines then I suggest that you resign. Will you accept our determination, our wishes on this matter?'

Mr Puritan was frightened. He had never seen such controlled anger, had never seen such an iron will, nor experienced such a devastating attack upon the whole core of his beliefs. But through his fear, through his amazement, there came his conviction that Justin Covinous was right, the power of red-hot capitalism could only be stopped when the greed for power, which Izzat obviously fed upon, was shown to be what it was in reality, nothing but a feeding frenzy of power. The rules, Covinous maintained, dulled the hungry, power mad beast's desires.

'Mr Izzat.' Puritan tried desperately to seem calm. 'There is absolutely no wish on my part to go against any single stipulation of the Association regarding the running of the Comity. I have, however, to administer the Comity in accordance with the legislation covering and indeed governing sheltered housing and community-based operations. Where these conflict with the Association's wishes, I must own my first duty to the regulations. St Margaret's Comity has to be run legally and in both the spirit and to the letter of the law, unless, that is, the Association gives me written instructions to break or contravene the law, and then I would indeed have to choose between obeying the Association's instructions and resigning.'

'And how exactly does that ridiculous Anti-Racist and Anti-Sexist Festival for the Third Age figure in the law or in the regulations, *Mr* Puritan?' asked John Izzat.

'It is against the law to discriminate on grounds of race, Mr Izzat. I made a judgement and decided that the festival would be a harmless way of highlighting this important bit of legislation. I assumed that the Association supported anti-racism. Am I wrong?'

John Izzat's eye narrowed and his mouth tightened. 'Mr Puritan, I have asked Mr Fribble to explain to you and to put in writing our wishes regarding the St Margaret's Comity and your duties as Administrator. They are a broad outline,' and here the affable, pleasant side of John Izzat was turned on at full power and bathed the committee and Mr Puritan with its radiance and good humour, 'and will not conflict with your laudable desire to keep the Association's sheltered housing complex within the letter of the law. Your admirable judgement on these matters of regulations and law will be given every opportunity to shine but, *Mr* Puritan, this committee has decided that following the very unpleasant events that have happened at St Margaret's Comity since your appointment, we will be forced to review your performance on a regular basis. You will agree, I am sure, that we cannot afford another mistake or problem between the residents, the Association or yourself. To this end we are asking you to sign a letter that states that you will conform to all reasonable requests by the Association regarding the running of the complex and should you fail to perform your duties to our satisfaction then we will be able to call for your resignation. Further, I have asked Mr Fribble to carry out and write an appraisal of your performance, which, when completed, will be considered by this Committee.'

John Izzat provided no opportunity for Richard Puritan to reply, but turned to Eric Fribble.

'Perhaps you would like to take Mr Puritan to your office, Mr Fribble, to explain the finer points that we might have missed.'

Mr Fribble would not have liked to take Mr Puritan anywhere and certainly not when the committee was still sitting. How could he know what was going on, what was being said, while he was out of the room?

'Would you like me to ask my secretary to take notes?' asked Fribble desperately.

'No, Eric, we have just about finished, I'll take any notes that are needed.' Izzat's charm was again at full power.

When Puritan and Fribble had left and Fribble's office door was heard shutting, John Izzat turned wearily to the other four members of the committee and said in a voice full of tiredness and sadness: 'I fear Fribble has let us down here, he should never have let this happen. Perhaps the job has grown too big for him; there is so much legislation, so many calls upon him, he's stretched almost to breaking point. Puritan is likely to be a difficult and tough nut to crack. I worry that Fribble will not be able to keep him in check.'

14

The Bishop Ponders the Problem

Joe Staunch and Laura drove down to Salisbury two days after they had planned, because Joe had heard that he had been selected for a show at the Serpentine Gallery in November.

They parked and then walked through the Cathedral Close to the Bishop's house. As they passed the cathedral, Joe and Laura were struck by its beauty, it seemed to Joe almost as if it was set in its place not only for God but by God.

'You'll think me mad, Laura, but if cathedrals had genders then I would say that Salisbury was feminine. Whereas a cathedral like Durham is masculine, Salisbury looks like a beautiful lady, so proud, so certain of its beauty. It truly is a holy place this cathedral, an awesome place because it seems totally perfect and nothing can be totally perfect, and yet if you wanted to add something to it you couldn't. There is nothing you could do to this cathedral that would do anything other than spoil it. Every stone is right, every window and every piece of ornamentation, and all of it crowned by that spire, so right, so perfect.'

Laura found Joe's statement far from mad, for she felt that the cathedral was the most beautiful building she had ever seen and had loved it ever since her mother had brought her to Salisbury as a little girl. Whenever she came near it she felt that it cast a spell over her that made her calm and at peace within herself. It was, like so much of the music of Bach; complete; indeed, so complete that not a single note could be deleted or added without spoiling it.

'It's one of my most favourite places, Joe. I'm so pleased you can see it as I see it. It is a perfect place, a timeless place and a place where there is great love, or so it seems to me.'

They walked on to the Bishop's Palace under the influence of this most perfect of cathedrals, and arrived feeling more optimistic and much calmer about Mr Puritan.

'Do you think you can just call upon a bishop like you call upon a friend or a relation Joe?'

Joe thought about the question. 'I should think that you can. The Church has become much more approachable and I get the impression that most bishops are a bit embarrassed about all the business of "My Lord Bishop" they tend to go for the "Call me Peter" attitude these days. Anyway, what have we to lose? Ring the bell.'

'No, you ring the bell.'

'Oh for heaven's sake, Laura!' And Joe rang the bell.

The door was opened by an elderly man in a dog collar and black suit. He smiled.

Laura explained that she and Joe wanted to see the Bishop. 'If it is about getting married, I'm afraid it's not the Bishop you should see, but your local vicar. The Bishop isn't involved in marriages.'

'It's not about marriage, it is about finding a vicar,' Laura replied.

'Have you lost a vicar then?' the ancient cleric asked, surprised. 'Well, I suppose you had better come in. Are you from the police?'

'No on both counts, but we would like to speak to the Bishop about a special problem we've got,' Laura replied.

A younger man in a dog collar and a purple shirt came up and smiled. 'What is it, father?'

'These young people want to speak to you about a lost vicar, Robert,' the elderly cleric explained. 'This is the Bishop, my son.'

'How do you do,' said the Bishop. 'I'm afraid I'm in a dreadful rush, but I'll ask my chaplain to see you – I have a service to attend and I can't be late for that or the choir will take it over and I'll be seen to be redundant. Father, will you take these young people to Neil?' He turned to Laura and Joe. 'Please excuse me but I really have to dash, but my father will introduce you to my chaplain. He is probably a better person to find a vicar than I am – they don't run away from him.' He laughed and opened the door and ran in the direction of the cathedral.

The Bishop's father took them to an office, where the Bishop's chaplain was working behind an imposing desk. 'Neil, these young people are looking for a vicar and Robert said you would try to help them find one.'

The Bishop's chaplain laughed. 'Have you any preferences? We've got tall vicars, short ones, fat and thin, high and low, male and female, young and old. Vicars come in all shapes and sizes, in all colours and to fit just about every opinion you could think of and even some you couldn't. Sit down and tell me what we can do for you.'

The Bishop's father left and Neil led them to a conference area, by the window, which looked out on to a beautiful garden.

Both Laura and Joe immediately warmed to this cheerful man with a sense of humour but also with a face that was full of gentle calm and kindness. Slim-built, not very tall and with thinning sandy hair, he seemed like the cathedral – complete.

Joe and Laura started to explain the problem of the Comity. 'Oh yes I know about St Margaret's Comity and the problems it is having. What is your interest?'

'My father is the president of the welfare trust that administers the Comity.'

'Surely, if something is to be done, then your father is the person to do it, isn't he?'

'My father is a very proper man,' explained Laura. 'He maintains there is nothing he or the trust can do unless Mr Puritan does something wrong. He says that Mr Puritan has been given responsibility and must exercise that responsibility with his best judgement, and as long as he does that then he cannot be sacked unless and until he breaks the law or behaves in a way that breaks faith with his duties as Administrator.'

'I would think that he is right in that. The main complaint you seem to have against this Mr Puritan would seem to be that his style is, in your eyes, wrong for a sheltered housing estate.' He saw Laura stiffen with annoyance. 'I'm not saying that you are wrong, Miss Izzat, but you can't surely expect your father or the Trust to sack a man simply because the way he does things isn't the way you would do them.'

'But the man is making the lives of the residents hell,' exclaimed Joe Staunch.

'It is unlikely that the Administrator's employment contract or job description contains anything that refers to the Administrator being loved or even liked by the residents, Mr Staunch.' Neil smiled and looked into the garden. 'But there must have been a reason for you to have come here, apart from telling us about the problems of the St Margaret's Comity residents. Why did you think the Bishop could help you?

Laura then explained that at the appointment interview Mr Fribble had pointed out to Mr Puritan that the head lease was owned by a Diocesan charity and that it had been, until the appointment of Mr Puritan, a stipulation by that charity that the Administrator of St Margaret's Comity should be a clergyman. Further, she recalled, having read Mr Fribble's minutes of the meeting, that it had been said that if a suitable clerical candidate presented himself or herself for the job then Mr Puritan would undertake to step down.

'A Mrs Kickshaw was the Diocesan representative who attended the selection meeting,' explained Laura. 'Presumably she would confirm this. We therefore came to the conclusion that the Bishop might see his way to finding us an ordained person – a vicar who would apply to the Trust for the post of Administrator.'

'With a view to getting Mr Puritan dismissed? Oh dear me, that would not be a very charitable thing to do, would it? Just because you don't agree with a person surely doesn't mean that they should be sacked from their job, even by a hidden means such as this. There is still the matter of knowledge – we would know that we had engineered Mr Puritan's dismissal, wouldn't we?' Neil again looked into the garden, seeking, it seems, some charitable and kindly answer to the problem.

'But the man's a monster, he's making the residents' lives miserable and causing endless pain.' Laura exploded with indignation. 'What do you want, Mr Chaplain? For him to go on causing untold grief, driving old men to kill themselves and old ladies to be too frightened to leave their cottages because they fear being insulted? It's preposterous!'

'Oh come on, Laura,' Joe interrupted. 'The Bishop's chaplain is right in one sense. It isn't right for the Church to go about getting people sacked from their jobs simply because it might disagree with their views.'

'You could have said that about Hitler,' retorted Laura. 'You have to stand up and be counted when you see something going on that is quite plainly wrong. Who was it who said evil flourishes when the good stay silent?'

'It is one thing to speak out, Miss Izzat, quite another to get somebody sacked for speaking out for what they believe in,' Neil commented.

Neil was not saying what Laura wanted to hear. Laura didn't want to learn that right had two sides, nor that compassion could be equally applied to the murderer and the victim. In Laura's mind there was right and wrong and the two had no common bonds, no more than judgements could be seen in a mirror reflecting back into the face of the judge.

Neil understood Laura's confusion and loved her righteousness. He saw that her solution would be ideal if only our morality could be projected as a beam rather than applied universally as a principle.

'We're back in Mr Puritan's territory, Miss Izzat, but the Church of England has never believed that the end justifies the means, although it is, I suspect, what Mr Puritan believes, and that is why he is prepared to pursue his causes in the face of clear evidence that it hurts and makes the residents of the Comity miserable. If we found you a vicar to replace Mr Puritan and engineered Mr Puritan's departure, would that stop Mr Puritan from believing that his way is right, or convince him that the pain he has brought to the people at the Comity is wrong? I doubt it. Would he not find another placement in a sheltered housing unit and with renewed vigour set about generating the same unpleasantness, promoting the same causes somewhere away from yours or my gaze? We would not have solved the problem of Mr Puritan, simply shifted the problem on and out of our responsibility.

'I know you probably think that I am being unhelpful. You are probably thinking to yourself, "That's the Church all over, do-gooding as long as it doesn't make waves, but never facing up to the fact that now and then you have to stand up and be counted". But principles and morality tempered with love demands, more often than not, that good holds back from striking evil, stays its hand rather than exacerbates the pain that evil has caused. There is an answer to Mr Puritan, Miss Izzat, but is it not an answer that you would want to hear, nor is it an answer that would satisfy you.'

'Too right,' Laura replied. 'I came here with a perfectly good and genuine solution to the problem that Puritan represents. All I wanted from the Bishop, or from you, was a name or two of a cleric who could be persuaded to apply for the job of Administrator of the Comity. I understand your argument, but in the final analysis it is not enough to simply say that the end does not justify the means. There is a problem and if the Church cannot answer it when it involves a Church charity, then I say again it is not good enough.'

Neil turned to her, no longer smiling. 'Miss Izzat, does your father know you have come here?'

Laura blushed. 'No, I am over eighteen and I have come here on my own account not on behalf of my father.'

'I think this is a concern of your father and the RRAWF and I do not believe that he, or indeed the trust, would thank you for approaching the Bishop over this matter. Further, I also think that it was a mistake for you to present the problem here. As you say, you are over eighteen – perhaps say twenty-three or so. If you were a little older you would know that a great many problems of this kind are not solved by brave and resolute actions but are solved by silent, almost unnoticed decisions. I can understand why you wanted the Bishop to help you with a list, but you will have to take my word for it that it would not be desirable for the Bishop to provide you with such a list. I am sorry that we cannot help you in the way you wish, but please be assured that the matter has not gone unnoticed, nor is it being ignored, but the Bishop and the Church have to act in matters like this in a manner that you very probably will never fully comprehend. It will, however, act.'

The chaplain rose from his chair and a smile came back to his face. 'Do you like our cathedral, Mr Staunch?'

'I think it is just about the most perfect building I've ever seen,' replied Joe.

'And what about you, Miss Izzat? Do you like the Cathedral?'

Laura regained her grace and charm and smiled. 'Oh yes, I adore it.'

Neil ushered them from his office. At the front door he paused. With his smile very much in evidence, he conspiratorially turned to Laura. 'I have some knowledge of you, Miss Izzat. My son is at the same college as you and has sung your praises both loud and very long – oh not to me, but to his sister over family meals. You have probably no knowledge of him – he is a year behind you – but from his description of you, I can now see that he does not, after all, exaggerate. You obviously brighten the college no end, but I am not sure that you contribute much to the male students' resolve to study hard and apply themselves to the law.'

'What is your son's name?' enquired Laura.

'Philip Thomas,' the chaplain replied.

'No, I am sorry, there are so many students, but I can't recall a Philip Thomas.'

'He will be distraught when I tell him I have met you, but then again he will hardly be surprised. After all, I am, in a manner of speaking, in the angel business.' He laughed. 'But perhaps I shouldn't mention this visit. It would, I am sure, be best for both his peace of mind and for all our peace of mind if we assume this meeting hadn't happened. Miss Izzat, Mr Staunch.' He offered them his hand and they shook it and left.

Once clear of the Bishop's Palace, Joe spoke. 'Well, it was a good try, but it is not, it seems, that easy to obtain a list of out-of-work vicars. Nice man, though, I thought.'

'Yes charming,' replied Laura. 'But useless.'

'Oh I don't know, he was aware of the Puritan problem. Let's get back to London.' They left Salisbury that afternoon.

When the Bishop returned, Neil Thomas discussed their visit

with him. 'They came about the goings on at St Margaret's Comity. She is Izzat's daughter, the Chairman of the RRAWF Trust.'

'Did they come up with any ideas?' the Bishop asked.

'Well, they pointed out that the head lease is ours, but we knew that. It did, however, set me thinking that perhaps there would be some leverage in your visiting St Margaret's and St John's and in the course of that visit you could ask the Reverend Palmer to arrange for you to visit the St Margaret's Comity; it would be a natural place for you to visit, and if you visited you could chat to the residents and hear for yourself what they feel about matters.'

'I could also find out a little more about this Development Enterprise Company and its chief executive, Ms Eristic,' the Bishop observed. 'I'm far from happy with this idea that the DEC has taken over the Council's provision for the care of the elderly and frail, and from all we hear about Ms Eristic, I tend to share Miss Izzat's view that we should take some bold action to safeguard the Comity.'

'We invited the lady to sit on our welfare committee, but she turned us down. We invited her to that special international seminar we held, and she turned that down. She does not appear to want to meet or talk to us right now, Robert.'

The Bishop nodded and pressed his hands together as if praying. 'Well, Neil, then we might have to be more active in asserting our point of view and it might just be that St Margaret's Comity is, for Ms Eristic, one sheltered housing trust too far. After all, as Miss Izzat reminded us, we do hold the head lease and we do have some say in the matter. But you are right about Mr Puritan, he is of no real consequence, he is simply a pawn in Ms Eristic's greater game. We should, I think, discuss St Margaret's Comity with the RRAWF Trust or at least the secretary of the Association. What's his name?'

'Mr Fribble,' and the Bishop nodded.

15

Mr Puritan Reflects

Richard Puritan had arrived back from his meeting with Mr Fribble and the trust committee exhausted and upset. The day had been just awful and he went straight to bed without even any boiled rice.

The next day had been a busy and messy day, allowing no chance to consider the matters discussed. It was on the third day following the meeting that he was able to reflect upon them particularly as far as they involved him, and cast either a good or bad light upon his stewardship.

He had been forced to employ some office help but had been unable to find a suitable candidate and so had had a series of 'temps'. The temp he had at present had been with the Comity for a week and knew enough about the place to allow him to close the door to his flat and just reflect upon the messages, both actual and implied, from the meeting.

This, in one sense, was fortunate because that very morning the minutes from Mr Fribble had arrived together with a letter from the secretary. This letter was the important part, although it is doubtful if Mr Puritan appreciated this, as it was one of Eric Fribble's more masterly compositions. It will assist the reader if I repeat it in full, as every word of such a letter from Mr Fribble carries its own point and poison.

Dear Mr Puritan,

I was concerned at the drift of the recent Trustee Committee Meeting, particularly at the criticisms of the management of the Comity.
I need hardly say that the events as detailed in the letter to the

Chairman reflect as badly upon yourself as Administrator as they do upon me. I must point out that I am not used to being faced with such matters concerning something under my overall control and intend that it should not happen again.

Whilst I can appreciate, to a limited extent, that being new to the job and indeed to full-time employment, you may not have been – or be – totally conversant with the way an administrator's job for a charity trust operates, nevertheless I have to warn you that due to the particular environment in which such trusts operate, the normal grace that any lapses from acceptable procedure might, in some other area of employment be allowed, cannot be extended to the area of the workings of a charitable trust.

One mistake might be tolerated if there is goodwill, but it is very unlikely that two mistakes could be allowed to pass.

I bring this up for your own good as I would be most upset to see you embroiled in trouble and unaware of the consequences.

The budgets you provided, I regret, are not acceptable as you have obviously mixed up 'current' and 'capital' expenditure. I have taken the liberty of recalculating the figures and deleting all 'capital' expenditure items on the specific grounds that such expenditure must always be submitted ahead of time to the trustees for approval and agreement before ever being contemplated or, of course, commissioned. Failure to follow this path in terms of the accounts, I need hardly add, constitutes a serious breach of acceptable operation and would most likely result in immediate dismissal. I am, however, not assuming that the proposals for such 'capital' expenditure in the budgets you sent me constitute such a breach as I am sure that they haven't been authorised or commissioned. I have, however, acquainted the Chairman with this, as I have a duty to inform him of matters of this nature. I am sure that I will be able to restrain him from taking any action on this occasion.

I would also point out that the committee felt that you did not fully appreciate that it is your duty to ensure that St Margaret's Comity does not become involved in political or popular causes; it is a sheltered-housing complex not a platform for changing society. Press attention should be discouraged if the Comity is to be run in a fashion acceptable to the trustees.

Finally, you can rely upon my support in what is a very difficult learning process, and should you have any further problems please feel free to chat them through with me as I am always available to help and advise.

Yours faithfully

Eric Fribble

Secretary to the Trust

It is obvious that Mr Fribble had taken John Izzat's instruction seriously and that he had sown the seeds for Mr Puritan's dismissal.

To Richard Puritan, the tone of the letter, rather than its content, was the thing that annoyed him, as he sat contemplating the meeting and its implications for him and for Felicity Eristic's campaign to take over the complex on behalf of the company she now headed.

Concerning the letter, he tended to dismiss it on the grounds that it was merely a confirmation of the conversation he had had with Fribble after the meeting. In reality it contained the ammunition, or rather a bomb with a timer that Eric Fribble would detonate when the time was right and he would gain maximum advantage.

Richard Puritan, however, saw little of this threat, for he was preoccupied with his own and Felicity's agenda. Once Felicity has taken over the total responsibility for this place, he thought, then Fribble can take a running jump.

His thoughts then turned to John Izzat, the chairman of the trust, and he suffered once more from the memory of the criticism that Izzat had made of his handling of the events at the Comity.

Had he no concept of the effort he had put into making the place conform to the current legislation, to ensuring that the insurance company was satisfied and that all the health and safety rules were now obeyed? There had been some unfortunate things along the way, but you can't make a cake without breaking eggs. Izzat was unreasonable, old or young, laws were there to be obeyed not flouted, age was no excuse and it was essential to administer the law with as firm and fair a hand as possible because if you didn't there was no point in making laws. Everybody agreed with anti-smoking, anti-racism, anti-sexism, he thought, and he knew not a single person who didn't believe in feminism or total freedom when it came to gender choice. Izzat was a fool, he concluded, and a bigot.

In vain, he searched his heart and mind for any scintilla of justification for John Izzat's reprimand or, for that matter, for the unpleasant things that Fribble had said to him in his odious office. He could recall no single instance where he, Richard Puritan, had overstepped the bounds or been in any matter remiss. Everybody knew that old people were difficult, and he had borne the rudeness, accepted the insults and the unpleasant attitudes that these old people exhibited towards him with forti-tude. He had tried to be good-humoured in the face of all their unkindness, and yet here was Izzat accusing *him* of unkindness. He had been diligent in enforcing the laws that had been set down, not only by him as Administrator, but by the Govern-ment and the local authority and the Health and Safety people, by the insurance company, the fire service and the European Union. These laws were not for his good, they were the *law* and *had* to be obeyed regardless of your age or infirmity. And yet, he thought, they were also the dead hand of capitalism upon the backs of the people. That is why he had sought to bring the Covinous insight into the Comity, the Covinous philosophy of freeing people of preconceptions about race and sexual orienta-tion, of sexual stereotypes and unhealthy habits. This was the way to free themselves of the capitalist yoke that weighed them down like tired old workhorses put out to grass and given scraps of charity.

This is how Richard Puritan explained the events of the Comity to himself, and the more he contemplated the unjust accusations that had been levelled against him, the more angry he became at the ingratitude of the residents and the trustees. Had Mr Puritan been familiar with the Bible he would have been able to cry out as in Psalm 41: 'All mine enemies whisper together against me: even against me do they imagine this evil', or perhaps, 'Mine enemies speak evil of me: When shall he die, and his name perish'. But, not knowing these things, he could only hold onto his repaired box and feel thoroughly sorry for himself.

He would have sat holding the lid of his box for the rest of the morning had Felicity Eristic not called into the office and been told by the temp that the Administrator was in his flat. Not one to stand upon ceremony, she had let herself into his flat and found a despairing Puritan sitting on the floor with his arms round the ridiculous wooden box to which he seemed so attached.

'Well, what happened at the trustees meeting, Richard?' she enquired. 'I expected you to ring me and tell me what exactly went on.'

'The minutes are on the table with a letter from Fribble,' he replied.

Felicity read them carefully, and as she noted the devious way Fribble chose to portray events and position comments within the structure of the minutes, she realised that Fribble was equal in every way to her. Here was a man who could manipulate the facts by placing them out of the normal order; here was a man who could omit certain obvious things, to leave only the poison of an unkind comment to stand and to be used later as an example of the feeling of the meeting. She admired Fribble's skill, his purpose to dictate his view regardless of the facts, and she noted the thread of fawning deference to Izzat running through these minutes.

Where Puritan only saw the words, Felicity saw the meaning and the plotting, she saw the traps laid for the luckless Puritan, and she realised that the game was now being played for far higher stakes. She also understood that Fribble, and possibly Izzat, perceived her strategy and was aware of her plans to take over the Comity and incorporate it into her Development Enterprise Company. She saw these things clearly and with certainty and she also saw Richard Puritan, hugging his wretched box for comfort, a victim in the war between Fribble and Izzat on one side and Eristic and the Development Enterprise Company on the other. The more she looked at Puritan sitting on the floor cuddling his box, the more she realised that he wasn't going to

133

be strong enough for her purpose. He was weak, self-doubting and unable to stand up to the combined forces of Izzat and Fribble, to the RRAWF and even to that snotty daughter of Izzat.

Puritan was not, she thought, enough of a man to be able to bend with the wind and spring back strong and tall.

The fact that this could have been construed as a sexist thought did not trouble her, because it was a thought held captive in the privacy of her mind and not open for public examination. She could use what metaphors and images she wished – in the privacy of her mind. Publicly it was a different matter and she was constantly aware that all such thoughts had to be edited and made politically correct when you spoke them out loud. It was, however, at this moment that she abandoned Puritan to his fate and determined that should he fall, then she would make his fall an opportunity and the moment when the Development Enterprise Company would rush in and grab the Comity from the control of the tiresome RRAWF.

Was Puritan aware that his refuge in times of trouble had cast him off onto the sea of his own fate? Did he realise that the strong arm of Felicity Eristic was no longer there to keep him afloat? Sadly he did not, for he still felt the knife wounds of unjust accusations and the righteousness of the Covinous philosophy. The greater cause still burned in his breast and his convictions still remained strong and bright in his mind. How could he have entertained the thought that Felicity Eristic, whom he had slept with and held in his arms, who had secured for him the job of Administrator and had plotted his festival, and supported him when the ungrateful residents of the Comity had turned against him, how could he have imagined that Felicity would turn against him and let him sink without a fight?

Although Felicity Eristic had given up on Richard Puritan, she was not prepared to allow him to go to hell in his own fashion. She was still the master puppeteer, the person in charge of the long-term strategy of the Comity, regardless of what the trust or anybody thought.

She read the minutes and the letter with intense interest and analysed the contents in her mind. 'Fribble is seeking to pull back the control here into his office, Richard. You must resist this, and there are absolutely no grounds for him to make these demands upon you. You know that, don't you, Richard?'

'I am an employee of the trust, Felicity, and as such I have to follow the trust's instructions.'

'You are an employee of the trust, but only as far it goes, Richard. Think about it. Before you can do anything, you must conform to the regulations and the local authority rules governing the running of sheltered housing units. Neither you, nor the trust, have a free hand in these matters. The Comity has to be run according to the web of regulations that cover all such dwellings, and it is not for the trust to change or alter these regulations. You are thus, on the one hand, a servant of the trust insofar as you are an employee, but you are also responsible for the implementation of the regulations, and in that sense you are a servant of the various bodies that make and police these regulations. You, Richard, have to decide on the split you make between the enforcement of the regulations and the time you devote to the implementation of the trust's wishes and instructions. Fribble will not be able to make a case against you if you use your time in making sure the regulations are honoured.'

Richard Puritan was not sure of this, he had faced John Izzat, he had dealt with Eric Fribble, not Felicity. 'I am not sure that you're right on that, Felicity. This is a private charity and it has the power to order its own affairs as it sees fit. Who is there to challenge it, if it decides that it wants to run things in a way that doesn't absolutely conform to the regulations? Mostly, the rules are in the form of guidelines not laws, often they are advice and nothing more.'

Felicity wondered at Puritan's lack of worldliness, at his innocence and his lack of guile.

'Richard, have you learnt nothing from Covinous's book? Power is about permission, the fact that somebody is allowed to say yes or no, that is all power is; and the greatest power in any sheltered-housing complex is the right to licence the damn place to continue. This power is in the hands of the Council. If my committee decides that the Comity doesn't fulfil the requirements set out in the various bits of legislation or in the regulations, then we oppose the renewal of its licence. The trust could continue to operate without such a licence, but it wouldn't risk it. Therefore I have the power to dictate what the trust does with the Comity. You can see that, can't you?'

Puritan could see that, and understood that Felicity Eristic had the power and would use it, but where would that leave him?

'It is my intention, Richard, to seek to persuade the Council that all homes for the elderly and frail should have, as a condition of securing a licence to operate, a qualified medical and social worker team backing them up on a twenty-four-hour-a-day basis. As you know, my Development Enterprise Company has such a team – it is only the Council's duty-call social worker in reality, but that social worker has access to the Council's medical officer and so, to all intents and purposes, it has a medical and social worker back-up team available. Now the Comity will never be able to afford such a back-up team simply for this one sheltered-housing complex. My DEC will offer to subcontract its back-up team to the Comity on condition that the DEC administers the whole complex on an annual contract. In this way I will control the Comity, and the DEC will make considerable profit from it because the charity will pay. Further, I will be able to nominate who becomes a tenant of the Comity on the basis of urgent need. The Council will thus be relieved of the cost of caring for a few of its old and frail, having shuffled it off onto the RRAWF, who will pick up the tab and pay through the nose. There are eight such private charity homes in the Council district and I intend to move in on each one. That, Richard, is what Covinous calls Directed People Power. The Council is voted in by the people and works to an agenda that frees the people of the need to rely upon charitable organisations like the RRAWF.'

How, wondered Richard Puritan, would John Izzat take that? Not sitting down, he was sure; but then Felicity Eristic's vision seemed so complete it would, he felt, be very hard to resist, and for a moment Puritan thought about the residents of the Comity and wondered what they would get out of such a take-over.

'I'm telling you this so that you can see that Fribble and Izzat have no future in this place, Richard. They are history and will simply become the purse but without any purse strings, so there is no real reason for you to worry about what they minute or write in letters to you.'

Felicity glowed at the cleverness of her plan, at the wonderful rightness of the deal, how she had within her grasp power, money and success, and there was little, if anything, anybody could do about it.

'I intended,' she said, 'to invite Covinous down here to hold a meeting and to explain some of the points of his ideas. We could hold it here at the Comity. It has that community room, which is a great deal more pleasant than any of the Council homes or properties I've got available. What do you think, Richard? Shall we hold it here? If you're worried about the trust, the Covinous Society of Wiltshire could pay you a pepper-corn fee – say, a pound – so you could say that you have let the place to a function. You let it out for weddings now and then, so it would be all right.'

Puritan agreed, but then he almost always agreed with anything Felicity Eristic suggested, it was his way, and he felt sure that with Felicity Eristic on his side he would be secure no matter what the trust or the world did to him.

'That's settled then, Richard. I'll set it in motion.'

Ms Eristic swept out of Puritan's flat and out of the Comity. Its Administrator was now alone as the temp only did half-days and had left on the dot of one o'clock, leaving a note for the Administrator which read – 'I have gone – Mary'.

16

Mr Pule Leaves the Comity

Arnold Pule was by all accounts a singular man. He had no immediate family alive and had come to the radio and television business late in his working life.

Born in Scotland, the only son in a close family, he had studied radio engineering. Upon leaving school he had gone to sea, taking, in the course of his career, a degree in electronics. He had for most of his working life worked for one of the major oil companies on tankers and had become, through the company's training schemes, a radio officer and then a senior radio officer.

During his years at sea, first his mother and then his only sister had died, leaving just his father and himself. His father ran a radio retail shop in Elgin, which was handy for Arnold when he was docked at Lossiemouth. As the years rolled on, his father's shop lost its sparkle and drive, particularly following the death of Arnold's mother, who had been the public face of the business. With the death of his daughter, Arnold's father had lost almost all his interest in the shop and had sent for Arnold to take over.

Always a solitary man, Arnold had made few if any friends and had become used to the lonely life of the radio officer on large oil tankers. He had not mixed with the rest of the crew and had simply studied radio and marine electronics, becoming over the years very expert, and in some quarters he was regarded as an authority on the subject.

He was not particularly commercially minded, but as his father rapidly left the business when Arnold arrived and then, having nothing to do and still missing his wife, died, Arnold redirected the business to cover the arcane but also more profitable marine radio side and, in time, Pules of Elgin became the leading shop for weekend sailors and yacht owners.

Reaching 65, Arnold, having no living relatives, had discussed his wish to retire with John Izzat, who was, at that time, interested in buying Pules of Elgin. Izzat had suggested that it would be possible for Arnold to move into the Comity. The matter was arranged, and within weeks of his retirement Arnold Pule had taken over one of the cottages in St Margaret's Comity. This had suited Arnold because of the closeness of Salisbury Cathedral and of St Margaret's and St John's.

During his travels Arnold had become a a practising Christian and took his religion seriously. He was one of the three residents at the Comity who regularly attended church in the village, the other two were Grace and David Cenobite.

Pule had lived at the Comity for seven years, and although a solitary man and one not given to socialising, he got along with the other residents and had been friendly with both the Reverends Hartwell and Palmer. When Hartwell left, Arnold still kept in touch with him, and when the Reverend Boon was appointed curate to St Margaret's and St John's, he had also found room for friendship with the new curate.

To the other residents of the Comity, Pule was thought of as a miserable man and one, moreover, who did not really enter into all the gossip and day-to-day Comity life. He was, however, respected, and as much as any solitary person can be – liked.

The business of Mr Puritan's statement about Arnold Pule's gender orientation had thus come out of the blue both to him and to the other residents. If, so the gossip went, he was 'that way', then who with?

For Arnold the very idea was repugnant to him and he felt the shame of it, although the implied accusation was said by Puritan in the most delicate way and without any attempt whatsoever to indicate any judgement. It was enough that the statement had been made, and made about him.

The actual words used were innocuous, but in the tense atmosphere that Puritan had generated with his ceaseless campaigns for political correctness over smoking, feminism, anti-racism and the rest, any slight remark was immediately construed in the new, politically correct battle climate of the Comity as a judgement.

What had been said by Puritan was: 'We make no difference here over gender orientation, we just don't care what a person is, male, female or anything in between – ask Arnold Pule. That's right, isn't it, Arnold?'

Arnold had replied with: 'What are you suggesting, Mr Puritan?'

Puritan had said: 'It doesn't matter to us, you can be whatever orientation you like, we don't judge here now.'

From that seemingly innocent conversation Arnold Pule had built a vast and terrible tower of insult that he had suffered at the hand of the Administrator. He had been accused, he told Ray Paladin, of being homosexual.

'I'm sure he didn't mean that,' Ray Paladin said, 'and you a sailor too. We all know what sailors have in every port!'

Ray Paladin had not made the most thoughtful of comments when he said this and it possibly angered Arnold as much as the Puritan accusation.

'Everybody should shut up about sex,' Arnold had thundered. 'At our age it's just plain smutty to keep on about it.'

Pule had confided all this to the Reverends Palmer and Boon following Matins, when they had commented on his depressed attitude. He had told them, I have to say, an edited version of the conversation, and in that edited version he had filled in the implied statement so that it became an observation of homosexuality, rather than an implied statement about tolerance of homosexuality by the Comity. Both vicar and curate were appalled for they knew it not to be true, but that is another story.

They had, like true friends, assured Arnold Pule that nobody could ever think that he was anything more than what they knew him to be and that Mr Puritan had, they were certain, never intended anybody to imagine that his gender orientation was in any way different than that of Ray Paladin or even their own. 'Just because you are not married signifies nothing,' they asserted, 'and anyway, Mr Puritan's opinion counts for nothing amongst the residents of the Comity.'

They could and indeed did say these things to Arnold Pule, but they didn't change how he felt and how ashamed he felt at what he saw as a slur upon him. Further, the longer he thought about it, the worse it became and he could well imagine that Mr Puritan would hold a festival for homosexuals and place his name upon the posters strung up over the Comity arch. Worse, he imagined the ridiculous Puritan holding talk-ins on gender for the residents where he would be used as an example. These and other fantasies were his constant companions through the days following his meeting with Mr Puritan.

About a fortnight after his conversation with the vicar and curate at St Margaret's and St John's, he sat down in his sitting room and took stock of the whole business. He had, he knew, more than enough money to leave the Comity and go somewhere else. He was 72 and still trim and healthy. He could comfortably buy a cottage anywhere he wanted, he could afford to furnish it and still have more than enough money to live very well for 20 years or more. He could buy any car he wanted and he could be shot of the odious Mr Puritan. What use, he reasoned, was his money if it wasn't to allow him to be free, to decide his own fate, to go his own way? Seventy-two did not mean he was finished; there was still 20 years more life for him, with luck. He had mouldered since his father's death, and almost rotted since his retirement. He would buy a cottage and in one room set up a small but expensively equipped laboratory to develop a marine satellite, a vessel recorder that would monitor the state of the vessel and its position every minute of the day, independent of the owner.

The thought was father to the deed and he decided to return to Scotland. He chose Lossiemouth and contacted an agent there. Within days he had received details of available property and he travelled to Lossiemouth to view the cottage he had selected. Impressed, he purchased it, arranged the building work and stopped off in London on his way back to buy his laboratory equipment and arrange for its installation.

Once back at the Comity, he pondered how he would inform the trust of his decision to leave. His problem was that he was loath to mention the reason for his wish to depart because it

141

would draw attention to the suggestion made by Puritan. He felt an obligation to John Izzat, who had secured the Comity cottage for him. It would be rude he felt to just leave without any statement to Izzat, and yet how could he tell Izzat of the monstrous suggestion made by Puritan? Indeed, he would have to tell Puritan, but that could be done with a simple letter that informed the Administrator of his intention to leave and on what date he would vacate the cottage.

After much thought, he could not resolve the problem and decided to discuss the matter with the Reverend Palmer, who already knew of the Puritan suggestion and so he would not need to put it into words. He ordered a taxi, having made an appointment with the vicar.

The Reverend Palmer is a kindly man and understands the fact that some people are intensely private and tell only the minimum, whilst others wear their hearts on their sleeves and share every last detail of a problem. With Arnold Pule, Palmer knew that he would be told the minimum, and that he would have to guess the rest and seek to confirm it obliquely. He was, however, surprised to learn firstly that Arnold Pule intended to leave the Comity and that he had made detailed plans for his future.

'Well, Arnold, you seem to have it all mapped out and, if I may say so, very well planned too. So what is the problem?'

'I need to tell John Izzat, he is now the President of the RRAWF Trust, but, I, I, I'm not able to tell him my reason for leaving, about what Puritan said, I mean, well, you know, I can't work out how to say it, I can't bring myself to tell him what, you know Puritan. I just can't.' He dropped his head dejectedly.

'But there is no earthly reason why you shouldn't tell Mr Izzat. It was wrong of Puritan to even hint at that, very wrong indeed. But there is no reason for you to feel bad, Arnold. You wouldn't feel bad if somebody said you were a shop thief, would you?'

'Yes I'm afraid I would, vicar, I'd feel dreadful. You see, I believe that people always believe things like that.'

'Do you think I believe it then, Arnold?'

'No, but you know, don't you.'

'Yes, John, I know about your daughter who died in Spain, but that doesn't change the thing. If I hadn't known about the girl and her mother, would you think I would believe something like that?'

'Probably not, but you're a vicar and therefore charitable in your dealings with people, but my experience of the world makes me think most people believe the worst of others.'

'That is a gloomy view, Arnold. Why do you think John Izzat would think the worst of you? Didn't he buy your business in Elgin?'

'Well, it was really my father's business, vicar, I just inherited it and ran it until I retired, but I always thought of it as my father's business.'

'Would you like me to write to John Izzat for you and explain the background, and then you could write to him and thank him for his help in getting you the tenancy and tell him that you're leaving. Would that help?'

Arnold Pule thought about the proposition, but was not certain. 'You see, vicar, I'm seventy-two years old and that's old enough, heaven knows, to be able to handle things. If I can't handle things at my age, then I'm not safe to be allowed out.' The two men lapsed into silence. There was truth in Arnold Pule's contention, but there was no resolution.

'Why don't you go to see him, Arnold. You don't have to mention the Puritan business directly, you need only say that you are unable to get on with Mr Puritan and, having thought about it, have decided to leave the Comity rather than live in a bad atmosphere.'

'Well I could, vicar, but it would still be avoiding the real reason, wouldn't it?' They relapsed into silence again and the Reverend Palmer realised that there was little else he could offer and thus stood up. Arnold Pule decide to walk back to the Comity and left the vicarage.

The matter remained unresolved and Pule worried at the problem for the next week, and then the week after that, and on the Sunday when the vicar asked him if he had done anything about it, he had to admit that he hadn't. 'Well, you can't keep putting it off, can you, Arnold,' the vicar observed, and Arnold Pule agreed.

In the third week, Pule made up his mind that he would phone Izzat from a public callbox and explain as best he could in the time allowed before the 50-pence piece ran out. In this way he could not be engaged in any lengthy conversation about the matter and would be cut off. He rang Izzat at work and got through at once. Izzat took the call. He explained that he had had an argument with the Administrator and had decided to leave and had rung to thank Izzat for his help in arranging the tenancy.

'What was the argument about, Arnold?' Izzat asked, but before Arnold could answer, the time the 50-pence piece had bought ran out and the call was disconnected.

Back in the Comity, Arnold hurriedly wrote out his letter to Mr Puritan, gave it to the temp in the office and then took the bus into Salisbury and spent the rest of the day in the cathedral.

When Puritan received the letter addressed to him he opened it and read its content, and although surprised was not worried. He filed the letter in his 'in' tray and decided to reply to it in the morning. Before he answered it he thought he would check the files to see how his predecessors had handled such resignations. He searched the files in vain, nobody, it seemed, had ever resigned their tenancy at the Comity.

At this point, Puritan became concerned. He had no wish to be the first Administrator in the whole history of St Margaret's Comity to have a tenant resign his cottage and he could not believe that this had never happened before.

What would Fribble make of this resignation? He wondered, and how would the trustees view it? The memory of his last meeting with John Izzat was still fresh in his mind and he started to imagine what Fribble would say. He went to fetch the letter and re-read it, Arnold Pule had given nothing away in his letter, it simply stated that he had decided to vacate the tenancy and leave in two weeks' time. He gave no reason for this decision nor did he express any thanks or recriminations, just that he would be leaving and the date.

Puritan faxed the letter to Eric Fribble at the RRAWF, and to

Felicity Eristic, and the information was to cause a ripple in the increasingly choppy waters of the administration of St Margaret's Comity.

When Fribble received the fax he immediately re-faxed it to John Izzat. When Felicity Eristic received the fax, she immediately saw a window of opportunity and determined to assign the tenancy to one of the people on the Council's waiting list. In Ms Eristic's decision lay the seeds of considerable later contention and the inevitable showdown between herself as chair of the Council's Frail and Elderly Committee and Eric Fribble on behalf of the RRAWF.

As for Arnold Pule, these battles would not affect him as by the time they commenced he would be safely in Scotland and away from the difficulties.

The most pressing problem Pule had to deal with was moving out, and to this end he once again shunned the other residents and sought to go it alone. It was in his nature to be self-sufficient and it had been a facet of his character all his life. He had never been an overt person, and in line with this he arranged for the packing and the cleaning to be done by outside people. The moving company did his packing and he contacted a firm in Salisbury to send in a team of cleaners on the day of his departure to thoroughly clean the cottage from floor to ceiling.

Mr Puritan had meanwhile been calling on Mr Pule to settle the various matters that were needed for him to resign his tenancy and so, to the residents, it seemed that Mr Puritan was spending a lot of time with Mr Pule.

Rumours circulated about the reason for the visits, and in view of the bad atmosphere in the Comity, the worst possible complexion was placed upon them and it was assumed that Mr Pule had become the object of some ridiculous campaign being waged by Mr Puritan against 'poor Arnold Pule'.

As Arnold was at all times taciturn and not given to conversation, the rumours fed upon themselves and in no time at all it became almost a fact that Mr Puritan was picking on Mr Pule over something, although nobody could say exactly what that something was.

None of the other residents therefore knew of his decision to leave the Comity until the van turned up two days before his departure, with the chests and crates for his furniture and possessions. On the next day the residents were surprised to see the packers turn up, and still they had no firm knowledge beyond that which they had seen.

Ray Paladin tried to discuss the matter with Arnold, but all he managed to find out was that he felt that he should leave and was therefore moving.

With such a lack of hard facts, the residents made up their own reason for his leaving and, remarkably, it did not concern the very thing that, had Arnold been asked, he would have said was the cause for his departure.

The residents' reason was that Mr Pule was known to have been against the Anti-Racist and Anti-Sexist Festival for the Third Age and his opposition had so angered Puritan that he had forced Pule out.

This version of Mr Pule's reason for leaving was relayed to all, and particularly to the drinkers in the Arms, and in time it found its way to the Reverend Palmer.

17

Joe Staunch Tells the Lovely Laura

Joe Staunch was in love, this much he knew, and being in love, he believed, was not the most comfortable state for a young man like him.

The free and easy lifestyle that he had enjoyed before being in love was definitely more comfortable, as was eating when and where he chose. Equally, it was more comfortable to dress in the clothes that pleased him and him alone. Now he dressed with care, now he ate meals at times that suited the lovely Laura. Now he had to keep appointments and get up in the morning in order to keep these appointments.

His work tended to get left and his male friends tended to be pushed out of his daily round of meeting, dining and escorting the lovely Laura. He was, he sometimes felt, little more than a driver, escort and messenger boy who had to keep a tight schedule and constantly watch the clock in order to be in the right place at the right time.

Today, thought Joe, he was also a cleaner as well, because Laura was coming to lunch at his flat and he knew that Laura did not much like dirty washing thrown about, or unmade beds or dirty dishes waiting to be washed up. She had even remarked upon his friend Lee Speer's studio floor, observing that a vacuum cleaner would help the artistic effort as much as a window cleaner would add to the available light in the studio. His own studio was, happily, not in his flat and he had been able to make excuses so that Laura would not visit what was little more than a pit of filth, viewed by her standards.

He had got up early in order to clear and clean his flat, and as the time approached for the lovely Laura to call, he had realised that cleaning was more than just a passing job and required dedicated and organised attention, rather than his more normal cursory shifting of things out of sight. It would not be an exaggeration to say that Joe Staunch had tired himself out making his flat fit for the beloved's inspection. He had even denied himself a cup of tea because he didn't want to muck up the kitchen. He now stood in the sitting room, unable to allow himself to sit down because it would untidy the cushions. He had showered and dressed and then re-cleaned the bathroom, he had polished the tiles and all the surfaces that he could see. The flat reeked of polish, spray cleaner, Brasso and room freshener. The windows sparkled, the sofa was vacuumed, as was the carpet, and the furniture polished. If brownie points were to be earned for effort and cleanness, then surely he would be top of the list and winner on all counts.

Punctually at midday Laura rang the bell of his flat and Joe, relieved that at last he could sit down, opened the door and proudly welcomed the lovely Laura into the sitting room.

Laura was in love and would probably not have noticed the state of Joe's flat had he not touched a surface with a duster or wiped a cloth over the floor. Laura was in love with Joe and had come as fast as possible to see him as she was filled with anger and concern over the news she had heard about the Comity.

It was the first time that Laura had visited the flat. She had, it is true, met him at his flat before, but it had been the sort of 'hello, let's go, I've a table booked at . . .' type of meeting and she had waited in the hall while Joe had picked up his coat or his wallet and then they had been off. Their loving had been carried out at Laura's house, where Laura had a sitting room, bedroom and bathroom to herself.

Laura threw herself down on the sofa.

'Do you know what that Eristic woman has done now, Joe?'

Joe did not know nor did he really care that much. What he wanted, after all the hard work of the morning, was for Laura to tell him how clean, tidy and totally sanitary was the flat on which he had spent so much effort. He could even have been satisfied with an observation that the meal, already laid out on

148

the table, looked good enough to eat. But this wasn't the thing that filled the lovely Laura's head.

'That Eristic woman is going to hold a seminar at the Comity addressed by the odious Covinous on his ridiculous theories about "community people power". It is outrageous that Puritan should allow the Comity to be used for political ends. What do the residents know or care about community people power?'

'How do you know that this seminar is taking place at the Comity?' asked Joe.

'It's in *The Guardian* with a profile on that creature Covinous. It seems he has proposed a programme to the BBC and they of course have accepted it. It's about how people must take back the power that politicians have stolen from them. One part will be filmed at the Comity when he holds his seminar. God knows what father will think or say. It is not the sort of thing that should happen there.'

'Why not?' asked Joe. 'It's not like the festival nonsense, it should be a simple seminar, no noise or stuff like that.'

'But it will be that man Covinous – he's poison. It's his ideas that Eristic and Puritan follow slavishly,' replied Laura.

'Oh, so you think that anything to do with Covinous must be bad, Laura?'

'You can't defend him, can you, Joe. I read his first book and it is popular nonsense without any intellectual originality whatsoever. He just rehashes the most successful bits from past dictators and rabble-rousers. Just because it worked for them, he assumes that it will work for him – which it probably will or does, but that doesn't make the man worth a second glance. He's rubbish, Joe, and you know it. He's just rubbish.'

'He's also my stepfather,' said Joe dejectedly.

Laura looked up at Joe, expecting it to be a joke, but saw instantly that he was serious.

'He's your stepfather?' she repeated, and Joe nodded. 'I'm sorry, I had no idea or I wouldn't have said those things.' Laura stood up, uncertain of what to do.

Joe moved to her and clasped her hands in his. He had known he would have to tell her about his stepfather but would have preferred a better, more suitable time to tell her, rather

149

than for her to find out as a result of some damn profile in a newspaper. He had rehearsed how he would tell her a thousand times in his mind but now he had been forced to just come out and say it.

'Yes, he's my stepfather. He married my mother after she divorced my father.'

The both sat on the sofa, Laura somewhat shocked and Joe somewhat apprehensive.

'My mother divorced my father when I was eight. It was pretty normal at my school to be told mid-term, either by your mother or your father, that they had divorced and that, oh you know, all the usual old lies about it not making any difference and all that guff. Anyway, my father went to Canada and I haven't really heard much from him since. Mother married Covinous when I was twelve, but it didn't mean a hell of a lot to me because I was at school and when I came home for holidays I didn't see a great deal of either of them. They had their careers and social scene which took up most of their time. Often for holidays I would go to my grandparents, maternal and paternal, although never Covinous's parents, who I have never met – I think he is ashamed of them. So you see, while he is my stepfather, I can't say I really know him all that well. Both mother and Justin now try to engineer a relationship but, although I have dinner with them every so often, I always feel like a stranger.

'The person who was important in my childhood was my grandfather, my mother's father. He died two years ago and I still miss the daft old fool. He was all those things that are unfashionable now, a gentleman in both senses, a churchgoer, mad keen on cricket and gardening, he read *The Times* and had apoplexy over the news, he read a lot, and his favourite composers were Bach and Perry. He used to say God made a mistake in making Bach German when he was obviously an Englishman – born in the wrong damn country. He used to call Covinous a fool in clown's clothes and say my mother wasn't clever enough to square the law with honesty and so had jumped into the midden to escape the smell of deceit.'

Laura wanted to ask Joe if he agreed with any of Covinous's

ideas but felt that it would compound her earlier rudeness, of which she now felt thoroughly ashamed. She would dearly like not to have said it.

'Your grandfather sounds the type of person I would have liked,' she said. 'I wish I could have met him.'

'He would have said that you were pretty as a flower. He liked pretty women and used to tell me that God had made women pretty because he was sitting on an English hill on a summer's day when he created them. He was a total romantic.'

'What about your grandmother?'

'Oh, I loved her because she organised my grandfather and kept his world in order. He could never have survived as long as he did if she hadn't taken the brutality out of the day-to-day world all around him. She hadn't a scrap of romance in her soul, she thought it was all nonsense and life was about living, getting things done the way you want it. She would say my grandfather lived with his head in the air and his feet on the clouds. Take no notice of him, she'd say, he knows as much about anything as the cat, but at least the cat catches mice. Since my grandfather died she isn't half as much fun. They were a double act, one played the other like a musician plays an instrument.'

There were hundreds of questions Laura wanted to ask Joe about Covinous and Joe's mother, but she realised that she had opened a box that would, perhaps, have best been kept shut until Joe had felt the time was right to tell her. She had stumbled into an area that was still full of pain for Joe and which she had no right to know unless he wanted to tell her. She looked away from him and saw the table and remembered that she was hungry.

'Did you prepare all that, Joe?' she said, pointing to table.

'Oh yes,' he replied, jumping up and going over to it. 'Would madam like to start with the smoked salmon and then maybe fish, or we can offer you a cold collation. And may I recommend the wine – Verduzzo '85, one of Italy's finest white wines, I'm told.'

'Gee, I'm just a country girl and not used to you city slickers. 'Ain't you got Coke, like we's always has?'

'My dear young thing,' he picked up his part, 'Verduzzo '85 is the Italian for a Coke that is white. Just one tumblerful and you'll never want the red stuff again.'

'Oh sir,' she drawled in an awful American Southern accent, 'you're so persuasive, I think I'll be putty in your hands afore too long.'

In this way the dreadful news of Joe Staunch's stepfather became known to Laura and, being a sensible girl, she allowed the lunch to be filled with inconsequential games.

Laura made the coffee and they sat at the table drinking it.

'Well, it seems that your stepfather is going to disturb the calm air of the Comity, Joe.'

'It would certainly seem as if he is, but knowing him, he would not take part in anything that was at all likely to end in a punch-up. He is mentally courageous but a physical coward. And if the BBC is going to be there, he will play up the elder statesman image for all he is worth. Oh yes, and he doesn't like old people, I think he is afraid of them.'

'Why?' asked Laura.

'Oh I'm not sure, but I think it is because they are like a time mirror for him. He can see himself old when he looks at old people and hates the thought. Haven't you noticed that it's only really children who can treat old people like ordinary people rather than like objects? I suppose it's because to children all adults are old, and they can see no real degrees of age in them.'

'But what game is that Eristic woman playing,' asked Laura, 'to hold the seminar at the Comity? There must be something in it – first the festival and now this.'

'Well,' replied Joe, 'it would certainly seem that she is involving the Comity in her company's affairs. She seems to be unofficially reaching into the day-to-day life of the place, weaving it into her business without actually having any right or any contractual ties.'

'That's just what she is doing, she is taking the place over, using Puritan to worm her way into the running of the Comity, that's what she up to.'

The realisation of the Eristic campaign for the Comity seemed to both Laura and Joe devious and dreadful. But in their correct assessment of the reason for Felicity's use of the Comity, they omitted to take into account Laura's father or indeed Eric Fribble, both formidable opponents and no less devious than Felicity Eristic.

The phone rang and Joe answered it. It was his mother asking if she could see him right away. He tried to put her off, but she was insistent and so he reluctantly agreed to her coming down by the internal stairs.

'It's my mother,' he explained. 'She says that she has something vital to talk to me about, although, knowing her as I do, I expect she saw your arrival and now wants to meet you.'

There was a knock at the internal door and Joe opened it, admitting his mother, who seemed to rush in.

'Joe darling, look, I have to meet your father and I've arranged for a bike to collect some papers. You know how it is with these court cases.'

'No, Tabby, I've not the slightest idea how it is with court cases. You and Laura here are the lawyers, I'm a painter.'

'Laura?' exclaimed Tabby, looking round and then seeing her. 'So you're Laura. My, but you're beautiful, and you're a lawyer, are you?'

'No, I'm reading law at university,' explained Laura.

'But you're much too beautiful to be a lawyer,' said Tabby with about as much conviction as a politician at a public meeting. 'Laura?'

'Laura Izzat, I'm a friend of Joe's.'

'Of course you are, my dear. Joe knows all the beautiful people, unfortunately not the committed ones. I despair of my handsome son – no commitment. He wouldn't care if the Government rounded up all the underclass and put them into concentration camps as long as he had canvas and paint. He leaves all the really serious matters to his father and me, but he's so handsome and gentle we forgive him anything and just fight all the harder for justice, don't we, darling?'

'Oh yes, mother, you certainly fight injustice for me – at Chez Jon, Wheelbites, the Café Royal and the Savoy. Tabby dines out with such startling regularity, Laura, that her fridge is full of ice and no food has touched its interior since it was purchased some ten years ago. Isn't that right, mother?'

Tabby could put up with a lot from her son, but the suggestion that she wasn't the perfect mother and housewife as well as the perfect community lawyer and committed worker for the disadvantaged was too much – as Joe very well knew. To challenge her sincerity was to challenge the core of deceit upon which her life was based and she could no more stand to look at that than she could face the reality of the contradictions in so many of the arguments which she so lovingly pushed.

'My darling boy, I hardly think that you can know much about anything as you have never managed paid work for a single day in your life. Living off a fortune left to you by your grandfather does not give you an insight into anything except privilege. Whereas Laura here knows that the Law is an unforgiving taskmaster that has to be persuaded and cajoled before she gives you even the time of day. You are a sweet boy Joe, but in many ways you're still a child when it comes to the real world.'

'Your real world is to patronise the ignorant, dressed in the rags of socialism and like some monstrous engine of lies running on the track of double standards, fool yourself that you, mother dear, are generating something other than self-deceit – or do I flatter you too much?' Joe turned angrily away and raised his eyebrows to Laura.

'The money we lavished upon your education has given you a vocabulary if no great sense. No matter, will you kindly make sure that you give the messenger these papers. I must fly, or your father will have given an interview without my carefully watching that he doesn't libel the Prime Minister or somebody of equal unimportance.' She lightly kissed his cheek and left, but this time through Joe's front door, waving graciously to them as she went up the stairs.

'Wow,' said Laura. 'Some lady that, Joe. Do you always fight like that?'

'No,' replied Joe. 'I don't know why we fought today, it's just that I seemed to have run out of the capacity to put up with her self-deception. All this flag-waving, woman of the people

154

nonsense when she behaves like the caricature of a duchess and Lady Bountiful when she's away from the law centre. She talks in Estuary English and mouths off about how wonderful all the fashionable "isms" are when she's at the law centre, but here she queens it. She's a total fake, and so is my stepfather.'

18

The Bishop Meets the Comity Residents

The meeting that had been discussed between the Reverend Palmer, Vicar of St Margaret's and St John's, and the Bishop was scheduled for October, just as the leaves on the trees started to turn russet and fall.

As we are aware, the meeting was not solely to do with parish or spiritual matters but was concerned in no small part with the events at the Comity and the Diocesan concern over these events.

The Bishop's right-hand man, the Reverend Neil Thomas, had been in touch with Mr Palmer earlier and it had been arranged that as part of the visit the Bishop would visit the Comity. The wish had been expressed that the Bishop would be pleased to meet both Mr Puritan and Ms Eristic, and this message had been passed on to Mr Puritan by the vicar. It had also been offered as a suggestion that the Bishop would appreciate a chance to talk with some of the residents over tea, and the Reverend Palmer had approached Ray Paladin directly on this, and had agreed with Paladin that the Bishop should take tea at Valery Curst's cottage.

The Reverend Palmer was not hopeful about the meeting, and had not in fact, been taken into the Bishop's confidence – not because it was felt that the vicar would be against the Bishop's and the Reverend Thomas's thoughts and initiative regarding the Comity, but rather because everybody at the Palace believed that Ms Eristic's agenda was not a matter that could be easily confronted. Rather it had to be circumvented, and in these circumstances it was better that the Bishop's Palace's agenda remained confidential to a very intimate and small group, headed by the Bishop.

Parish business dominated the morning at the vicarage, and in a change of arrangements, it had been agreed that Mr Puritan and Ms Eristic would have lunch with the Bishop at the vicarage. Mrs Palmer had thus been forced to turn her hand to something like mass catering as there were six to lunch in the dining room, as well as the normal meals for the children in the kitchen.

Mr Puritan and Ms Eristic had arrived precisely on time at one o'clock and had thus wrong footed the vicar and the Bishop, who were running late. However, against this eventuality, Neil Thomas had been dispatched to be there in time to greet them on their arrival.

The party sat down to lunch at fifteen minutes past one, and after a vegetable soup, Mrs Palmer brought in a fine steak and kidney pudding, which it was common knowledge was the Bishop's favourite. It happened to be the vicar's favourite as well, and so Mrs Palmer was both pleasing her husband and his bishop in the same pudding, so to speak. To accompany it there were carrots, cabbage and boiled new potatoes, and the Bishop had contributed some very good Italian red wine.

Ms Eristic was the first to greet the pudding.

'God! That's not meat, is it?' she exclaimed. 'I don't eat meat, I'm against it, I can't stand the cruelty and the killing. I wouldn't have thought a bishop would have condoned the vile butcher practices of abattoirs either.'

Mrs Palmer was mortified, Mrs Palmer was embarrassed, Mrs Palmer wished herself safely in the kitchen with her children, eating hamburgers and away from Felicity Eristic.

'I also don't eat meat,' chirped up Mr Puritan smugly. 'I think we should respect all God's creatures rather than kill and eat them. I'm sure you agree, Bishop?'

Mrs Palmer was wounded, but now after the knife of criticism had cut at her soul, an anger rose in her breast and she became not the vicar's wife but an insulted and criticised party.

'Miss Eristic, you will, I am sure, forgive me for inviting you to share our food when it is obviously not to your liking. However, I shall happily cook you and Mr Puritan an omelette or I will even go into my kitchen and bake you some other vegetarian dish. Naturally, I am sure the Bishop and the vicar will excuse me, for they, Miss Eristic and Mr Puritan, have been well brought up and abhor any display of atrocious manners and ingratitude. They would much sooner I left the table to cook for you than witness your discomforture, whether it is born of ignorance or malice.'

Upon completing her speech, she collected the plates from in front of Ms Eristic and Mr Puritan and left the room with them, silently calling both people names that it would not be proper to write here.

The Reverend Palmer smiled and suggested that those already served should eat up as it would spoil if they waited for his wife to reappear with the vegetarian food.

'Well, Bishop, do you agree with killing animals for food?' demanded Ms Eristic just as he had taken a mouthful of Mrs Palmer's wonderful pudding.

He chewed reflectively and then when his mouth was empty observed: 'Ms Eristic, I have been to China, where they eat monkeys, and was offered some at a formal dinner. I was flattered that they had taken so much trouble to offer me something they considered a delicacy. In Australia, I was invited to an Aboriginal celebration at which I was given a roast pupa of a grub to eat, I ate that because I felt that the kindness displayed by my hosts was something that I needed to honour. In the many countries I have visited I have been treated to dishes that I would not normally think of eating. I have, however, learnt that there is much that is wrong with the world, and much pain and violence is the daily lot of a great many people. When I then encounter kindness and generosity I treasure it and try to make it a rule always to pay in the same coin. I would not question your right to be a vegetarian, not only because it would be bad-mannered but also because it might well embarrass our host, who is obviously not.'

The Reverend Neil Thomas commented to the vicar that the pudding was the best he had tasted for a long time, in an effort to make the scene caused by the vegetarians less hurtful.

'And I'm sure that your wife has had a quite a morning of it, Mr Palmer, doing all this cooking. Two small children take up a great deal of time even if you're not entertaining. She must have been up extremely early to have produced this wonderful meal.'

The table fell silent with nobody prepared to speak in case the meal became more acrimonious. Mrs Palmer returned with two plates of pasta with a vegetable sauce.

'I truly hope that this will be to your liking, Miss Eristic and Mr Puritan. It is a simple pasta dish that I believe vegetarians enjoy.' She set it down before them and took her place. 'Oh dear, my own meal is quite cold. Never mind, I've lost my appetite.' She pushed her plate away. 'I hope my pudding was to your liking, Bishop?'

Dessert was able to be eaten, even by vegetarians, as it was a plum tart, made from the plums that grew in the vicarage garden.

With the ending of lunch, Mrs Palmer left, having cleared the table. As neither Mr Puritan nor Ms Eristic elected to lend a hand, the vicar and the Bishop's chaplain carried the various plates and trays out to the kitchen. When the table was clear, the Bishop asked Mr Puritan how the Comity was progressing: 'I understand from Mr Palmer that you have only recently taken over the Administration of the Comity, Mr Puritan. The Diocese has an interest in St Margaret's Comity, as I believe you know, so I felt that as I was making a visit to St Margaret's and St John's, I should pay my respects to you and wish you well. I am so pleased that Ms Eristic was able to join us as I believe she has a most important role in the Council and, indeed, has lately taken an even more enlarged interest in the provision of care in the Council's area.'

'Yes that's right, Bishop, or Reverend – look, I'm sorry, but I don't know what I should call you. You see, I'm not a member of the Church, so I'm not up to calling bishops anything.' Felicity Eristic was also uncertain, and she didn't like being uncertain.

'Please call me Robert, Ms Eristic. If you wanted to be formal you could call me My Lord Bishop, but then I would have to respond by calling you Mistress Eristic, or possibly something else, and communication would become dogged with titles, so call me Robert.'

'Right,' replied Eristic. 'As you say, the Council is enlarging its community commitment to the frail and elderly in its area, and in line with the Government's policy the Council is subcontracting its responsibility to a company – DEC Ltd, which stands for Development Enterprise Company – and they have appointed me to be its managing director.'

'How very innovative of the Council,' observed the Bishop. 'And what are the advantages for the elderly and frail in this development, Ms Eristic?'

'Well, the company is still really in its infancy, Robert, but we are expecting to be able to buy care very much more cheaply and thus make savings in the cost of running the service.'

'Yes, I can see that, Ms Eristic. But how will the DEC spend the money it saves on buying in care and other services? Will it perhaps offer more services to those under its care, or perhaps upgrade the facilities and improve the conditions of some of the homes, or perhaps buy in more carers?'

'Well no, that is not the intention. Firstly the Council grant will be reduced. We have a very full agenda in the Council and have been forced to cut the education budget already. The Council is also a very dedicated equal opportunities employer and we are dedicated to mounting a substantial campaign to stamp out sexism and racism. All that costs money, Robert.'

'I see, Ms Eristic. The money you save on the frail and elderly will be reflected in an increase in spending on such causes as anti-racism and anti-sexism. Is that right?'

'Oh, not only on those areas.' Felicity warmed to the Bishop, he seemed to understand the need for priorities in Council spending. 'There's battered wives – they need a grant for refuges – and there's the gay community. Did you know the Council had no counselling provision whatsoever for the gay community and in order to provide it we've had to cut the street-cleaning budget and the library budget, but even so there's not nearly enough for the gay community? It is shocking how tight all the budgets are. We haven't made any provision this year for immigrant housing. Can you imagine that Robert?'

'And what about youth, Ms Eristic? Surely there is a budget for youth?' Neil Thomas asked somewhat ironically.

'Well, we had to cut the education budget in order to help our local football club rebuild its stand, and we also cut the frail and elderly budget to help the football club.'

'I can see that the calls upon the Council are very great indeed, Ms Eristic, and if this is so, how will bidding to run the private sheltered housing organisations help resolve this problem?' The Bishop smiled his most winning smile at Felicity.

'Well there's a lot of charitable money in the private sheltered housing sector, and if the company I head up took them over we would be able both to charge the charities for our administration services and make savings on the basis of economy of scale over our total operation. To a large extent the whole strategy is set out in Justin Covinous's book on community people power.'

The Bishop smiled at Felicity and then looked at his chaplain.

'It is a very ambitious scheme, Ms Eristic. I'm indebted to you for explaining these things to me. Now, Mr Puritan, how about you and the St Margaret's Comity. How are you finding things?'

Mr Puritan, seeing that Felicity Eristic had obviously impressed the Bishop, and seeing how pleased with herself she looked, immediately took his cue from her. 'Well, it has been most interesting, Robert, I have had to contend with some pretty difficult problems. There is an awful lot of smoking amongst the residents and I have tried to curb this, and then there is a fair degree of sexism too.'

'Oh dear me,' murmured the Bishop. 'Sexism and smoking, Mr Puritan. And what have you been able to do to control this?'

'Well, they are elderly people and so I have had to move slowly, but I have sent every single resident a regular newsletter that has tried to put the right approach about these things, you know.'

The Bishop nodded, and smiled at Puritan, inviting him to continue.

'We have recently staged a very exciting, and I think stimulating, Festival for People of the Third Age.'

'The third age?' queried the Bishop's Chaplain.

'The elderly. There's the young age, the middle age and old age, that's how we come to the term the third age,' supplied Mr

161

Puritan helpfully. 'Our little festival focused on anti-sexism and anti-racism, but we had many other attractions. We had a herbal beauty consultant, new age therapy, and alternative medicine and white witches.'

'How did that go down in terms of anti-racism, Mr Puritan?' asked the Bishop.

'Oh, I see what you mean,' smiled Mr Puritan. 'No, this was white magic as opposed to black magic.'

The Bishop put his hands together seemingly in thought. 'Exactly, Mr Puritan. Is the word itself not racist in its definition?'

'Good lord no, Robert, white and black magic has been around since the birth of time, since man first walked upright. It's about good and evil, right and wrong, er . . .'

Mr Puritan suddenly started to experience a glimmer of understanding as to where the Bishop's question had taken him.

'I believe they officially called themselves good magic or good witches.'

'As in *The Wizard of Oz*, perhaps, Mr Puritan?' Neil Thomas offered.

'Well yes, or rather no, they are serious people, sincere.'

'So many people, Mr Puritan, can be said to be sincere. Stalin, for example, was, I believe, very sincere. Sincerity is sadly no guarantee of goodness, nor is seriousness. Indeed, I find I have more faith in people with a good sense of humour than serious people, but that is probably a weakness in a bishop. How then did the residents take to this festival of the third age? Did they attend and support the venture?'

Mr Puritan realised that he would either have to tell the truth or lie, and in his heart, he didn't relish the prospect of lying to the Bishop. Felicity Eristic spotted the problem and intervened: 'We are now going to have a lecture by Justin Covinous, the TV pundit and writer. He is going to speak on his latest book *Community People Power*. Perhaps you have read it Robert.'

'No, Ms Eristic, I can't say that I have, but Neil, my chaplain here, has. He is a man that keeps up to date with all the latest social thinking. Indeed, he is so up on all the latest social studies that I sometimes have to employ an interpreter when he talks to me about it all. Is that not right, Neil?'

'The Bishop has not been empowered to empathise or relate in an in-face situation, he just seems unable to put out, to get past his stereotype denial and realise his positive personal subconscious agenda,' Neil replied, winking at the Reverend and Mrs Palmer.

'You see, Ms Eristic, he becomes almost a social worker talking in tongues. But Mr Puritan, are the residents of St Margaret's Comity appreciative of all your considerable efforts to bring them your enlightenment?'

'It is slow work, Robert,' answered Puritan. 'You see, they keep harking back to the last Administrator, Mr Hartwell, who, quite frankly, was sacked because he just couldn't get on top of the job and let matters slip. Hartwell left things in a shocking state. He had no policies on any of these important issues, no policies on anti-racism or anti-sexism, he had made no effort at all on the whole subject of gays or smoking or even on the role of women.'

'Sins indeed,' murmured Neil Thomas.

'I think that would be the Reverend Hartwell, would it not, Mr Puritan? And I believe he resigned to be nearer to his daughter. He certainly was not sacked. I am right in this, am I not, Mr Palmer?'

'Yes Bishop, he resigned in order to be closer to his daughter and his grandchildren, a first-rate man and a very fine preacher. We certainly miss him at St Margaret's and St John's.'

'A sweet man, a gentleman, and certainly one of the kindest men I have ever known.' Mrs Palmer had returned to hear Mr Puritan slag off the Reverend Hartwell and could not contain herself at such a vilification.

'Yes, he resigned, Robert, but I have to tell you he left things in a pretty bad state, especially in the area of Council and Government welfare regulations and safety requirements. I've had a hell of a lot of work to do to get the place in line with the latest regulations. It's not been easy; the residents have not liked the changes because they have had to be introduced in a great lump rather than bit by bit.'

'Yes, I can see that presented as a body of changes, the residents must have felt that most of the changes and new regulations were both unnecessary and pointless. It is the way of governments and bureaucrats to introduce small, pin-prick changes, and before you know where you are they have stood the whole operation on its head so it is unrecognisable. It is the same in the Church, Mr Puritan. The modernisers start by suggesting small changes in the liturgy and before you know it, we have no liturgy at all. It has all been changed, and Neil's beloved Book of Common Prayer has been thrown in the rubbish skip. He constantly complains to me about it, don't you, chaplain?'

'Indeed I do, Bishop. But do you listen, do you fight?'

'Neil, the Book of Common Prayer has stood hundreds of years of attacks. It is and has always been a fighter, it has always won, and will win. Fashion Neil, is the transitory thing; it comes and goes like political beliefs. It is ephemeral.'

Neil Thomas snorted and looked pained, and the Bishop smiled at him.

'You see, Ms Eristic, to some people like Neil here, certain things are too precious, too special to them and they will fight to the last breath in their body until that which has been taken away is restored to them. My philosophy, my arguments, my logic might well convince Neil that the Book of Common Prayer that he loves so much will win the battle against fashion and silliness, but that will not stop him fighting day in and day out for its return. I doubt if you could sympathise with Neil over the BCP, but in your life, as indeed in most people's, there is just one thing that is their cornerstone.'

'Certainly not the BCP, Robert. I'm afraid I am not a religious person, I'm more concerned with today, the here and now. And here and now I have Council business to attend to. I must fly – the business of the day to day and all that.' Felicity Eristic wished them all goodbye and the Reverend Palmer escorted her out.

'Well, Mr Puritan, if Ms Eristic has things to do, I am equally sure that you have too. I have to finish my parish visit. I'm calling on some of your residents for tea shortly. Perhaps I shall see you at the Comity.'

The Bishop thus helped Mr Puritan on with his anorak and wished him goodbye.

Returning to the dining room, he sat down heavily and sank his head in his hands. 'Nothing I have heard from those two is designed to put me at ease, Neil. The Comity is in danger from them, and the poor residents must either dance to their tune or be broken. They are not easy people, they are zealots.'

'What can be done for the residents, Bishop?' asked the vicar. 'Already they seem dispirited.'

'Well, we will have to do something, that's for sure. I am reminded of Miss Izzat's suggestion, Neil. Tell me, Mr Palmer, how is Mr Boon, your part-time curate, getting on? He wanted to do something that would help but not be too strenuous. You're not working him ragged, I hope, Mr Palmer?'

'I don't think so, but as you know, I have three churches to run.'

'So you do, Mr Palmer. You could probably do with a younger man and full-time too, with three churches. You know, Neil, I have a feeling that we might have put too much on Mr Boon; he is not, I feel, totally recovered from his illness. Remind me to see him, not on this visit but later. A very keen chap is Boon, Mr Palmer. He ran a very successful church school, you know, until his wretched illness forced him to retire early. He was loved by the parents, pupils and governors, kept his school running like a well-oiled clock, pupils passing examinations, winning sports cups and competitions, nothing but good reports about Boon, and his wife is his match in every respect. Between them they could run the country better than the Government, but then again, anybody could.'

Later in the afternoon the Bishop, Mr Thomas and Mr Palmer called for tea on Mrs Curst at her cottage.

When they arrived they found that several of the residents were already there and waiting. David and Grace Cenobite, Valerie Curst, Philip Dabster and Ray Paladin were squeezed into Mrs Curst's sitting room. Given the smallness of the room and the shortage of chairs, Robert declined the offer of the easy chair and he and Neil Thomas sat on the floor, whilst the vicar sat upon a small linen box. Mrs Curst poured the new arrivals' tea in her best cups and saucers, and when they had refused cake, Mrs Palmer's pudding having been more than enough to fill them up for many hours, the Bishop, smiling, asked them how they found the new Administrator.

'He's full of change, Bishop, full of change, and I for one don't like all the change,' answered Valerie Curst.

'He's always on about sex and race and smoking, although what that's got to do with us we don't know, do we, Grace?'

Grace Cenobite agreed with her husband. 'It's all about homosexuals, begging your pardon, Bishop, and you too, vicar, but what with all his posters about race and sex and smoking and the leaflets he keeps pushing through the door and the bell things and taking the gates off the front...'

The Bishop then heard the stories of Mr Pule and Mr Hall, he heard about Martha Preen and Sangeta Patel and the rest. It was all related to him, and not much embroidered either, and he was told about the festival and about the burglars. Indeed, such a great wail of anguish came out that, although the floor was hard, none of the clergy present felt the least bit uncomfortable.

When there was a pause the Bishop turned to the vicar. 'You will have to keep a sharp eye on these parishioners for me, Mr Palmer. It seems that they could well need an helpful friend.'

Ray Paladin laughed. 'We'll be fine, Bishop. We are old, and have passed the point where anybody considers we have any usefulness. We are therefore here simply to pass the days before we die. Contributing nothing, adding nothing and using up resources.

'In past times, the old were considered to be a resource. They had seen it all before and therefore if they could not "do", they could at least warn and explain, interpret and digest the information the younger people brought back. But now nobody wants to be warned of possible dangers, they prefer to hear lies and then, when faced with inevitable disaster, they choose to react by analysing the situation. It isn't the wisest way but, I suppose it is a way.

'Mr Puritan is young and doesn't know an awful lot about life. He believes that it is possible to change people by pressure and exhortation, and he doesn't much care if the people do not want to be changed or that there is very little point in changing them because people, happily, will never be perfect. But Mr Puritan wants perfect people, and believes that they are flawed simply because nobody has pointed out to them that there is a better way. So he reasons that, if he points out the better way and forces the poor souls down his signposted route, then they will gain enlightenment. The paradox is, of course, that Mr Puritan has not lived long enough, nor seen enough, to know that the ideas he pushes are as old as the hills and have always failed whenever they have been tried. To him they are new and to him they will produce perfect people.

'The Church, Bishop, knows, as we know, that Mr Puritan's ideas are false, knows that they will not work, knows that the only way forward is the gentle, careful, loving way. It is your duty, Bishop, to point this out to Mr Puritan because he does not hear us when we tell him, because we are old and of no value in his eyes. He discounts our pain for the sake of his new Jerusalem. We suffer from his ideas, but we have to accept the world's opinion of us that we are of no value, and so our suffering is, I suppose, of no real account.'

The Bishop had listened to Ray Paladin with great care and it was obvious that what he heard was more than a little painful. He looked thoughtfully at his chaplain.

'If I were writing a sermon on Mr Paladin's thoughts, Neil, I would use as my text St Paul's letter to the Romans, Chapter 12. But we must go on. Mr Paladin, Mrs Curst, Mr and Mrs Cenobite, thank you for the tea and thank you for telling us about the situation here at the Comity. I can say this, that as far as the Church's influence exists in the affairs of the Comity, it will be used to improve and return your lives to the happier administration you experienced under the Reverend Hartwell, who, you tell me, you both respected and loved.'

They all wished the visitors goodbye and the Bishop and his party left, observed by Mr Puritan, who wondered what had been said and why the three clerics looked so serious as they walked up the path to Mr Palmer's car.

19

Ms Eristic Makes her Play

The Secretary of the RRAWF was surprised to hear mid-morning that Ms Eristic was waiting in reception and would be pleased if Mr Fribble could spare her some time.

It was, I have to admit, not convenient for the Secretary. John Izzat, the Chairman of RRA and the President of RRAWF, was just finishing the review of the accounts for the last three months and would expect to spend an hour or so going over outstanding matters.

It is not, he reflected, convenient, nor is it good manners to just turn up without an appointment. The unpredictable was, to Eric Fribble, profoundly threatening and uncomfortable. It was enough that he had the President there; to now have an unexpected visitor who demanded a meeting was more than flesh and blood could, in all conscience, countenance.

Fribble consulted the President, who enquired what did Fribble think she wanted?

'I've absolutely no idea, Mr President. She has no right to visit. If it is anything to do with the Council, then she should write, they always write. We're in London and her Council is in Wiltshire. I just can't imagine what she wants. I could tell her I'm too busy and ask her to make an appointment.'

'No, Eric. Seeing as she has come to London, I think perhaps we should see her. Let's see her together, here in the conference room.'

Ms Eristic entered the conference room, power-dressed in a black trouser suit with a white blouse and carrying a briefcase. Gone were her social worker jeans, gone was her shapeless sweatshirt. Both men stood up and John Izzat welcomed her.

'Ms Eristic, I believe you wanted to see the Secretary, and I also understand from Mr Fribble that it is about the Comity. As the President of the Welfare Fund, I have taken the liberty of joining the meeting. I trust that's all right?'

Felicity Eristic smiled her assent and Mr Fribble pulled out a chair for her.

'Now, Ms Eristic, what can we do for you?' continued Izzat.

'I am here to offer you a rather tempting deal concerning the Comity, gentlemen.'

'Really,' asked Fribble, 'and what is the deal?'

'The Development Enterprise Company Limited, which has been contracted by my Council to run all the sheltered housing and elderly care homes under the Council's control, can offer your Association or Welfare Fund the opportunity of our taking over the management of the St Margaret's Comity for a very reasonable management fee, and further ensuring that the St Margaret's Comity does not fall foul of the many Council and National Health and Safety regulations that are now in place covering matters such as accommodation and care.

'As you are no doubt aware, the Council has a duty of care to ensure all such accommodation meets certain well-defined standards, and this can mean very costly building alterations and construction work. Under the management of the Development Enterprise Company Limited this work would be managed over a longer period and carried out without upsetting the existing residents. Naturally the cost would have to be borne by the Welfare Fund; however, under the management of my DEC, you would be assured that all such work would receive Council approval and would pass all Council inspections.

'Our management fee would not be excessive, and would, after the necessary work had been satisfactorily carried out, be pegged for a contract period of three years. Thereafter it would be reviewed. My company would assume all responsibility for wages of the staff at the Comity and for such matters as cleaning, maintenance and administration and all other costs involved, which would naturally be reflected in the management fee. I have all these matters detailed in this proposal.' Felicity took from her briefcase a stack of glossy proposals. 'I expect you

169

would like to circulate these to the members of your management council or committee.'

John Izzat and Eric Fribble both picked up a proposal.

'You know, Ms Eristic, were I not a plain simple businessman, I would say that your proposal was tinged with threat, although I am willing to put money on the fact that the bit about meeting the Council's H & S requirements does not appear in this fine proposal.'

Felicity Eristic had cut her teeth in local radical Socialist Workers Party politics and had learnt the business of the exploitation of power. She had negotiated with the police, with local Labour middle-of-the-road councils, she was tough in the art of getting her own way for a cause.

'Look, cut the shit, Izzat,' she hissed. 'If your tuppenny-ha'penny outfit wants to take on the Council it will cost you money one way or the other. I'm Chair of the Frail and Elderly Care Committee of the Council and I'm also MD of the DEC, plus a fully paid-up member of the local Labour Party and will be a Councillor after the next election. If you dream that you can jerk me around, have another dream – probably a wet one for Fribble. What options have you got? By the time my committee has finished with the Comity, demanding back exits from every cottage, a wider arch to allow the fire engine and ambulance through, closed-circuit security TV, full-time medical staff and qualified nursing cover twenty-four hours a day, plus a full-time health and safety officer, fire officer and proper food preparation facilities, it will break your fund and you will have to turn the place over to the Council. And then there's all the European Union, Brussels Directive crap. The Council will be expected to enforce all that rubbish and that will cost, oh boy will it cost.

'You're white, male elitists, racists, middle-aged and middle-class, but you're playing in a new league, the great European Union league, where regulations and rights rule, not sodding traditions and emotions. Get real, gentlemen. The playing field has changed and you're not even in the team. Your power base has been given away by the politicians and the civil servants, so it's time for the whining to stop and the reality to bloom. What alternatives have you?'

170

Mr Fribble cleared his throat. He was not used to being insulted in his own conference room, but that did not signify. It was irritating, nothing more; this challenge to his divine right to determine what was and what was not important in the matters he directed *was* important and a matter that he took extremely seriously. So, too, was the assumption, albeit implied, that anybody could just walk in off the streets and erode his organisation, take away the instruments of his power. That was totally unacceptable and something that was to be resisted by all possible means in his power. He had not reached the age he had without being more than a match for some jumped-up woman from some unimportant council.

John Izzat also reflected that whatever Ms Eristic might think, she did not indeed hold in her hand the ace and straight flush that she imagined. Mr Fribble spoke first.

'Ms Eristic, whilst the Association is always open to any business proposal, the Welfare Fund is unfortunately governed by its rules and its complex relationship with its founding Association. It is able, for example, to determine the minutiae of the day-to-day running of its sheltered-housing unit, but is unable to alter its constitution. That, my dear Ms Eristic, is a matter for the National Council of the Association, which has to have a notice issued of an intention to meet at least six months in advance. That notice, my dear, is only able to be issued once the General Council has agreed to hold such a meeting, and this has to be done in consultation with the Welfare Fund's trustees, both past and present, who must meet prior to the General Council meeting.

'Now we would all probably say that is a lengthy and bureaucratic process that must be able to be short-circuited; however, it is required by the Charity Commissioners, and were it to be short-circuited, we would endanger the Fund's tax position, which is essential to its ability to finance the management of the Comity. Things, Ms Eristic, have to be done in a certain order if they are to be done at all, and indeed done well. This proposal,' Fribble lifted it up as if it was too hot to touch with the very points of his fingers, 'this proposal must go through the proper channels at the proper time and in the right sequence of

171

events. There is just no other possible course open, no other way, no other options. We are locked into a system that is set in the constitution of this Association. Things can continue but not change, as far as the rules are concerned.'

John Izzat smiled at Fribble and Fribble smiled at Ms Eristic.

'Ms Eristic.' Izzat's eyes were cold; there was no smile, no warmth, the words came as if on a computer screen. 'You accused us of racialism. You, said, if I remember correctly, that we were white, male elitists, racists, middle-aged and middle-class.

'You wave the flag of racialism in the same way as the Grand Inquisitor waved the crucifix. You seek to make racialism a votive force, as if by simply stating the word it settles an argument – it doesn't. Racialism is an argument that is divisive; it seeks to separate groups into two sides, and that is the first falsehood generated by your use of the word. The second is that in almost every case you demote the value of a complaint, be it an injustice or a plain lack of caring. That is the second falsehood of the use of the word racism, as you call it. Thirdly, by using the word, you obscure, to the benefit of nobody, one very real reason for a lot of discrimination, namely performance – differences between one person and another's ability at a given task or skill. Poor performance is not made better and good performance is demotivated. But even worse, Ms Eristic, is the fact that by raising the accusation, you force those not involved in your complaint to take sides, thus fanning the very prejudice and resentment that, before you raised the racist banner, never existed and which you claim to hate.

'By constantly crying racialism, you generate, foster and then exploit what you've produced; hatred, bigotry and complaint. It is iniquitous, evil, cruel and cynical and I refuse to even consider your falsehoods. As for your proposal, I fail to see your threat that the Council will not pass St Margaret's Comity as satisfying the meaningful regulations. There are, Ms Eristic, standards that can be measured and assessed. A fire door can be seen, a medical call-out agency can be contracted to cover, an exit can be constructed. The true test is not the Council withholding a licence, it is the validity for the Council taking such action and

172

then justifying it in front of independent judges. The Association has no fear whatsoever of its legality, Ms Eristic, and as long as the Council has no fear either, there can be no cause for concern.'

Felicity Eristic was put out. She had not expected the meeting to develop in this fashion, she had expected capitulation and a measure of gratitude. She questioned, in her thoughts, the wisdom of her earlier outburst, and for the briefest of brief moments, she even considered the possibility that she may have been wrong in her strategy and even in her approach. But Ms Eristic was not given to introspection and was quickly able to see that she was being manipulated by the sickening white middle class, who felt they had a divine right to rule and govern. She vowed she would show them who was the master now.

'I will leave the proposal, gentlemen, and I would urge you to think long and hard on it, because the Council has, as far as the Comity is concerned, a bottomless pit of legal expenses and a fantastic ability to create numberless problems for you should we become locked in battle.' She rose and walked to the door. 'And Mr Izzat, when I want a lecture from you on social matters or philosophy, then I will, as Mr Fribble said earlier, put it in writing. Your analysis is wrong, but then again, that is to be expected from a racist,' and she left before John Izzat or Eric Fribble could utter a word.

Mr Fribble was speechless for a minute, then he phoned through to reception to satisfy himself that she had left the premises.

'She has gone, Sharon, you're sure? Well, should she come back, I am not able to see her. If she does come back – at any time – ask Mr Flight to see her and take a note of anything she asks, but I am *never* in to Ms Eristic. Mr Izzat, what a dreadful woman, so coarse and foul-mouthed.'

Fribble looked at John Izzat for confirmation, but John Izzat was deep in thought, his eyes set on the ceiling.

'You know, Eric, she has a point has our Ms Eristic. We couldn't hope to take on the Council and win, and if the Council demanded all the alterations she indicated and which

173

are no doubt spelt out in this proposal, we would be hard put to raise the necessary finance to pay for it all.'

'But, that is the whole point, Mr Izzat? They are not necessary, they have never been necessary and the regulations haven't changed that much. The Comity is totally adequate for its purpose.'

Izzat remained silent and, had Ms Eristic unexpectedly returned, she would, no doubt, have been gratified by the fact that her strategy seemed to have worked, if that strategy had been to force the Association and its servants into a defensive position. Both men contemplated the prospects of Ms Eristic's DEC taking control of St Margaret's Comity with profound dismay and distaste.

'We shall have to take legal advice, Eric. But even more urgent is the need to get rid of Mr Puritan. He is nothing but Eristic's puppet and also her access to the affairs of the Comity. While he remains in place as the Administrator, we are constrained in our management of the place and are unable to do anything without Eristic knowing fully what we are doing, when and how.'

John Izzat stood up and paced about the room, clenching and unclenching his fists. His face was set and his eyed blazed with anger. To Fribble, it seemed that he was engaged in a private and internal battle, fighting some giant foe in his head. Fribble could not recall ever having seen him so angry, so stretched and so determined.

Eric Fribble feared to even move let alone speak to the President. He remained motionless while Izzat paced and thought. Finally, with a characteristic nod of the head, he moved beside Fribble and stood quiet, both hands clenched, and then he smashed his fist down on the table, causing the ashtrays, water glasses and blotters to leap into the air.

'I will not allow this Association to be manipulated for political purposes nor for the overweening ambition of that woman, Fribble. We will not lose the Comity or its management. I will not be known as the President who sold the Comity into vassalage. I will fight for the Welfare Fund's assets like a tiger and the Association will go head-to-head, fist-to-fist, blow-for-blow and we will win. Do you hear, Eric – we will *win*.

'Bring the matter of Puritan to a head as quickly as possible and set up a meeting with our solicitors. I will also need to see the Bishop of Salisbury. They own the head lease and need to to consulted. We will win, Eric, we *have* to win for all the charities in this country and for all those thousands of people who have contributed in the past and, damn it, for the residents of all the sheltered-housing complexes throughout the country, but especially for the residents of the Comity.'

The tone of Izzat's voice and the strength of the man's conviction was enough to reduce Fribble to what, in truth, he was, a mere functionary, in the preparations for a battle. He had not the courage, nor the strength of belief in anything, to do more than march behind a flag. He was no general, no leader.

'I will get on to it right away, Mr Izzat. Mr Puritan's removal may not be that quick, but . . .'

'It has to be that quick, Eric. I'll not be delayed on this. You have to bring it to a head at once. Every minute provides Eristic with the opportunity to wound and attack us. If you can't or won't do it, I will. Puritan has to go. Is that understood?'

'I will do it quickly, Mr Izzat. We will get him out.'

Izzat nodded, and his manner changed back to the approachable and mannered President of the Welfare Fund. He picked up one of the proposals Ms Eristic had left on the table and placed it in his briefcase. He turned to Fribble, who was collecting the papers and straightening the various things that had become overturned and dislodged when Izzat pounded the table.

'Miss Eristic will have to learn that we white, middle-class, middle-aged, elitists have found, in the course of gaining our experience of life, that a single issue is never in reality a single issue, it is always ringed about with a galaxy of other interrelated issues. Did I not see that DiHsui was planning a factory in Wiltshire? Set up a meeting with them, would you, Eric, and with the Department of Industry – I think the Permanent Secretary wanted a word. After all, the Government is investing a lot of money in the DiHsui deal.'

20

The Establishment Stirs

The offices of Barratry, Barratry and Simony, solicitors, were in the Aldwych. The firm enjoyed some reputation amongst businesses as it was very aware of the need at all times to be discreet, often ruthless and nearly always successful, Barratry, Barratry and Simony was the anvil upon which commercial causes and private grudges were hammered out from coin into lethal swords. There were two senior partners, David Fetor and Ruston Olid. Both were comparatively young, having forced the last and remaining Barratry from the firm and into early retirement. Those who dealt with the firm did so because of its results not because of its partners.

The more senior of the two equally senior partners was Ruston Olid, an ugly man, bull-necked, with thick black oily hair, a sallow, almost yellow complexion and sleepy eyes. A slow man in his physical actions, his voice was rasping and indeterminate as far as an accent was concerned. Those who listened closely stated that English was not his first language. His background was not something that he spoke about and few had either the desire or the courage to probe far beyond the matters that had brought them to his office.

David Fetor was the suave front man of the firm. Highly polished and elegant, his social ability and brittle cynicism made him seem attractive. However, his private life and sadistic attitude soon repelled any who would have rashly considered any relationship other than formal business.

It was to the offices of this firm of solicitors that John Izzat came to seek advice and help concerning his battle to save the Comity. Izzat had used Barratry's before, not as his company's or the Association's lawyers, but for specific actions that required the skills upon which the firm's fame rested. He had an appointment and had asked to consult both senior partners as he wanted their joint opinion.

The meeting took place in Ruston Olid's office, which was the largest office in the company and decorated in the most modern and functional style possible. There was no single personal item that could provide any clue to the man whose office it was. No single photograph or personal effect was allowed to distract the visitor, and the staff had strict instructions to remove any evidence of humanity – such as coffee or tea cups – as soon as empty. There was only one thing that could be said to be personal to Olid, and that was an ashtray, for he smoked Turkish cigarettes, which were kept in a silver box on his desk.

Izzat was shown straight into Olid's presence. He rose and offered his hand and gestured to a chair in the conference section of the office. Fetor had followed Izzat in and sat opposite him. Olid, however, chose to walk the office whilst he listened intently to his client.

Izzat told the story of the events at the Comity to the two lawyers in a dry monotone, for he knew that firstly all conversations were recorded and secondly that the two lawyers would only want the details and would be uninterested in any feelings – emotion was the tool the lawyers manipulated in their opponents, not something they were interested in themselves or their clients.

'And your objectives in this matter, Mr Izzat?' asked Fetor.

'I wish to maintain the Association's total control of the Comity and to ring-fence the charitable status of the place in such a way that whilst it will not seek to fight the local Council nor contravene any regulation, it will not be possible for it to be wrested from us.'

Olid smiled. 'And what else, Mr Izzat? What else do you want, or should I rather say, who else do you want? Perhaps the troublesome Ms Eristic, or perhaps Mr Puritan?'

John Izzat felt uncomfortable. He was not used to being transparent, not used to having people one jump ahead of him.

'The chips will fall where they fall, I suppose. But I must

admit that I would not weep should either of those two people fall off the branch of the tree of my argument.'

'Would there still be an argument if they did fall, Mr Izzat, as you say, off the branch of the tree of your argument?' enquired Olid.

'No, I suppose the argument would cease if they were removed from the matter. But it is not within possibility that Ms Eristic could be removed from either her Council position or from the board of her company, is it?'

Olid smiled; the smile that his opponents had long learnt to both loathe and fear.

'Oh, I think that is exactly the answer to the problem, Mr Izzat. Indeed, were it possible to achieve Ms Eristic's removal, the Comity would have no problems whatsoever. Mr Puritan, as a servant of the Association, would either fall into line or, better still, be removed.' Olid looked over towards Fetor. 'Don't you agree, David?'

David Fetor did agree. 'Ms Eristic is undoubtedly the key to the problem, Mr Izzat. What do we know about her? Where is she from? What is her past?'

'I know nothing about her at all,' admitted John Izzat, 'although she knew Mr Puritan before he came to the Comity and, indeed, she was instrumental in his appointment. Beyond that, I fear we took her on face value as being an employee of the Council.'

'Well.' Olid rose and walked over to his desk. 'I think we have been briefed adequately. It is for us now to progress the matter as we see fit. It would serve no purpose for you to know what action we will propose until we have carried out some research. I need to know, however, who we are acting for – are we acting for the Association, the Welfare Fund or are we acting in this instance, Mr Izzat, for you?'

'You are acting for me, and all communications should be sent to my private address, which you have, Mr Olid. I do not want anything from this office to go to the Association.'

'It shall be exactly as you say, Mr Izzat. We shall be dealing with you exclusively. Now, unless there is some other matter with which we can assist...?'

Izzat left and hurried to catch the train to Salisbury, where he had an appointment with the Bishop.

Ruston Olid and David Fetor remained in conference in Olid's office.

'Izzat is firmly tipped for an honour in the next list, Ruston. It would be advantageous for the firm to make sure that we clear up this matter as a swiftly as possible, to allow the honour to be conferred without any possible chance of background chatter. Eristic has to be removed and discredited so that there are no ghosts to haunt the tabloids with lurid accusations.'

'Are you suggesting that there might be some sexual dimension between Izzat and Eristic, David?'

'No, not for a minute. Izzat has a young daughter who is something of a belle, certainly the object of all the marriageable young men in London. The man himself is as straight as it is possible to be without being an actual ruler. He was deeply in love with his wife, and I suspect has never recovered properly from her death. It has slowed him down greatly and taken the commercial shine off him. He is, however, still a formidable man – not somebody to cross, for he has contacts in almost every sphere of society.'

'His wife's death, how did that happen?'

'Cancer. She was ridiculously young and, as so often, by all accounts a most gentle and lovely woman, better than Izzat because where he made money, she was born to it, although she was never rich.'

'You say her death has taken the commercial shine from Izzat. Where does that leave him?'

'Well, he is contemplating retirement, that's common knowledge, and if the honour comes his way, which is highly likely, then he will enter the ranks of the Great and the Good and thus head up numerous commissions and quangos. I have also heard that he is interested in the Church, although that is simply chatter. I cannot think that the head of the UK's TV retail world would happily forsake the small screen for the sky and God bothering.'

'Is that sky with a capital S or small s, David? I will write to Chase to ask them to undertake a thorough investigation into both Eristic and Puritan; I shall tell them that this has top priority and they must put everybody available on it. We'll want photographs, criminal, school, further education and employment records, birth certificates and reports on parents. I will want interviews with everybody who has any personal knowledge of either of them, and we'll want financial information on both of them. Chase's will have to work damn hard and long on this, we'll want every scrap of information that is available. They can also look closely into the Development Enterprise Company, and we can get the accounts picked over by that market analysis company, the people that check every telephone call and sales invoice – we used them in the DiHsui *v* Ahmids case.'

David Fetor nodded. He knew exactly where Ruston was going and was content that Olid should handle that side of the matter.

'I'll bone up on charity law and charity land law, and put the two juniors downstairs onto researching all the areas of the rights of charities over councils and social legislation. I have a feeling that if the charity is more directly related to a religious objective, then Councils have to back off as religious freedom takes precedence over Council bylaws, although I'm not certain about it. Anyway, it will take some examination. There's also the EU. There is certain to be some wretched EU Directive that is just waiting to be brought into play.'

'Well, it's a matter of getting on with it then, David. Let's call for a report session in two days.'

Fetor left Olid's office, and the wheels within Barratry, Barratry and Simony started to turn at a rather quicker rate than most people would have imagined solicitors could or would ever work, but that was part of the secret of the firm, they were not so much solicitors as engines of retribution, and sought to improve upon the biblical account of the Mills of God by grinding faster and harder.

Nearing Salisbury, John Izzat started to feel a shade better. His meeting with Barratry's had heartened him and now he was on his way to see the Bishop, another plank would be hammered into the wall to save the Comity from the terror of Felicity Eristic and Council control.

He expected that his meeting with the Bishop would place another barrier in the path of Eristic's headlong rush to build an empire of sheltered-housing units. He planned to spend the night in Salisbury at the White Hart, an hotel that he had long felt was a great deal better than any of the guidebooks gave credit to. It was very comfortable, well run and close enough to the cathedral to allow guests to attend services if they wanted or just to look at the building and stand and wonder. His beloved wife Elizabeth had loved the cathedral and had sold it to him lock, stock and barrel on one of their visits. She had enthused and wondered, had sighed at its magnificence and had been entranced when walking by it. On one visit they had had dinner and decided to walk past the cathedral; it was a summer's night, the building was wonderfully floodlit and Elizabeth had looked up and had seen the cathedral's shadow upon a large cloud. This had seemed then to Elizabeth, and he now admitted to himself as well, as nothing less than a miracle, a divine statement privately witnessed by just the two of them.

It had changed his view of the cathedral in some subtle way, and now as the train neared the city he was eager to renew his relationship with the giant building. Perhaps, he felt, he might find something of Elizabeth there, some echo that would warm and comfort him. He also reflected that he would attend Evensong, which was sung at the cathedral each evening. He was not a religious man, but since Elizabeth's death he had found himself drawn to the certainties of the Book of Common Prayer. The fact was that these words had been said through centuries and were still just as meaningful to an electronically dominated world as they were to a world that had relied upon candles. The verities, he felt, never really changed: birth, childhood, marriage, old age and death. The microchip couldn't alter or change this process, and at each stage of the way there were dangers and chances, at each step on the path you could slip or climb, and all too often some unkind fate would deal a card that brought you low, as it had brought Elizabeth low. This is where the Book of Common Prayer scored because it explained and calmed, entreated and raised you up, partly because it was about such commonplace events, but also because it had over its long, long life acquired the very holiness with which it dealt. The words themseslves now held a holiness that spoke directly to his soul and joined him with Elizabeth.

He took a taxi to the White Hart and found, as usual, that the staff were attentive and cheerful. His room had been booked for him by Laura and she had made certain he had a large double room with windows that opened. He rested for a little, ordering tea and reading a book that he called his sleeping pill because he always read it last thing at night and would often wake to find it just one page forward on the blankets where it had slipped from his hands. His tea was brought to his room, and thoughts of Elizabeth came flooding back to him as he poured just one cup for himself.

His meeting with the Bishop was scheduled for three forty-five, and upon looking at his watch he realised that he had time to walk to the Bishop's Palace, so he drank his tea and left the hotel.

The walk took him through the cathedral grounds and past the statue by Elizabeth Frink of a walking woman. From there he could see the cathedral most clearly. As there almost always was scaffolding over parts of the building, he longed to see it without this haze of poles that always seemed to spoil one part of the view, but he was realist enough to know that a building of that age couldn't be left standing for any length of time without maintenance.

His walk to the Bishop's Palace was pleasant and it allowed him continuous views of the cathedral, and by the time he arrived at the gates of the Palace he was in a tranquil mood. The gardens were not as well cared for as he would have liked, but his taste in gardens was one that was very labour intensive, easy enough for a man with money and time, but not so easy, he reflected, for a bishop in today's active Church.

The Palace itself was well cared for, he noted, and nestled comfortably into its plot. The years had been as kind to it as it had to the cathedral, and it seemed to welcome the visitor as soon as it came into view.

The whole close told of another world, one that was less angry, less dramatic and warmer than the world John Izzat inhabited.

Walking up the driveway, he wondered if the people that inhabited this religious cathedral world could ever be a match for the ambitious and careless Eristics of today, but even as this thought crossed his mind, he recalled that Salisbury Cathedral had witnessed and seen off the over-riding ambition of kings and politicians, all who had sought to bend the cathedral and the Church to their will had been defeated and seen off, while the cathedral had continued quietly changing a little but always remaining true to its foundation and true to its beliefs. These people are experts at taking the world on and winning, or at the least holding on to those things that they think are important. If dictators and kings can't move them, the Eristics of this world will be small beer indeed, he thought.

He had judged the time of his walk from the White Hart to the Palace well, and as he rang the bell, he noted that it was exactly a quarter to four.

The door was opened by the Bishop's chaplain, Neil Thomas, who recognised the visitor.

'Mr Izzat, thank you for making the journey to Salisbury. The Bishop is delayed, but come in and we can review the situation while we wait for him. I am sure you'll understand that bishops these days are usually scheduled to attend more meetings in a day than there are timeslots available, and that most meetings overrun by at least ten minutes. We try very hard to build into his diary the likelihood of this kind of delay but it still always seems to defeat us.'

The chaplain showed Izzat into his office and offered him a cup of tea, which Izzat declined.

'I think we have reached some understanding of the Comity's position, Mr Izzat,' Neil Thomas said. 'The Bishop has been able to have a meeting with both Ms Eristic and Mr Puritan and he was also able to visit the Comity, although I expect Mr Puritan has already reported to your committee about our visit.'

'No, Reverend, I fear that kind of report is not one of Mr Puritan's strengths. It would seem that he favours lengthy documents about the needs to change the residents' attitudes concerning smoking or sexual orientation to reports of the day-to-day business of the happenings at St Margaret's Comity. And I have to tell you that the Welfare Committee does not seem all that interested in his thoughts on the lack of political correctness.'

21

The Head Lease

John Izzat and Neil Thomas were sitting in the conference area of the chaplain's office, which overlooked the garden. On the table was a folder headed 'Property Services, St Margaret's Comity and Lands'. Neil pointed to it. 'You will, I hope, understand, Mr Izzat, that the Bishop was most disturbed at the things he was told by the residents of the Comity. Indeed, perhaps a stronger word would better fit the Bishop's reaction to his meeting, but for the purpose of our discussion here, we will let "most disturbed" cover his feelings. The whole of the body here was distressed to read his report and plainly felt that we had a duty to do something about the situation.'

Izzat had expected a deal of sympathy, but from the tone of the chaplain's voice it seemed clear to him that *he* was about to be told off.

'You see, Mr Izzat, as the Bishop will explain, as the owners of the head lease, and in view of the nature of the deed of gift surrounding this parcel of land, the Church has a significant duty bestowed upon it. Further, with the present state of adverse publicity that is generated whenever the Church, as property owners, is mentioned in the press or in Government, we see that there is a very grave danger indeed, should the affairs of the Comity become public, that the Church would find itself beaten with a stick not of its own making, but with a stick of your Association's making. This is, I am sure you will agree, profoundly worrying and not something that we can let pass. This is the background against which I would beg you to view our thoughts and the Bishop's observations when he comes to make them to you.'

'Good Lord, chaplain, that is the very reason I have come to see the Bishop. The Association is deeply unhappy with the whole situation – deeply unhappy – and is actively seeking, right now, to produce a solution. However, we are not free. There is legislation – rules and by-laws. We are not free, surely you can see that we have to work within the rules – within the law.'

The chaplain nodded his head. 'Yes, yes, we understand all that, but how has this matter reached this pass, Mr Izzat? It is your Association that has the responsibility; you have the lease, you own the building, your employee is the Administrator, you have the care of the residents under your wing. If things have gone wrong, then we have to look at the responsible body.'

It would be wrong to say that John Izzat became angry with the chaplain, because he became angry with himself, he became as mad as hell with the truth that the chaplain was telling him, and this anger gnawed at him, for he knew that this meeting was premature, he should have taken action sooner and had this meeting later. As it was, he had no defence to the charge of negligence, and worse, much worse, he had stirred up a hornets' nest, prodded the Church into taking action not against Eristic and Puritan but against the Association. Perhaps he had lost his commercial shine, as Fetor had said of him to Olid, certainly as he sat in the Bishop's Palace he was aware that he should have acted sooner, should have blocked Puritan's appointment as soon as he had received Fribble's report.

The Bishop arrived in a rush of clerical garments and stopped at the door of his chaplain's office to look searchingly at Izzat.

'Ah Mr Izzat, I've heard a great deal about you from many quarters and now I have the chance to meet you. What a delight. I expect that Neil has already briefed you about my visit to St Margaret's Comity. Have you offered Mr Izzat some tea, Neil? Come in, Mr Izzat, I'm so pleased to meet you at last. I trust the retail world is still generating healthy returns? I believe we are considerable shareholders of yours, Mr Izzat, but happily such matters are not left to bishops, because we would only make a great mess of it.'

Izzat was ushered into the Bishop's office and was surprised to see how Spartan it was – a desk at one end by the window, a conference table and a prayer desk.

'Let's sit at the table, Mr Izzat, it is more comfortable.' Neil Thomas had followed them in and he placed the report upon the table and in front of the Bishop.

'Please let's not be formal. My name is Robert and I hope I can call you John.' The Bishop sought agreement from Izzat, who nodded his head. 'Good, well then, John, as Neil here has explained, I was very shocked by my meeting with the residents of St Margaret's Comity and greatly disturbed by my meeting with Ms Eristic and Mr Puritan. It would seem that you have a very real problem with those two people.'

Izzat had had enough time to marshal his thoughts and he was determined that he would not take the guilt for Felicity Eristic, although he could not avoid taking it for Puritan.

'Ms Eristic is not our responsibility. She is I fear, outside our control and try as we might – and we have and will continue to try – I can assure you, there is little or nothing the Association can do about firstly the DEC, secondly the Council's Welfare and Frail and Elderly committees, and lastly about Government legislation. We are targets not engines in the battle, Robert, and whilst I readily accept responsibility on behalf of the Association for Mr Puritan, although even with his candidacy we were inveigled into his appointment by Ms Eristic, I refuse to accept responsibility for legislation and its implementation by the Council.

'The situation is that we are presented with demands by a body which has a vested interest in ensuring that those demands exceed our capabilities. For example, to widen the archway requires the demolition of the St Margaret's Comity central building. This in turn means that we would have to close the cottages and find alternative accommodation for the residents. That is not an option open to us.'

The Bishop toyed with the report in front of him. 'The problem we have, John, is that the public has an inability to see much beyond the first tree in the wood. Should events at the Comity become public, the focus would stay upon the Comity and not widen into the whole picture. Few people see a moral climate when they read of a crime, and should the events at the Comity reach the press, then it would be Mr Puritan and St Margaret's Comity that would make the story, not the Government's legislation or the difficulties facing administrators of sheltered-housing complexes, nor yet the stupid demands made on carers by ignorant civil servants.' The Bishop paused and a look of sadness crossed his face. 'Our position in this matter is complex insofar as we are the head leaseholders and have leased the ground to your Association on certain conditions and with certain restrictions. The Association and the Church have had no difficulties in the past. We have found the arrangement mutually satisfactory and we have had no cause for complaint, no reason to worry. However, as a result of my visit to the Comity, this happy situation has now changed and I am in the unpleasant position of having to formally require from the Association certain actions that will, I trust, return our relationship to its former happy state. We are not unreasonable people, John, but I cannot allow a situation, once it is drawn to our attention that it is clearly wrong, to continue without our intervening. I hope you can understand our position in this.'

Izzat was deft at reading between the lines. His commercial experience had honed his mind so that he was able to strip out the flattery and fill in the blank pauses. He summarised the Bishop's statement as saying: 'Because we are involved in St Margaret's Comity, we have to make certain that we appear faultless, should the dirt hit the fan, and as we can't do anything about the two main players, namely Felicity Eristic and Richard Puritan, we find that we can only do something to the Association, and this we have to do in order to save our reputation, regardless of the results of our action.'

In his mind Izzat rapidly surveyed the position and considered the best course of action he should and could take in these circumstances. He had taken from his briefcase Fribble's report on the situation and the accounts of the Comity, which were the cornerstone of the impending case against Puritan. He opened the file and pretended to read it. The Bishop and the chaplain waited and the silence was almost audible. Suddenly Izzat looked up and directly into the Bishop's eyes.

'Robert, I completely understand your position. Naturally it is impossible for you to ignore a situation that has been forced upon your attention. To do so would be both negligent and possibly also morally wrong. No, you have to act, and of course you have to act against the only body that you can reach – the Association. The problem I see with such action is that it could be very counter-productive and could well play directly into the hands of the one person who is now causing us problems. Should the Association, for example, pull out of St Margaret's Comity and make it over to Ms Eristic's DEC, why then, like a tower of playing cards, your own interests in the field of sheltered housing would also come crashing down under Ms Eristic's DEC attack. Simply, what is a problem for us today could well become a much larger problem for the Church tomorrow.

'Now I wouldn't, for a moment, ask you to hold back on any action that you may feel you have to take against the Association, you must act according to your conscience. But I would suggest that it could probably be more beneficial if, rather than fighting against each other, we joined together to settle the cause of the problems that have arisen, and then you would be free to issue the Association with the list of your requirements that would, I am certain, be readily agreed and implemented. I am not seeking to deflect you from the course of action that you have decided upon, but I do feel that there is more to be gained for us both, and St. Margaret's Comity, before we settle any other matters in your report.'

The Bishop looked at Izzat for a long time without speaking and then said: 'John, you have a fearsome reputation and both Neil and I prepared for this meeting with tremendous care. It is not that either of us felt we would be bested, but that even if we held our own, we could not win against a man with such a reputation of negotiating and business skills. We had looked at almost every eventuality and had decided that there was little to be gained by setting down conditions and demands from you on behalf of the Association. The suggestion that we discuss these affairs seems to me to be invaluable. How do you see the problems?'

Izzat, seeing that he had already won his point and secured his position, pushed any notion of self-congratulation from his mind.

'We appointed the wrong man to the post of Administrator and carer to the Comity. From the moment he took up his position, the situation at the Comity deteriorated. On the one hand we lost control and on the other, we had never had that kind of control in the first place. We have now put into place a whole series of measures that seek to regulate and restrain the man's excesses, but he has never been *our* man, always Eristic's man. Everything we've tried to do has only been done if Eristic approved. Puritan is merely a puppet and Eristic pulls the strings, not the Association.

'Our problem is made more complex by the relationship that there has to be between the Council and the Comity. The relationship between the Comity and the Association is through the Administrator, as is the relationship between the Comity and the Council. Thus Puritan is pivotal, and if he is not to be trusted then in many ways the Comity is out of control.'

Throughout Izzat's statement the Bishop had been nodding his agreement and the chaplain had been taking notes. Izzat became aware of this note-taking and stopped talking, then, gaining eye contact with the Bishop, inclined his head towards the chaplain and raised his eyebrows. The Bishop placed his hand over his chaplain's notebook.

'I don't think we'll take notes, Neil. This conversation is off the record.'

Neil Thomas tore off the sheets, crumpled them up and threw them into a waste-paper basket.

'I'm sorry, John. Please continue.' The Bishop smiled at Izzat, who now understood why Robert was a bishop.

'I have said we have taken steps to resolve the problem of Puritan. In this file I have the accounts of the Comity that will, we believe, place his position as Administrator beyond salvage. However, with the Council backing him to the hilt, we will have to do more than simply get him out, we have to be able to replace him with a candidate that satisfies the Council and, naturally, the trustees of the Association. It is here where I believe that you can very usefully help. When Puritan leaves, it is imperative that we have a new Administrator ready to fill the position and one who is not connected with the Council and Ms Eristic. Previously, as you know, we have had a cleric and we are most anxious that we should seek another ordained person for the job. Further, should you be able to help us with such a candidate, we would increase the salary and make provision for the refurbishment of the living accommodation.'

The Bishop smiled and placed the fingers of his hands together. 'We have reached an identical conclusion, John, and Neil here has been very busy searching for just such a person. Strangely and coincidentally we think we have an ideal candidate who would fit your needs, and indeed ours: the Reverend Boon, who is at present a non-stipendiary priest at St Margaret's and St John's in Newell under Lea. I must stress that we have not approached him; however, I am confident that if offered the post he would be inclined to accept. He has never been in charge of a parish but has been a schoolmaster and then a lecturer at a college of further education. He has two sons and a daughter and has, for the last fifteen years, been a non-stipendiary curate and lately a stand-in priest.'

'Is he sound?' Izzat asked.

'Yes, he is and, what is more, he has the academic qualifications that makes him unable to be contested by Ms Eristic. The only requirement, John, is that you have to get rid of Mr Puritan first. I cannot move on the Reverend Boon until I have an assurance from you that Puritan is leaving.'

'I hope to be able to give you that assurance shortly, Robert.'

'Then if that is agreed, I have another meeting to attend. The life of a bishop is much more concerned with being seen than being seen doing something. I often think that the ideal bishop would be a robot dressed up in all the robes and with a permanent smile on its face. Neil will see you out, and when you have some news contact him – and don't make us wait too long, John.' He tapped the report in front of him and Izzat knew that if Puritan was not removed quickly the Association would become the target.

'It's good doing business with you, Robert, and I can see that you too should have a fearsome reputation.'

191

The Bishop smiled and waved his hand to dismiss the idea. The chaplain opened the door and Izzat left with the picture of the Bishop looking serious and watching his leaving from eyes that were summing him up.

Neil returned to the Bishop's office.

'Well, Robert, what did you think?'

The Bishop had sunk down into his chair and tiredness seemed to drape his face.

'He is a very clever man indeed, Neil, and I think an honest one. But he is also a fighter. I am glad that we chose not to seek to lay down conditions and demands, for had we done so he would have taken us on as well as the world. If I were a king in the Middle Ages, I would have chosen John Izzat as my champion.'

'But you have, Robert,' interrupted Neil. 'For who else will fight the demon Eristic for the Church if not John Izzat?'

'I don't believe he knows that, I believe he only sees his fight against Eristic as the Comity's fight.'

The two men looked out of the window into the Palace garden.

'I do like roses, Neil, but they are not right for the Bishop's Palace garden. Too many thorns, too many thorns.'

As Izzat walked back to the White Hart, he thought, Robert is frying bigger fish in this than St Margaret's Comity. He decided to walk through the city and left the Cathedral Close, going past a row of almshouses that proudly stated that they had been given to the city by the cathedral some three centuries ago, and he noted that they were still administered by the dean and chapter of the cathedral.

22

Mr Puritan Loses a Carport

Richard Puritan woke up to find that Felicity Eristic was having a bath. It would not be right to say that she had moved in, but she did seem to spend a great many nights at his flat, and the residents of the Comity could have been forgiven if, seeing her car almost always parked on gravel, they thought she had.

It was true that she spent a great deal of time at the Comity, using both the office facilities and Richard Puritan.

The DEC had offices, but they were shared with the Labour Party's local branch, and Ms Eristic was not happy about what she felt would seem to be a very overt connection, and so a great deal of the DEC's business had been carried out from the Comity address.

For Puritan, this state of affairs was less than perfect because it seemed to him that he had been demoted to more or less an office-boy-cum-stud to Felicity. Added to this was the fact that all the domestic chores had devolved to him, and so as well as doing secretarial duties for both the Comity and the DEC, he was also acting as housemaid, making meals and washing and cleaning.

No job, he reflected as he lay in bed, was too lowly for him to perform in a relationship in which his heart was no longer committed. His thoughts constantly strayed to the lovely Laura, and Felicity's constant demands on him put him in mind of slavery rather than joy.

A further problem nagged at his thoughts, and that was the fact that every memo he received from Mr Fribble of the Association seemed to demand more and more information and was charged with antagonism. Whereas the early months had been full of trust and understanding, now everything he sent to the Association came back with questions and restrictions. Felicity ignored all this and insisted that he took no notice of the flood of restrictions and demands. However, she was not an employee of the Association and he was.

Matters at the Comity had not improved, although they had not got significantly worse. The only difficulty that was current was that of the vacant cottage. Felicity Eristic had insisted that it should be awarded to a young immigrant family from Nigeria who had tripped up to the Council offices demanding to be housed because they were homeless. She had sent them along to the Comity, but at the time Richard was attending a meeting in London with Mr Fribble, and when Richard's part-time secretary had phoned through to ask him about furnishing the cottage, Fribble had overheard the conversation and had strictly forbidden the tenancy. The young couple concerned had therefore had to go back to their uncle, who was, it transpired, an attaché at the Nigerian Embassy with a very large house in the district. This uncle had turned rough with the Council, saying that his nephew was homeless because he was not prepared to let them stay in his house.

Eristic had taken up the couple's case and was insisting that they should stay at the Comity. Fribble threatened Puritan with his life if he allowed them to spend so much as 30 minutes in the area of St Margaret's. With a rare display of independence, Richard Puritan had hidden the keys to the cottage and was refusing to tell Felicity where they were.

The tenancy of the vacant cottage, although a matter of contention between the couple, was not enough to make Felicity sacrifice the comforts and convenience of the Comity or Richard Puritan. She would win in the end, of that she was certain, and so she waited until she could find out where the keys were, and then Fribble and the Association would have the job of eviction rather than agreement.

Such problems weighed upon the mind of Richard Puritan as he lay in bed listening to Felicity taking her bath. Uppermost in his thoughts, however, was a palpable longing for Laura Izzat. She was what he needed, he felt, to make his life worthwhile.

194

With her at his side he could do anything, go anywhere, be anything he chose to be. He admitted that he had only seen her once but still, he thought, you only needed one look for it to be love at first sight, and for him it had been love at first sight. He had not, he also admitted, liked her father. He was unsympathetic to enlightened views, and Felicity had said he was a racist. But that had nothing to do with Laura, who was, he knew in his heart, a thoroughly wonderful person.

Felicity called from the bathroom for him to get breakfast as she would not be very much longer, and grudgingly he got up and started to prepare her food.

After breakfast he sat down to prepare and submit the accounts for the last four-week period. Last month Felicity had done it for him as she had wanted him to run an errand, he had simply signed the completed sheets when he returned. He looked at the bills in front of him and the invoices that had been sent for payment and was amazed to see that there was an invoice from a builder for the construction of a carport. Even more surprising was the fact that the invoice stated that the sum required was the remaining £2,000, £1,500 having been paid in advance.

Distractedly he rapidly looked back to the previous month and saw that indeed he had shown the prepayment on the accounts. He then feverishly looked at the cheque stubs for that period and found in Felicity's writing a cheque stub made out for £1,500. He recalled that she had asked him to sign some cheques, which he thought were for normal supplies such as milk, tea and electricity. This cheque must have been included in that group.

Where was the carport? he wondered. He had not seen it, although he had to admit he did not usually take a very close look at the building, but surely he would have noticed a carport. Felicity came into the office and he questioned her about it.

'Well, the carport isn't actually built yet, Richard, but that company had done some work for me and the bill overran the budget and so, because I couldn't show the increased costs on the Palmerstone House accounts, we agreed that we would show it as a carport here, and later, on another job, I would accept a quote that was higher and they would carry out the work and then build the carport out the back. I don't mind about not having the carport yet so there's no problem.'

Puritan was aghast. 'You mean this money is to cover up overcharging on the work at Palmerstone House and you've put it through the Comity's books, Felicity?'

'Yes, if you like, although it wasn't overcharging, they had had to do more work than they originally thought, and I agreed it without realising that it breached the budget at Palmerstone House. There's no problem and, anyway, we will get the carport if we push through the alteration works needed here. I can't see what you're worrying about. I'm going to get the management contract for this place and then it will all be squared up.'

'But it's a capital project, Felicity, and I have no power to initiate or agree any capital project without the Welfare Fund's written agreement. I only have power to sign for current costs – day-to-day expenses. Something like this is a sackable offence. I can't think how it went through last month without Fribble burning the phone lines over it. And the fact that there is no carport – it's impossible.'

'I've told you, Richard, I'm going to get the management contract for this place. I've seen Fribble and Izzat, I've given them my proposal and it is simply a matter of time. Once they have signed, then the whole of the finances both capital and current expenditure come under my control and I can assure you, should you continue to worry, that I will not put you in the dock over the wretched carport. Now there must be something more valuable for you to do than worrying about the carport. You can go downstairs and see if the milk has been delivered and make us a cup of tea. Sheila Cam is coming over this morning to go over the agenda for this evening's meeting of the Welfare Committee on the Frail and Elderly and so I have to look at those papers before she comes. There's also the newsletter to write and get out. This week we should concentrate on anti-foxhunting and animal welfare. Go on, Richard, there's no point in sitting there like a sick pig.'

Richard went to get the milk because he felt so sick and he hoped the walk would do him some good. That and the fresh

196

air, he thought, might make the whole problem of the carport seem less dreadful and less threatening. It did not help, and as he made the tea, he thought about all the threats that Fribble had made to him about ever letting any capital projects slip through the accounts, and the dire warnings as to what would happen if he did not obey the rule to the very letter.

He also cast about for some way of getting round the problem, some means whereby he wouldn't have to submit the invoice to Fribble. If he hasn't spotted last month's prepayment, perhaps if I don't send in the invoice it will pass without notice, he thought. These were the hopes and fears that filled his mind as he went over the carport problem again and again.

Puritan could find no answer and could not settle down to the newsletter. He would have to send in his accounts, and the only course of action that seemed in any way possible was for him to lose the invoice for the carport. He made up the accounts, leaving out the carport invoice, and although Felicity was hovering he sealed the envelope and placed it in the post tray. Regarding the invoice, he simply dropped it into the waste-paper basket and hoped with all his heart that it would go away and never come back, although in his heart he knew that this would not happen and that in time the carport would come back to haunt him.

Felicity Eristic's co-committee member Sheila Cam arrived more or less at the appointed time and Felicity and Sheila took over the general office, leaving Puritan to kick his heels and spend some time wandering round the cottages. This was a lonely pursuit because he had noticed that whenever he walked round the cottages all the residents had their doors shut and the place seemed deserted.

These days he seldom saw the residents unless he left a note for them to see him, and even then the meetings were tense and very short, with the tenants giving monosyllabic answers to his questions and looking very uncomfortable sitting in his office.

On one occasion he had tried to get Mrs Hall to talk to him about how she was getting on following her husband's death, but she had sat in her chair and simply repeated that things were all right.

Ever since Felicity had more or less decided to make his flat her home, he had found himself increasingly sidelined as she took over his space and minimised his functions. He had always been a solitary person but now, although living with Felicity, he found himself lonely. Her friends became, in theory, his, her schedules became his schedules, her daily activities crowded out his, and it seemed to him that he was becoming more and more invisible until Felicity needed him to perform some action or run some errand. His job had become simply a minor matter in her day and his priorities had been demoted to things he had to fit in between Felicity's needs and Felicity's demands.

Most of all he felt lonely. He knew her job was bigger and more important, that her income was higher and her influence greater, but lurking in his mind was always the thought that if he could only win the heart of Laura Izzat, he would not be lonely and would be able to grow in his own as well as her estimation.

Lately, he had entertained the thought that if he adopted the ideas of Izzat, the great man's daughter might come to see him in a more favourable light. Change, he felt, could right his wrongs and find a way into Laura's affections. He had contemplated the notion that he would visit the Reverend Hartwell and ask his advice. But always Felicity was there to make him do this or that and run him about like some battered motor car.

Now the matter of the carport returned to his mind and he saw that it was a time bomb waiting to blow him up and scatter him in little pieces all over the Wiltshire countryside. How, he wondered, had Fribble let the last report slip through without comment or investigation? Perhaps Fribble was waiting for the report by the surveyor who had visited two weeks previously to prepare a report on the fabric of the building. But the surveyor wouldn't have reported on the carport because there was no carport there to report upon.

He had left out the invoice for the completion of the carport and this, he felt, would go in his favour if the matter did blow up. The builder would get on to Felicity for the money rather than on to him, so he could string the matter out for some months, promising Felicity that he was sending the invoices to

198

Fribble and waiting for Fribble to pay them. But what of the first invoice that was now in Fribble's office?

There was nobody about the Comity as he walked round it. All the front doors were shut and he could have been in a ghost town.

He remembered his mother and knew she had been, and probably still was, a very sociable woman. She had once said to him when he had asked her why she was always going out and leaving him alone: 'Because when I'm out and in the pub I don't have to be myself, I can be what other people want me to be. When I'm here with you, I have to be myself and I'm not very interesting, and you're not either.'

He had after that tried very hard to be interesting. He had read the newspaper from cover to cover and tried to speak to her about the things he had read, and he had tried to take an interest in his mother's dress and the way she looked. But it had not worked and she had still gone out almost every evening leaving him alone.

At that time he had decided that he wasn't interesting, and it had coloured his whole life. As he grew up and went into other classes at school and then left and went into a squat and then on to university, he had always known that he wasn't interesting, and there was nothing he could do about it. When his uncle turned him out, he reasoned then that it was because he wasn't interesting. Later, he should have worked out that it was because his uncle and his mother were finding it hard to have the sort of sexual relationship that they wanted with him constantly in the small flat, but Richard Puritan believed that it was because he wasn't interesting, and it became another confirmation of this bald and inescapable fact.

That he entertained an idea that with the lovely Laura Izzat he might stop being uninteresting and become a person others would like to know says more for the optimism that exists in the human condition than any sense of reality.

As he trudged back towards the main Comity building he was surprised to see two photographers taking pictures of the buildings. He had certainly not ordered any photography and wondered why they were there and who had sent them. As he came up to them, he asked them what they were doing.

199

'Taking photographs of the buildings. What did you think we were doing?'

'You can't just take photographs of buildings without permission,' Puritan asserted. 'You have to ask permission and then wait until it's either granted or refused.'

'We've got permission from the owners, the RRAWF in London. They asked us to take the photos. Here, it's in this letter, and there's an order with it, see.'

Puritan looked at the letter. It was on the Association's headed notepaper and asked the company to take photographs of all the buildings on the Comity land. The letter and the order were signed by Fribble, and the firm, Puritan saw from the address, was a firm of architectural photographers.

'What do they want the pictures for?' he asked.

'Search me,' said the young man who was obviously the assistant and the one that carried the boxes and set up the camera.

'Probably a brochure,' said the man taking the photographs. 'A lot of our work is used in brochures. Will there be any problem in going into the fields to take pictures of the back of the cottages?'

'No,' Puritan replied. 'Both are fallow right now and won't be sown for a few weeks. It should be all right.'

The young man had started to pack up the equipment and the older man smiled at Puritan and started to walk out of the Comity through the arch. He stopped and turned. 'If you're speaking to Mr Fribble, tell him the pictures should be with him in two days, OK?'

Back in the Comity office, Puritan told Felicity about the photographers and that he had been told that the pictures were for a brochure.

'I can't believe that they are for any brochure,' she retorted. 'If we're taking over the management of the place, they won't need brochures.'

'Well if it's not for a brochure, what else could it be for?' he asked.

'How do I know?' she said. 'I'm not that snivelling Fribble. But they're wasting their money anyway, because by the time I've finished with this place it won't look anything like the sleepy

200

run-down place it is now. We've just completed our plans for the Council's submission, and I can tell you Sheila is impressed. The key to it is to set down a rigid set of guidelines for all sheltered housing in the area and to place the inspection of such housing under the control of the Council. The guidelines are so health and safety geared that nobody could object, and once they are in place I doubt if a single voluntary or charitable body will be able to afford to implement them. Along with the guidelines, we're also asking the Council to adopt a policy of awarding the management of all such housing to my company if the bodies running them fail to implement the guidelines. It will be a short step from there to being able to buy the freeholds of the properties, and before you can say frail, we'll have a portfolio of very valuable sites ripe for development.'

'What will you do with the people in the sheltered housing, if you sell the land?' Puritan asked.

'Move them to less valuable places. The old mental hospital is vacant now. We could refurbish that a bit. The idea is to concentrate them, which will produce economies of scale. If instead of being spread about they were all gathered together, one medical team, one cleaning group and one catering unit could service them. It's about economies of scale, Richard. These scattered places use up too much resource. The cathedral, for example, has got some sheltered houses that contain just two or three units. That's just plain uneconomic. The optimum number is somewhere about a hundred units to each site, and they certainly don't need to be in prime residential areas either.'

Puritan noted that Felicity had become a very different person since she had been appointed managing director of the enterprise company. Even the holy Covinous had been pushed onto the back burner of her mind. Certainly, apart from sexual couplings, he had become nothing to her. Only the other Labour Party members and nominees on the board of the company received any respect nowadays from Ms Eristic.

'I don't think it's so much about economics as it is about keeping these people happy and independent for as long as possible, Felicity.'

'You're soft and stupid, Richard. You don't get anywhere by

playing the game by other people's rules; you make the big time by playing by your own rules and making other people think that they're *the* rules. Any fool can be a failure, you know. It doesn't take brains, ability or talent. Success, on the other hand, only comes if you fight for it tooth and nail, twenty-four hours of every day, and once you've got it you still have to fight to keep it.'

Puritan was not sure if he wanted success on such terms.

23

A Peal of Alarms

The arrival of the Reverend Boon at the Bishop's Palace coincided with a downpour of rain that rendered Mr Boon very wet and very apprehensive. He had no idea why he had been summoned to the Palace, and although he had met the Bishop when he visited the parish, his recall of the gentleman in question was hazy. He did, however, remember Neil Thomas in greater detail and recalled that he had instantly liked him.

The rain had dampened his spirits, and chilled him and he wondered if this invitation to visit was in some way associated with the fact that his clerical career was a classic case of always being the bridesmaid and never the bride.

Since his retirement from full-time teaching he had not, he felt, been able to settle. He liked being the curate at St Margaret's and St John's well enough, but he was used to a more senior role in matters and his position as curate precluded this.

Neil Thomas was waiting for his arrival and had the door open before he reached the steps. He was welcomed warmly and his coat was taken from him as he was ushered into Neil Thomas's office and placed next to the radiator to warm up. A cup of tea was produced, and all the time Neil Thomas fussed over his comfort as if, rather than being a lowly curate from an out-of-town parish, he was an archbishop.

Ten minutes after his arrival, the Bishop rang to tell his chaplain to bring the visitor in and, as he entered, the Bishop stood up to greet him with the warmest of warm smiles.

'It really is very good of you to make time to visit me, Mr Boon. Let's sit at the table and discuss our business and then I have arranged for lunch, which I do believe you will find as good as any meal you have eaten for a very long time, although I think we should agree not to compare it with Mrs Palmer's excellent cooking which is truly superb.'

Mr Boon sat at the conference table and the Bishop sat next to him, while the chaplain sat opposite.

'A problem has arisen, Mr Boon, and after a lot of thought, we felt that you would be the ideal person to share this problem and perhaps even provide the solution.'

Boon was wary; he knew the way that the top brass in the Church spoke about problems when they really meant disagreements or even conflicts. The Church had its own vocabulary. For problems read conflict, for challenge read correction, for unity read submission and for interesting read disagreement. There were many other euphemisms that littered ecclesiastical speech, all of which attempted to prevent the accusation that the words were deliberately designed to wound the listener or the listener's interests.

'If I can help in any way, then of course I will,' he assured the two men. 'What is the problem?'

'Well, Mr Boon, it is the St Margaret's Comity in your very parish. We are perplexed with several aspects of the way the place is being administered.'

'As you know,' Neil Thomas spoke for the first time since entering the Bishop's office, 'the Bishop visited the Comity. The residents' story alarmed us, and as we are the owners of the head lease, we cannot allow the matter to go on. Something has to be done.'

'But surely it is a matter for the Administrator and the trade association that runs the Comity.'

The Bishop rose and walked to the window and spoke from there. 'Well, it is rather complicated. You see, one of the conditions in the lease we granted was that the Administrator should be a member of the clergy. At the time of the present Administrator's appointment we had no suitable candidate and so we were prepared to allow a lay person to take the position. And there is the nub of the problem; we still have no candidate, unless we make one. Normally, had the appointment been successful, we would have been happy to let the matter ride, but following my visit, I am convinced that it would not be right to continue. We have to have a suitable candidate if we are to set the Comity on the road to becoming what it should be – a tranquil ark for its residents.'

'How can I help, Bishop?'

'I would like you to consider the possibility of becoming the Administrator of the Comity, Mr Boon. Naturally I am unable to offer you the post, because at present it is not in my gift, but I have every confidence that it is only a matter of time. Would you be able to consider such a post? I know it is not a parish of your own, nor is it directly under the Church. However, the salary would represent an improvement and I am anxious to incorporate all such sheltered housing into our "out-reach policy": what do you think, Mr Boon?'

'I would be very happy to be both of use to the Church and to the residents of the Comity, Bishop.'

'Well, that's splendid, isn't it, Neil? I think we deserve our lunch now, Mr Boon. After lunch, Neil here will fill you in on the details, but right now let us eat. You are an excuse, you know, Mr Boon. When I have visitors I can order much better lunches than when it is just Neil and me – I expect it's wicked, but the cook is so good when given his head that perhaps we can put it down as staff motivation. What do you think?'

In the offices of Barratry, Barratry and Simony, a briefing meeting was under way. Both partners were in attendance and a draft report was in the process of being made ready for submission to John Izzat.

'I have to congratulate all concerned with this report. It has fulfilled our expectations and we now have a solid base from which our client may proceed, if he sees fit. I will run through the main points again so that we may collectively see how the information weaves the main threads of our findings together into the possibility of action.'

Rustin Olid gave, what some cynics in the offices described as a *rigor mortis* smile.

'Firstly, Mr Puritan has convictions for minor, but neverthe-

205

less, significant public order offences committed at various civil disturbances. The so-called poll tax riot notched up a court appearance, as did a disturbance outside the South African and the American embassies. A road-widening scheme also added to his tally, as did Greenham Common. In all these cases he was bound over to keep the peace, which naturally he ignored.

'There is also a civil action against him, with a court appearance for squatting. In this matter he had to be forcibly removed from a council flat in Camden. Youthful excesses, perhaps, but they do represent a picture of a not very law-abiding person, a drifter on the radical political waves of society and a failure. There is also a criminal conviction for possessing a small amount of a controlled substance. It is, however, important to notice that none of these events were mentioned on his application form for the job of Administrator of the St Margaret's Comity, which is important in the light of the fact that the form in question calls for specific information of any civil or criminal actions involving the applicant in the last ten years. His own mother's comments on her son are not important in a legal sense however, they might play a significant role when it comes to preventing Mr Puritan from taking further action against his employer. Few of us would like such a comment read out at an industrial tribunal, namely "He was always a little shit and bloody devious. He caused trouble at school and at home."

'Turning to his education, there seems little of interest here. Regardless of what his mother says of him, the schools thought him more sinned against than sinning, and he was generally considered a rather quiet and withdrawn boy with few friends or interests. At university, again he was seen as a misfit but harmless, although he joined in the radical student union activities, but never as a prime mover, always as one of the bloody infantry.

'What is interesting is the confidential report we have obtained about the man's relationship with the DSS – his only source of income for most of his life. The DSS viewed him, it would seem, as untrustworthy and are convinced that he conspired with others to defraud the benefit system. They could never catch him out but remain convinced that his many claims

206

were largely bogus and were part of a far larger scam master-minded by others. How he received his instructions or passed on the money was never established. The DSS investigators thought it was by some kind of code as he seldom met anybody else on their list. It is interesting, though, to note that he was usually in the first ten claimants for every new benefit claims trend that became established.

'Ms Eristic has proved much more fruitful. Her family loved and indeed loves her dearly, although she has shunned them and refuses to have anything to do with them. An only child, she was doted on and spoilt to the point which some may think was absurdity by both parents. She still receives a monthly allowance from her mother of one thousand pounds.

'Good at school – which was a girls' public school – Felicity shone, and although never popular with her peers, she was popular with her teachers. As is often the result of being grossly spoilt as a child, Felicity's academic track record was not good, she just scraped through her exams and then left as soon as possible. She did the travelling bit, although there was always financial support from her parents, and when she returned to Britain, she lived with a young man who was on the extreme left of the Communist Party. She has espoused almost every radical cause and has a string of minor convictions for breach of the peace, motoring offences, drunk and disorderly, possession, criminal damage and even shop theft. Whilst this is of passing interest, it is what we would expect. However, it is when we look at the people with whom she has had relationships that we find real gold for our purpose. A Labour MP for a riot-prone inner-city North London area was once her lover, and there are two active members of the Socialist Workers Party, one who has recently become the agent in a far left constituency in Liverpool. There has also been an Italian politician, who is now in jail, our Mr Puritan and a French mayor who marched through Paris with various student groups. But when Felicity discovered that she was really a lesbian, that's when we find the true pay-dirt for our case. Her lover was and perhaps still is *Mrs* Covinous, wife of the TV presenter and tame academic. Felicity and Tabatha Covinous have been having an affair for some years.

But more amusing, Felicity has also been having an affair with Mrs Covinous's husband Justin, without, we believe, either husband or wife knowing of the other's affair.

'The Covinouses were the two key players in Felicity's appointment to her present position. They signed her application and were the referees she used. They both lobbied behind the scenes for her and endorsed her policies and bailed her out, as far as we can tell. Ms Eristic plays husband against wife when there is a need, much as she has always played her parents against each other to get her own way.

'Of late we have discovered that there is a far more serious game afoot. It seems that Mrs Covinous and Ms Eristic are engaged in a very complicated plot to firstly move Mrs Covinous's considerable fortune safely away so that Mrs Covinous can divorce her husband, who would not be able to claim any part of it. How we have obtained this information is naturally very confidential, but we have been able to verify it and know it to be true.

'In the course of these transactions, Ms Eristic has committed perjury. She has sworn affidavits that she knew were false and she has even forged Mr Covinous's signature on a delivery note for some documents. The transfer of Mrs Covinous's wealth is almost complete, and we believe that Mrs Covinous intends to cite Ms Eristic as the cause of the marriage breakdown. If the divorce does proceed, then Mrs Covinous will claim half of her husband's estate. It seems, on the face of it, foolproof, providing both Mrs Covinous and Ms Eristic stick together, which is our lever.'

David Fetor then spoke: 'In relation to the actual management of the Comity, we have discovered that it is possible to locate the management company of the Comity in any EU desired country. We have made a thorough search of the legislation governing such charitable housing schemes in the EU and believe that were it to be registered in Spain or Italy, it would be completely illegal for a local council in the UK to enforce its will without extremely expensive and protracted negotiations in the country of registration. If the management company was, for example, located in Sicily, it is our belief that its distinct regional independence and almost total lack of accountable civic administration would prohibit any possibility of a take-over. Further, we have established that should the Council seek to exercise control, we could change the status of the place from sheltered housing to a religious order responsible for caring for the elderly. This would prevent any incursion.'

The report was finalised and despatched to John Izzat by special messenger, with a special letter suggesting a recommended course of action.

John Izzat's bill would be massive, but Barratry, Barratry and Simony were specialist solicitors, exclusive, and provided a unique service for those who could afford it.

In the Council offices, the Council leader was in a less than happy mood. She had received a phone call from Party Headquarters and she had in front of her a letter from the MP for the area. Both the call and the letter had expressed the same point to the leader, namely that the much heralded and needed inward investment by the DiHsui Company was turning pear-shaped because of concerns voiced by DiHsui's major customer in Europe, NTR plc.

It had always been understood that the massive DiHsui factory would be built in the Swindon area, given generous Government grants and Council and regional help, as well as a major grant of EU money. The DiHsui Corporation made electronic components that were used in hi-fis, radios and TVs and other electronic leisure products. The company would employ some thousand workers in the factory but would spawn other services and attract other companies to the area, as well as provide an injection of cash to the local university for research and development work. It had been the dream inward investment project and something that both the Party, the Council and the Government had worked very hard to achieve. The key to the project was that National TV Retailers plc, or NTR plc, as it is known in the City – was DiHsui's distributor in Europe and the company that incorporated its DiHsui components into its own branded goods – would guarantee DiHsui a long-term contract. This, it now seemed, was a matter that was in some doubt.

The DiHsui negotiating team had tried to discover what it was that caused the doubt, but all the NTR people would publicly say was that the contract might infringe EU law on competition. Privately, however, the whisper was that the NTR chairman was unhappy with the Council and felt that it had social policies that were likely to be disruptive to its interest.

Officially, the problem was the EU competition problem and the other matter was not spoken of, and yet it was made plain by the DiHsui negotiating team to the DTI negotiating team that the Council could resolve the problem by stepping back from certain proposals. The problem for the leader was that she had no clear idea what those proposals were. Indeed, nobody identified the proposals because nobody concerned in the negotiations really knew what they were. Even DiHsui did not know, and thus the leader of the Council was faced with the prospect of being held responsible for a breakdown in a vital inward investment project all for the want of a little flexibility on her Council's part.

The answer for the leader was to call a meeting of the heads of all the Council departments. They assembled in her office and she asked the question – 'How have we upset NTR plc?'

The majority of the heads of department looked remarkably blank, although there was a minority who could not swear that it was not something their department had or had not done. Simon Tottery, Head of Social Welfare, was particularly concerned, because he knew of the efforts being made by Felicity Eristic to purloin the sheltered-housing complex owned by the trade association headed by the chairman of NTR plc.

'It could, leader, be the activities of the Frail and Elderly Committee,' he suggested.

'What have they got to do with NTR plc, Simon?'

'Well, the chief executive is the Chairman of the trade association that owns the sheltered-housing complex know as St Margaret's Comity at Newell under Lea, leader.'

'And what are we doing to this St Margaret's Comity, Mr Tottery?'

'We, the Council that is, are doing nothing whatsoever to St Margaret's Comity, leader, but Ms Eristic's Development Enterprise Company – the DEC – has proposed – and it is only a proposal, leader – to take over the management of St Margaret's Comity in order to bring it into line with the latest legislation and regulations of the Social Welfare Department. But they are only proposals and Ms Eristic has only submitted them to the trade association, nothing more.'

'And how were these *proposals* received by the association, Mr Tottery?'

'I gather not very well, leader. It seems that Ms Eristic and the association's secretary, Mr Fribble didn't exactly hit it off, if you know what I mean.'

'No, I don't know what you mean, Mr Tottery. We have in front of us what is perhaps the biggest inward investment project that this council, no, damn it, the *country*, has seen, and Ms Eristic and her DEC have upset the chief executive of the major company involved in this whole project. Is that what you're telling this meeting, Mr Tottery?'

'On a point, leader.' The Head of Finance observed, 'It is not Ms Eristic's DEC, I believe it is your DEC. You are the Chairman of the Development Enterprise Company, Ms Eristic is simply an appointed servant, albeit managing director.'

'I know all about the structure of the DEC, thank you,' answered the leader, glowering at the Head of Finance. 'What I don't know is how this matter has been allowed to foul up the effing DiHsui project without any of you involved having the wit to see the ramifications and firing off a maroon so that we could delay or alter the damn proposals that Eristic was putting forward.'

'But they went before the Council in early September, leader, and were agreed and passed,' a mild-mannered department head stated.

'Well, the whatsit's hit the fan now and we'll have to move to defuse the matter – and quickly. I've already had our beloved MP bending my ear as well as Party HQ, who have been contacted unofficially by the DTI. Get Eristic in here.'

'She's out, leader.' Simon Tottery, it seemed, could only give bad news to his leader, and the fact hurt him a great deal more than anybody else in the room.

'Contact her and have her come back from wherever she is. I want to see her and thrash this thing out. I want it settled.'

'But we don't know that it is the matter of St Margaret's Comity that is the problem,' the Head of Public Relations said. 'It would seem likely but we don't *know*, and it could be something a great deal worse – a planning matter or a trading standard blitz on NTR shops. We don't know that it's this Comity place, Leader.'

'Well, until you come up with something else, I will assume that it is and try to sort it. Meanwhile, every department head should look through all the business of their departments to see if they can come up with anything else that involves either NTR or the DiHsui or NTR top people.'

The heads of department left to search every nook and cranny for NTR plc and the name Izzat or Fribble.

Simon Tottery made straight for the phone to call Felicity, and only now did he allow himself a slight feeling of happiness.

Passed over by the Chair of the Social Services Committee, ignored by the likes of Felicity Eristic, treated as an irrelevance by almost everybody in his department, he now knew that his way had been the right way. The advice he had given and which had been regarded as nonsense had been advice that should have been heeded not ignored. He knew it would make no difference now, because he had agreed to early retirement on, he admitted, very favourable terms.

He would soon be gone and there would be no trace of his ever having worked all those years for the Council. He had reached the top, and having climbed the ladder, had found that his ladder led to nothing but a blank and cheerless wall.

He rang the Comity, and after five rings, the phone was answered by Mr Puritan.

'Could I speak to Ms Eristic? It's Simon Tottery.'

Ms Eristic was no longer at the Comity, she had left to visit Palmerstone House. He rang Palmerstone House but Felicity hadn't arrived, and so he left a message. He debated whether to inform the Council leader that Ms Eristic had not been reached and decided that his day had been too full of difficult meetings, and so he found a pressing appointment that he just had to attend and left the office, telling his secretary that when Ms Eristic phoned in to tell her to come back to her office, as the leader was very anxious to talk with her.

In this fashion the fate of Mr Puritan and Ms Felicity Eristic was being settled without their knowledge or their agreement.

In offices in many parts of the country, matters were in train that would bring about a challenge for both people – and they would need more than their normal wit and intelligence to overcome it.

24

The Falling Leaves of Love

As autumn shades into winter, London is not a place of unalloyed pleasure. The pavements are wet, the streets often windswept, and there is about the people a pinched and hurrying gait that suggests that they have little or no time for anything other than to get where they are going with as little fuss as is humanly possible. The daylight is often in short supply and the days of themselves are shortening. Any English city is joyless at this time of year, but London, because it is larger and the capital city, lacks perhaps that warmth that is generated by people who know and love their home city, come rain or shine. London is a city of strangers, strangers to London and often strangers to Britain, and that fact tends to take away any softness that even adversity produces.

It is surprising, therefore, that whilst, for all the other residents of London, the dreary fact of late autumn forced them into the particular scurrying London gait, for two people, namely Laura Izzat and Joe Staunch, the dullness of London streets disappeared, and for those two brave souls, London was awash with colour and bright with expectation.

I might be cynical and indeed jaundiced about love, but I have to admit that love had, for these two cupid-touched individuals, transformed the capital city and turned it into a wonderland of discovery and adventure.

Almost every evening now, Laura and Joe were engaged in some new delight and some new discovery. The chance finding of a road called Saffron Street off Farringdon Road sidetracked them into finding out the reason for its name, and this led them to discover Old Sea Coal Lane, connecting Farringdon Road with Cheapside. It was these interesting quirky historical facts that served as grouting for their love, and so, joined together, the young people spent days and evenings delving ever deeper into the joys of their emerging relationship.

Love is, or so the wisdom of old folk says, either all honey or all muck, and for Laura and Joe it was all honey. Some more sour people might indeed have said that they were working a honey seam, so sweet were the days and nights, so joyful were the pleasures they managed to find in each other's company.

John Izzat had been surprised at this turn of events, but had grown to like Joe Staunch and was happy that Laura had found somebody who could wipe away the dark memory of the death of Elizabeth. He was not inclined to take a view regarding his daughter's blossoming relationship with Joe Staunch beyond the thought that it produced in his daughter a joy and happiness that he had not seen since her mother died.

When it came to the Covinouses, Tabatha was aware of her son's preoccupation with Laura, but as she was engaged upon a business that might shortly cause her to revert to her maiden name, she found little time to express even a mild curiosity. Justin Covinous was in the middle of writing a new book and was thus totally unaware that his stepson Joe was even going out with anybody. So Joe's epoch-making, world-revolving, season-bursting love passed almost unnoticed – proving, perhaps, that there is no better guardian of privacy than indifference.

Such considerations did not trouble the two lovers. Love is blind and very often daft as well as deaf. This happy felicity allowed Joe and Laura to act and behave as if all the known world was both aware and approving of their new-found love. In part this view had some validity as the lovely Laura was no longer in circulation, forcing all eligible young men to search for a new object of their love and fortune.

While Laura and Joe discovered London and love, they also drew closer and closer to each other. It thus became obvious even to the two lovers that the journey they had embarked upon would lead to an unsurprising conclusion.

Matters came to a head not in some romantic restaurant but in a bookshop in Charing Cross Road. They had gone to the

215

shop to look for a book on Bridget Riley, a painter who enchanted both Laura and Joe. The book wasn't available and the shop assistant offered to get it in for Joe.

'When it arrives, I'll ring you or your wife,' the assistant said in a rather bored voice, and at that moment Joe looked at Laura and Laura looked at Joe, and both of them knew that something had been said that was massively profound to them. The presumption had been made about them by the rather bored shop assistant, and the simple fact of this presumption seemed all at once to both of them, so blindingly obvious, so magically right, so wonderfully exciting, that for a moment both lovers could only stand and stare at the shop assistant and then into each other's eyes.

This truth dawns upon most young lovers, and whether it is seen as marriage or simply living together, the fact in itself becomes inescapable, and when that happens suddenly, what was until that moment a matter of choice has been lost and the joining together has become an imperative.

Laura, realising this, blushed – something that she did not usually do – and the feeling of blushing, plus the truth of the discovery that she was to become Joe's wife, stopped her heart for a second. She knew that the shop was still there, she knew she was an adult and well beyond the blushing age, and yet simply because by his look Joe had acknowledged the fact that neither had faced until that very moment, she was blushing and looking down at the floor in a confusion that, had she been asked, she would not have been able to explain.

Joe also knew that he had reached that point when there was no need to formally ask the question, because Laura had answered him with her eyes.

The shop assistant somehow managed to miss this earth-shaking business and, having all the information needed, turned away to serve another customer.

Love, as I have said, is blind, and this singular lack of reaction on the part of the shop assistant and the other customers did not cause a flutter of concern in the minds of the lovers. Joe and Laura had recognised the inevitability of their engagement, and this central fact had suddenly turned their world upside-down and changed, perhaps for ever, their lives.

Readers should not scoff or laugh at this knockout blow of fate upon Joe and Laura. Most of us have travelled along the self-same road, have gazed moon-struck into the eyes of our beloved and felt that now, at last, the world would be a different, better, more manageable place. Just because we have found that love does not cure every ill and solve every problem cannot devalue the experience nor yet blunt the hope that love brings – even in a bookshop in Charing Cross Road.

Now the question that raced through Joe's mind was where they both could go to talk about this world-shattering development. He recognised that a bookshop wasn't the ideal place to hold hands and pledge – well, his love to Laura. There were a thousand things that needed to be said, discussed and settled. Also, he felt, the occasion had to be marked. He thought of champagne or something but his mind was in such a whirl he had no idea what he should do.

For Laura, too, there was an equal uncertainty. They had to get away, out of the shop. They had to talk, to settle the hundreds of questions that this unspoken agreement to get married had raised. She wondered if she should take charge of the situation, or whether it would be better to leave it to Joe – a question that wouldn't have crossed her mind when they walked into the bookshop together.

One thing was certain, she could not stay in the bookshop after blushing. In this, although Laura Izzat was probably one of the most intelligent people in the shop, she was still, at that moment, a girl who had seen the inevitability of love and had blushed at her own immense feelings of joy and happiness.

They almost ran out of the shop and up Charing Cross Road towards Oxford Street, which they reached without stopping, so great was their need to be away from the bookshop. They came to a sandwich bar which had an empty table and went in. Laura sat at the table and Joe ordered two cups of tea.

Strangely now they were both shy about the whole thing. Neither wanted to say that which they had never said, to admit that they intended to be married.

Laura, however, somehow knew that she would have to raise the subject.

'Well, so the shop will be phoning you or your wife, Joe. Does she know?'

'The assistant obviously saw us as an old married couple, or they're in the marriage brokerage business.' He looked uncomfortable, knowing that he should have addressed the question directly not tried to be flippant.

'Well, if they are into marriage brokerage, then they should have instructed you on asking for my hand instead of selling arty books.'

'Will you marry me, Laura? Not that I think I'm much of a catch, but I would like to marry you.'

'Of course I'll marry you, Joe, but not until I come down from Cambridge – with a first, naturally.'

'God, Laura, that's years in the future. I want to marry you tomorrow, later this evening if it can be arranged. I don't want to wait until hell freezes or until I'm old and grey.'

'I couldn't give up law just to marry some starving artist. My future's all planned out, and anyway I seriously believe that everybody should have some skill, some profession, or some way of earning a living – even if it's only being able to paint an approximate likeness.'

'There's more skill than you'll ever know in being able to paint a likeness, Laura – there's years of drinking and hanging around with absolutely mindless people who have only one ambition and that is to get drunk. I've put time in on my art and I don't want to wait for you to take your finals simply so that you can earn a living.'

'One of us has to be able to pay the rent and the bills, Joe. And anyway, we have to tell my father and your parents, we have to sort out a whole mass of things before we could possibly get married.'

The world had spun for Joe and Laura, had tilted on its axis, and the thousands of details that had to be settled would all be finalised by the time they were married.

While Joe and Laura were discovering the remarkable newness of love, in a sandwich bar in Oxford Street, Felicity Eristic and

Justin Covinous were engaged in another altogether more jaded form of the same condition.

The location was in a hotel near Victoria Station, and Justin had met Felicity to have both sex and, more importantly, a discussion on the way her business empire was going. The two met regularly and clandestinely – or so Justin believed.

They spent the whole afternoon together, and after the sex, which was an urgent and almost animal business for them both, they relaxed and drank wine and their conversation ranged over Justin's latest work and Felicity's schemes and ambitions.

Such talk was always useful to both parties, and because it was held in the afterglow of passion, Justin was never watchful or on guard. This is often the reality with powerful men who convince themselves that because the girl has given herself to him then she is under his total control and there is no need to be on guard or even circumspect. In the case of Ms Eristic this was certainly not the case and, had Justin but known it, the information gleaned by Felicity at these meetings was noted and committed to her diary the same evening, whilst an edited version was not infrequently passed to Tabatha.

Justin, however, lay in total ignorance of Felicity's double or even triple dealings and tended to congratulate himself on his powerful sexual attraction and his ability to carry on the affair with the utmost discretion and the utmost pleasure and, further, at a fairly reasonable cost.

This afternoon, Justin was full of two matters of importance. Firstly, he had this odd feeling that Tabby had a lover, although all his efforts to trace or find out about this untraceable person had come to naught. He now contemplated employing a private detective but was uncertain of the way to go about it. He was thus very relieved when Felicity offered to do it for him and, as long as he picked up the bill, she would provide the detective's reports to him when they were together on their regular weekly meetings. In this way, Felicity said, he would never have any papers or reports on him and Tabby could never find out.

'If only I had married you, Flicky, rather than Tabby. You're so supportive and practical, but on a teacher's salary there is just no way I could keep us.'

This, of course, was Justin's public face of poverty, and although he knew that Felicity knew all about his really lavish lifestyle, he could not change from his constant dirge about low pay, even in bed with his mistress.

The other matter that concerned him was that Peter Oser, another pundit used by the television companies to sound off on subjects of political philosophy, had been appearing more often than he had, and Justin was deeply worried that he was fading as the resident 'independent' authority on matters political.

'Peter was on the BBC twice, on Channel 4 and on BBC 2 and, I hear has been approached to make a full-length programme called *Great Thoughts and Great Thinkers Who Shaped Our Lives*. That's a provisional title and Oser has suggested a better title, *Ideas Power*.'

'I think both titles are rubbish,' commented Felicity.

'It's the idea that irritates me so. I floated out an idea that is a thousand times better, and so was my title – *The Shape of Ideas*. That's a title that would sell and the idea is so much more attractive – looking at the common backgrounds of great thinkers and the things that formed their writings, and then looking at their ideas and the impact that such ideas have had on societies. That's much more powerful, isn't it, Flicky, and yet those creeps at the Beeb have chosen Oser. I should complain, but I've so much on and my publishers are chasing me for copy for the new book, and I also have to do Open-Uni stuff as well.'

Felicity was concerned, and shared the problem, but she had problems of her own and now was the time to air them.

'I've been ordered by the Council leader to lay off the Comity take-over. It seems that some megga-important inward-investment deal is being held up because our suggestion to take over the management of the Comity clashes with the interests of the RRAWF, under the ever watchful of eye of John Izzat. She was not pleased with our upsetting the godly Izzat and not over-keen on the whole idea of the company taking over the other sheltered-housing units. She banged on about account-ability, or rather the lack of it. If I lay off, it will put the whole schedule back a year, and that means the DEC will be pushed to show a profit – in fact, it will make a loss.'

Covinous understood the seriousness of this development. Hiding behind Eristic, he had been able to manipulate the affairs of the DEC, which was his own particular form of entryism. Ever since the local party had floated the idea he had instructed Eristic to support it and had spoken – as a disinterested observer – to the various people both on the Council and in the Party, endorsing the proposal and even suggesting Eristic for the post of MD.

The purpose was to establish a working example of his own theory on what he called 'people capitalism'. He had been instrumental in the thing from the start but had remained always very much in the background, pushing it forward through his various contacts both on the Council and through the Covinous Society.

'We can't allow the project to be put on hold, Flicky. It is essential that you take over the management of the Comity and then all the others in your area. It is already detailed in my new book, which will come out in the summer of next year – you have to have it up and running by then. It's what we believe in, it's the way forward, independent of the Party but with the spirit of socialism. I've devoted two chapters to it in order to rebut the critics who are always saying that it might seem good in theory but wouldn't work in practice. The bloody woman can't hold us up, it has to take place. We've spent weeks thinking through our every move, second guessing Izzat's moves and Fribble's reactions.'

'But I'm an employee of the Council, Justin. I have to obey an order that is given to me by the leader of the Council – or risk losing my job and the position of managing director of the DEC. If I am told to put it on hold, I have no choice.'

'She only said on hold, she didn't say stop it all?' he asked.

'No. After all, she is Chair of the DEC, so she knows what's what, and I've formed the impression that once this forward-investment project is running, then she will give me the nod to continue as if nothing has happened. She said that once they had started to build, it would be too late for them to abandon the project, and then all their complaints could fall upon very deaf ears as far as the Council was concerned.'

'But it has to be running in time for the publication of my book, it just has to be running by the time I publish, or I'll have to take out those chapters and fill in with something else.'

Justin Covinous could see hours of work being thrown out simply to please some political leader of a tin-pot council. The thought that it might also concern the residents of the Comity never once crossed the mind of the very revered and much admired Justin Covinous. Not once did he stop to consider that it was their lives that would be part of his experiment, nor did he entertain the thought that they should be consulted and their agreement sought before his ideas were implemented. He did, however, think about his book and the work he had put into writing the two chapters and about the loss of face should his book be published and the DEC not be in control.

For her part, Felicity was now more worried than she had been for a long time. She had expected the resourceful Justin Covinous to reassure her, to tell her that he would speak to somebody who knew somebody and that the pressure would be removed. He had done this before and she wanted him to do it again, for she had not liked the interview with the Council leader one little bit and felt more than a little insecure. Things had been said at the interview that caused her to worry. Accusations had been levelled at her for which she had no answers, and now here was her lover, the mighty Justin Covinous, whingeing on about his damn book.

If she had never been straight with Justin, she expected him to be straight with her, and now he was simply behaving like a baby.

'Can't you ring somebody, Justin? You have contacts in the Council. I can't act on this without the leader's agreement. You will have to try to get her to let me continue with the DEC business.'

Justin knew that he couldn't be seen to be overtly taking sides on the issue without declaring that he had an interest, and that would never do for his image or for countless other reasons. He would support a cause and fight for it but he would never sacrifice his status of being an independent thinker.

'I might enquire how things are going and then suggest some

solutions, Flicky, but you know that I couldn't be identified directly with the DEC. It would give the impression that I was involved, and that would cut me out of a lot of future TV work.'

'But if things go wrong on this, my arse is in the firing line not yours. I need your support, I need you to go in fighting for the DEC and for me. Frankly, I'm worried. The leader of the Council indicated that if heads have to roll on this, it will be my head. I've backed your ideas all along the way and now's the time for being counted.'

'Oh come on, Flicky. No job's that important, there are always other jobs. Be realistic. There is too much to lose.'

'Who for, Justin?'

'Darling, for both of us. You believe that people capitalism is the way for us, don't you? I know you do. Well nothing ever happens without a hitch or two, and that is when we have to be ready to make sacrifices.'

Felicity understood then who would make the sacrifices.

25

Premonitions

I have written that Richard Puritan is not, in any meaningful sense of the word, sensitive and yet, that is not to say that he has no feelings, or indeed that if cut he will not bleed. Rather it is that in his normal day-to-day existence, Richard Puritan does not sympathise with people who cross his path. He sees them and hears them when they address him, but he fails to appreciate that they might suffer as a result of his or anybody's actions unless they are violent or particularly overt.

He does not, for example, comprehend that he might easily offend a person by talking about the dreadful colour yellow, when they are wearing a yellow dress or shirt. He does not wish to offend but does not quickly register the downcast look nor yet surmise that the person may be dejected or sad.

It is odd, therefore, that when he woke up on the day in question, he experienced what most people would call a premonition of something awful, and he had not been able to rid himself of the thought all morning.

We can readily appreciate that there are reasons for this anxiety. We know that there are great engines of change turning within the greater interests of St Margaret's Comity, designed to bring about his removal and replacement. Richard Puritan, however, knows nothing of this and thinks only that he is feeling down as he tries to implement his grand plans to bring a clinical legality to the affairs of the Comity, as well as establishing his own brand of heaven for the residents of the place.

To this latter end, Mr Puritan has tried to organise a midday course for the residents on vegetarian cooking for single people or those on limited budgets. This has mostly failed because, in the course of promoting it, he has rushed into print with one of his now famous newsletters extolling the virtues of rejecting meat because it involves the killing of small, or at any rate, not massive animals. Mr Puritan has waxed eloquent on the subject of slaughtering, and having researched the subject has listed all the means whereby farm animals are killed.

The research on the subject has done much to reinforce his own views, has made him almost fanatical about the brutality of slaughtering animals. It has prompted him to rush out further newsletters explaining the gruesome ceremonial and religious ways that animals are despatched. He has shared these revelations with the residents and has only mentioned the cookery course as an afterthought.

The residents have been sickened by the newsletters' content and have binned them as soon as they have seen that, yet again, their carer is caring for something other than his job.

Now the day had come for the first of the cookery lessons, and the demonstrator from the Vegetarian Society was due to arrive, and once again Mr Puritan was faced with the almost certain possibility that this would be yet another venture which would demonstrate that his plans enjoyed absolutely no support from his residents. In his zeal to promote his views of the cruelty of slaughtering methods, he had, he now realised, forgotten to sweet-talk one of the residents to allow him to hold the demonstration in their cottage. Also, he had forgotten to purchase the ingredients the demonstrator had asked him to buy, and had only a very short time to drum up interest and send somebody out for them.

Had Felicity not left early that morning for a meeting in London, he could have asked her to help. It was not even a day when his part-time secretary worked, and so he was well and truly on his own.

This was not the reason for his dreadful premonition, because he had not remembered the demonstration until after he had made his breakfast.

He had tried unsuccessfully to recruit Valerie Curst and Sheila Truckle, but both had been out and had not responded to the note he had left for them. Feeling unequal to the task, he had rung the lady who was to give the talk and put her off and was now miserable because he had failed to get his great campaign for vegetarianism off the launchpad.

This, however, was not his reason for the dark feeling of despair that engulfed and wrapped him in a feeling of foreboding; it was something that nagged at the back of his mind and wouldn't let him lift his eyes to the horizon, but kept his head bowed and his eyes cast down.

Having settled the matter of the vegetarian teach-in to nobody's satisfaction, least of all his own, Mr Puritan returned to his office and was sitting disconsolately when Mr Boon knocked on his door and asked to see him.

Whilst Mr Puritan had been seeking a resident to host his teach-in, Mr Boon had been in conversation with Doris Hall and Rachel Malapert.

Rachel Malapert had developed a friendship with Doris Hall, following the death of Doris's husband John, and the pair had spent an increasing amount of time together.

Doris had taken a greater interest in the Church since John's death. She had met Rachel Malapert on Sundays as Rachel was one of the few regular churchgoers from the Comity. It was therefore perfectly natural that the women should have struck up a friendship and, as both were widows, their interest in the church tended to cement the friendship.

Mrs Hall was still very angry with Mr Puritan, who she saw as the cause of her husband's death, and would go to extreme lengths to avoid him. She used every means at her disposal to ensure that she had no contact whatsoever with the crusading Administrator.

Mrs Malapert has always been implacably opposed to Puritan and had never made any bones about her dislike for the man. This was due, in no small part, to her membership of the Church, as she had been a very firm supporter of Lionel Hartwell and believed that the job of Administrator should have been given to a cleric.

This common cause and an affinity with each other's situation drew the two women closer together, and in this drawing together they had found a comfort in the face of the continued attacks upon what they saw as 'their security' by Mr Puritan and his new lifestyle for the 'third age'.

Since the suicide of John Hall, Mr Boon, who had been very sympathetic at that time, had become a very welcome guest at Mrs Hall's cottage and, what is more, an eagerly awaited visitor. It was normal that Mrs Malapert should also visit when Mr Boon was expected, and therefore he was not surprised to find Rachel Malapert with Doris Hall when he visited that day. Mrs Hall had asked him to visit and he had been happy to oblige.

The purpose of the request, it had been explained to him, was the fact that the two women wished to share the one cottage, to live together. They were, however, very worried about making the request to the Administrator, mainly on account of his seeming total preoccupation with the sexual orientation of his charges, or as they put it, his constantly going on about homosexuality.

'We're not homosexuals, Mr Boon,' Doris Hall explained, 'or these lesbian people either, yet we know that no matter what we say, Mr Puritan will think we are.'

'We are much too old for that kind of thing anyway,' chipped in Rachel Malapert. 'But even if we weren't, we were married women and mothers. But you know what Mr Puritan is like and he will imply that we are – "funny" – no matter what, and we don't want any of that sort of discussion with him.'

'So we wondered if you could talk to him about our moving in together and make it very clear to him that it's got absolutely nothing whatsoever to do with sexual orientation, homosexuality or anything like that.'

'It's just that we would be happier being together, especially after the robbery and what happened to the Cenobites,' explained Doris.

Mr Boon did understand and appreciate the couple's problem. He too had read Mr Puritan's and Felicity Eristic's newsletter on the subject and knew what trouble Mr Puritan had caused Mr Pule, who had become so upset that he had been forced to leave the Comity rather than suffer the constant insinuation that he was a homosexual.

'I'm not sure what I can do to stop Mr Puritan from talking

227

about sexual orientation to you both,' he said. 'He is his own man and believes very strongly that this is a matter that should concern us all. However, there can be no harm in my talking to him and explaining your situation. I shall stress the fact that you are both widows and mothers and were very happily married. Beyond that, I don't believe that there is much that I can do. Naturally, if he raises the question with me, I will assure him that you would both be very upset at the slightest hint that either of you are motivated by anything other than the wish for the companionship that such a move would provide. But I have to say that, from my observations, such assurances would do little to change his mind once he has made it up. He is a very singular man when it comes to his pet ideas.'

Both women knew the truth of this and they could do little else than cross their fingers and trust that Mr Boon would succeed.

As far as Mr Boon was concerned, he didn't relish the task, the more so as he knew that there were already moves being made to remove Mr Puritan from his post as Administrator of the Comity and, moreover, that he had been earmarked to supplant him in the position.

These were the thoughts that boiled up in Mr Boon's mind as he climbed the stairs to the Administrator's office and knocked upon the door. He would have preferred to have let the matter take its own course because, whatever happened, he felt that the ladies would not have moved permanently before he was installed as Administrator, and then there would be no problems for the two to worry about. He had, however, given them his word, and Mr Boon was not a man to shrink from anything once he had given his word.

Mr Puritan was not really in the mood to consider other people's problems. The black mood that had enveloped him upon waking had now deepened, and he sat dejected and he felt bones destroyed in his body, for such was the despair that racked him.

Mr Boon, upon entering the office, seemed to understand that here was a man, if not in actual torment, then riven with a multitude of doubts and misery. Perhaps he recalled the part in the Epistle of Saint Peter that says 'having compassion one of another, love as brethren, be pitiful, be courteous; not rendering evil, or railing: but contrariwise, blessing.'

'I wondered if you could spare me a moment, Mr Puritan?'

'What is it, Mr Boon? I'm afraid I'm a bit down just now, I can't seem to shake off a great feeling of worry.'

'What about?'

'That's the problem, I don't know, it's just a general anxiety, a kind of mood. I woke with it, feeling, you know, really down, as if the day offered me nothing but misery, and it just seems to get worse.'

He looked at Mr Boon and Mr Boon wondered whether it was possible that Mr Puritan knew in his heart, if not with his mind, that his days as Administrator were numbered and that it was this that he was communicating.

'Well, we all have off days, don't we? I have them myself, days when nothing seems to go right. Perhaps you are having one of these off days.'

'Yes, that could be it. But you know, Mr Boon, things haven't gone as I had hoped they would. When I started here I thought that this was a wonderful opportunity to change things, to make ... well, you know, a new kind of sheltered-housing complex, to mould it into a better place for the residents, a place where they could get rid of all the old, bad things in their lives and take on some good, worthwhile things. They have all got out of the rat race and this is their last chance to take up things that are socially right.'

'Ah yes, but they have lived a lifetime in their old ways, they have got used to them, and are confident in what they know. I'm not sure that the elderly make very good revolutionary material, Mr Puritan.'

'But it is their last chance to change from the old, bad ways and adopt the new enlightened ones. How many times will the old ways have let them down, have caused them problems? In his book Mr Covinous says that we get set in a track of wrong ways and dig the track ever deeper for our own children until it's almost impossible to climb out. Have you read any of Mr Covinous's books, Mr Boon?'

Mr Boon admitted that he had not found the time to read any Covinous book.

'Then you should, because I think you'd find them very powerful. They deal with the social problems that we all face in this modern society.'

'I'm afraid that my ideas for changing society are not at all in line with any new ideas, Mr Puritan. I believe that we don't need any new ideas for society, we already have the blueprint, it is just that it is very hard to follow.'

'Well,' replied Richard Puritan, 'it is all right for you, you're a Christian, but that really is an old faith, hardly suited to the situation that we find ourselves in today. With our new technology and with the way that power is all in the hands of a few international companies, we need new methods, new ways.'

'Perhaps, but I believe that the challenge is not about structures but about people. If we, as people, have the right approach, we can tackle anything, any structure, no matter what. I recall when I was teaching at university, it became the fashion amongst students to gamble. They would gamble on almost everything. Some of the students ruined themselves and had to leave, some ruined their parents, and some just never became involved, they carried on along their own paths and didn't follow the fashion. I am not saying that they were Christians, not all were, but they all exhibited a common attitude towards life; they were in charge of their own lives and took their decisions for themselves, regardless of what the other students were doing. That's what I believe is important, to be in charge of your own life no matter what the world does or says. After all, when you are past eighteen there is no one you can blame but yourself.'

Mr Puritan did not believe that the rest of the world could escape responsibility that easily. He was used to blaming everything, from international business to governments, from creeds to birth. His whole adult life had been built on the solid fact of blame. Somebody was always the cause of every disaster, every injustice, and he could no more accept the fact that the whole ethos of finding somebody to blame was pointless than he could accept the fact that not every Conservative was a criminal. This was how he had always seen life, and whereas he believed that the residents of the Comity should welcome new ideas, in his own world he could not entertain the thought that not everything was somebody else's fault.

'I wish it was that simple, Mr Boon, but those with their hands on the levers of power have, unfortunately, the means of shaping society as they want it, of forcing us all to do their bidding. We are pawns in a great game, we are not, I fear our own masters at all.'

Mr Boon realised then that it was very unlikely that Mr Puritan would ever be reached by the bright light of belief or the comfort of religion, he was bound to a system that looked for conspiracies, and there was no way that he could bring comfort to such a set mind.

'I came about Mrs Hall and Mrs Malapert. Mrs Malapert would like to move in with Mrs Hall. They are worried about the robbery and would feel safer if they shared.'

'I would need to consult the Association, but I can't see anything against it, Mr Boon. Mrs Hall has been very strange since her husband's suicide. I think she needs somebody with her, although Mrs Malapert is hardly the person I would choose – she is a very difficult person, always prepared to speak her mind, and she's very rude.'

Mr Boon reflected that he had never found Mrs Malapert rude, but then he seldom experienced rudeness from people. Mr Puritan, or so it seemed, often encountered rudeness in his daily round. If there was a reason for this, or even a conclusion to be drawn, Mr Boon was too gentle a man to draw it.

'The winter is never a good time for me,' he observed. 'The days are too short and too cold. It could be that, being tall and thin, the cold gets to me sooner. When I was at school, the other boys used to ask me what the weather was like on account of my height.'

This effort at small talk fell upon a morose ear as far as Mr Puritan was concerned and, getting no response, Mr Boon stood up and made to leave.

'I wanted to rename this place the Nelson Mandela Comity, but the Association turned it down. They said that it already had a name, St Margaret's Comity. Bloody silly name that. Who's ever heard of St Margaret, anyway? Everybody has heard of Nelson Mandela. Everything I suggest seems to be turned down. They just don't want to try anything new or exciting. I'm very tired of always fighting, and no matter what I suggest it's turned down. I'm tired of it, Mr Boon. A year and half of having everything turned down.'

'Well, maybe this isn't the right place for you then, Mr Puritan. Maybe you need to go somewhere where the authorities appreciate your talents and will welcome your suggestions and improvements.'

'Jobs aren't that plentiful these days. The Government has broken the back of new social initiatives. Nowadays everything has a price, everything has a cost. It's a money-based society now, Mr Boon. Money is the only bloody thing that talks.'

'Oh, I don't know. There's still caring, I find the Church is very caring and very socially minded. Often, to tell you the truth, too much so. I think religion should be more about spiritual things, not simply social caring.'

'Well, that's your trade, isn't it.' Mr Puritan was not prepared to view the world of caring and religion, his mind was set upon the injustice that he felt he had suffered and, rather than cast his mind wider, he wanted to focus it ever more closely upon imagined hurts and insults. He should never have confided in this parson, he thought, the man was obsessed with his religion and couldn't see the wider issues of the way society is organised, nor even who controlled the show. He shut his mind to Mr Boon and wished him away.

'Well, I must get on.' Mr Boon made for the door, and this time Mr Puritan made no conversation that might hold him back. 'I'll tell Mrs Hall and Mrs Malapert that you have no objection to their arranging to move in together then?'

Mr Puritan nodded and returned to his brooding.

Once downstairs, Mr Boon returned to Mrs Hall's cottage and told them that as far as he could see, Mr Puritan was both in agreement and had not raised the dread subject of sexual orientation.

'He never mentioned it once, and apart from saying that he

would need to get the agreement of the Association's Welfare Committee, he seemed to completely understand the matter.'

Mrs Hall and Mrs Malapert exchanged a look that was both smug and satisfied.

'I knew that you could arrange it, Mr Boon,' Mrs Malapert said. 'I expect it's because you're a curate, even that Mr Puritan wouldn't be rude to a curate. People still respect the cloth, don't they, Mrs Hall?'

Mrs Hall agreed that even Mr Puritan would stop short of raising homosexuality with a curate and observed that decent people didn't talk about such things anyway.

For his part, Mr Boon was not totally convinced, but rather than raise his doubts about the power of the cloth, just smiled and made his normal excuse to leave.

'I'm afraid parish business drags me away, I still have a lot of visits to make and there's only twenty-four hours in every day. Surely God should have made the clergy's day thirty-six hours with all the work he expects us to do – but don't you dare tell him, ladies. Remember what he did to Job when he complained!'

It was, he knew, an old joke that he'd said many times before, but it always raised a smile and there was just that grain of truth in it that made it not seem to be challenging God too much.

They showed him out and he promised to call again shortly. As he walked across the Comity garden and towards the now infamous gateway, he thought to himself that, if he was appointed as the Administrator, he would find the job very rewarding and, although he did not deceive himself about his own ability to be a shepherd of the flock, he did entertain the idea that he might just be able to make a contribution to the lives of the residents, to demonstrate what caring was all about; responding to their needs, listening to their problems and trying to show that God is not an all-action proposition, but a reaction proposition.

If they seek him out then they shall certainly find him close at hand, he thought as he walked home.

26

The Mills of God

Eric Fribble and John Izzat both had the means to bring Eristic and Puritan down, but both waited. Why they waited is not clear but, to be charitable, it was probably that Christmas was not too far away, and thus they waited to allow the festive season to pass before they fired the guns that they held loaded and ready.

Christmas was just two weeks away, and both men had their minds fully committed to the various functions and activities that it demands of busy people.

In Lossiemouth, however, things were taking a different turn and, if it can be said that the mills of God grind exceeding slow but exceeding hard, then perhaps it was in Lossiemouth that the mills were slowly grinding Ms Eristic and Mr Puritan's fate.

Arnold Pule had settled in and had found that his skills were in great demand, since the yacht owners were anxious to upgrade and increase the radio equipment and rigs that they had already installed on board. He had only worked on two projects but had found that after mouldering at the Comity, his new, albeit light working week, invigorated him and blew away most of the bad memories of Mr Puritan and Ms Eristic's slurs.

He had taken to going to the local Presbyterian church on Sundays and had found in the pastor a man with whom he could form a friendship. During the course of time he had entertained the minister in his cottage, and the two men had chatted about his time at the Comity and about the events that had caused him to buy the cottage and start up his little business.

The memory of the events at the Comity had continued to

preoccupy Arnold Pule's mind, even though he was now far removed from that place, and it was natural for him to discuss and worry over these things with his newfound friend the pastor of his church.

What Arnold Pule never knew and, even if he had known, it is doubtful if he would have cared about it, was that his pastor was a *Thought for the Day* speaker on the local radio. So, the pastor retold the Comity story, being careful not to mention Arnold's name or his particular problem but simply called him one of his congregation. The thrust of the tale the pastor told, with more than a little embellishment, was of the tide of political correctness washing away the normal caring and close relationship of a sheltered-housing complex.

A local stringer for one of the Scottish tabloids smelled a story and it didn't take her too long to trace Arnold, as the rest of the congregation had never moved more than five miles from where they were born.

As for Arnold, he had no idea where the stringer had obtained the story, and from the stringer's questions could see that she had no idea of the special reason for his departure and so, again embellishing the story a little himself, told the Comity residents' side of the business. He also provided the name of St Margaret's Comity and its address.

The headline read: LOONY LEFT PURITAN DRIVES OLD PEOPLE OUT OF HOMES. It was a good, well-written story that was almost as accurate as that Arnold had told the stringer. However, the sub-editor had added a little colour here and there, and had indulged in a shade of sneering at 'those English', and those people down South.

The bones of the story were, however, all there, with the exception of Arnold Pule being harassed on sexual orientation grounds, for which we can forgive Arnold because there is no profit in throwing mud at oneself. Arnold had been assured that his name would not be used in the story and, in this, fate played a cruel trick because he was named as Mr Arni Poole, and it is impossible to know if this was a cunning ploy by the delightful lady stringer or a plain mistake on her part, when keying the story in.

It did not take very long for the story to be picked up by other newspapers, and what had started as a local story rapidly escalated into a 'national story'.

Both Ms Eristic and Mr Puritan, however, were not aware that there was a story brewing on the affairs of the Comity, nor that editorial researchers were busy searching back issues of the local paper.

The two were delighted, indeed, to tell a reporter who contacted them by phone that yes, they had indeed banned smoking in the Comity meeting room, and when the reporter asked about other important issues that they had addressed, Ms Eristic took the phone from Mr Puritan and explained her views, and therefore Mr Puritan's, on the issues that faced the administrators of sheltered housing. She was, she explained, working for the Council in the area of the frail and elderly and had introduced many new innovations in the Council's sheltered housing units. When asked for the reason for her speaking for the Comity, which was a privately run sheltered-housing complex, she was rash enough to state that the Council was concerned with the management of all sheltered housing in its area.

It would have been more circumspect had she remembered that the leader of the Council had issued very strict instructions to her regarding this matter, but the chance to air her views to someone she imagined was a sympathetic member of the fourth estate was too great an opportunity for her to be able to pass up. Mr Puritan, also, should have recalled that Mr Fribble had instructed him not to issue any statement to the press on any subject concerning the Comity without the Welfare Fund's express permission. The possibility, however, of fame and high public profile was too great for either of the two fighters for heaven on earth to miss, and they explained fully their own total commitment to the establishment in Wiltshire of a fairer and more just society for the frail and elderly.

With such open and frank views, the reporter cannot be blamed for taking down their every word. And probably even if he had wanted to tell them that the idea of the piece was to show the absurdity of their kind of political correctness, it is very doubtful if they would have noted it or, indeed, trimmed their opinions by so much as a jot.

One week before Christmas is not normally a fruitful time for newspapers. News stories are usually short on the ground and editors have to search for entertaining items that often contain more by way of gossip than enlightenment. It was thus too tempting to devote more space to this Comity story than the facts really justified.

It is not an exaggeration to say that both Felicity Eristic and Mr Puritan looked forward to the morning papers, confident that at last their views would be published and that the world would nod its collective head at the wisdom and sagacity of these two leaders of political correctness for the frail and elderly.

When they bought copies of the paper, they were totally unprepared, therefore, to see that rather than lionised they were pilloried. Under the subheading WILD-EYED ZEALOTS CLAIM TO BE RIGHT, Their views were set out side by side with large stars against what the editor considered were the most extreme points. The headline for the whole page was even more terrible, it was – 'THE *HELL* OF BEING OLD'.

Over his breakfast Eric Fribble read the story and sensed disaster. Unlike Mr Puritan, Fribble was under no illusion how the Association Welfare Committee would react to this news and, more to the point, who they would blame. He abandoned the toast and left for his office without one shred of hope. He knew in his heart that his day would be one of fighting for survival. As he travelled into London, one thought was uppermost; Puritan would go before the day was out. He reviewed, in his mind, the various instructions that had been issued to the man, all of them written and posted, and as the train sped towards London, he composed the note that would be issued and despatched that very morning, telling Mr Puritan that he was instantly sacked and would have to leave.

The problem was that there was nobody available who could take over the job at a moment's notice. But that, he considered, was a mere detail. If needs be, he would stay there until he could find a suitable replacement. One thing, and one thing only, was vital to Eric Fribble and that was that Richard Puritan left the Comity and got out of his life before the day ended. Even the fact that, officially, he could not presume to sack Mr Puritan without the agreement of the President of the Welfare Fund did not intrude upon his total determination to be rid of the man by nightfall, if not sooner.

The Council leader was also determined to rid herself of Felicity Eristic. Seldom had she started the day so upset, so totally shamed by a revelation. She had, she recalled, warned Ms Eristic that she was not to continue with the matter of the Comity, and certainly she had given her to understand very clearly that she was to play down any activity concerning the DEC. And now here was the woman sounding off about the Council's plans for taking over the management of sheltered-housing units in the Council's area as well as being associated with this man Puritan, who was running, or so it appeared, a sheltered housing complex that was a living hell for the residents. The Council leader squirmed at the thought of the questions that she would have to answer, and determined to move Ms Eristic as far away from any possible further complication in the Council's Frail and Elderly Care Department and, what is more, she determined to do it that very morning.

Another Council employee was not upset, and he was Mr Simon Tottery, notional head of the Council's Social Welfare Department. The news was, for him, the vindication of every-thing he had stood for, and against which he had so ineffectually fought. He had warned the Chair of Welfare that the way she was letting Ms Eristic organise the Frail and Elderly Department was dangerous and could cause problems, but he had not been listened to and no notice had been taken of his warning. Now the very thing he had always feared had struck, not him but the department, and it gave him considerable pleasure to contem-plate that there were on file countless memos from him advising and cautioning his Chair of Committee that Ms Eristic's policies were riddled with likely problems that might rebound upon the department.

Had he been a wiser man, he might have known that when it comes to a departmental enquiry then the head of Welfare Service – even if he is to all intents and purposes purely 'notional' – is highly vulnerable to the charge that: if he takes the money he takes the responsibility. But for Simon Tottery, nearing the end of his career and in sight of early retirement, at worst, the pill – even were the blame to be piled high upon his head – was still sweet when he contemplated the downfall of Felicity Eristic, who had treated him like dirt and sneered at his every memo and taken over his car park space, in which she had parked her battered and ugly Renault.

Simon, however, could not see clearly that Ms Eristic's departure would force his own even earlier retirement with a reduced pension and a deal of shame, when the independent inquiry had delivered its final verdict on the DEC and the ease with which it had been allowed to infringe upon the welfare provision provided by the Council. All this was, however, some way distant from the publication of the infamous article. All Simon felt on that morning was elation that the dreadful Ms Eristic had dug her own grave with her own tongue and her own words. In Council terms, she had committed suicide by her own memo.

In the Comity itself, the residents were both surprised and more than a little put out by the article. They had no wish to see their Comity displayed as if it was some kind of death camp, nor did they welcome the suggestion that they had been forced to suffer – although all agreed they had, at the hands of the awful Mr Puritan and the horrible Ms Eristic.

Their dignity was damaged by the article and they feared, both collectively and individually, that they could never go into the village again without being gushed over by the middle-aged and young. They deeply resented the tone of the article and the manner in which they were shown as being less than able to fight their own battles and keep their own end up. They were demeaned by the whole thing and felt the shame deeply. Surely, they felt, it was enough that they suffered Mr Puritan without their disgrace being shouted out from the rooftops.

There was no comfort in the exposure for the residents of the Comity.

Not far away, in Salisbury, the Reverend Lionel Hartwell was shown the paper by his daughter. It is hard to describe the sadness that this kindly man felt as he read the article and gazed at the painting that he had been presented with by John Izzat and the rest of the trustees. He wept, and the tears were such that his daughter grew concerned for him and wondered if her father's heart would break. He had missed the company of the Comity and had often wished to return, but felt this would have pained his daughter and so had stayed away. Now he felt that he had been remiss, had let both the residents and Mr Puritan down. I could have guided Mr Puritan, he thought, and I could have guarded the residents from the excesses of the dreadful regime, and he wept again until he, too, thought his heart would break.

The ripples thus sped outward from the story, touching everybody concerned with affairs of the Comity during Mr Puritan's stewardship. If justice had a heart, then certainly the publication of the article did little to demonstrate to those involved that there was much good in the brutal exposure of the Mr Puritan's tenure of office as Administrator.

In Winchester a rather seedy builder had woken to discover that Ms Eristic was in the newspapers and not shown in a very good light. He had hurried to his office and was spending a great deal of effort erasing the name 'Eristic' from invoices and works notes, for he was wise in the ways of the world.

When John Izzat saw the paper, he remained calm and an intense anger grew in him. He was angry that he had let the matter slide and had misjudged his moment. He was angry that he had not been firmer, and he knew that whatever happened now, he would need to act with a degree of resolve that he had wanted to avoid, for he saw that the business had to be settled and settled at once. He also knew that there would be three victims, Puritan, Eristic and Fribble. He did not think he, too, would suffer from the affair.

He rang the Bishop, and while he waited for him to answer his call, reflected that his feeling of unease when he had first read the minutes of the selection meeting months ago had been right and that he should not have allowed the appointment to stand.

Speaking to the Bishop, he was aware that he wanted a favour and needed the Bishop's co-operation if he was to get out of the mess with anything like a satisfactory result.

He admitted to the Bishop that things had gone wrong: 'I was hoping to let Christmas pass before I acted, Robert, but obviously that is now impossible. I intend to act today and to have Puritan out by this evening, Did you speak with your Mr Boon?'

The Bishop, whilst cautious, was still much taken with Izzat. He'd liked him from the moment they'd met and was prepared to suspend judgement or a quick-fix reaction from the Church, should it be called for. He was, however, very aware that the Church could be made the scapegoat if the media decided to keep the story going.

'I must have action immediately on this, John,' he told Izzat. 'And yes, I have reason to think Mr Boon is prepared to take over as Administrator. However, I must have an assurance from you that there will be no industrial tribunal or litigation that will suck Mr Boon into court. I cannot leave him open to or involved in any legal actions. I must have your word on this, and it must be an unequivocal commitment on your part.'

Izzat knew that he couldn't give such a guarantee, but he also knew that he could almost give one, and, so pushed, he said: 'I give you my word that he shall be shielded from any such actions, and that I will ensure that his appointment is not joined to Puritan's dismissal. Naturally, I can't guarantee that Mr Puritan will not seek to involve Mr Boon, if that is what he decides to do, but I can assure you that very great pressure will be placed upon him to undertake no such action. I can do no more, Robert.'

The Bishop was satisfied with this assurance and the call ended.

Izzat's next call was to Ruston Olid, of Barratry, Barratry and Simony. He recounted his conversation with the Bishop and engaged the firm to look after Mr Boon's interests over his appointment and Puritan's dismissal. It was during this conversation that Olid told him about the car port.

'You can't just stop an investigation, Mr Izzat. Information still comes in, and we have heard from one investigator that we used for our original report that there has been a carport charged to the Comity and part paid for, although there is no

241

carport at the place. The builder concerned laughed about it, saying that it was all part of a deal with Miss Eristic.'

'You say it has been part paid for, Mr Olid?'

'So I'm informed. It was, it seems, part of a kind of contra-deal for some work done at another sheltered-housing unit under the Council's control.'

'Fax me the details please, here to my home, Mr Olid. Can you do that?'

'Yes, but it is only a transcript of a conversation.'

'That will do. Do you have any more on it?'

'No, only that the investigator checked up at the Comity and could find no carport.'

Izzat then instructed the firm to be at the Comity at noon and discussed the form and means of Mr Puritan's dismissal.

'Who can you send me? I suppose both you and Fetor are too busy?'

'For a client of your standing, Mr Izzat, either Mr Fetor or I will be there, rest assured on that.'

Relieved, Izzat then rang Eric Fribble, who had been expecting the call and dreading it. Fribble explained that he was arranging to send a messenger down to Wiltshire with Mr Puritan's notice.

'Do nothing yet, Mr Fribble. I want you to take the next train and to meet me at the Comity, and bring with you the last three months' accounts submitted by Mr Puritan, covering all costs and payments. I shall be leaving very shortly. Oh yes, would you please phone Mr Puritan and ask him to be sure to be in his office at noon. Tell him I am travelling down and I must see him.'

Izzat then rang the other trustees and put them in the picture regarding his proposed action. They agreed to it and faxed their assent to him at Ideality. It was nine thirty when Izzat left his home and started the drive down to St Margaret's Comity.

In Whitehall at half past ten a senior civil servant took a list from a folder on his desk and deleted the name of John Izzat. This was the final list of names for the next honours. These names had passed every test. John Izzat would not receive an honour that year, for once your name was deleted, there was no possible way the name could ever be reinstated. The civil servant looked up, having deleted the name, and smiled at his secretary. 'He's fallen at the last fence, poor chap,' he said, closing the folder and pushing the newspaper under it into the wastepaper basket. 'A pity, really. He's done a lot for this country.'

In Lossiemouth, Arnold Pule studied the paper and was generally very pleased. He had not planned to 'get his own back' when he had left the Comity, but as things stood, he was not sorry to see Puritan and Eristic damned by their own words. It seemed to him that he had struck back for John Hall and Sangeta Patel, for the Cenobites and all the other residents who had suffered for the cause of Mr Puritan's politically correct zeal. He too missed the community of the Comity, but he didn't miss Mr Puritan, and considered it a trade-off worth the sacrifice. In an ideal world, he thought, I could have finished my time out at St Margaret's Comity.

27

Retribution

It is possible that readers will think that the chapter heading is unjust. Mr Puritan and Felicity Eristic have never acted out of spite, they have not behaved badly because they were in any sense 'bad' people. They may have experienced troubles with the police on demonstrations, but that is the lot of radical protesters.

If they are judged to be guilty, it is crimes of omission rather than commission, although the residents of St Margaret's Comity would not see it in that light. Both Eristic and Puritan have only sought to make the world a better place, to improve the lot of those who have come within the orbit of their influence. They believe that it is not enough to let things be, rather they believe that we are born to improve the world and make it better for all its inhabitants.

I believe that the crimes, as the newspaper article called them, that have been perpetrated against the residents of the Comity have happened because both Puritan or Eristic have not got the perspective necessary to treat people, as the Church has vainly tried to teach, as flawed creatures, imperfect examples of a perfect plan. Rather they are convinced that if they can change the elements around and about people, then the people will become perfect.

Had this been possible, then the churches in the land could have produced perfect people long ago and the world would now be on course for heaven on earth. But it is not so, people are flawed and the fault lines in us all continue from one generation to the next, however manfully we struggle against them. It is this basic misunderstanding that caused Puritan and Eristic to fail and falter, and in the course of their mighty struggle with the inherent weakness in mankind, they were forced to ever sillier and sillier extremes.

Such philosophical thinking was not, however, in the mind of the Council leader when she summoned Mr Simon Tottery and Ms Felicity Eristic into her office following the publication of the now infamous newspaper exposure of the goings-on at St Margaret's Comity.

'I demand to know why you thought, Ms Eristic, that you were empowered to speak to the media on the Council's plans for the frail and elderly?'

Felicity couldn't answer.

'We have a policy regarding speaking to the media, and we also have a whole department that deals with media enquiries. What is more, after the inward investment problem, I specifically spoke to you and instructed you to play down the whole subject, and now you have allowed yourself to be featured in a national newspaper sounding off on the subject and implying that you were speaking for the Council. The damage you have done to the Council and also the DEC is immeasurable. So much so that we will be winding up the DEC, and in so doing we will have presented the opposition with its biggest opportunity for years. You have ruined the DEC, you have damaged the Council, you have brought shame upon your department and I am sick to death of you. Personnel tells me that I can't sack you, Ms Eristic, but I can, and I am going to place you completely out of harm's way as far as this Council is concerned. I have arranged that with immediate effect you will be transferred to the Stationery and Administration Supplies Department stock audit office. In that office there is only an internal telephone and so you will not be able to contact your friends in the media. The salary grade is considerably lower and there is no provision at that grade for car parking within the Council property area and so you should remove your car straight away and find a parking space outside.'

The Council leader paused for breath, and also paused because the sight of the two people in front of her so infuriated her that she was finding it hard to maintain her normal and well-known composure.

'And Mr Tottery, as head of the Welfare Department, you have singularly failed to control and organise your department so that this kind of thing doesn't happen. There are no possible excuses and I intend to make an example of you so that all the other departmental heads are left in no doubt whatsoever that I will not tolerate sloppy and accident-prone management. I understand that you are two years off your planned early retirement. I am offering you the chance to take immediate retirement and I expect you to write to tell me that you intend to do so. Personnel has worked out a package and it is the best that I am prepared to offer, so there is no point in trying to negotiate with the Council over the terms. I am very, very upset and angry. Have either of you anything to say?'

Felicity Eristic had seen the possibility of a better life for herself when she had headed up the DEC. The prospect of working in the Stationery Department did not enthral her, nor did the idea that she would be working with this leader who had failed to support her and had, at the first sign of trouble, ditched her and now sought to humiliate her. As she stood there, she recalled their cosy conversations when the idea of the DEC had been first mooted, and their subsequent planning and meals together as the shares had been issued and the company structure worked out. Now, here she was being spoken to in the same manner as the leader spoke to Tottery, with the same disdain and contempt.

Felicity Eristic looked hard at the Council leader, drew back her lips in a sneer and leaned forward so that her hands were on the leader's immaculate desk.

'Yes, I have something to say, but I am uncertain whether to say it to you or to the press. The policy that you now deny was agreed with you and the other board members of the DEC – all councillors. Your attitude towards me is disgraceful and I shall be reporting you to the union, who will, I am certain, have something to say on this. You sit there believing yourself to be somehow better than the rest of us because a group of politicians thought you were less likely to be a nuisance than anybody else. Not because you have any special abilities or special talents. You try to impress us with your position rather than your talents. As for your job in the Stationery Department, on the basis of ability it would seem to be too taxing *for you* but the union will no doubt tell you that it is unsuitable for my grade and for me. You are, like all politicians, blown up with your estimation of your own importance; as Covinous says, you have the mind of an idiot, the stamina of a mule, the vanity of a peacock, the mouth of a sewer and the sincerity of a cockroach. I know about you, leader – I have the minutes of the DEC board meetings – so think before you do anything and consult a little. I will not be jerked about by you. What you do to Tottery here is between you both, but be careful of me.'

She turned on her heels and, white with anger, stormed out of the office, leaving Tottery and the leader with their mouths open and their brains numbed.

By four o'clock that day Simon Tottery's letter asking for immediate retirement was on the Council leader's desk. For him the trials of having Felicity Eristic in his department would soon cease to be a matter of importance or a generator of problems.

Felicity's advice to the leader had been powerful and when the leader had time to cool down and to consult and reflect a little, she realised that perhaps she had been hasty and that Ms Eristic would be better suited to another senior post within the Council, one, however, without any responsibility for welfare. and so Ms Eristic's name was put forward for the post of Property Services Department Head that became vacant as a result of another convenient early retirement.

At the Comity Richard Puritan waited for the coming of John Izzat. He did not wait hopefully and was aware that the meeting would be neither pleasant nor profitable for him. Several times he said to himself, why should I wait, why don't I simply pack up and move out? That's the sensible thing to do. They're going to sack me anyway, so why wait? And in this thought he was right, it would probably have been best if he had simply written a letter of resignation and left it in a prominent position and gone. Nothing but grief and pain could he expect from the meeting, and thus it was surely something that he could, in all

247

conscience, spare himself, but he waited, perhaps knowing that until you meet the thing you fear most you cannot look yourself in the face.

He had made mistakes, he had handled things badly and he had made life miserable for the residents of St Margaret's Comity. He had also done much good to the organisation of the place. The fire inspectorate now gave the Comity a clean bill of health, certain maintenance work had been carried out to the cottages, although most of the residents felt that it was a waste of time and money. The offices of the Comity had been thoroughly sorted and a book-keeping system based upon today, rather than yesterday, had been implemented. There was now a fax machine and a computer, and a nurse-call system joined every cottage to the office on a 24-hour-a-day basis. The local bus now stopped outside the Comity entrance, rather than down the road, and a regular medical team had been introduced that cared for everything from feet to eyes and hair.

Richard Puritan's ability at organisation and his love of a tidy 'ship' had been largely beneficial and there were many innovations that residents had reason to be grateful for, but they had been obscured by his ham-fisted and often silly campaigns for political correctness and fashionable causes. He would probably have been an ideal bursar at a college, where he could have identified with the more far-out radical student groups whilst running the college for the good of all. But Richard Puritan wanted to be part of the 'real world' not the putty world of student politics where demonstrations and protests were organised as much for the fun as from conviction. Puritan wanted to be amongst adults not silly children, and this was just one more of his conceits.

Rustin Olid arrived first, and his chauffeur parked at the back of the Comity building. Olid climbed the stairs, following the signs to the office. Mr Puritan was surprised to see him and asked who he was and what he wanted.

'I am here to meet Mr Izzat. If he hasn't arrived yet, I will wait.' Olid appraised Richard Puritan. He looked somewhat different from his photograph. His enormous bottom, he noted, had not been apparent on the photographs.

'I didn't catch your name, Mr er, er?' Puritan tried.

'No, I didn't give my name, Mr Puritan. Most people who need to know me know my name, and those who don't will either learn it in the course of time or never need to know it.'

'Well, you seem to know my name. I am Richard Puritan.'

'Yes, I know that.' Rustin Olid did not engage in small talk.

Puritan found the man disconcerting and vaguely threatening. He wished that he could sit somewhere else and decided to go to his own flat, rather than sit in the room with this stranger, whose bulk and hooded eyelids heightened his feeling of impending doom.

'I am just popping over to my flat for a moment. Would you keep an eye on the office and an ear on the phone, do you think?' Puritan asked.

'No, I do not keep an eye on other people's responsibilities. It is your office and you should take responsibility for it, Mr Puritan.'

A noise on the stairs indicated that somebody was coming up and Mr Fribble came through the door.

'Good morning, Mr Puritan.' From the way that Fribble greeted him, Mr Puritan could tell that the temperature of the proposed meeting would be decidedly cold. 'And who is this?'

'This gentleman is waiting for Mr Izzat, he never gave his name.'

'You are, sir?' Mr Fribble asked Rustin Olid.

'Waiting for Mr Izzat, as Mr Puritan has told you, Mr Fribble,' the lawyer replied.

'Damn it, if you know Mr Puritan's and my name, why don't you tell us yours?' Fribble fumed.

'Because I choose not to, Mr Fribble.'

They waited silently for John Izzat to arrive, looking at everything rather than at each other. Mr Fribble would have liked to raise the question of Mr Puritan's words in the ill-famed article, but felt it was better to wait for his President. Mr Puritan entertained the hope that the meeting was not, after all, about the article, but about some new initiative. Rustin Olid enjoyed waiting in silence as it afforded him an opportunity to observe both Fribble and Puritan under stress.

249

When the telephone rang, it seemed that it was twice as loud as it in fact was. Puritan picked up the receiver and heard Felicity's voice. She was incandescent with fury and she related to Puritan her interview with the Council leader. Both Olid and Fribble could hear most of the conversation. Puritan tried to tell Felicity that he had people in his office, but she was too angry to hear anything he said and continued giving a blow-by-blow account, until Puritan, thinking he heard Izzat, said, 'I must go now, Felicity,' and put the phone down.

The sound of John Izzat's car produced a charge of excitement amongst the assembled players of this particular game. They heard the door of his car slam shut and then heard each footfall on the stairs as he climbed them. I suspect that each one felt something different as the footsteps drew closer, and then John Izzat opened the door and walked into the office. He recognised each person with either a nod or a smile. Seeing that they were all together, and wanting to speak with Rustin Olid, he hesitated a moment and then turned to Eric Fribble.

'Mr Fribble, it would be helpful if you and Mr Puritan would check the Comity to see the work that has been done. Could you list the various building jobs and see that they have been done to your satisfaction?'

Slightly mystified by the requirement to physically check each job, Eric Fribble got up and Richard Puritan followed him out.

When they were alone John Izzat turned to Rustin Olid: 'It's good of you to have come, Mr Olid. On the journey down I was thinking how best I should proceed, and have decided that it should be very calmly, without any heat or anger, just quietly and resolutely. Would you agree?'

'Yes, Mr Izzat, I would. These things are always better done without temper or passion. Anger always obscures the purpose and confuses the issue. It has no place in business or, I would imagine, in life, but I am considered to be a very passionless person.' He laughed. 'Indeed, when I represented the Duke of – well, the Duke – he described me to his wife as the only man who makes a dead fish seem positively active.'

'I will want you as an official witness, Mr Olid.'

'It is in that role that I am here. Here is the letter that you asked me to draw up, I believe that it achieves your objectives and will prevent any after-taste of this matter lingering in the public's mind as far as Mr Puritan's tenure at the Comity is concerned. It will place a straightjacket round his activities so that he should be no further problem.'

Olid passed Izzat a lengthy document and Izzat read it at speed.

'I see you have required two witness signatures, your own and Mr Fribble's.'

'I believe that it will allow the other matter to proceed smoothly if Mr Fribble witnesses this document, it will be a tacit acknowledgement that he was aware of the lack of the carport and thus he will have agreed that a fraud was committed and that he knew about it.'

'Thank you, Mr Olid, it is exactly what I wanted. Should Mr Puritan not agree, then we will have to call the police, and again your presence here will be invaluable.'

Mr Fribble and Mr Puritan returned and John Izzat rose and offered Mr Puritan his chair in front of the desk.

'Mr Puritan,' Izzat said quietly and deliberately, 'the papers today are full of your thoughts on how sheltered-housing units should be run. That is unfortunate because whilst I deplore the views you expressed in the article, it has come to my attention that in your monthly accounts you have falsified some building work and made a payment to these people.' He placed a copy of the invoice into Mr Puritan's hands. 'You will see that it's payment for the preparation of a concrete base and drain for the erection of a carport on the standing behind this building. Did you see any evidence of this work, Mr Fribble?' He looked at Eric Fribble, who shook his head. 'This is very serious, Mr Puritan, on many counts, but specifically because all such work needed the full Welfare Fund Committee's agreement before such works were carried out. It is also very serious because you authorised the invoice for payment when no such work had been done. It is my understanding that the work was ordered by Ms Eristic, and that Ms Eristic knew that no carport base has been laid. Mr Olid here is a solicitor, and he tells me that this constitutes a very grave criminal offence. I also have here your application form, and again I find that under the heading about any convictions, you have written 'none', and yet that is not true, is it, Mr Puritan? No, it is not and yet here you are in the newspaper talking about the moral rightness of the correct attitudes. The point I am making, Mr Puritan, is that as Chairman of the Welfare Fund Committee, I find the contradiction between your public statements and your private dealings too great to tolerate.'

Izzat traced the wrongdoings that had been going on at the Comity and finally came to his solution. Mr Puritan was to leave at once, and the RRAWF would take no action providing he agreed to remain silent about his period of employment at the Comity and paid back regularly the money that had been swindled for the carport.

'If you agree,' explained Izzat, 'then you must sign this undertaking and it will be witnessed by Mr Fribble and Mr Olid here.'

Mr Puritan considered his options, and came to the conclusion that he had little or no choice in the matter. There had been no angry scene, no shouting, simply a reasoned and unpleasant statement of a set of facts. He wanted to tell Izzat that he thought that the way his trustees had run the Comity was lax and old-fashioned, he wanted to tell him that his manner was patrician and arrogant, he wanted to say that even old people can take a challenge and that there was nothing wrong with presenting them with challenges – some nice and some nasty. He would have liked to explain about Covinous and his insight into the structure of the society that they live in. But he had not been asked to justify himself, to explain or to put his side. He had simply been presented with some unpalatable facts.

'Well, Mr Puritan, do you agree to Mr Izzat's proposal?'

Rustin Olid's voice was hardly above a whisper, yet all those in the room heard it.

Puritan felt like a caged animal. There were no friends there for him, there was no independent advice. It was, as so often, him against the world, and an unfriendly and vengeful world at that.

'Yes, I will sign the document and leave this afternoon.' He was beaten again. He had raised himself up only to be knocked down by people with power, people with money. Richard Puritan felt very, very sorry for himself. He looked around him at the other people in the office and, apart from Mr Fribble, could not see any evidence of victory in their faces. Olid sat without any expression on his face; Izzat looked exhausted – there was no hint of triumph or of victory, just a tired man.

The document was signed and witnessed, and Mr Fribble was instructed to accompany Mr Puritan through the rest of the day and to take the keys and stay at an hotel overnight and open the Comity office in the morning.

28

Good News

One week after Mr Puritan left the Comity, the builders returned and started to decorate the Administrator's flat.

Eric Fribble had stayed for the afternoon of Mr Puritan's last day, returned the following morning, and left shortly after lunch, having arranged with the part-time secretary that she would, for a limited period, increase her attendance to five days per week – just to keep the office ticking over. Beyond that, Mr Fribble had sent a note to each resident, stating the affairs of the Comity would be run from the offices of the RRAWF in London until a new Administrator was appointed. The note further explained that anybody wishing to speak with Mr Fribble, who would be acting Administrator until an appointment was made, could telephone him from the Comity office free of charge.

In this manner, the residents learnt, first that Mr Puritan had left and second that a new Administrator would be appointed. Most of them were pleased with the news of Mr Puritan's departure and few stopped to think very much about the reasons for it, or what Mr Puritan would do.

Nobody had seen Mr Puritan leave, which was not surprising as the residents tended to be home well before it got dark and to stay there for the rest of the day, not venturing out again no matter what. The winter was hard that year, and the cold seemed to increase as the light faded. They had not therefore seen the taxi call for Mr Puritan, nor had they seen the box he so loved loaded. He did not have a great many things and so, although they had filled the taxi and its boot, he could still think of it as travelling light.

Puritan had thought about staying in Salisbury, but had

decided to go back to London. He wanted to shake the dust of the Comity from his feet and start afresh.

Had Eric Fribble been a more observant man, he would have noticed that Puritan had changed, or more probably was in the process of changing. The meeting had been the catalyst in a kind of mental chemical reaction for Puritan and he recognised that there was a sea change happening in his whole philosophy. It was, he would reflect later, as if the scales had been removed from his eyes and he started to see that a great many of his old ideas were unproductive and often stupid.

What was happening to Richard Puritan was that he was finding, through his own humiliation and pain, charity and compassion. He was starting to see that people, although imperfect, were fragile and were in all probability more noble than the pigeonholes into which he had, in the past, pushed them. With this realisation he was also seeing that all those icons that he had relied upon in the past were flawed and brittle. They had not given him a formula for dealing with real people in a real world, but a worthless formula for dealing with cardboard cut-out people who never existed and were convenient pegs that people like Covinous and Eristic used to justify their actions.

This realisation contributed to his pain and was straightforward shame, for his past actions, his mentors and himself. This is why he decided that he wanted to go to London to lick his wounds and rediscover the better side of himself. He had no idea what he would do, how he would survive, nor even where he would stay, but he did know that now things would be better and now he would start to be a person he could like and of whom he could be proud.

For Eric Fribble, the sacking of Richard Puritan had left him, after the Administrator's departure, free to wander about the office and through the flat. It also gave him an opportunity to think about his own life. He did not, however, take advantage of this opportunity and worried instead about having missed the carport entry in the monthly accounts that Puritan had submitted to him. He realised that such an error was not a matter that could be ignored; the fact that Izzat had found it and not told him before facing Puritan with it meant that Izzat had been watching him with the same fine eye that he had watched Puritan. Further, he had always prided himself on the fact that he was the watcher who watched the watchers. He did not normally make such errors, and anyway he knew that he had failed to engineer the sacking of Puritan, a job that he had specifically been given by Izzat. He would not be forgiven for such an error and so it became a matter of when he would offer his resignation.

These were the thoughts that engaged Eric Fribble as he contemplated the empty Comity offices and flat.

In the Bishop's Palace there was a feeling of quiet satisfaction. Neil Thomas had taken Izzat's call from his mobile phone as he drove back to London and had told the Bishop.

'You must get straight on to Mr Boon, Neil, and tell him that he will be appointed as Administrator, and should therefore start to ready himself for the move. Obviously, Mr Izzat will have to make the appointment, or rather the Welfare Fund Committee of the Association will make it.'

Neil Thomas also told the Bishop that Ms Eristic had left the Council's Frail and Elderly Department and that the leader of the Council had taken over her responsibilities.

'That's even better news, as far as we are concerned,' the Bishop observed. 'I can work with her. We meet on several committees already so there should be no problems.' The affair of St Margaret's Comity had been resolved for the Bishop in a very satisfactory manner.

Readers might note a contradiction, insofar as Mr Boon was to be appointed to the post of Administrator without there seeming to be an open field of selection – indeed, in much the same manner as Mr Puritan – but here the top echelon of the management had agreed the appointment, whereas when Mr Puritan was appointed it had not been so. There was the feeling that this made all the difference, perhaps it did.

Whatever the means of Mr Boon's appointment, there was a feeling of peace at the Bishop's Palace, and the sense that a problem had been met and solved, and it was one less that

Robert the Bishop had to contend with and that made for a sound sleep and a cheerful morning.

At Wimbledon, John Izzat had arrived home late and gone straight to bed without seeing Laura. He too had slept soundly.

The following morning he came down late for breakfast and found Laura already up and his breakfast under way. She was particularly attentive towards him, and whilst he enjoyed her fussing, he knew that she wanted to tell him something important.

'I have something to tell you, father.'

The fact that Laura was all smiles told Izzat that whatever it was that she was going to tell him, it was not bad news.

'Joe and I intend to marry in the summer.'

'I see. I'm not sure what I am meant to say. Are you asking my permission as proxy for Joe, or will Joe ask me if he may marry you later, when you have established that I do not object?'

'Well, yes, something like that. You are allowed to be surprised, you know.'

'But I'm not surprised, Laura. You've both been behaving like a pair of lovesick doves for the past three months. When you become as old as I am, you will know that when two people behave like lovesick doves, either they have some massive argument and vow never to see each other again, or they decide to marry, or perhaps live together, which is the same as marrying without the security for either person.'

'That's remarkably old-fashioned of you, father. You don't need a piece of paper to love each other, so why should you need one to live together?'

'Because property is all about contract of ownership, Laura, as you well know, studying law. Property remains when love changes, fades or blooms in another garden, and that is when that piece of paper comes between the incontrovertible fact of breakdown and salvaging what is left of pride and self-esteem. Without that "piece of paper", injustice, brute force or duplicity creeps into the equation and there is little or nothing that can

257

be done about it. That is why that so despised "piece of paper" has been found over hundreds of years to be not only important but vital, insofar as it protects the weak against the strong.'

'Oh father, you sweet old thing, but I think I can look after my own interests well enough.'

'It's is not you I am worrying about, you young dolt, it's Joe. Such a nice lad. It would be a real shame to see a nice young man like Joe in the hands of a scheming woman like you.'

Laura tried to swat her father with the *Telegraph*, but he dodged out of her way laughing.

'When you say the summer, Laura, when exactly are you two thinking of getting married? If you want a quiet wedding I suggest August, then most people will be away on holiday, and I will also be on holiday in Italy, and so all you would need to do is pick up a couple of strangers as witnesses and best man and you'd be wedded and bedded without any of the people who know and love you being there. Or if you want a big wedding, then I suggest the end of September; almost everybody is back from their holidays by mid-September.'

'We haven't thought about the actual date yet, but probably late September, while there are still flowers out and leaves on the trees.'

'You romantic old thing. What about your career? You will have passed your finals by then and be starting in chambers, won't you?'

'That's another thing I want to discuss with you. I don't think I want to be a lawyer. I've been thinking a lot about it and I think I would sooner go into business, the professions are so ... oh, I don't know, so damned nothing. There's nothing there when you really look at them. The law is just other people's trouble. The Church, well, you need a calling. Medicine, well, that's just other people's troubles again. Accountancy, that's just writing the history of others' financial successes or failures. Teaching, well that's pretty thankless, isn't it? You're always working with other people's raw material, and never really producing anything yourself, at first hand. It's never your success, always theirs.

'No, I want to be doing something where I can make my

mark, achieve something. You've done it, you know, I want to build something like you, something that wasn't there before you came to it and is there after you've left. I won't find that in the law or in a profession, but I will find it in business.'

'It takes a lot of your life, Laura, and contrary to most young people's beliefs, you really don't have an awful lot of time in one life.'

Laura smiled at her father, for she knew she had an eternity, she would live for ever, she had years and years ahead of her, time wasn't something that worried her, it came every day in 24-hour chunks.

'I can tell Joe that you approve then, can I, father?'

'Yes,' Izzat laughed at his daughter. 'Tell Joe I expect him to come with his hat in his hand and to stutter and shuffle about and then, all red-faced to blurt out, "Mr Izzat, I love your daughter Laura, and want to marry her, say that you have no objections, Mr Izzat". If he does that I will give him my answer by late June.'

Laura managed to swat him this time and went to phone Joe Staunch to tell him the good news.

Left alone in the kitchen, John Izzat suddenly felt very alone and very sad. He longed for Elizabeth and was close to tears. How would he be able to arrange all the thousand and one things that a daughter needed arranging for her wedding? Elizabeth would have known what to do and would have taken charge of the whole thing, and all he would have had to do was mildly complain that the whole thing was taking the house over, turn up on the day, proud as Punch, and take Laura – lovely Laura – down the aisle and then, later, pay the bill. Oh, why did you have to die Elizabeth, he said to himself, as he had said so many times before.

He resolved, sitting there, that come what may, he would have to try to sort out all the wedding things for Laura. He would try to find out about wedding dresses and go through the family address book and search for cousins and relations that he hadn't seen for years, but whom Laura had sent Christmas cards to each year since Elizabeth's death. He would make a fist of it, he thought, if he put his mind to it and worked at it.

Laura came back into the kitchen.

'I have a confession to make, father. I told Aunt Grace before I told you, because we will need her to do all the arranging and stuff. Do you mind?'

'Of course not, she's the ideal person. All her daughters are married and she's in her element organising. What a brilliant daughter you are – but you should have told me first. It would have been wonderful if your mother had been here, she would have loved to see you married.'

'Aunt Grace said you would get all sad about mother, but you're not to. Of course, I would sooner mother had been here, but she's not, and that's all there is to it. I've got just about the best father in the world and I've got bossy Aunt Grace, who won't give you a moment's peace, so I'm not in the least disadvantaged. And anyway, had mother been here, ten to one Aunt Grace would have taken over and done it all anyway, but once removed.'

John Izzat smiled and hugged Laura, holding very tightly to him, and she couldn't see the tears that filled his eyes and ran down his cheeks. He let her go and walked quickly to the door.

'I forgot my watch, I'll be back in a moment,' he said over his shoulder, and ran upstairs so Laura wouldn't see he was crying. He returned after ten minutes and found her already making lists.

'You know what, lovely Laura, we must have a party to celebrate your engagement, here in Ideality. We'll invite all the rellies and all your friends and mine and have a party to end all parties. We'll invite Joe's parents and Joe's friends and go on all night.'

'But you hate parties, father. You've always said that parties are for people without brains to demonstrate the fact, and for those without friends to show the world why.'

'Ah yes, but I've only got one daughter, and only one life, and so a bit of mindlessness and mass stupidity should be used to mark her engagement. Or maybe I need one more party to confirm my opinion of them – who knows? But we'll have the party and I shall have an opportunity to show off my wonderful daughter before she becomes Mrs somebody or other and I have to share her with some young and disgustingly talented artist.'

'You will never have to share me with anybody, father. I'm your daughter and no matter what, I've only got one father, and if you thinking you're going to shrug me off to that boy Joe, you've got another think coming. I might get married to him, but I was born to you and mother, so don't get any ideas about getting rid of me.'

The party did take place, and John Izzat did not really enjoy it very much, but he did enjoy not enjoying it. It proved to him that parties were not something he liked very much. Laura and Joe liked it, as did most of the guests, and it cost a great deal of money.

The Covinouses did not attend as they were engaged in a battle of wills with each other. Matters had come to a head, and although Tabby Covinous hadn't made a decision to part from Justin, a great deal of acrimony had found its way into the relationship.

Joe had told both his mother and his stepfather that he was engaged and intended to marry Laura Izzat, but neither his mother or stepfather could find the time to attend to his affairs as they were so busy with their own.

For his part, Joe was not desperately upset by the lack of interest on the part of his parents. He had crossed over the line between those who supported the Comity and its fight and the Covinous side of Puritan and Eristic. While the fight had been going on, he had come to understand that it was a fight about letting people be what they are and not what they might be. In understanding this, he had found an insight into his parents and their lifestyle and had made a choice.

For Mrs Hall and Mrs Malapert, it was good news indeed to know that Mr Puritan had left.

Rachel had moved some of her most precious things into Mrs Hall's cottage and the two women had found that just being together was a tremendous improvement for both of them. They felt a great deal safer than when they had been in their separate cottages. They also contemplated a reduction in their living costs as they would only be burning one lot of lights and cooking one meal at a time instead of two.

Now that Mr Puritan had left, the one black cloud that had hung over them had been lifted. There was nobody to accuse them of being homosexuals or lesbians. There was no longer any pressure on either of them to have to feel guilty about living together, two widows of uncertain age.

They were also free, as were all the other residents, of being constantly nagged at, over racism, smoking, feminism, vegetarianism, environmentalism and road safety. All that was behind them, but most of all, for the two women, the monstrous slur of sexual orientation and whatever that encompassed was gone from them.

Now they breathed an air free of political challenges and accusations. They could just go right on being themselves, thinking their own thoughts and not caring about what was or was not acceptable in the eyes of the rest of the world outside the closed and comfortable world of St Margaret's Comity.

Of course they were not free of it all, for now they knew that certain things were acceptable and others were considered unacceptable. The worm of knowledge was now firmly implanted in their brains and sadly they would never be as they were before Mr Puritan arrived. But now they had a choice as to whether or not they abided by the canons of political correctness. Now they could choose to accept or reject any part of that ugly philosophy.

It was not much of a contest really, as, for the most part, they had always been reluctant to swim against the tide of social thinking. It is probably true to say that, had Mr Puritan and Ms Eristic stopped to observe the residents before they had started their campaign, they would have seen that the residents of St Margaret's Comity were largely politically correct. Only in matters such as smoking could they have found a sizeable number of incorrect people. The residents were not much given to making distinctions or to indulging in radicalism. If they didn't keep themselves to themselves, then they struck up friendships that lasted because they had been formed over long periods of time, rather than a couple of days.

The dark shadow of Mr Puritan had been lifted from them and they were free to be themselves, and there was nobody to point the finger at them should they fall by the wayside on any particular point.

There was no party or celebration, except that they now smiled more, and more smiles must mark a celebration of some sort, even if it is just the return of good humour.

The residents were not aware that Mr Boon was to be appointed the next Administrator, but had they known, I am certain that they would collectively have approved, as indeed they did when they were told later.

The winter at the Comity was on the way out, as far as the residents were concerned, and spring was just around the corner.

29

A New Beginning

The long dark evenings had started to shorten and it was obvious that winter was moving away from the Comity.

Mr Boon and his wife moved into the flat at the end of February, although they had been appointed on the first of February.

The builders had completed several important changes to the flat and it now had its own entrance on the other side of the arch, and so it wasn't necessary for Mrs Boon to go through the Comity office every time she wished to leave or enter the flat, as had been the case prior to the changes.

A further change had been suggested, the reinstatement of the gates, and the builders had been installing various mechanisms connected with these new gates. It was intended that they would be dedicated to and by the Reverend Hartwell, and money had been raised in the parish under the prompting of Mr Palmer, the vicar. The residue had been provided by the Association.

The new gates were to be electrically driven and controlled by a switch in the Comity office and was also able to be opened by the emergency service vehicles.

A personal letter to every resident had been written and sent by John Izzat as President of the RRAWF, telling them about Mr Boon's appointment and explaining a new organisational approach suggested by Mr Boon and to be implemented by him.

There would, the letter explained, be a Residents' Panel which would meet with the Administrator twice a year and look at all matters concerned with the Comity's running and affairs. It would not have the right to make changes, but would be consulted and listened to over changes that were likely to be made.

Three people would sit on the panel, and John Izzat had enclosed in the letter a slip for nominations for membership of the three places. It was proposed that if there was no consensus, then an election would be held by Mr Boon when he took up his residence.

A further change had been suggested by Mrs Boon, who was a landscape gardener with a thriving local business. She had suggested, and the trustees had agreed, that the Comity garden should be totally redesigned and made a visual 'high spot' of plant excellence and tranquil beauty – a tranquil ark. The best of the existing garden would be retained and the shrubs and plants – particularly the wisteria, which had suffered from neglect under Mr Puritan's tenure, would be pruned and brought back to its former and full glory. Residents agreed with this plan and supported it fully. Work on the new garden had started and it was hoped that planting would be completed by the end of March.

A company starting up near Swindon had donated a wonderful set of specially designed garden furniture and some statues. Mrs Boon was to be seen most days supervising the creation of the new garden, the design of which she was responsible for and which she had donated free to the Comity.

The Bishop had been active too, and the cathedral had donated some shrubs and a part of the extensive Comity community hall had been converted into a small chapel, a development that especially pleased Mr Boon as well as the Bishop.

'The place is starting to look respectable again,' Sangeta Patel had remarked, 'and when the new gates are installed then we shall feel safe in our beds again.'

This was the view of all the residents. Mrs Boon had already struck up relationships with most of the Comity folk, who saw her supervising the new garden as they went about their normal activities. Although 'plain speaking', her tendency to call a spade a spade was not thought of as a difficulty and the general feeling was that she was an asset to the community of the Comity.

Most of the residents did not really know Mr Boon, but Mrs Hall and Mrs Malapert were able to sing his praise on the strength of their knowledge of his visits and sermons, and their recommendation of his sterling qualities counted for much.

Mr Boon thus came to the Comity in a rosy glow of endorsement and a feeling that whilst there was no way that the place could return to the more carefree days of Lionel Hartwell, at least the worst was over and the Comity could go back to sleep in its rural setting, and, with a pair of new gates and a lovely new garden, there would be a gradual return to contentment amongst the residents.

As far as John Izzat and Laura were concerned, the engagement party proved to be the moment when the problems of St Margaret's Comity ceased to figure very largely in their thinking. John Izzat had resolved the problem of Mr Puritan, had seen off Ms Eristic and had lost his chance for an honour. He was, however, content, and felt rightly that his stewardship of the Comity had not been a total disaster. Mr Puritan had been a blip in an otherwise positive contribution. The standing of the sheltered-housing complex was now on the mend and the new Administrator was a person who would build wisely upon the foundations that were now in place. Later, John hoped, the Comity would win an award and become a model for other sheltered-housing units up and down the country.

The Association was also happy with the new management of the Comity and with its new Secretary, Mr Fribble having retired early, there was a general feeling that the Association could lift up its collective head and hold it up. The mistakes of the past were just that – past and its Welfare Fund Committee could now take a pride in providing the kind of support that its membership expected of a moderately rich trade association.

Felicity Eristic would not have said that she had been a player in the business of the Comity. She had certainly stayed there, but only as Richard Puritan's lover. She had been interested in the Comity but that was only as a part of a wider plan for all sheltered-housing units within the Council area. At the DEC she had been concerned with the place, but again that was part of the DEC's drive to expand its business into the private sector. If she reflected at all about the Comity it was to reassure herself that she had been misunderstood and very badly treated indeed.

Her time as managing director of the DEC had, however, given her a taste of a better life, and whilst she was totally committed to the socialist revolution and the empowering of the people to rise up against the tyranny of the Establishment, she knew that she would have to wait. Whilst she was waiting for that much promised and most glorious moment to arrive, she did not feel that there was any real harm in improving her own career and financial situation.

In her new position in the Property Services Department of the Council, she could see that many opportunities existed. There were the companies that supplied the Department and she felt sure that they could well do with her very special expertise.

I am confident that Ms Eristic will not need any extended period to lick her wounds and get back on her feet in the centre of the property services market. She will, I am certain, make her mark and become very rich in the service of her Council.

All these considerations were of little or no importance to Mrs Hall, who one warmish night in February, having put out the empty milk bottles, looked up at the stars and remembered how her husband had been fascinated by the fact that man had walked upon the surface of the moon and had come in to her and explained that the technology that had been used to get the first man on the moon was already out of date. He had said to her, she recalled, 'Doris, if we can get a man on the moon with our technology, we can go anywhere and do anything.'

'We can't do "anything", John,' she said to the passing stars, 'we couldn't stop you dying and we can't mend a broken heart, or fill the gap you left.'

'Are you all right Doris?' Rachel Malapert called from the door of the cottage. Doris Hall waved into the room and turned to go back inside.

'I'm not all right, am I, John, but I'm as good as can be expected,' she whispered to the night air and walked back up to her cottage and went in, closing the door to keep out the chill, the dark and the memories.